BRATVA BRIDE

BY T J MAGUIRE

Copyright © 2021 by T J Maguire

All rights reserved.

No part of this publication may be reproduced, distributed, or transmitted in any form or by any means, including photocopying, recording, or other electronic or mechanical methods, without the prior written permission of the publisher, except as permitted by Australian copyright law. For permission requests, contact T J Maguire

The story, all names, characters, and incidents portrayed in this production are fictitious. No identification with actual persons (living or deceased), places, buildings, and products is intended or should be inferred.

Book Cover by Faera Lane

Edited by BLD Editing

CONTENT WARNING

Before you continue, please be advised that this book has a content warning. If you are a sensitive reader, please proceed with caution.

-Extreme violence

-Harsh language

-Hand necklaces

-Murder/death

-Graphic sexual scenes

-Talk of sexual abuse

-Torture

CHAPTER ONE

Illayana Volkov

"Illayana Volkov! Get your ass out of that bed! Now!" a deep voice boomed from outside my bedroom door. Three loud bangs against the door followed after, making the walls shake.

I bolted upright, my hair dishevelled and legs wrapped up in the blankets. My hand flew to my forehead as I closed my eyes and groaned.

Ugh, too fucking early. Another bang at my bedroom door snapped me out of my haze, my eyes flying open. The heat of a body next to mine made me jolt straight out of bed.

Oh, fuck. There, lying in the middle of the bed was—fuck, what was his name? My one-night stand. Let's just call him that.

After a kick-ass night at one of our nightclubs, *Distoria* (where I celebrated turning twenty-one with a few of my closest friends), I must have stumbled home, taking this guy with me.

How the fuck did I get him past the guards at the main gate?

My eyes wandered over the sleeping male in my bed. Was it just me, or did he look way more attractive last night?

Beer goggles, Illayana. Those damn beer goggles. He wasn't unattractive, just not the usual man I go for. He was lean, but more so on the skinny side. He had long brown hair that went to his shoulders with streaks of blonde running through it. *Yuck...did I think that was sexy?* His face was round (kind of like a baby face) and his nose was flat, like he had been hit with a shovel repeatedly and his nose never healed properly.

What the fuck was I on last night? Looking down at my body, I realised I was naked.

Fuck.

I quickly ran across the room to my closet and plucked a robe off a hanger. Tying the rope around my waist, I made my way back to the bed just as another bang reverberated throughout the room.

"Illayanaaaaa," the voice growled, which I then knew to be my older brother, Aleksandr.

"Just a second!" I yelled back, reaching for my phone. I quickly dialled my best friend, Tatiana. She answered on the fifth ring.

"You better have a damn good reason for calling me this early in the fucking morning," she grumbled, her voice thick with sleep.

"Dude, what the fuck? You let me bring a guy home last night? Are you insane?!" I hissed, cupping the receiver.

"Bitch, I didn't let you do anything. I tried to stop you. You said, and I quote, 'if I wanna get laid, ain't nobody gonna stop me.' Then you stumbled off, dragging him behind you. What was I supposed to do? Tackle you?"

"That would have been preferable, yes. My father is gonna lose his mind when he finds out!"

"So don't let him find out then. Duh."

If I could have slapped her, I would have. Granted, it wasn't exactly her fault. I should have had enough common sense not to bring him home. But still, she was the sober one last night, the DD (designated driver), not me. So, she should have had enough of her brain cells working to realise what a horrible mistake this would turn out to be.

"And how the fuck am I supposed to do that?"

"I dunno, figure it out and call me later. I'm going back to bed."

"Tatiana, don't you dar—"

She hung up.

That bitch.

Tatiana has been my best friend for as long as I can remember. Being raised in the Bratva, it was sometimes hard to make friends unless they were in the life, which, luckily for me, Tatiana was. Her father has worked for mine for over twenty years, since before we even moved to America. As one of my father's advisors, he was always around, and he would bring his daughter along too. Tatiana and I clicked instantly. To put it bluntly, we were both bat shit crazy and loved to stir shit up, even when we were kids.

The man was still fast asleep on my bed, his upper body completely bare and the blanket just barely covering his lower half. I placed my phone on the bedside table, brought my foot up and kicked him in the leg, trying to rouse him.

"Oi," I hissed, kicking him again.

He groaned, rolling his body to the side to face me, and opened his eyes.

Ahhh, that's why.

His eyes—one blue, one brown. And a complete fucking turn on.

He blinked a few times before those sex bomb eyes focused on me.

"If you value your life, you'll get up and jump out that window," I said, pointing to the large window to my left.

My room was on the third floor, so it wouldn't be a pleasant fall. But compared to what lay in store for him should my father find out he was there, I think I'd prefer the jump out of the window, to be honest.

"What?" his voice came out raspy and thick with sleep.

A loud bang followed by a string of Russian curses had Sex Eyes jumping out of the bed completely buck naked. My bedroom door had been kicked open, and the force of it caused the door to smack into the wall.

Next thing you knew, in strolled big brother Aleksandr, in all his 6'7 glory.

He's a bigggg dude, built like a pro wrestler and tall enough to have to duck his head whenever he walks through a damn door. He is my father's pride and joy, the next Volkov to take the throne and continue our legacy. He has the entire world at his fingertips. Doesn't hurt that he's good looking either, and he damn well knows it. His black hair is cut short and styled neatly. His chiselled jaw is always a winner with the ladies, as well as his piercing bright blue eyes.

Aleksandr walked in like he owned the damn place and stopped right in front of me. His gaze flicked from Sex Eyes to me, and back to Sex Eyes, his signature scowl plastered on his face. You could feel the intensity of his presence fill the room, almost to the point where you felt suffocated by his sheer masculinity.

Sex Eyes started to squirm under the scrutiny of his gaze, shifting from one foot to the other. He lowered his head in submission, his dick hanging placid between his legs and his arms limp at his sides.

Aleksandr turned fully and pinned me with his gaze. "Really, Illayana?" he growled.

Even though I'm 6'2, I still have to raise my head to look him in the eye. "What?" I asked innocently.

Think of something to distract him.

"Did you forget today's my birthday?"

Aleksandr narrowed his eyes and then scowled at me, turning his focus back to Sex Eyes.

Oh, ho, ho, he did forget. And I was going to use that to my advantage.

"Oh my god, you did forget!" I chastised, poking my finger into his chest. "My own brother forgot my birthday! I'm hurt!" I yelled dramatically, bringing the back of my hand to my forehead and swaying like I was lightheaded.

He looked back to me, his face clearly radiating annoyance at this entire situation. "What do you want, Illayana?"

Ah, big bad brother knew me well. Obviously I didn't give a shit if he forgot my birthday, but I knew I could play the card to get what I wanted. And he knew I did, too. Let's just say, it wasn't the first time.

"Why don't we forgo presents this year and instead you help me out with a teeny, tiny problem I've got," I said, not at all subtly, pointing my thumb over to Sex Eyes.

Aleksandr closed his eyes and inhaled deeply, as if he just needed to take a moment to collect himself before finally looking back at me. He turned and started making his way over to the naked man in my bedroom.

Sex Eyes' head snapped up and he started backing away, his hands flying up in surrender. "What the fuck is going on?" he yelled, as he continued to back away. His legs hit the end of the bed and Aleksandr placed a hand on his shoulder, forcing him to sit.

Without hesitating, Aleksandr pulled his gun from inside his suit jacket and clocked Sex Eyes right between the eyes.

A solid *umph* came out of Sex Eyes—right before he fell back onto the bed, unconscious.

"I'll take him to the pit and we'll deal with him later," Aleksandr said as he picked up the limp body and flung him over his shoulder. "You need to hurry up and get ready, or did you forget that Father called a meeting this morning?"

"Oh, fuck!" I yelled, sprinting to my closet.

"'Oh, fuck' is right," Aleksandr muttered as he walked out the door.

Ignoring him, I quickly put an outfit together—simple black jeans and a blank tank—and ran to my en suite. After a quick shower, I got dressed and made my way downstairs.

Our house (although people would say it's more of a mansion) is built on several hundred acres of land. The whole property is gated off and guarded by my father's men twenty-four hours a day. It's every bit as ostentatious as one might expect of the leader of the Bratva; three-story house, built in the Victorian Era, and every bit deserving of the name. With towers, turrets, wraparound porches, decorative railings and a stone exterior, our home is everything my mother ever wanted it to be.

Making my way down our large, circular staircase, I tried to get my head back in the game. My father told us all yesterday he wanted to meet this morning to discuss something important. Of course, I'd hardly paid attention because I was getting mentally prepared to get fucked up that night.

Now I was paying the price for that.

I had no idea what this meeting was about, and I hoped to God he didn't tell us yesterday. Otherwise I'd be the next one to go a few rounds in the ring with him.

Growing up, my brothers and I used to get into all kinds of fights. From screaming matches to full on blows, we would argue over the tiniest little things. Not to mention the fact that we used to prank each other all the time, and our pranks sometimes got way out of hand.

One year, Lukyan and I decided Aleksandr really needed to loosen up a bit, so we spiked his vodka with Rohypnol (commonly known as Roofies). Once he passed out, we tied his ass up and left him buck naked in one of our strip clubs with lipstick kisses all over his body from one of the strippers.

He woke up pissed and disoriented, with no clue as to how he got to the strip club, and a simple note taped to his chest, *'Lyubov, Lukyan & Illayana.'* Love, Lukyan & Illayana.

When he got home, note in hand, he was ready to wage war. Instead, we settled it like we always do: in the ring. When our father realised he couldn't contain our habit of picking fights with one another, he decided that any disagreements would be settled in our boxing ring at our personal gym. He also used it as a form of punishment. If we fucked up a job or disrespected him, we would have to go a few rounds with him—the devil himself—and Father never goes easy in the ring. It doesn't matter if you are his own flesh and blood, he'll knock you down to teach you your place.

Reaching the bottom of the staircase, I pivoted left and made my way down the long corridor towards my father's office. Coming to a stop in front of a large, wooden door, I raised my hand and knocked twice.

"Enter," my father's voice boomed from inside the room.

I immediately lowered my hand to the handle and opened the door.

The smell of smoke and alcohol instantly hit my senses (not surprising, even for nine o'clock in the morning). My father was seated behind his large mahogany desk in the middle of the room. Wearing his signature three-piece Armani suit, he looked like he was a model for GQ, not a cold-blooded Russian mobster.

His black hair was kept neat and tidy, only a few grey hairs starting to make their appearance. His face was set in his usual neutral expression, giving off the epitome of a man who had no care in the world. His bright blue eyes locked onto me as soon as I stepped into the room.

Father rose from his chair and made his way around his desk, heading towards me. "*S dnem rozhdeniya, printsessa,*" *Happy Birthday, Princess,* he said in Russian as he embraced me in his arms. Placing a small kiss on my forehead, he gave me one quick squeeze before letting me go. Reaching into his suit jacket, he pulled out an envelope, handing it to me.

Ah, the perfect gift. Money. I can always count on Daddy Dearest to deliver the goods every year.

Leaning up on my tiptoes, I kissed him on the cheek and whispered, "*Spasibo, otets*" *Thank you, Father.*

He straightened his body, fixing his tie and running his hands down his suit. A clear sign he was uncomfortable. My father loves me, there's no doubt in my mind about that, but he isn't the greatest at showing it (or at showing emotions or feelings in general).

He was raised to be tough. To show no weakness. To be every bit the ruthless killer a *Pakhan* ought to be. That kind of upbringing cemented him as the tough love type of parent instead of the nurturing type.

He walked back to the desk and sat in his large leather chair, pouring himself what I'm guessing was his second or third shot of vodka. As I walked in, I tucked the envelope in my back pocket and took stock of my surroundings.

Lukyan was sitting in a chair in front of Father's desk, slouched back with his ankle resting comfortably on his left knee. He had a thick brown cigar sticking out of his mouth and a glass half-filled with vodka in his hand.

He was the youngest boy, and he definitely acted like it. He was carefree with an 'I don't give a fuck' attitude that wafted off him like a bad smell. He was always the first to make light of a bad situation with dark humour and crappy jokes, never taking anything too seriously and generally always being a shithead. Only a few years separated us. He was older (but you wouldn't think it, based on his childish behaviour half the time that drove me absolutely fucking mad.)

Swirling the glass, he brought it to his lips and chugged the remains of his drink. Placing the glass on Father's desk, he stood quickly and made his way over to me.

He was just as tall as Aleksandr, but instead of being built like a bloody brick house, Lukyan was more on the leaner side. His dark hair was tied back at the nape of his neck with a few strands cascading over his face. His blue eyes connected with mine and his lips curved up in a smile.

"Happy Birthday, baby sister," he said, his thick Russian accent coming through clear as day. No matter how long we lived in Las Vegas, his accent never changed, his true heritage always shining through.

"Thank you, brother," I replied, wrapping my arms around his waist.

Nikolai emerged from the shadows behind Father's desk, and I had to work hard not to flinch in surprise. Father would have been furious to know I didn't pay attention to my surroundings.

Nikolai walked over and shoved Lukyan to the side. He wrapped his big, muscular arms around me and rested his chin on top of my head. At 6'6, it was easy for him.

"Happy Birthday," he whispered, before letting me go and slinking back to his usual spot against the wall.

If Lukyan was the crazy idiot of the family, then Nikolai was his polar opposite: quiet, smart, driven. Nikolai was the brains whereas Lukyan was the headache, the one that drove us all mad. Not only was Nikolai incredibly smart, he was also unbelievably strong. We always used to place bets as to who would win in a fight between him and Aleksandr. I'm talking about a real fight, not just a friendly spar. Not only was he our resident tech head, but he was also head of security, responsible for any and all surveillance-related queries. He invested all his time into the Bratva, never doing anything for himself. The Bratva was his life. It was who he was. He lived and breathed for the Bratva.

I thanked them both and moved to sit down in the chair next to the one Lukyan was just occupying. Father poured another shot of vodka in a glass and handed it to me. I picked up the glass and downed the drink without hesitating. The burn of the liquid as it slid down my throat was comforting and familiar.

Lukyan took a seat next to me and returned to his position prior to my arrival. He brought his cigar to his lips, inhaling for a solid few seconds before releasing his breath.

"So, Father, what's this meeting about?" he asked casually.

Our father turned his head and pinned him with a sharp gaze. He said nothing. He remained absolutely silent. The only indication he'd heard Lukyan's question was the subtle raise of his eyebrow.

Lukyan immediately back-peddled. "Not that I'm demanding answers from you or anything, Father," he said quickly, sitting up straighter. "I mean. . .I was just. . .you know. . .oh, fuck," he said, lowering his head.

"'Oh, fuck' is right, you moron," I whispered in his direction, though I knew Father could hear me.

You *never* asked Father what was going on. He would tell you when he was good and ready, not a moment before.

"We'll discuss your insolence later, Lukyan," Father said, his voice low and threatening. His entire demeanour was cold and menacing. Just being in his presence made you want to tuck your head between your legs and fucking run. He was my father. I loved him. I respected him, but I also feared him. You'd be a fool not to.

"Once Aleksandr returns, we'll begin. Speaking of which, where is your brother?" Father asked, turning his killer gaze towards me and arching an eyebrow.

Oh, fuck. Oh, fuck. Be cool. If he finds out you brought a guy home, you'll be in the ring.

"He had to go to the bathroom after he came to wake me. Massive case of the runs. Full-blown diarrhoea," I said quickly, mimicking an explosion with my hands and adding sound effects. "Kabooooooom!"

Father remained still, his face impassive, but I could see the slight twitch of his lips. He was trying hard not to laugh, to keep his 'Russian Mobster' persona intact.

Three quick knocks on the office door and any trace of laughter from him disappeared as quickly as it had arrived.

"Enter," he bellowed.

Aleksandr opened the door and walked in. With a slight head nod to Father, he moved to the far side of the room and took a seat on the three-seater couch. Leaning back, he stretched his arms out over the back of the couch and crossed his ankle over his knee.

Father focused back on me while the room filled with silence.

"Let's begin."

CHAPTER TWO

Illayana Volkov

Father picked up his glass and took a long swig of his vodka before beginning. "Our contacts in New York have reached out with a message. Alessandro De Luca, head of La Cosa Nostra, requested a meet."

Silence. Complete and utter silence. I mean, what other reaction was he expecting? It's not every day that an Italian family tries to establish some sort of alliance with the Russians. We're not exactly enemies, but we're not really friends either. We coexist with each other. We stay in Las Vegas, they stay in New York. End of discussion. We don't cross each other, we don't engage each other and we're all better off for it. So why change things?

Aleksandr was, as always, the first to break the silence. He leant forward, placing his elbows on his knees and interlocking his fingers. "La Cosa Nostra? Are they sure?"

"They are," Father replied, leaning back in his chair. "Vincenzo De Luca, Alessandro's son, delivered the message in person to solidify its authenticity. He was adamant the request was genuine, and would end in a mutually beneficial agreement between us both."

"Mutually beneficial?" Lukyan scoffed, taking a puff of his cigar. The smoke swirled around in the air between us, the stench lingering and filling my nostrils.

"What kind of agreement?" Aleksandr continued as if Lukyan hadn't spoken at all.

"Vincenzo didn't go into specifics. He merely requested a meet with us on neutral ground," Father replied. "Our contacts have been keeping an eye on New York, and they've reported a lot of carnage between the De Lucas and another Italian family, the Gambinos."

"You think that's why they're requesting the meet? For help against the Gambinos?" I asked out loud, tilting my empty glass towards my father.

He lifted the large glass bottle of vodka and poured me a shot.

"Makes sense. What's the beef about?" Lukyan asked.

"That, I do not know," Father replied. He looked around the room, taking his time and dragging his eyes over us all, making sure to maintain eye contact for a few seconds with each of us. "But I *will* find out."

Father's word left no debate about his intentions.

"You've agreed to meet with them?" Aleksandr asked, raising his eyebrows.

"It has always been an unspoken agreement between us to steer clear of each other. If Alessandro is reaching out, I'm curious as to why," Father explained easily. "And it has been so very boring here. Maybe a little war will liven up the place a bit," he added, winking at me.

I winked back and took a sip of my drink.

"When and where?" Aleksandr asked.

"Kansas City, tomorrow. You, along with Maxim and your sister, will accompany me."

"Oh, man!" Lukyan hissed, slamming his foot on the ground. He always hated missing out. Such a spoilt brat.

Father pinned him with a glare, letting the fury from his outburst show on his face. With his jaw and fists clenched, he looked like he was gonna blow at any minute.

"I mean, they're totally the better choice. So right, Father, so, so right," Lukyan quickly said, lowering his head.

Kiss ass.

Father ignored Lukyan altogether and opened his desk drawer with his right hand, pulling out several folders. He flung them along his desk, letting them spread out in different directions.

Lukyan jumped to his feet and grabbed them, handing them out to each of us, clearly eager to try and get back in our father's good graces. Pointless. If he felt like you disrespected him, there was no fixing it unless it was in the ring.

I took a folder, making sure to scoff loud enough for Lukyan to hear me. He narrowed his eyes at me, but stayed quiet. He knew he was on thin ice as it was.

As he moved to give Aleksandr and Nikolai their folders, I opened mine and was greeted with a family portrait of the De Luca family.

Standing square in the middle were who I assumed were Mr and Mrs De Luca.

Alessandro stood tall and proud, his left hand holding the middle of his tie, like the photo was captured as he was fixing it. His right arm was bent ninety degrees, with Mrs De Luca's arm looped through it.

He was wearing an impeccable grey three-piece suit, clearly tailored to fit his build. He looked like he was in his late fifties or early sixties, with a fresh head of dark hair. His million-dollar smile might fool others, but I knew better. I could see the evil lurking in his eyes as clear as day. This man was manipulative, conniving and ruthless.

Mrs De Luca was about as much as I expected. Such a small little thing, with pale skin and long, black hair. Her round face and doe-eyed expression showed her for what she was: weak, unimpressive, docile. Her only outstanding feature was her entrancing green eyes. So vibrant, unlike anything I'd ever seen before.

Standing beside Alessandro was another man a few inches taller. His eyes hooked me in straight away. *No. Fucking. Way.* Another bi-eyed beauty! But this guy? Oh, fuck, this guy was leagues ahead of Sex Eyes.

Even in his suit, you could tell his muscles had muscles. His suit bulged in all the right places, clearly tailored like his father's. A faint trace of ink peeked out of the neckline of his suit, and I was dying of curiosity to find out what lay beneath his damn clothing.

My eyes went back to his face and *fuck me,* he was so fucking delicious. High cheekbones, full, luscious lips, his jaw so incredibly defined you could cut glass on it.

His eyes…oh, god, his eyes. One green, the colour as captivating as the rarest emerald in the world. One blue, so bright and sparkling, like the ocean on a hot summer's day. His black hair was short and slicked back, styled neatly, and he looked to be in his late twenties or early thirties. He was without a shadow of a doubt the hottest fucking man I'd ever laid eyes on. All I wanted to do was run my tongue down that delectable body and feel that powerful frame tremble from my touch.

Next to Mrs De Luca was another man. Just as tall as his father, and just as handsome as his brother. But he didn't capture my eye like the gorgeous specimen before him. His suit was nice, tailored to fit him to perfection. His black hair was styled messily and his bright green eyes seemed to be the same shade as his mother's. His lips were curved up in a sly smile, like he knew *exactly* how good looking he was. The guy screamed 'man whore'.

Sitting on a couch directly in front of the De Luca adults were two small children. A boy and girl who looked to be about ten, maybe? The little boy was dressed in a suit, matching his father and brothers, and the little girl was wearing a white dress with a matching white bow in her hair.

The photo seemed to have captured them right in a moment where they seemed to be arguing. The little boy's face was scrunched up in anger, his little fist heading straight towards his sister. The little girl didn't look much happier either. Her foot was hanging in mid-air, almost striking him.

How. Flipping. Cute.

After taking a good look at the De Luca family, I raised my head and waited for my father to continue. Aleksandr, Nikolai and Lukyan were each studying the photograph as intently as I was, like they could get all the information they needed just from that one shot.

Father cleared his throat, demanding our undivided attention, and we all obliged. He held the photograph up in front of him, so we could all see it. "Alessandro De Luca and his wife, Isabella De Luca. Next to him is his eldest, Arturo De Luca, rumoured to be his underboss. Vincenzo, as I'm sure you've guessed, is the male next to Isabella. From what I can ascertain, he's an enforcer for his father."

"I've heard of Arturo De Luca. They call him Shadow throughout the Vegas Underworld," Lukyan began. "Apparently, Alessandro paid $5 million a year to have him go to Switzerland to study under Elias Huber."

"Elias Huber? The Assassin Trainer?" Aleksandr asked, surprised.

"The one and only. He was there between the ages of thirteen to seventeen," Lukyan said, relighting his cigar that had gone out. "That's what I heard, anyway," he finished, shrugging his shoulders.

Elias Huber was a legend in the criminal underground. Known for his skills as a fighter and weapons expert, people came to him when they needed to take somebody out. It didn't matter how important or how high up the individual was in the world. Rumour was, he could take out anybody. There wasn't a single bad mark to his name.

"Vincenzo is quite well known as well. Even a few of our own soldiers have heard of his brutality," Nikolai began. "Demyan told me once that he heard Vincenzo had come across a rat in the family. Not long after that, the rat's body had been dismembered, the pieces spread throughout New York as a warning to others."

I whistled, low and long. "Damnnnnnn...that's my kinda justice," I said, smiling.

"Fuck yeah!" Lukyan agreed, raising his hand and fist bumping me.

I laughed and turned my attention back to Father. "So, this is who we're meeting tomorrow?" I asked, trying to get my head back in the game and focus.

"Da," Father replied, as he poured yet another shot of vodka. "Be prepared. I want you both armed and wearing your Kevlar Vests. I doubt this is an ambush, but I won't take any chances."

Aleksandr and I both nodded.

In my mind, I was already ticking through all my weapons I would be taking with me. My switchblade, my push dagger, as well as a couple of my favourite blades and some throwing knives. Couldn't forget my good old Smith and Wesson handgun. That beauty has gotten me out of some tough strides. Part of me hoped for a fight. It had been a long time since the Volkovs had been at war.

"Nikolai and Lukyan, I need you both to head to *Russian Roulette* and settle some discrepancies with our high rollers," Father said, motioning his hands towards my older brothers.

Russian Roulette is one of many casinos we own in Las Vegas, as well as some high-end strip clubs and restaurants. To be honest, we have enough businesses and revenue to get out of the mafia life and go legit, but where's the fun in that?

"Yes!" Lukyan said, pulling out his gun and a knife. "How would you like it settled, Father?" he asked, raising his right hand with his handgun, then his left with his knife.

Father tapped his fingers along his desk, pursing his lips in thought. He flicked his head towards Lukyan's knife and smiled. "Don't make it too quick, boys," he said, chuckling.

Lukyan stood gracefully, buttoning up his suit jacket as he went. Nikolai rounded the desk and came to a stand beside Lukyan. They both gave a small bow and left.

Aleksandr moved from the couch, coming to sit in the chair Lukyan was just in. Father stood as well, moving to stand in front of his desk and leaning back up against it. He crossed his arms over his chest and pinned me with his hard glare.

"I'll need you to pay extra special attention at the meeting tomorrow, *doch'*." Daughter.

I raised an eyebrow but remained silent. I knew he wasn't quite finished yet.

"There's a chance a marriage proposal could be offered. It's the only way to solidify an alliance between our two families that can be trusted. We value the sanctity of marriage just as much as the Italians, and neither of our people would disrespect such a union."

Ah. That explains why he wants me to come tomorrow. If a union was suggested, it would most likely be one of the De Luca men to engage in the marriage.

"I would never force you to marry. The choice will be yours, and yours alone," Father continued, placing a hand on my shoulder. "I won't lie to you, we would benefit a lot from an alliance with the De Lucas. New York would be open to us, and the amount of money and power to be had would make our family even stronger than it is now."

I nodded, listening intently.

"But the choice in the end is yours, Illayana. Always."

I smiled up at my father. It was so rare to see that side of him—the loving, caring side—when most of my life, I've known the tough, badass Russian mobster side. I took his hand from my shoulder and held it.

"I'm curious about the war between the De Lucas and the Gambinos as well, Father. I'll pay close attention tomorrow, and if a marriage is what they propose, I'll weigh all the pros and cons before making a decision."

Father chuckled, a small smile forming on his lips. "Those damn pro and con lists. Your mother was always so good at those." His eyes glazed over, as if he was suddenly caught up in a memory of the past.

I tried not to let the mention of my mother bring me down, especially because I knew how much it hurt my father that she was gone.

The Voznesenskys—a rival Russian family—tried to overthrow us and take everything we have. They hit us simultaneously at our home, casinos, strip clubs and restaurants. We still don't know how they pulled it off, but they hit every one of our businesses, hoping it would be enough to beat us.

It wasn't. We lost a lot of good men and a lot of damage was done to our properties, but in the end The Volkovs prevailed. Unfortunately, it wasn't all of us. My mother was kidnapped, raped and murdered.

After finding her body, my father went into a rage unlike anything I'd ever seen before. He vowed justice, revenge on the Voznesensky family. He promised blood and retribution.

It was exactly what he got.

It took a few months, but my father hunted down every single member of the Voznesensky family here in America, as well as in Russia. He slaughtered every single one of them. He didn't spare the women or the children. He killed every single person with the last name Voznesensky, effectively wiping them off the face of the Earth.

Or, that was what a lot of people *thought* anyway.

What my father *allowed* them to believe.

Truth of it was, even in his state of anger, he could never harm a child. But he had no problem letting people *believe* that he had. It made him look like a bigger monster in their eyes, and who wanted to go to war with a monster?

Word quickly spread throughout the Bratva. Throughout the entire crime underworld. And now everyone knows that if you fuck with the Volkovs, it's not just you who suffers. It's your entire fucking family.

"She was," I whispered.

Father's eyes landed on me and his face softened. For a moment, it was completely silent in his office, my father, Aleksandr and I all stuck in memories of the woman whose death shattered us all.

Father quickly shook his head, like he was trying to banish his thoughts from his brain, and his face returned to the hard, cold face I've known for all my life. He pointed a finger at me and sternly said, "Be ready in the morning, Illayana. No fucking around."

I nodded, but said nothing in return.

"Good. Now go and enjoy your birthday," he said, waving a hand towards the door, effectively dismissing me.

I rose from my chair and leant forward, placing a kiss on his cheek. Turning around, I slapped Aleksandr on the shoulder. "Later, big brother," I said with a cheeky smile on my face.

"Later, brat."

CHAPTER THREE

Illayana Volkov

After leaving Father's office, I was absolutely brimming with excitement. The possibility of going to war with another mafia family had my fingers twitching and my blood running hot. It had been *so long* since the Volkovs had had a worthy challenge.

After my father's rampage over my mother's death, no one had the guts to challenge us, and I can't really blame them. When you hear an entire family has been wiped out, you tend to stay away from the people responsible.

Heading down the long corridor outside my father's office, I started to think about the meet the following day. *What are the De Lucas like? What exactly do they want from the Bratva?* It could be a simple means of trading. La Cosa Nostra were well known for their drug trade, whereas the Bratva specialised in arms trafficking and money laundering.

Could the De Lucas simply be looking to upgrade their weapons for their war against the Gambinos? A simple trade off, drugs for guns? I hated the fact that I'd have to wait until tomorrow to find out. I wondered if the bi-eyed beauty would be there.

Passing the kitchen, I watched as the maids rushed around trying to get lunch prepared. I barely paid attention as I made my way through the large open space, heading towards the back door.

"Illayana, wait."

I turned and frowned. "Nik? I thought you were leaving with Lukyan to deal with the high rollers."

"I am," he said, coming to a stop in front of me. "Have to talk to you first." He glanced around the room and leant in close so I could hear him whisper. "What the fuck was with last night?"

"What do you mean?" I asked, playing dumb.

He glared at me, not believing for a second that I didn't know what he was talking about. "You know exactly what I mean, Illayana. You threatened to castrate Ivan and Donat if they didn't let you through the gate with that little fucker you brought home from the club."

I winced. "I did?"

"Yes, you did. Why would you do something so stupid? You know Father is going to lose his mind when he finds out a norm passed through the gates."

My father classified anyone who wasn't in a criminal syndicate as a 'norm'—someone who lived a completely normal life, instead of one filled with violence and bloodshed.

"Look, I'll be honest. I barely remember the night, Nikolai. I'm sorry, okay?"

He shook his head, disappointment flashing on his face. "Just get rid of him before Father finds out. Otherwise it's both our asses."

I saluted him. "Yes, sir."

"I'm serious, Illayana. He's your responsibility. And if you don't handle it, we'll all be in deep shit."

"Alright, alright, I'll deal with it. Don't get your panties in a bunch."

"Nikolai! Hurry up already!" Lukyan yelled from the front of the house.

My brother narrowed his eyes and pointed his finger sternly at me before turning, plucking a banana from the kitchen counter and jogging away.

I blew out a breath and reached for the handle on the sliding door that led to the outside veranda. A deep voice called out to me from behind. Turning around, I found my father's *Sovietnik*, Maxim, heading towards me.

A *Sovietnik* is a councillor, someone who helps the *Pakhan* in making decisions and gives another point of view. Maxim has been with the Bratva for as long as I can remember, and he's one of my father's most trusted advisors.

My eyes travelled up and down his long, muscular body as he stopped in front of me. His full lips curved into that devilish smile that always made me hot, and his chocolate brown eyes lit up with excitement.

Maxim and I have had a bit of a sexual relationship over the past few years. He may be a little older than me. . .okay, a lot older. At thirty-nine, there's a solid eighteen years age difference between us, but I didn't give a shit. He was sexy as all fuck, and age doesn't matter to me if they're older.

"Happy Birthday, Miss Volkov," he said, giving me a slight bow and arching an eyebrow in amusement.

Even though we passed onto a first name basis years ago, in public he always addressed me as he should. My father would have killed him if he were to find out one of his men—his *Sovietnik*, no less—had slept with his daughter after she just turned eighteen. Actually, killing would be too quick. Knowing my father and his need for revenge, I'd say he'd make Maxim suffer for a long time before letting him meet his end.

"Maxim," I replied coolly with a slight tilt of my head.

Maxim scanned the kitchen, taking note of who was around us before his brown eyes focused back on me. His eyes roamed up and down my body, and I could see him undressing me in his mind. "Heading to the gym?" he asked, a hint of seduction in his voice.

The gym was our usual go-to place. There's an entire workout area specifically designed for me that only my brothers and I have access to. My father can be a tad bit overprotective sometimes, and he likes to make sure all precautions are met when they concern his only daughter.

Truth be told, I was heading to the gym, but not for the workout he had in mind.

"I am," I replied, before turning on my heel and making my way outside. The Las Vegas sun bored down on me the second I stepped foot on the veranda, and the heat instantly brought sweat to my brow. I hated the fucking heat with an unbelievable passion. If it's too hot and muggy, you better stay the fuck out of my way. I've been known to shoot a person or two who pisses me off on a hot day.

"Keen for some company?" Maxim asked, following behind me as I headed towards the warehouse a few yards behind the house. "I need to give you your birthday gift," he said, winking.

If I knew Maxim—and I did—his "gift" was his cock.

"Not today," I said briskly. "I have a meeting tomorrow with my father, and I need to get a proper workout in beforehand."

Maxim stopped dead in his tracks, a look of confusion plastered all over his face. "The De Luca meet? *You're* going to that?"

His tone of voice irritated the fuck out of me, and I couldn't help clenching my teeth.

"Yes. Father asked me."

"Why?" He immediately asked, and his line of questioning was really starting to piss me off.

Growing up with three overbearing brothers and a father who was head of the Russian Bratva, I learnt very quickly to stand up for myself and not take crap from anybody.

"Because Father said so."

Like I need any other fucking reason?

I continued on, a little frustrated, and he followed close behind me. I said nothing.

"Why would he want *you* there? You hardly ever come to meets. You're always off with Lukyan, doling out punishments."

This was true. I never had any particular interest in the meets my father would organise with other families or gangs within Las Vegas. I much preferred being out with my brothers, enforcing Father's word. That's where the *real fun* was.

I was debating whether or not to tell Maxim about my father's thoughts, about how there could be a possibility of marriage. How would Maxim react? He'd always shown a bit of possessiveness towards me. Would he flip out? God, I hoped not. I didn't want to have to deal with his jealous ass.

In the end, I decided to just keep my mouth shut. If my father wanted him to know, he would have told him himself.

"I don't question my father's orders, and neither should you," I said briskly, effectively ending the rest of the conversation.

The warehouse finally came into view and I turned around to face Maxim, who was only a few paces behind me.

"I'm not questioning him," he said quickly. "I just have no idea why he'd want *you* there."

I felt the rage his words brought on flow throughout my entire body. *What, does he think I'm not good enough to meet with the De Lucas? That I'm not strong enough to handle it?* I closed my eyes and clenched my fists at my sides. Taking in a deep, calming breath, I opened my eyes again to see Maxim watching me intently.

"What?" he asked, cocking his head to the side.

I shook my head and turned back around, heading towards the gym. Just as I reached for the handle on the door, I spoke. "I'm going inside to train. Don't follow me." I opened the door and stepped inside, slamming the door behind me.

Maxim had always been that way. He'd always questioned my involvement with the Bratva. I don't know if he thought I was incapable of doing what needs to be done, or if he just didn't want me in danger. Either way, he needed to mind his own fucking business. Maybe I'd let what had been going on between us get too far.

I felt along the wall next to the door. As soon as my fingers found the light switch, I flicked it on. The room immediately started to come into focus as light flowed throughout the warehouse. It was a large space—about 25,000–50,000 square feet—with a high tin roof and concrete flooring. Gym mats were placed strategically throughout the building, and an endless amount of weight sets were stacked haphazardly around the room.

I walked in, making my way to the space at the very end of the warehouse. I opened the door, flicked on the light and stepped inside. It was my safe haven, the only place I could truly calm down and let myself relax.

Ever since I was a young girl, I've been doing gymnastics. Apart from doing work for the Bratva, gymnastics is my ultimate passion. If I wasn't born into the mafia, I know I would have pursued it as a career. There's no way to describe the happiness that flows through me when I fly into the air, twisting and turning my body, only to land back on the ground with complete ease. Such pride, such accomplishment. It's a truly wonderful feeling.

When my mother saw the love I have for the sport, she built me my very own gymnastics gym, fully loaded with the very best equipment money can buy.

I headed straight for the large open space, ready to kick off and just start flying, ready for my mind to disappear and let my body take over.

I stood dead centre on the large blue mat, feet planted firmly on the ground with my hands at my sides. I cracked my neck and shook my hands out, jumping up and down on the spot. I pulled my phone out of my back pocket, connected it to the Bluetooth speakers and clicked Spotify.

Music immediately started blasting throughout the room, the walls almost shaking from the vibrations, but I didn't care. The louder the better. I just wanted to drown out everything and focus on the task ahead of me.

I tossed my phone to the side and ran forward, immediately starting a constant stream of front handsprings until I reached the end of the mat, and then a full-twisting layout, landing solidly on my feet. Without missing a beat, I flung my body back towards the centre of the mat and ended up in a handstand, my body completely straight with my toes pointed towards the roof. I waited five seconds, maintaining that position, staying still until I slowly moved my hands, heading back the way I came. After moving ten metres on my hands, I arched my body backwards and flipped, landing back on my feet. Then I spun around and did it all over again.

For hours and hours, I worked my body, pushing it almost to its breaking point. I flipped, I flew, I twisted my body in every direction it could go, working on making it as flexible as it could be. By the time I was finished, I was lying on my back in the middle of the mat, sweat coating my body and my breathing ragged. My muscles ached beyond belief. I couldn't help the smile coming across my face. It was a good session.

The sound of someone doing a slow clap pulled me out of my thoughts and my eyes scanned the room, trying to pinpoint the location of the noise. My brother, Lukyan, stood leaning against the far wall with a smirk on his face and his hands clapping in front of him.

"What the fuck do you want?" I grumbled, closing my eyes.

Lukyan stayed silent. I thought he might have left, until I heard his large body plop down next to mine. I turned my head to face him.

"Whatcha doin'?" he asked, rolling his body to face me and propping his head on his hand.

I couldn't help the smirk that came on my face. "Nothing, just thinking," I replied, turning my head back up towards the ceiling. "How were the high rollers?" I asked.

Truth be told, I was a little pissed that I couldn't go with. Usually, it was Lukyan and I who handled the clients. Sometimes people step out of their place, either mouthing off to someone they shouldn't be or refusing to pay their debts. That's where Lukyan and I come in. As Father's enforcers, it's up to us to keep people in line.

Lukyan pulled out a knife from the sheath on his hip and held it up high. It was still dripping with blood. "Not as much fun as I would have liked it to be, but entertaining enough."

I nodded, staying silent. Eventually, Lukyan sighed loudly.

"You're pissed I had all the fun, aren't ya?" Even though I couldn't see his face, I knew the bastard was smiling.

"Fuck you," I grumbled.

Lukyan stood up in a flash and extended his hand to me. I placed my hand in his and he helped me to my feet.

"Come on," he beckoned as he led me back to the main training area.

"Where are we going?" I asked, dragging my feet behind him.

To be honest, I was tired and cranky, all my muscles aching from my workout. All I wanted was a nice, hot bath and some vodka. Maybe even a joint. *Definitely* a joint.

"I haven't given you my present yet," Lukyan replied, a wide smile spreading across his face.

Excitement bubbled through me and all my other feelings disappeared. I love presents, and Lukyan always gives the best gifts.

I've always been close to Lukyan, more so than I have Aleksandr and Nikolai. I don't know if it's because he's only two years older than me, or if it's because we have the same quirky personality. Either way, he's my go-to brother.

He led me over to the large steel door at the very back of the warehouse. A small fingerprint scanner was on the right-hand side of the door, and a few metres up was a thin black camera, recording every movement within ten feet of the door.

Lukyan placed his right index finger over the scanner and the red light above it turned green, the door swinging open. A long wooden staircase led downwards into the pitch-black basement. Lukyan took point, walking down the stairs with ease. I followed behind, making sure to shut the door after me.

Once Lukyan reached the bottom, he flicked a switch on the wall and the hallway lit up. He led me down the long corridor, walking past several closed doors until he got to the one he wanted. Opening the door, he swept his hand out in front of him and bowed slightly, a playful expression on his face. "Your present awaits, Princess."

I glared. "Don't call me that. You know I hate being called that."

"Oh, come on, we both know you're Father's favourite. His little Princess," Lukyan laughed and I elbowed him in the ribs as I walked past, stepping into the room.

I took in the scene in front of me. The room was completely bare—except for the one male suspended from the roof. His hands were bound in a thick layer of chain that was being held up by a beam running along the roof. His feet just barely touched the ground as his body swayed slightly through the air.

He was completely naked and already had several cuts and bruises on his body. Blood dripped onto the floor, heading towards the drain at the centre of the room.

Lukyan walked over to the man, gripped his hair and flung his head back. He slapped his face a few times, trying to rouse him. "Wakey, wakey," he sang, slapping him a few more times for good measure.

The man groaned.

Lukyan let him go and turned to face me, a wicked smile on his face. "Best birthday present ever, right?"

I grinned. "Who is he?" I asked, walking forward and circling him like prey. My eyes roamed his body, looking for all those vital weak points.

"Some local gangbanger. Got caught roughing up one of our girls at *Strip*," Lukyan replied, backing up.

In case you couldn't tell, *Strip* is the name of one of our strip clubs downtown, in one of the worst parts of the city. Occasionally gangs stopped in to partake in certain services we provide.

"Ready to have some fun?" Lukyan asked, tying up his long hair at the nape of his neck. His eyes shone with excitement.

I slowly walked over to him and held out my hand. Lukyan reached for his knife and handed it over. It was a small dagger with a black leather hilt that had *LV* engraved along the blade.

I ran my thumb along the sharp edge, watching the blood drip down my hand. I turned and made my way back over to my present, my blood pumping with anticipation.

My eyes locked with Lukyan's and I raised the blade, a smile crossing my lips. "Where should we start?"

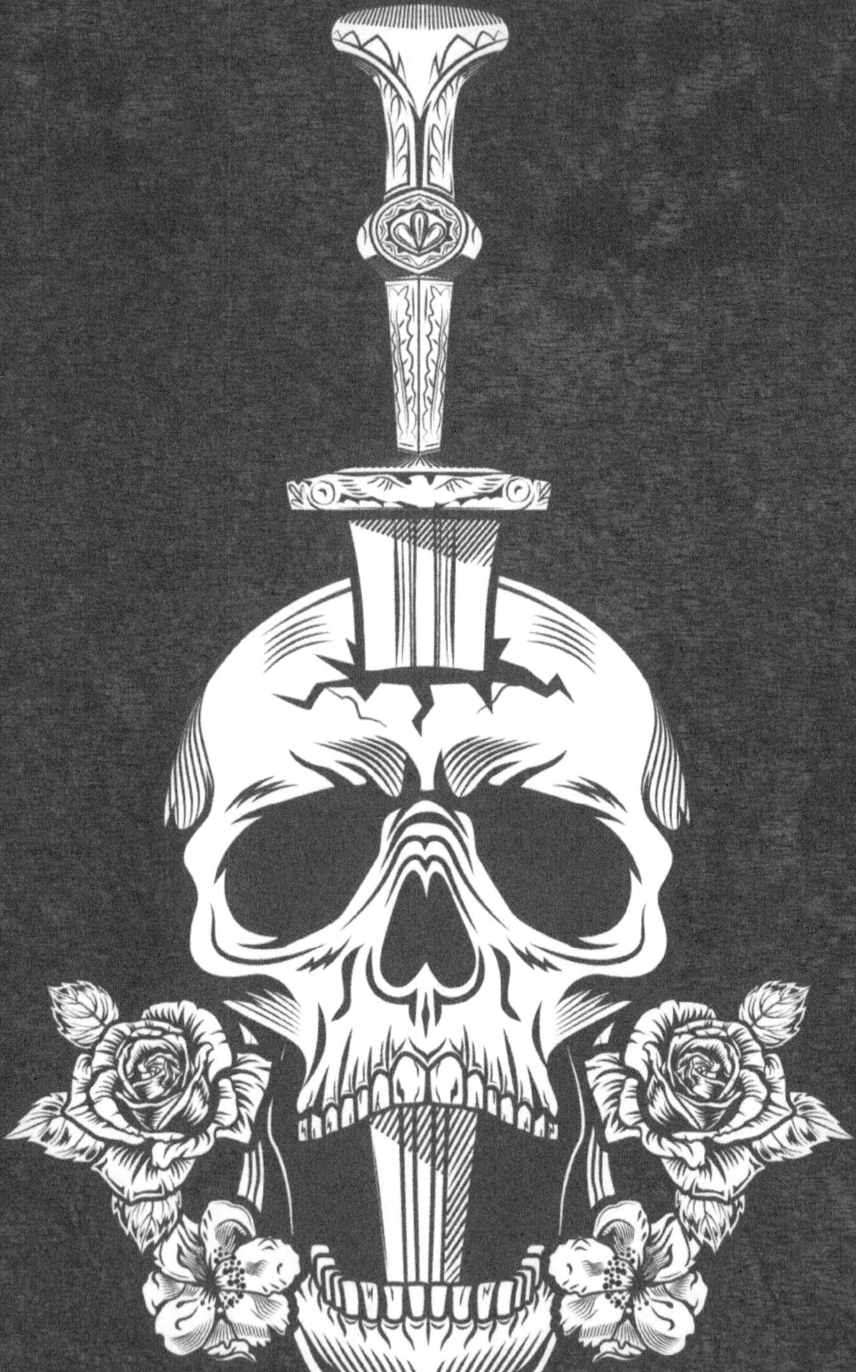

CHAPTER FOUR

Illayana Volkov

I woke up the next morning bright and early at two o'clock. I couldn't help it, I was too amped up for the coming day.

The night before, I'd spent hours researching everything there was to know about the De Luca family. Every single bit of information I could get my hands on now flowed through my brain.

For example, I knew Vincenzo De Luca was known around New York as the city's biggest man whore. He'd never had a serious girlfriend. In every photograph online and on his social media accounts, he had a different woman on his arm. His face was always plastered all over the tabloids with articles about some stupid, reckless stunt he just pulled off. It was easy to see how he'd gotten his reputation of being aloof and carefree. But then he had another side to himself...a dark, vicious side. Word on the street was he *loved* to get his hands dirty. He was the Cosa Nostra's official punisher, the one who inflicted all the pain on those who deserved it. And he could be quite creative with it, too.

His brother, Arturo De Luca, seemed to be the face of the family. And what a pretty face it was. He was CEO of a range of different companies throughout New York City, and he was known for being a real pit bull in the business world. He was lethal, cutthroat and didn't like being told no. If he wanted something, he got it. Even if he had to step over others to do it. Although there weren't many rumours about him on the streets, I had a feeling he was even more dangerous than his brother. There was something about him, something lurking behind those gorgeous mismatched eyes that screamed danger.

As the information about the De Lucas flowed through my brain, I started to get ready for the day. I quickly jumped out of bed and made my way to my bathroom for a quick shower. Once I was finished, I dressed in the outfit I had laid out the night before and did my usual hair and makeup routine.

Standing in front of my full-length mirror, I took stock of my appearance. I was wearing one of my favourite business outfits: a long-sleeved black blouse that clung to my chest like a second skin, matched with a knee-length pencil skirt that accentuated all my curves. I had on my favourite pair of black Louis Vuitton pumps that added an extra few inches to my height. My long black hair was left free to flow down my body, ending just above my waist.

I kept my makeup minimal; just simple eyeshadow, eyeliner and blush, my full lips painted with a bright red lipstick.

After strapping a holster around my chest, I placed two fully-loaded semi-automatic handguns in the pouches. I placed another holster around my waist and put my favourite switchblade in. Walking over to my closet, I pulled out a stylish long coat that matched my outfit and, pulling it on, concealed my weapons. After stashing a few more knives into my coat, I was ready to go.

My phone rang. Frowning, I picked it up.

"Yes?" I answered.

"You're meeting with the De Lucas today?! Why didn't you tell me?!"

Tatiana screeched. I had to pull the phone away from my ear, it was so loud.

"Who told you I was meeting them?"

"Irrelevant! Is it true?"

"Yes, it's true. They reached out requesting a sit down."

"Oh my god! Oh my god, you lucky bitch! Do you have any idea how hot the De Luca brothers are?! They're spank-your-ass-and-fuck-you-til you-can't-feel-your-pussy hot!"

I rolled my eyes. "Calm down, they ain't all that." I was lying through my teeth. They were sexy as all hell. "How do you even know who they are, anyway?"

"Um, hello, they're two of the most eligible bachelors in New York! Who doesn't know who they are? Argh, I'm so jealous of you right now, I could kick you."

I laughed. "Thanks? I think. Anyway, I gotta go. We're leaving soon to meet them."

"Take pictures!" she yelled.

"Pictures? Are you serious? I can't just take pictures of them in the middle of a meet."

"Yes, you can! Just do it on the sly. Come on, I need some material for my spank bank."

"Dude, they're not going to be naked!"

"Doesn't matter. They're that hot, I don't need them to be. Just snap a few for me."

"I'll try."

"You better!"

I hung up, shaking my head.

She was fucking nuts.

I walked out of my bedroom and made my way downstairs without another thought. I knew that if I were to stand around and dwell, my mind would start to go crazy and the nerves would kick in.

Stepping into the foyer, I saw Aleksandr waiting next to the front door, dressed in a sharp black suit that looked like it was moulded to his large, muscular frame. His black hair was cut short and neat, his blue eyes narrowed in thought. I couldn't see any weapons on him, but I knew he was packing.

The only sound that could be heard was the click-clack of my heels as I made my way over to Aleksandr. He stuck his fist out for a quick fist bump as I took up position next to him. We were only waiting for a few minutes before we heard the door to our father's office open and shut.

Making his way through the corridor towards us, flanked by four of his men, my father looked just as menacing as the *Pakhan* should. His face was set in stone, portraying no emotion whatsoever. His body moved with grace, his shoes making no sound at all as he walked on the marble floor. He was wearing a stylish, dark three-piece Armani suit with a grey tie and matching pocket square.

He didn't say a word as Aleksandr opened the front door for him and he stepped out. We followed close behind him, heading straight for the black Range Rover parked in front of the house.

Maxim stood waiting next to the car, feet planted firmly on the ground and hands clasped behind his back. "Boss," he said in a deep voice, opening the back door of the car.

Father acknowledged him with a slight tilt of his head and climbed into the back seat. Maxim extended his hand to me and helped me inside, with Aleksandr following close behind me.

Maxim climbed into the passenger side while another one of my father's men took the driver's seat. "Let's go," Maxim told the driver gruffly. "The helicopter is waiting."

The driver nodded and started the car, driving down the dirt pathway that led away from the house. Just as we arrived at the main gate, the large iron-wrought fence swung open, allowing our departure.

After a quick car ride, we arrived at a large open field where our MD 500 Helicopter was waiting for us. The rotary-winged aircraft was prepped and ready to go, wind flowing around the blades as they sliced through the air.

We all rushed out of the car, heading for the helicopter. This wasn't the first time we had to take the chopper somewhere. We all knew what to do.

Making sure to keep my head low, I jumped inside the black aircraft, strapping into the seat straight away. After chucking on the headset and double-checking my seat belt was clicked into place, I looked to Aleksandr, who took the empty seat next to me. He gave me a quick wink as he put his headset on.

My father sat in front of us with Maxim at his side. After a signal to the pilot, the helicopter started to rise into the air with ease.

I leant back in my chair and closed my eyes, running through everything I knew about the De Lucas one more time.

I felt my phone vibrate in my coat pocket and quickly pulled it out to read the text.

Maxim: Don't be nervous, baby, I'll keep you safe ;)

My eyes flicked up to connect with Maxim's dark brown ones, which were already on me. He had his phone in his hand and a sly smile on his face.

I scowled at him and looked out the window. He knew I hated being called 'baby'. Furthermore, I hated the fact that he was treating me this way. I'm not a fucking child, and I'm not weak. I don't need protection. My father taught me to protect myself.

Maxim was continuing to step out of line. I'd let our arrangement go on for too long, and it was clear he was laying a claim to me. One he was most definitely not entitled to. Even if I wanted to be with him—which I didn't—it could never happen. My father would never allow it.

An idea popped into my head and, before I could question it, I raised my hand and pressed a button on the side of my headset and spoke.

"If I agree to marry into the De Luca family, what will you ask for in exchange, Father?"

My voice flitted through their heads and three sets of eyes landed on me.

Maxim's face was one of pure confusion that morphed into anger within seconds. "Marry? Why would you *marry* a De Luca?!" he asked, showing a bit too much emotion.

Aleksandr arched an eyebrow at Maxim's reaction to my question, and I mentally slapped the fool. If he wasn't more careful, they were gonna catch on real fucking quick. I just wanted to torture the fucker for a bit, not completely blow our cover.

My father's bright blue eyes were on me, the orbs twinkling with excitement. "Expansion," he replied, one side of his mouth quirking up into a smile.

Maxim's eyes flew between my father and I, like he couldn't believe we were having this conversation. I could see the anger radiating off him, feel it climb over me and cling to my skin.

He was pissed.

"The Italians would never agree to a marriage," Maxim said stiffly, turning his head to look out the window. "They're sticklers for tradition. They never marry outside of the *famiglia*."

That was true. The Italians were well known for only marrying within other Italian bloodlines. I myself had never heard of a union between La Costa Nostra and the Bratva before, but that didn't mean it wasn't possible.

Aleksandr's deep voice came through next, clear as day. "Is marriage what you want, *sestra?*" Sister. I turned my head to look at him. He had a smirk on his face and his eyes were shining with amusement.

"Wouldn't be the worst proposal in the world, big brother," I replied, winking at him. "Me, married to the future head of La Cosa Nostra? Who knows how much fun I could have!" Because I had a sneaking suspicion that, if a marriage was proposed, it would be to the eldest De Luca. Which meant that when Alessandro eventually stepped down, I would be Queen of New York. Not a bad thought, considering I would never get that here. Aleksandr was the one who would inherit our father's title.

Aleksandr's face broke out into a full-blown smile, his big body shaking as he chuckled.

"They won't ask for marriage," Maxim interjected. "They just won't. It's not how they do things."

I looked back over at him. His eyes were fixed firmly on me, his hands clenched on top of his knees. His body was tense with anger, and I could see the tick in his jaw from where I sat across from him.

"If an alliance is proposed, the only way to solidify that would be with marriage. It's the only logical course of action," Aleksandr replied stiffly, narrowing his eyes at Maxim.

"They won't do it because she's not Italian!" Maxim hissed, pointing straight at me.

My father frowned at his outburst. "Control yourself, Maxim," he scolded, like he was talking to a child.

Maxim lowered his hand and straightened his big body. He narrowed his eyes at me accusingly, like I orchestrated this whole thing.

Well, I kinda did.

"They won't ask," he muttered. "They won't."

It sounded like he was trying to convince himself more than us, but either way I stayed silent, letting the conversation drop.

A little while later, we touched down in a wide-open field. A black SUV was parked and ready to go as soon as we landed. We all piled in and headed to our destination.

The car ride was tense, the conversation from the helicopter still hanging in the air. It was clear Maxim was still pissed about the whole thing. He didn't even try to hide it. The fucker. If my father and Aleksandr didn't know about our relationship before, they sure as fuck did now.

After a short time, we pulled up in front of a large commercial building. I had no idea who owned it, but I trusted my father had the whole thing handled. The second we parked, Maxim jumped out and opened our car door, and we all climbed out. Another black SUV pulled up behind us and four of my father's men got out and took up position behind us without a word. Knowing how prepared my father always was, he would have had the men here earlier to scope out the building before we arrived to make sure it wasn't an ambush of some kind.

As we made our way into the building, my mind started going into overdrive. My eyes moved around the room we'd just walked into, looking for any type of threat, but there was none. The place was completely empty.

We walked along the main floor, not a single soul in sight, not a single sound to be heard except for the click-clack of my heels.

Father led us to an elevator on the far side of the building. It was a tight fit, but we all crammed inside. As the door shut and the elevator began to rise, I felt something touch my hand. I looked down to see Maxim wrapping his fingers around my wrist. I looked at him in confusion and tried to pull my wrist back, but his hold immediately tightened.

His lips were pressed in a tight line and I could see the vein in the middle of his forehead start to throb. He squeezed tighter to the point of pain, and I tried hard not to react. As soon as the elevator dinged announcing our arrival at our floor, I narrowed my eyes at him and pulled my wrist free. This time he let it go, but I could tell by the look on his face that it wasn't over.

Father walked out first, followed by Aleksandr on his right and me on his left. Maxim took up position behind us, along with my father's other men. We walked in complete silence, no one making a sound. We passed several different conference rooms, each one completely empty. The place was completely deserted.

At the end of the hall, a woman was waiting with her head down and hands clasped in front of her body. She was dressed in a stylish black pantsuit and her blonde hair was up in a tight bun. She kept her head down as we approached, not saying a word. I could see her body shaking and I knew she was scared—terrified, more likely.

I mean, who wouldn't be? You're about to be trapped in a building with two of the most ruthless mafia leaders in America. If you weren't the tiniest bit freaked out by that prospect, you were a fucking fool.

The double doors beside the woman swung open as we stepped closer, and we walked in. The first thing I noticed was the huge conference table in the middle of the room. It could easily seat fifty people, but at that moment it was empty. The only thing on it was a basket of fruit centred in the middle.

I followed my father to the head of the table with Aleksandr as Maxim and the other men fell back to take up position behind us against the wall. My eyes moved around the room, taking in every bit of detail I could.

Alessandro De Luca stood dead centre at the other end of the table, his lips pressed together and eyes narrowed on us. He was wearing a suit similar to the one in the picture I saw yesterday, and it looked even better on him in person than it did in the photo.

His two sons were standing beside him, Vincenzo on his left, Arturo on his right. I had to work hard not to stare openly at his eldest son. In fact, I tried to not even look at him at all. But the second I felt his gaze on me, that flew out the bloody window.

Arturo stood tall, a few inches more so than his father. His suit clung to him like a second skin, his muscles bulging and contracting as he moved. His large, muscular body was screaming for my attention. I didn't think there was a man out there as big as Aleksandr, but Arturo could definitely give him a run for his money.

His eyes—one blue and one green—were firmly on me, running up and down the length of my body. When his eyes finally locked onto mine, his lips curved up into a coy smile. God, he looked even more handsome in person (if that was even possible). The intensity of his gaze started to make my palms sweat.

He had a certain aura about him. A dark, dangerous presence that surrounded the guy. Power. That's the first thing that came to mind as I stared at him, admiring the rough, sculpted lines of his face.

I couldn't get over how gorgeous the man was! The fact that he didn't stop staring at me started to make me nervous, but I worked hard not to show it.

Vincenzo was dressed in black slacks and a white button-up dress shirt. His bright green eyes were sparkling. They were mesmerising. His black hair was styled messily, like he just got up this morning, ran his fingers through it and said, "Yep, I'm done." But surprisingly, it looked good on him. Of course, it would. With a face like that, I'm sure he couldn't look bad if he tried.

At first, no one said a word. Everyone was too busy sizing the others up. The De Lucas were watching us, and we were watching them.

"De Luca," my father's deep voice filled the room.

"Volkov," Alessandro replied in the same tone.

They both stood there, staring at each other for a few more seconds before they simultaneously pulled out their chairs and took a seat.

Aleksandr followed our father, easing his big, overgrown body into the tiny chair they'd provided. Just as I was about to take my seat, Maxim came over and pulled my chair out, sweeping his hand over it like he was my Prince Charming or some shit.

I narrowed my eyes at him but said nothing as I sat down. I looked across the table to find Arturo's gorgeous mismatched eyes scrutinising Maxim's every move. His icy glare was fixed permanently on Maxim as he took his seat next to his father.

Vincenzo turned his seat around and sat down, leaning his arms against the back of the chair. He cocked his head to the side as his eyes locked onto me.

The room filled with silence once more until my father spoke again, stretching out his hand. "The floor is yours, De Luca."

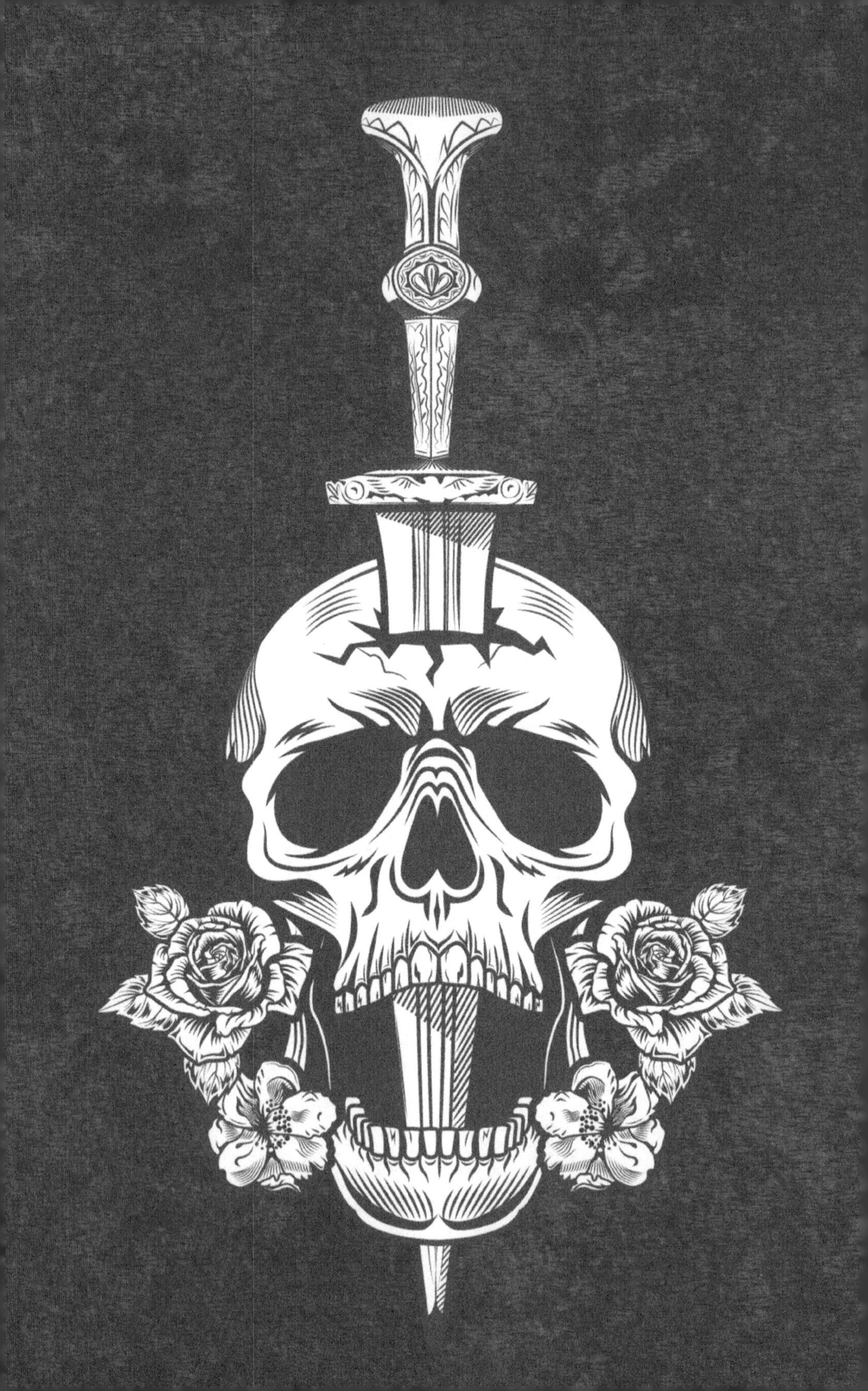

CHAPTER FIVE

Illayana Volkov

I watched as Alessandro tapped his finger on the table, pursing his lips. It was like he was trying to figure out where to start.

"It's been a long time, Dimitri," he eventually said, tilting his head to the side, studying my father. His thick Italian accent came through clear as day.

"It has," my father replied coldly.

"How's the family? And business?" Alessandro asked.

"Cut the shit, De Luca, and get on with it," my father snapped, his icy blue eyes lit with fire.

Alessandro shook his head and chuckled, his big body shaking in his seat. "Ah, still as patient as ever, I see," he said, scratching his chin. "Alright. No more pleasantries then." He took a deep breath before continuing. "If you're going to understand exactly what it is we're doing here, I'm going to need to explain a little bit of. . .De Luca family history to you," he said, waving his hand in front of him. "Twenty-nine years ago, my wife, Isabella, was arranged to be married to Nero Gambino, son of Matteo Gambino, Don of The Chicago Outfit. It was a contract agreed upon by their families at the time she was born. She was set to marry him a few weeks after her eighteenth birthday. That was, until she met me." A sly smile broke out over his face, his blue eyes twinkling with amusement.

"We fell for each other instantly, kindred spirits and all that. But I knew the Gambinos would never let her go. She was, for all intents and purposes, theirs. Nero's," he sneered, shaking his head, anger starting to take over his body at the memories playing through his mind. "There was only one way I could see out of it, out of her arrangement with the Gambinos," he said, placing a hand on Arturo's shoulder.

"You got her pregnant," I said, my eyes fixed firmly on Arturo.

His gorgeous blue-green eyes were already on me, watching me. His lips were set in a slight frown that made him look even sexier.

Alessandro smiled, showing his gorgeous, straight white teeth. *"Sì,"* he replied, nodding his head. "Nero was, well. . .not happy to hear his bride had not only slept with another man, but was pregnant as well. He was ready to come and take her by force. To challenge me for her," Alessandro scoffed, shaking his head like the mere thought of that was idiotic. "But his father wouldn't allow it. Matteo was already at war with an MC gang that was selling drugs in his territory. He couldn't afford to start another war with us. He was by no means happy with how things were playing out. The Russos—Isabella's family—had agreed to a union with the Gambinos, but he didn't have a choice. He simply didn't have the numbers to fight a war on two fronts. In the end, he compromised and agreed to take another Russo woman in Isabella's place—Isabella's younger sister, Mia. It meant waiting a few years until she came of age, but the agreement suited everyone."

"Everything in the end worked out, and our families were able to put aside what happened. My father, Antonio De Luca, the head of La Cosa Nostra, apologised in person for my 'behaviour' and agreed to supply Matteo with a years' worth of free drugs as penance. Everyone was able to forgive and forget. Except for Nero," he said, pressing his lips firmly together. I could see the veins pulsing in his neck, and I knew his anger was building.

My father remained quiet as Alessandro spoke, his hands clasped together on the table in front of him. Aleksandr hadn't moved at all, his icy glare stuck firmly on the De Lucas.

"Nero was never able to let go of the past. He could never accept the fact that I won, and he lost. Over the years, his anger continued to build, until he was finally able to do something about it. A few months ago, Matteo was murdered in a drug deal gone bad. His people think it was us who killed him, and I bet you can guess who started that bullshit," he said, shaking his head, clenching his fists on the table. "Nero quickly became Don of The Chicago Outfit, taking over from his father. His first order was to attack us. He claimed it was revenge for what happened to his father, but I knew better. It was, and always will be, about Isabella."

"I was prepared for it and planned against his attack. It was easy. Nero was nothing more than a child playing dress up in his father's clothing. He may have been his father's successor, but he didn't know anything about being a leader. I had already been head of La Cosa Nostra for years, taking over after the death of my own father, when Nero stepped up. I know how to lead, how to plan, how to fight and how to win."

"Even though he wasn't successful the first time, Nero continued to attack us, but it was never anything more than a nuisance. He just didn't have the experience to take me on, or the guidance. He lost a lot of support after the first few attempts failed, and to be honest, I was having fun slowly stripping him of everything he had," Alessandro said, shrugging a shoulder, chuckling.

Then he took a deep breath in, closing his eyes. He exhaled loudly, letting all the air back out. "That is, unfortunately, until my ego got the better of me. I should have stopped toying with him and just finished the job, but I was having too much fun!" he yelled like a petulant child. "I didn't anticipate him approaching The Los Zetas for aid," he said, scowling.

Vincenzo chuckled at his father's behaviour, and I couldn't help joining in. It was funny to see a big, bad mafia boss sulking because he was having fun destroying someone's life and he couldn't continue to do so.

"The Los Zetas? The Mexican Cartel?" Aleksandr asked, speaking for the first time since we entered.

"*Si,*" Arturo replied, speaking for the first time as well. His voice was deep and thick, seductive. It felt like it was crawling all over my skin, giving me goosebumps.

"With their help, he's managed to hit us back. Hard. He's not only fucked up a few of our trade routes, but he's ambushed several of our suppliers as well. They were either murdered, or turned to work for him," Alessandro said, gritting his teeth. "I've had enough of this fucker, and I'm ready to do what I should have done years ago," Alessandro said, straightening in his chair. "That's where you come in, Dimitri."

My father arched an eyebrow at his last statement. "Oh?" he questioned.

Alessandro narrowed his eyes and scowled. "Don't play dumb, Volkov, you know what I want. As much as I wish I could do it on my own, I simply don't have the contacts. I need your guns. Nero has declared all-out war on us, and with the Los Zetas aiding him, he's becoming more and more of a threat."

My father chuckled, shaking his head. He raised his hand in the air, clicking his fingers. Immediately the woman from outside came in with a glass of what I could only assume was vodka. She placed it down in front of him and stepped back two steps.

"Would you like a drink?" my father asked, raising his own glass to his lips and draining the contents.

Alessandro remained silent.

"Fine. Just trying to be hospitable," Father said, waving the woman off. She quickly scurried out of the room like a mouse. "What kind of guns do you wa—"

"What do you have?" Vincenzo interrupted.

"Raspizdyay," Stupid fucker, I whispered in Russian.

Arturo narrowed his eyes.

Did he understand what I said?

My father immediately pinned his dark glare on Vincenzo the second he spoke. I could see the rigid cords in his neck, see his eyes bulging with anger. He *despised* when people interrupted him. It was one of his *biggest* pet peeves, and if I was Vincenzo, I'd be shitting my fucking pants under that death glare.

"Watch who you're talking to, boy," my father hissed, spit flying across the table.

"Maybe it's *you* who should watch out for *me*, old man," Vincenzo said, grabbing an apple from the middle of the table and kicking his feet up.

Did this kid have a fucking death wish?

Arturo's gaze was on me and my pulse spiked as I felt his eyes crawl all over me, but I kept my focus on my father. His blue eyes looked to me and he gave me the slightest nod. Barely recognisable, but I saw it.

As Vincenzo brought the apple to his lips and bit into it, I quickly pulled out a throwing knife from inside my coat and flung it straight at him. The blade flew through the air, piercing the apple with textbook precision.

Vincenzo sat frozen in place, the apple in his mouth, his hands still gripping the sides with my blade stuck right in the middle. He slowly pulled the apple away from his face and held it up in the air, looking at it with bewilderment. His green eyes landed on me and I could see the fire burning within.

"V sleduyushchiy raz eto budet tvoy glaz." Next time, it'll be your eye, I said in Russian, my eyes fixed firmly on Vincenzo.

"I have no idea what the fuck you just said, and I don't care. That was hot as fuck," he breathed, his green eyes sparkling with desire. His lips curved into a sly smile and he waved his fingers in the air at me, like he was saying hi.

"Enough, Vincenzo," Arturo barked.

"Enough, both of you!" Alessandro snapped, slamming his hands on the table. "My apologies, Dimitri. Please, continue."

My father leant back in his chair, tapping his fingers on his chin. "Which guns do you want?" he asked, repeating his earlier question.

My eyes locked onto Vincenzo's to make sure he kept his mouth shut this time. He smirked and winked at me.

"Your standard MP5s and M60s, as well as some higher ordnance pieces for my boys and I. DAR-701-4s, to be precise. A few high-powered rifles, and some semi-automatic handguns as well should do the trick," Alessandro said casually, like he was ordering a meal at a fucking restaurant.

In the corner of my eye, I saw Aleksandr pull out his phone and begin texting away, most likely to see exactly what we had available. I knew we had plenty of MP5s and M60s, but the Canadian submachine guns (the DAR-701-4s) might be a little harder to track down.

"And in return?" my father questioned, arching an eyebrow.

"What do you want?" Alessandro asked, leaning back in his chair.

Expansion. My father's voice fluttered through my brain.

"I want more, Alessandro. More territory, more money, more power. If you can't help me with that, then this negotiation is over," Father said briskly.

Maxim chuckled from behind me, amused at my father's words.

Arturo's blue-green eyes flicked up to Maxim. A dark, evil look crossed his face. One that screamed danger, pain. It was a look you gave your enemies before you stepped out onto the battlefield. One used to intimidate, to make them cower.

I sucked in a breath at the darkness radiating from him, my heart thumping loudly in my chest. Arturo glanced at me and his gaze turned predatory, like a man honing in on a woman he wanted to fuck.

Maxim grumbled loudly enough for the whole damn room to hear him, causing a smile to break out over Arturo's face.

"That, I can most certainly help you with, my friend," Alessandro chuckled. "More territory? Simple. Take Chicago once this is all over. I don't want it, nor do I need it. One of your sons can rule in your place if you see fit. More money? Easy. With our distribution already set up in New York City, we'll sell your guns for a small percentage. More power? Well, that's something perhaps you and I should discuss in private," Alessandro finished, his gaze sweeping over the men standing behind my father.

I couldn't figure out if he was just a cautious person, or if he genuinely didn't trust our men.

My father tapped his fingers along the table, pursing his lips in thought. I could see he was seriously considering this, but there was still a part of him that was holding back. "You said The Los Zetas aided Nero. How so? Was it just with weapons, or did they supply Nero with men to help take you on?" I asked Alessandro, leaning forward on my elbows.

A sly smile broke out over his face as his gaze landed on me. *"Intelligente e bella."* Smart and beautiful, Alessandro said in Italian. *"I preferisco mortale."* I prefer deadly, I replied in Italian. I watched in amusement as all three of the De Luca men looked at me in surprise, their jaws dropping open. They hadn't anticipated that I could speak their native tongue.

My father always thought it was important to know your enemy. And how can you know your enemy if you don't speak their language? So, he made sure my brothers and I learnt the basics: Italian, Spanish and Chinese (and Russian, obviously).

"To answer your question *Principessa, Princess,* it was with reinforcements. The Los Zetas provided a stream of men to help in his crusade against us," Alessandro replied.

"And is that what you need from us? Men as well as weapons?" Aleksandr asked, continuing my line of questioning.

My father leant back in his chair and let us take over. He never minded when we asked questions. If anything, he preferred it. He always used to say the best way to learn something was to do it firsthand.

If Alessandro cared that we were the ones asking questions, he didn't show it. He continued as if my father himself had spoken. "*Si.* I'm not asking to pluck your men from your territory and bring them to mine. No, no, no," Alessandro began, his thick Italian accent coating his words. "I'm merely suggesting that when certain situations arise, I can call upon you and your men to aid us. We would extend the same courtesy to you as well, should you need it."

My father remained silent as he processed Alessandro's words. I could see his brain running through every possible scenario that having an alliance with the De Lucas could bring.

He raised his hand and clicked his fingers, bringing forth the woman from earlier, a new drink in her hand. She took the empty glass from before, placed the new one down in front of my father and quickly made her exit.

He brought the glass to his lips and sighed with satisfaction as the liquid moved down his throat. He remained silent after finishing his drink, letting the suspense build in the air. The four men standing behind the De Lucas started to shift from foot to foot, unable to hide their discomfort.

Father watched as the men squirmed before him. He didn't show it, but I could tell he was pleased at their reaction. The only ones seemingly unaffected by my father's powerful presence were the De Luca men.

"You've given me a lot to think about, Alessandro, a lot to consider. But I do still have one question for you," my father spoke low, his voice rough.

Alessandro arched an eyebrow, waiting.

"How do you plan to solidify our alliance? A blood oath, or a union of marriage?"

At Father's last question, I heard a sharp intake of breath come from behind me, and I knew it was Maxim. I didn't need to turn around to know exactly the kind of look that would be on his face.

A low growl started sounding throughout the room and it took everything in me not to stand up and slap him across the face. I clenched my fists on the table and closed my eyes. Taking three deep breaths, I opened them again to find Arturo's gorgeous eyes looking directly at me.

A frown flashed on his face, his eyes darting quickly between Maxim and I. It was clear that he could tell there was something going on between us. Only a fool wouldn't recognise the signs. And if Arturo—a complete stranger—could figure it out, that meant my father could.

Alessandro opened his mouth to respond and Arturo tapped him lightly on the shoulder, stopping him. Alessandro leant over so Arturo could whisper in his ear. After a few seconds, Alessandro pulled back and stared at his son, frowning.

Arturo held his father's gaze, not backing down from whatever he'd just said.

Alessandro's blue eyes narrowed on me before returning to his son. He gave a swift nod and then turned back to face my father.

"An alliance such as ours has never been attempted before. It stands to reason that there will be those not happy with a truce between our people," he said, waving his hand in the air. "To guarantee a strong alliance, and to show we mean business, I suggest we do both."

"Both?!" a voice shrieked.

It took a second for me to realise it was Maxim. My father, Aleksandr and I all slowly turned around in our seats, staring at our father's *sovietnik* in disbelief.

Maxim quickly regained his composure and lowered his gaze to the floor, but it was too late. The damage was done. I didn't even have to look at my father to know he was seething. I could hear him grinding his teeth. I watched as he clenched and unclenched his hands, the act showing how desperate he was to wrap his hands around Maxim's throat.

"Yes," Alessandro continued. "Both."

We all turned back around, ignoring Maxim's outburst (for the moment) and refocusing on the matter at hand.

"I'm proposing a blood oath between you and I, Dimitri. And a union of marriage between my son and your daughter," he said, inclining his head towards me.

My eyes locked onto Arturo's. His gaze roamed over my face, then my body, like he was taking inventory. A dark, predatory look crossed his face before he gave me a panty-melting smirk, one that made shivers dance over my skin. Looking at the man, you could just tell he would be amazing in bed, that he knew the way around a woman's body. That he would give you a night you would never forget.

My body was frozen under Arturo's scrutiny. I couldn't move, couldn't think. My mind was like jello. *Holy fuck.* They really were suggesting a marriage! Before I could even think of a response, Father spoke.

"I see," he said, rising slowly from his chair. Aleksandr and I quickly followed. "Like I said, you've given me a lot to think about. I'll let you know my decision in two days." With a final nod in their direction, my father turned and headed for the door.

Aleksandr bowed slightly before pivoting on his heels and walking away.

My eyes connected one more time with Arturo's as I made my way towards the exit. Just as I reached the door, I heard his deep, seductive voice call out to me in Russian. *"Uvidimsya, kotenok,"* See you soon, kitten.

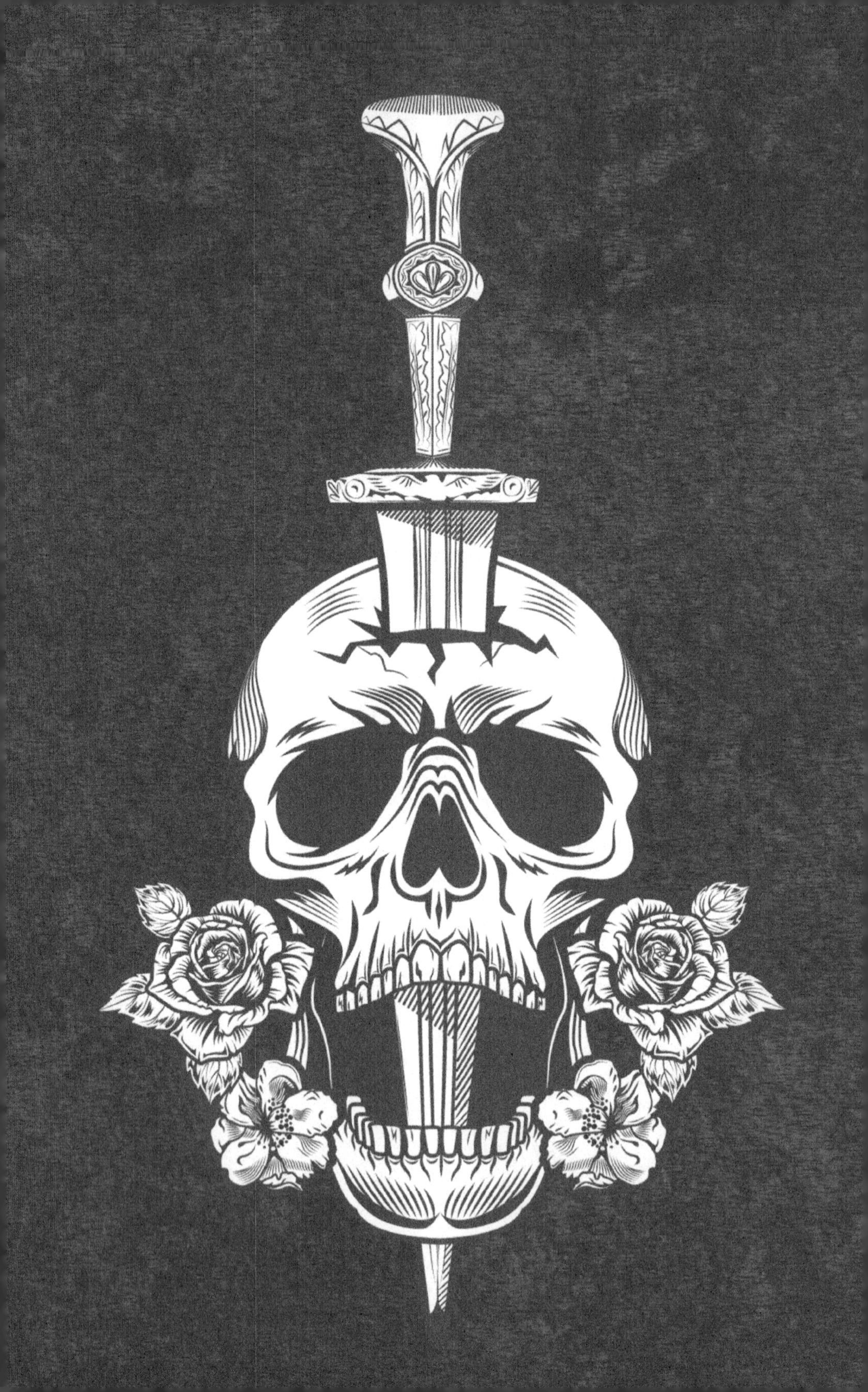

CHAPTER SIX

Arturo De Luca

I watched in awe as the tall Russian beauty walked out of the room, her long black hair flowing behind her.

Illayana Volkov.

Even though we weren't formally introduced, I knew who she was. I knew who they all were.

The second she'd first walked into the room, she had my undivided attention. I couldn't keep my eyes off her. Her gorgeous tanned skin, her beautiful, piercing blue eyes and those enticing full lips had me screaming in my head for a little taste.

Never in my life had any woman caught my attention the way she had. The way she moved. The way she talked. The way she walked into a room commanding your attention. It all called to me. She called to me.

I could tell straight away she wasn't anything like the other women I'd dated. She was a fighter. A warrior. A soldier. Even though I could see she was armed, it still surprised the fuck out of me when she pulled a blade from her coat and threw it at Vin.

She reminded me of a kitten; a vicious little thing that, when threatened, would rip you to shreds with her teeth and claws. Oh, I had no doubt she was dangerous. Lethal. The fact that she could throw a knife with such speed and precision proved that. But that's what made her so captivating.

All the women in the famiglia were timid, docile, boring. None were anything like her. And I was supposed to marry one of them?

No. That's not what I wanted. I didn't give a fuck if it broke tradition, I didn't want a weak wife. I wanted someone strong who could match me, challenge me. And I knew that woman was Illayana.

Her sweet, sexy voice as she spoke in Russian (and Italian) made me want to fuck her so hard, she screamed my name.

I could tell by the way she kept looking at me that she was just as affected by my presence, as I was hers. She tried her best to hide it, to hide the lingering gazes and the blushes that crept onto her face, but I saw it. I saw it all.

Even that stupid fucker at the back, Maxim. I saw how he looked at her with hunger and desire. His eyes never left her body the entire time we were in that fucking room, and it took everything in me not to march over there and shove my gun down his throat. He might not have known it, but the second she walked into that room, she was mine.

Her brother, Aleksandr, was a quiet one. I kept an eye on him, even though the majority of my attention was on his gorgeous younger sister. He was a big guy, packed with muscle like a damn marine. I knew it would be in my best interest to avoid pissing that dude off (not that I was worried I couldn't take him. I could, I just didn't really want to go toe to toe with the dude).

According to the information Vin acquired about their family, she had another two older brothers, Nikolai and Lukyan. I was hoping they would be there as well so I could assess them, but no matter. I was sure there would be plenty of time to get to know my future brothers-in-law.

Vin let out a low, long whistle of surprise as the double doors slammed shut. "Damn," he breathed, running a hand through his thick black hair. "She was somethin', huh?"

I turned around to look at my younger brother. To me, he looked exactly like our father, only a much younger version. His startling vivid green eyes were locked firmly on me as I stared him down.

"Don't even fucking think about it, Vin," I grumbled, shoving his shoulder as I walked past.

"What?" he asked innocently, arching an eyebrow. "The deal is to marry a De Luca son," he stated, walking forward, stretching out his arms and turning in a circle. "Uhm, hello? That's me." He pointed his thumbs at his chest, a sly smile spread out over his dumb, handsome face.

"It was my idea, stronza, asshole, therefore I'm the one marrying her."

"No fucking way! Just because you suggested it? Nuh-uh," Vin said, shaking his head aggressively. I swear, sometimes you would think he was bloody five years old.

Alessandro's deep, throaty chuckle made Vin and I look at him in confusion. "What's so funny?" I asked, frowning.

Alessandro shook his head, his big body still shaking from laughter. "I find it amusing that you think the choice is yours, my sons."

"Why wouldn't it be? When Dimitri agrees, I'll take her as my wife. End of discussion. There is no choice in the matter," I stated firmly.

"It is not Dimitri who must agree to the marriage," Alessandro replied. His blue eyes locked onto me as he waited for me to figure out the hidden meaning behind his words.

"Then who?" Vin asked, scratching his head. His nose was scrunched up, like he was working his brain overtime to try and work it out himself.

Alessandro sighed. "Illayana, of course."

Surprise flashed across Vin's face. "What? That can't be right. As a matter of fact, what was she even doing here? Since when does a woman get involved in our world?"

I could see where he was coming from. In La Cosa Nostra, the women are never involved in the day-to-day operations of the world we live in. They're to be kept safe, to be protected. At the slightest hint of danger, they were taken away and hidden in our safe houses until the danger had passed. It's the way it's always been…for us, anyway. But a part of me knew the Russians didn't work that way. At least, from what I'd seen so far of their beautiful Russian Princess.

"The Russians are different, Vincenzo. They do not hide their women away. They are raised in the life, like you and your brother," Alessandro replied, heading towards the exit.

"Bullshit!" Vin snapped. "I've never once since a woman out on the streets."

Vin and I followed behind Alessandro as we made our way down the long corridor, heading towards the elevator. My father's men dropped into position behind, flanking us.

The blonde woman who brought drinks to Dimitri throughout the meet was standing beside the elevator with her head down, hands clasped in front of her body. At our approach, she quickly pushed a button on the wall, calling the elevator.

Vin narrowed in on the woman instantly. His lips curved up in a smile as he stood in front of the blonde. "Well, here I am," he said, sweeping his arms out in front of him. "What were your other two wishes?"

The woman slowly lifted her head and her jaw dropped open.

Yeah, my brother always had that effect on women. I shook my head, chuckling.

"Uh-uhm. . .what?" she croaked.

"Aw, don't be shy, darlin'. How about we head back to your place and you can tell me your other two wishes." He leant forward, bringing his lips to her ear. "I'll do everything I can to grant you your every desire, bella," he whispered.

"Vincenzo! Enough!" Alessandro barked as the elevator appeared and he stepped inside.

Vin pouted as he followed us in. He turned around and waved his fingers in the air at the now-pale and frozen blonde. "Next time," he whispered seductively, blowing her a kiss.

I brought my hand up and smacked the back of his head just as the doors closed.

"Ugh, what the fuck?!" Vin hissed, massaging his head.

"Can't you keep it in your pants until we get home? She's a Bratva woman. If she wasn't, she wouldn't be waiting on Dimitri hand and foot," I snapped.

Vin shrugged his shoulders and pulled out his phone. "I would have given her a better time than that wrinkly old man. Just sayin'."

"Jesus Christ, Vin," I breathed, releasing a frustrated sigh. "Just keep your mouth shut until we get out of this building, okay? Who knows if they've bugged the damn place."

The elevator arrived on the main floor and we all stepped out. Two large black SUVs were parked right out front of the large commercial building, waiting for us. My father, Vin and I took the first one, and our men took the second. Once we all climbed in, the cars took off, heading for our hotel.

"So, if Illayana really does get to decide about the marriage, does that mean she gets to pick the groom?" Vin asked, waggling his eyebrows.

I glowered at him and folded my arms across my chest, staring him down. The image of Illayana and my younger brother together was making my blood boil.

"What makes you think she would even choose you? She threw a fucking knife at your face!" I yelled, my anger getting the better of me.

Vin pulled said knife from his pocket and started flipping it around his fingers. My eyes watched, entranced as the blade moved effortlessly around his hand. "So? Maybe that's her version of foreplay," he replied, winking at me.

I leant forward and grasped his wrist, halting his movements. I grabbed the knife and plucked it from his fingertips.

"Hey!" he chastised. He extended his arm, trying to get the knife back, but I just swatted his hand away. "What the fuck, Turo?!"

"Children, stop," Alessandro said halfheartedly, his eyes glued on his phone in front of him.

We both ignored him.

"Shut up," I snapped at Vin as I held the knife in the air, inspecting it.

It was a small thing, nothing special. The blade was about five inches long and had a black leather hilt. The letters IV were engraved on the side.

"This is hers," I stated, staring at him.

"Yeah, and? She didn't try to take it back after she threw it at me. Finders' keepers," he huffed, leaning back in his seat and crossing his arms.

"What are you, twelve?" I scolded, shaking my head.

Vin pouted as I tucked the knife into my pocket and straightened my body.

"So what now, Father?" I asked, tuning Vin out.

Alessandro kept his body still, his hand holding his phone in front of him. He flicked his fierce blue eyes my way as he spoke. "Now. . .we wait."

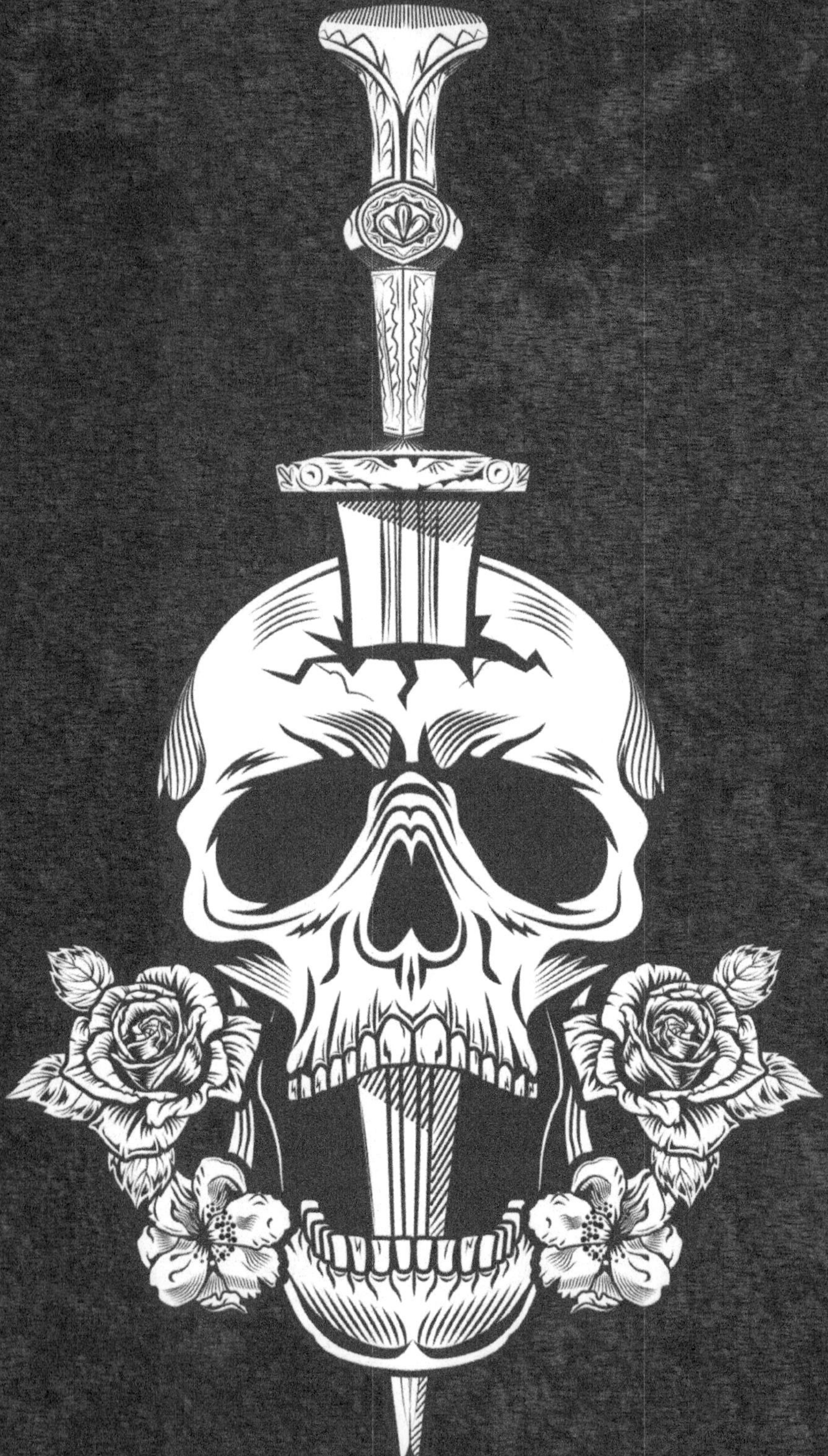

CHAPTER SEVEN

Illayana Volkov

The entire way home, no one spoke a word. Nope. Not a single. Bloody. Word. From the car ride to the helicopter, from the helicopter to Las Vegas, and from the drive to our home, it was complete and utter silence.

Talk about awkward.

My father was fuming. That much I could easily tell. His big, muscular body was seated next to mine on the drive home to the mansion. He didn't say a word to me, didn't even look in my direction. But by the way his jaw kept clenching, I knew the quiet wouldn't last forever.

I pulled out my phone, dying for some sort of distraction right now. I opened the Instagram app and decided to do a little bit of cyberstalking. There's no harm in checking out my future husband, right?

I typed 'Arturo De Luca' into the search engine and wasn't at all surprised to find hundreds of fan accounts made about him. After sifting through all the junk, I finally came across his personal page. I clicked his profile.

Oh, my lord.

The most recent upload was a photo of him shirtless, standing in front of a beautiful, prestigious yacht. His entire upper body was covered in tattoos. As I zoomed in, I couldn't help the blush rising to my cheeks. Fuck, he was hot. So, so hot. I wanted to lick him all over like a bloody ice cream cone.

His tattoos ran from his wrists all the way up his arms, snaking out over his chest, down his torso and around his back, entwining together to form a beautiful piece of artwork; a complex design of patterns and swirls. I was dying to run my hands along that body, to trace his intricate tattoos with my hands. Or my tongue.

Definitely my tongue.

He had a sly smile on his face and his gorgeous blue-green eyes were covered with sunglasses. His face was sharp, with sculpted lines and dark eyebrows. He looked dangerous, sexy. Deadly.

After taking a quick screenshot (because come on, who wouldn't), I sifted through his other photos. Nothing too crazy. Him in expensive tailor-made suits at functions or business meetings. Some shots of him next to fancy cars. In a few photos he was with a woman, but I skipped past those. No need to get myself even more pissed off than I already was.

The sound of a large gate being opened pulled me from my stalking and I realised we were finally home. My father still hadn't moved. His fists remained clenched on his knees the entire time and the scowl never left his face.

My eyes flicked to Aleksandr, looking for support. He gave me a small smile and then shook his head ever so slightly, as if to say "don't fight him, just take the punishment."

Uh, yeah fucking right.

Before the car had even come to a stop, I flung the door open and bolted. I barely acknowledged our head housekeeper, Flora, as I ran up the porch steps and inside to the house. If I could just make it to my bedroom, maybe

I'd be safe.

Fat fucking chance of that, Illayana.

I barely made it halfway up the stairs before I heard the front door slam open. My foot stopped midair above the next step as my father's deep voice boomed throughout the house. "Illayanaaaaaa!"

Fuck, he sounded mad. Really mad.

I took a deep breath and slowly turned around to face my father. He stood in the foyer with Aleksandr at his side. His bright blue eyes locked with mine as he stared me down. "Get back here. Now," he ordered, pointing to the ground in front of him.

I slumped my shoulders and lowered my head. I hated being told off by my father. The look of disappointment and anger on his face was almost too much to bear.

A look of sympathy flashed across Aleksandr's face as I made my way back downstairs and stopped in front of them.

"My office. Go."

The second the words left his mouth, my feet moved almost of their own accord. I walked down the long corridor heading towards his office. I felt his presence behind me, looming over me like a dark shadow. I felt the anger rolling off his body as he followed me. At this point, I was fucking petrified.

I stopped in front of his office door and he leant over me to open it. I stepped in and moved to sit in front of his large mahogany desk while he walked behind it. He shrugged off his suit jacket and placed it neatly over the back of his leather chair. He placed his palms on the desk and slowly lowered himself into the chair, closing his eyes and taking a deep breath.

I stayed frozen in my spot, sweat rolling down my neck, my nerves so bad I felt like I was going to throw up. My leg twitched uncontrollably and I cracked my neck.

"How long?" my father asked, his jaw clenched.

Fuck...Fuck...FUCK! What should I do? What should I say?! Do I admit to what I did? Or play dumb?

I was 99% sure he was talking about Maxim. After the way he behaved at the meet, it couldn't have been more obvious that we were involved. *But there was the small chance he wasn't talking about Maxim, and if I went blabbing, I not only gave him another reason to be pissed at me, but I blew my cover.*

In the end, I decided to play dumb.

"How long what, Father?" I whispered.

He narrowed his eyes and bared his teeth like a fucking animal. "Do not play dumb with me, Illayana Rae Volkov. You know exactly what I'm talking about. How. Long?"

*Oh, shit, he full-named me. I'm **definitely** in trouble.*

"Father, I don—"

"How fucking long, Illayana?" he growled, not even letting me finish the lie that was about to come out of my mouth.

My head lowered in shame. "A few years," I croaked out.

Father cursed in Russian. "Aleksandr!" he barked.

A few seconds later, Aleksandr and Nikolai came in. Each had a hand wrapped around Maxim's arms as they escorted him inside. Lukyan followed close behind, a look of pure menace on his face.

I kept my eyes to the floor as they brought Maxim to stand in front of us. Aleksandr gave a swift kick to his legs and he fell to his knees with a grunt.

My father circled Maxim slowly. He was the predator and Maxim was the prey. There was no way around that. He came to a stop directly in front of him. "Talk," he demanded.

Maxim said nothing and I silently cursed. Keeping quiet was only going to piss him off more. Father stuck out his hand and Nikolai placed a gun in his palm. With unbelievable speed, he pistol-whipped Maxim straight in the face. His head flung back, the sound of his nose breaking filling the room as blood spurted onto the floor.

"Talk, Maximoff, or what we did to The Triad will seem like fucking child's play," my father growled.

Even though blood was dripping down his face, Maxim smiled. "We both know you're going to do that anyway."

"Maybe," my father shrugged, "but I'll make it hurt a hell of a lot more if you don't talk."

Maxim laughed but otherwise stayed silent.

Father studied him, his eyes moving from Maxim to me and then back to Maxim, his mind working overtime. "The only reason why you wouldn't talk would be if the truth was worse than your silence." Father moved and began circling him again, that evil smile of his getting bigger and bigger. "Luckily for me, I don't need you to talk."

Father pinned me with his icy glare and I knew he was referring to me. I looked over to Maxim, still kneeling on the floor, his deep, chocolate brown eyes begging me to keep quiet, but he should have known I would always do what my father asked.

"Talk, Illayana. Start from the beginning," my father ordered, his voice demanding obedience.

Aleksandr and Nikolai stayed beside Maxim, watching his every move while Lukyan moved to my side. He lowered down to his hunches and took my hands in his, offering me his support. His long brown hair was tied up in a bun on top of his head, a few pieces cascading over his rough, masculine face.

I took a deep breath and started. "It was the night of my eighteenth birthday party. You and Aleksandr were out of town on business," I said, pointing at my father. "Maxim was left in charge to watch over the party. I don't remember much. I drank a lot, got high with a few friends. You know, the usual," I shrugged.

Father's jaw clenched, but he stayed silent and allowed me to continue.

"As the night went on, I got more and more drunk. I remember Maxim coming over and offering me another drink, and even though I knew I shouldn't, I was pretty fucking wasted already. I took it. I always thought he was kinda hot, and I didn't want to seem like a wimp who couldn't hold her liquor."

"Where were your brothers during all of this? Where were Nikolai and Lukyan?" Father narrowed his eyes accusingly at my two older brothers.

Lukyan tensed at my side and muttered, "Fuck."

There was no way I was going to let either of them get in trouble, so I covered for them.

"They were with me most of the night, but when the party started to die down I told them they could go."

Father looked at me for a few seconds before deciding to believe me. He gave a swift nod for me to continue.

"Like I said, I was having a drink with Maxim when I started to get really tired. It was like all those drinks finally caught up with me at once. He offered to carry me to bed, and I said yes. I don't really remember what happened after that, but I woke up with him in my bed with me. We were both naked. I asked him if we had sex and he said yes."

"Wait," Nikolai interjected. "You don't remember? Having sex with him?" His brown eyes narrowed on Maxim.

"No. Like I told you, I was drunk. Everything is fuzzy."

"What about now? Can you still not remember anything?" Aleksandr asked.

I frowned and tried my hardest to pull any memory with Maxim from that night to the forefront of my mind, but it kept coming up blank. "No," I replied, confusion laced in my voice. "It's like every time I try to reach a memory, it slips from my grasp. Everything is like a haze I can't see through."

There was a brief moment of silence and then a deep, terrifying roar hit the air as Aleksandr pounced on Maxim and started hammering into him, his fists connecting with his face over and over again. Blood dripped down Maxim's face, making a pool of blood on the floor beside him.

Lukyan looked at me and mouthed, "*What the fuck?*"

I just shrugged my shoulders. Aleksandr had a short fuse. Who knows what set it off this time?

Maxim groaned, trying to bring his hands up to block his face, but it was useless. Aleksandr wouldn't relent, and eventually Maxim went limp. But that didn't stop my brother. He just kept pounding him with his bloody fists.

Father grabbed Aleksandr by the back of his shirt and pulled him off Maxim. He gave him a quick pat on the shoulder and then moved to stand beside his *Sovietnik*. He nudged him a few times with his foot, but he was out cold.

"Could someone please explain to me what the fuck is going on? Why did you snap like that, Aleksandr?" I asked.

He turned to look at me and I gasped at the look of pure rage on his face. His eyes were bulging, the vein in his neck was pulsing and his lip was curled up in disgust. His big body was shaking with anger.

"He fucking roofied you, Illayana!" he yelled.

"What the hell are you talking about?" I asked, confused. "No he didn't."

"Did you forget that you and Lukyan fucked me up with that damn drug a few years ago? I know what it feels like. It's exactly like you described. That fog, the haziness. I still can't remember a single fucking thing from that night, and every time I try it just comes back in a haze."

"That doesn't mean I was drugged, Aleksandr. I was drunk, I could have just blacked out."

"Either way, he shouldn't have laid a fucking hand on you! If you were drunk enough to be passed out, he took advantage of you! Can't you see that?"

I looked over at the unconscious man bleeding all over my father's floor. I sighed, shaking my head. "It doesn't matter. The past is the past. Nothing we can do about it now. Besides, I've been the one to initiate half of our encounters over the last three years."

"It doesn't matter?!" Aleksandr roared. "Of course it fucking matters! He took advantage of you!"

I looked around the room and watched as my father, Nikolai and Lukyan started to get just as worked up as Aleksandr.

Fuck, I need to get out of here.

I stood up and brushed my hands down the front of my blouse, even though there wasn't a speck of dirt on me. I looked into my father's bright blue eyes as I spoke.

"Can I be excused? It's been a long day and I just want to rest."

Father looked like he was going to protest, but then his eyes softened a fraction and he gave me a quick nod. He moved to stand in front of me and wrapped his arms around me. *"Prosti, doch,"* *I'm sorry, daughter,* he whispered into my hair.

I wrapped my arms around his torso and whispered back. *"Vse khorosho, otets,"* *It's okay, Father.*

He pulled back and gave me a small smile before kissing me on the cheek. I slowly moved around the room, stepping over Maxim's unconscious body in the process, and said my goodbyes to my brothers. I could feel the tension in them all as I hugged each of them. I knew that as soon as I left, they planned to have some fun with Maxim.

I made my way out of the office and headed straight for my bedroom. That day...ugh, that whole fucking day! I was ready to wash it all the fuck away and start again. It was not how I pictured the night ending. And I can damn well bet it wasn't how Maxim thought the night would end, either.

I opened my bedroom door and slammed it shut behind me, frustration boiling within me. The fucking idiot! If he had just kept his fucking jealousy in check, none of this shit would have happened.

As I walked into the room, the hair on the back of my neck stood up and I got the distinct feeling that I wasn't alone. Someone was in my room. But who?

Before I could form another thought, a large hand clasped over my mouth while an arm of steel wrapped around my waist, pulling me into the huge body that was now standing behind me. He was a tall motherfucker, that was for sure, and his body felt like it was made of pure muscle.

Shit! Don't think, just react.

And so, I did.

With as much force as I could gather, I drove my elbow deep into his ribs. He grunted and his hold loosened slightly, but not enough for me to escape.

Okay, fucker, you wanna play? Let's play.

I picked up my foot and slammed my spiked heel down on top of his shoe. My heel cut through nicely and stabbed him in the foot. He cursed and let me go, pushing me forward. But I didn't stop. I knew from experience that it only took one second to fuck up in a fight and have it cost you your life. That wasn't gonna be me. No fucking way.

My room was still encased in darkness, so all I could see was his silhouette, but it was enough for me. I ran forward and jumped into the air, wrapping my legs around his neck. Using my body's momentum, I twisted and flung him to the ground in one quick manoeuvre.

He grunted as his big body hit the floor, the ground shaking from the impact. I straddled his large frame and pulled a blade from the sheath around my waist, holding it to his throat

The moonlight shone through the curtains at just the right angle, revealing his face. His mouth curved up in a sexy smile, his eyes dancing with mischief and desire.

"Ya ze govoril, chto scoro uvidimsya, kotenok." I told you I would see you soon, kitten. His deep, sexy voice said it in perfect Russian.

Arturo fucking De Luca.

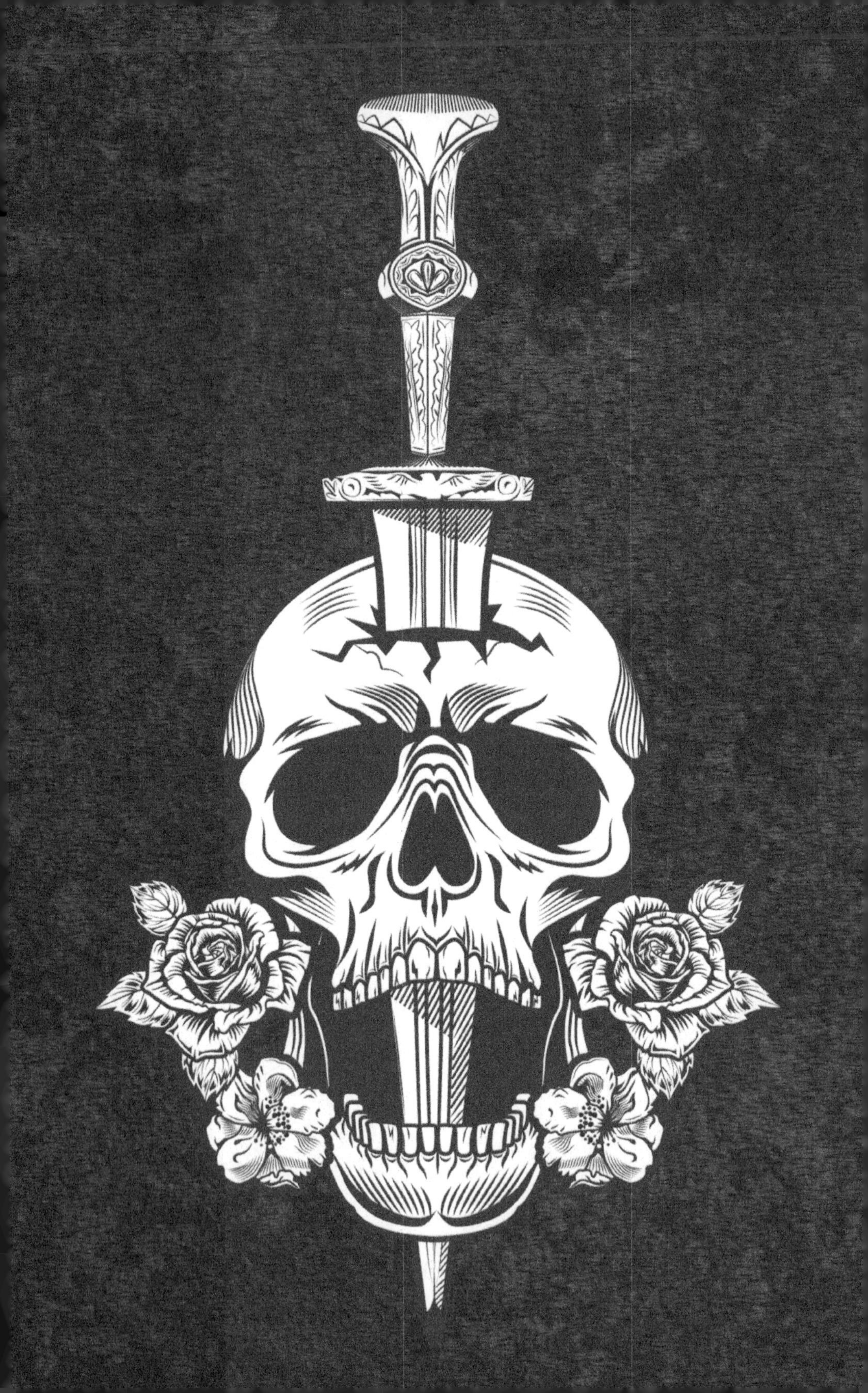

CHAPTER EIGHT

Illayana Volkov

If you had told me that morning I would be ending the evening straddling Arturo's chest with a knife to his throat, I would have said you were fucking crazy. Yet there I was. Knife in hand, legs on either side of his body, staring into those entrancing blue-green eyes.

His stupid handsome face looked just as appealing as I remembered. Just staring at him made my body heat with lust and attraction. His gorgeous mouth curled up with an expression that looked like half a smile, and half a challenge. I didn't like that cocky look on his face (even if he did look hot as fuck).

I dug my knife a little further into his throat, a faint trickle of blood starting to drip down his neck.

He arched one of those perfect eyebrows (I don't even know how someone can have perfect eyebrows, but he fucking does) and that cocky expression stayed plastered on his face. It was like he was enjoying it.

"What the fuck are you doing here?" I hissed.

"Isn't it obvious, *Kotenok?*" *Kitten,* he chuckled, those gorgeous eyes of his staring me down. "I'm here for you." I tried to ignore the tingle that ran through my body at his words, but who was I kidding? I fucking liked it.

The sound of footsteps came from just outside my bedroom door and I tensed.

Arturo's eyes flicked to the door and he stiffened.

Fuck. If my brothers walked in with me straddling Arturo with a fucking knife to his throat, they wouldn't react very well. No, not well at all.

A soft knock followed by my brother's voice filled the space of my bedroom.

"*Sestra? Sister?* Are you alright? We heard some banging," Lukyan asked.

Goddamnit! Must have been when I slammed him into the ground.

"I'm fine!" I yelled back. My eyes darted down to the sexy male beneath me and he winked at me, mouthing *"Yes, you are."*

Bastard.

I snapped my head back towards the door as it began to slowly open. I tightened my grip on my knife and flung it forward with as much speed as I could. It embedded deep into the doorframe, straight down to the hilt just as Lukyan's head appeared.

"Jesus fucking Christ!" he shrieked as he pulled his head back and slammed the door shut again.

"I told you, I'm fine!" I yelled back.

Arturo's big, muscular body started shaking beneath me and I looked down to see him laughing silently.

"Fucking hell," I heard Lukyan mutter behind the door. "Is it that time of the month or something?"

I ran my hand down my face, groaning. Of course he'd say some stupid shit like that. My second time properly meeting Arturo and he's already hearing all about my period. Fucking joy.

"Don't be an idiot," I heard Nikolai reply. *Great! They're both fucking out there.* "You know we monitor that shit." *They fucking what?!* "Calendar says it's still two and a half weeks away."

"Right. Right." I could just imagine Lukyan nodding along. "I forgot that we started doing that after she tried to burn me with that blowtorch. Damn Shark Week," he grumbled.

Oh my god, I'm gonna kill them. I'm going to fucking kill them. They track my menstrual cycle?!

Arturo laughed outright and I clamped my hand over his mouth, narrowing my eyes in warning.

"Go the fuck away!" I roared.

"Are you sure she's not on her period? She sounds pretty fucking hormonal to me," Lukyan asked Nikolai.

That's fucking it!

I wrapped my fingers around the handle of my gun and pulled it from the holster. I pointed it at the door, making sure to aim high enough so I wouldn't hit them, and fired two shots.

"Fuck!" One of them yelled (not sure which), the sound of their big bodies dropping to the floor following next.

"I told you, I'm fine!" I growled. "Now fuck off before I fire again. This time I won't miss!"

"She's fucking mental!" Lukyan yelled.

"What Volkov isn't?" Nikolai replied, the sound of his voice fading until the only thing I could hear was Arturo's breathing and my heart beating.

My body relaxed as soon as I realised they'd left.

Seriously, what else is this fucking day gonna throw at me?

I rose to my feet, ignoring Arturo's heated gaze as I stepped over him, and sat on my bed. I leant over to my bedside table and flicked the lamp on, then I started undoing the straps on my heels, desperate to get out of them and relax my feet.

Arturo picked his big body off the floor and stood gracefully. He lowered his head and looked at his left foot, and that's when I remembered I stabbed him with my heel. I should have felt bad, but I didn't. The fucker broke into my house. He deserved it.

"How did you get in here?" I asked, dropping my heels to the ground. His only response was to look at the large window in my room.

My eyes followed his gaze and I shook my head. "Bullshit. That's a three-story drop."

He arched an eyebrow, that sexy mouth of his curling up in a sly smile. "You wanted an answer to your question, I gave you one. Whether you believe it or not is up to you."

I forgot how damn sexy his deep voice was.

"And what about my other question?"

"What question was that, *kotenok?*" I swear I could hear a hint of seduction in his voice.

"What the hell are you doing here?"

"Ah," he chuckled. "but I did answer that question already. I told you, I'm here for you," he pinned me with his gaze and the intensity of it sent shivers down my spine.

Just his mere presence made my body tingle and my stomach flutter. What the fuck was this man doing to me?! I've been around plenty of hot guys and none of them made me feel like some giddy school kid talking to their crush.

I stood up, not liking the fact that he was looming over me. He was a good few feet taller than me, even standing, but at least this way it wasn't as bad.

I didn't realise the first time I met him how broad and wide his shoulders were. How his hips narrowed, showing that he wasn't just muscular but lean as well. He was still wearing the same suit from that morning, and I could see the faint traces of his tattoos just under the collar of his shirt. It took every bit of willpower I possessed not to reach out and trace them with my fingers.

"What does that mean? That you're here for me?"

He answered my question with another question. "Have you thought about my proposal?"

"You mean your father's proposal?" I asked, arching an eyebrow.

Arturo shook his head, chuckling. He slowly started circling me, similar to how my father circled Maxim. Like I was prey. Fuck, I felt like prey right then. I stayed rooted in place, refusing to show any sign of discomfort, following him with my eyes.

"My father may have put the proposal forward, but it is my proposal nonetheless." His beautiful heterochromia eyes were roaming up and down my body as he continued to circle me. I couldn't ignore the desire burning from within them, or the way his heated gaze made my blood boil with excitement. "Have you?" he whispered, and this time I knew for sure there was seduction lacing his voice.

"I have," I replied, keeping track of him. "Have you?"

He froze, his face twisted in confusion. "Of course I have. It is my proposal, after all."

This time, it was my turn to chuckle. I moved forward, circling him like he did me. He stayed still, watching me as my eyes roamed over every inch of his body.

Fuck, I wanna climb that like a jungle gym.

"I don't think you have. You see, I won't be the type of wife you want."

"Oh?" he arched one of those perfect eyebrows. "And how do you know what type of wife I want?"

I continued to circle him, secretly loving the fact that he stayed completely still, allowing me to peruse him as much as I wanted.

"You want what every made man wants: a woman who worships the ground you walk on. A woman who will do what you say, when you say it. A woman who won't argue with you, who will be content waiting at home day in and day out for you." I stopped dead in front of him, letting him process my words. I leant in slightly and whispered, "That's not me."

His eyes roamed over my face, pausing slightly at my mouth before going back up and meeting my gaze. "I know," he whispered back. "And I'm not like every made man. I know exactly who you are, exactly what you're capable of, and it only makes me want you more."

He took a step forward, his body almost pressed up against mine. I had to work hard to control my breathing. I could feel my heart beating erratically in my chest and I prayed he couldn't hear it, couldn't feel it.

He raised his hand slowly and wrapped his fingers around my throat, squeezing slightly, making heat curl down my spine. Want and need blazed inside me, right through me down to my core.

"I don't want a docile woman, a weak woman. I want a queen. A woman to help me conquer and rule. A woman who will stand by my side, not cower behind me."

My eyes moved down to his mouth and I involuntarily licked my lips. For a split second, I forgot what we were talking about and imagined what it would be like to kiss him, to taste him. I knew he'd taste fucking amazing.

"And how do you know I'm that woman?" I whispered, my voice a bit huskier than I would have liked.

Staying close, he studied me for a few moments before reaching into his suit jacket and pulling out a knife. He held it up in the air and as I watched the blade shine from the light in the room, I saw the letters *IV* engraved into it.

My knife!

I reached forward to take it, but he pulled his hand back out of my reach. With one final squeeze to my throat, he released his hold and stepped back. I missed his touch instantly.

"I've never seen a woman—a beautiful woman, at that—throw a knife with such precision."

I was listening to him, but my eyes were on my blade. It was one of my favourites. I couldn't believe I'd forgotten it! My father gave it to me the day he made me a made woman.

"I knew from that moment that you were the one I've been looking for," he smirked.

I frowned. "So, you're telling me all it took was for me to throw a knife at your brother for you to decide to spend the rest of your life with me?" I hoped he could hear the scepticism in my voice. "Any woman in the Bratva could do that."

He tsked and placed my knife back inside his suit jacket.

Uh, excuse me. I want that back.

Now that he wasn't so close to me, I felt like I could finally breathe again.

"No, *kotenok*, that's not all it took. There are many things about you that helped sway my decision."

"Oh yeah? Like what?"

"I never pegged you as the type of woman who fishes for compliments."

I scowled, narrowing my eyes. "I'm not! I just don't think you've thought this through."

He sighed. "Think what you will, woman, but I've thought it through plenty."

I studied his face, looking for any sign of deceit, but I couldn't see any.

"I won't be an easy wife, you know. I'll probably drive you mad," I said, shrugging my shoulders. "I hate being told what to do and I despise being underestimated. I know La Cosa Nostra are not used to women being in the life. I can guarantee you, your men won't like me around."

"I don't give a fuck what any of them think," Arturo stated with complete conviction.

"Nevertheless, I won't tolerate it. I will not be disrespected. Should any of your men do so, I hope you're prepared to lose them."

His eyes lit with fire, desire and lust rolling off him in waves. He clearly liked his women vengeful. "If any of my men disrespect you, there'll be nothing left of them by the time I'm finished."

"And the fact that I'm not Italian?" I arched an eyebrow. "Will that not be a problem?"

"To some, it may. But like I said, I don't give a fuck what they think."

I studied him for a few seconds before giving him a slight nod. I believed him. He didn't strike me as the type of person to care about what other people think.

"There is one thing you should probably know before you agree," Arturo said hesitantly.

I locked eyes with him, curiosity flowing throughout my body. "What?"

"My father will be stepping down as head of the La Cosa Nostra as soon as we've dealt with Nero."

Okaaaaay. That, I had not expected. Alessandro was still young by mafia standards. He could continue to rule for at least another five to ten years before needing to step down. So why hand over the reins early?

"Why?" It was the only question I could ask.

"My father has ruled for a long time. He was only twenty-nine when my grandfather was murdered and he was made Don. He's ready to let go of his empire. Ready to move on in life with my mother." A sad smile formed on his face, like he was happy for his parents but sad to be losing his Don. "I'm ready to take over. It's what I've been raised for, what I've been training all my life for. However, one of his stipulations was that I was to be married beforehand. Don't ask me why, I have no fucking idea. It was just one of his rules."

Hang on a second.

My brain started working overtime, trying to find the right combination of words to express what was flying through my mind.

"Requesting a marriage between our families was an impulse decision, made by you. I saw when you spoke to Alessandro, and then he put forth the proposal."

"Yes?" he asked, confused by my train of thought.

"So if he was already planning to step down when this whole mess ended, you must have had a woman lined up to marry." I phrased it as a statement, but he answered like it was a question.

"Yes," he sighed. "There was a woman I was prepared to marry instead."

I couldn't help the unbelievable jealousy I felt at his words. Fuck, I'd only met the dude that day. I knew I had no right at all to be jealous, but fuck, I was.

"Who?" I asked, making sure to keep the jealousy out of my voice.

"Her name is Gabriella. She's the daughter of one of the high-ranking men in the *famiglia*."

Eh, Gabriella. Bet the bitch is fucking gorgeous.

"So she's a Cosa Nostra woman? Does that mean there's gonna be people pissed that you're marrying an outsider instead of her?"

Arturo shrugged. "There's always going to be someone who's mad about that. They'll get over it."

Maybe, but I highly doubted it. Depending on their level of anger, it could mean I've already gained enemies in a place where I would spend the rest of my life. Did I really want to move somewhere I'd constantly be looking over my shoulder?

Another thought tore through my mind and I stiffened. "What kind of marriage will this be? A business one or a personal one?"

"What do you mean?"

"A business one means we're husband and wife on paper, but not in real life. A personal one means that in every sense of the word, we're husband and wife. That means loyalty, fidelity. I know Mafia men have the predilection to do whatever the fuck they like, including cheating on their partners. I won't take that. You marry me and you're mine. You don't go sticking your dick in other bitches."

He chuckled and tapped my nose. "So, just this bitch?"

"Yes."

I should probably be insulted that he called me bitch, but I wasn't. I am a bitch. And proud of it.

"If I'm getting what I need from you, I don't see why I'd need to get it somewhere else."

"And by getting what you need, you mean?"

He cupped my pussy roughly and I gasped in shock.

Jesus fucking Christ.

"This. This is what I need. I am a red-blooded man, Illayana. I need sex. If this is going to be a proper marriage, one where we stay faithful to one another, are you going to give me what I want, when I want it?"

"That depends."

He ground the palm of his hand against my clit and I moaned. He stepped close, his breath hot on my skin as he nuzzled my neck. "Depends on what?" he breathed.

"How good you are at it."

He chuckled again and ran his tongue up the side of my neck, capturing my earlobe in his mouth. He tugged slightly with his teeth and I shuddered. "I don't think that will be an issue, *kotenok.*"

Why does he keep calling me kitten?

"From the goosebumps on your skin, the flush in your cheeks, the way your breathing has increased, I'd say you'd agree. Wouldn't you?" His free hand travelled up my body and collared my throat again, unleashing another moan from my lips. He chuckled. "Oh, yes, you definitely agree."

Yeah, I sure fucking do.

My body begged for his touch, passion heating my blood and making me so fucking hot I just wanted to tear his clothes off right then and fuck him on my bedroom floor. I felt dizzy, lust consuming my entire soul as my heart hammered in my chest. I could feel the bulge in his pants, his cock hard as stone against my leg. I wanted nothing more than to grab it, feel it throb in my hand. To play with it and hear him moan. There's nothing sexier than a man moaning in pleasure.

With one final tug on my earlobe, he released me, pulling away from my body. I missed the contact instantly. "So, will you be my wife?" he asked seductively, his eyes filled with desire.

I looked at the man in front of me. Really looked. His unbelievably good looks and his fun and mischievous personality would make it sooooo easy to be his wife. I mean, I'd be fucking crazy to say no, right? By the way my body was buzzing, I knew we were sexually compatible—from my side, at least. Not only that, but the realisation that I would be married to the head of The Cosa Nostra had my blood bubbling with excitement.

I locked eyes with him, a similar smirk to his forming on my face. I ran my tongue over my bottom lip, watching as his eyes followed my movements, burning with lust.

His nostrils flared and his jaw clenched, like he was fighting a war within himself not to move.

"I hope you're as badass as they say. You'll need to be, to handle me."

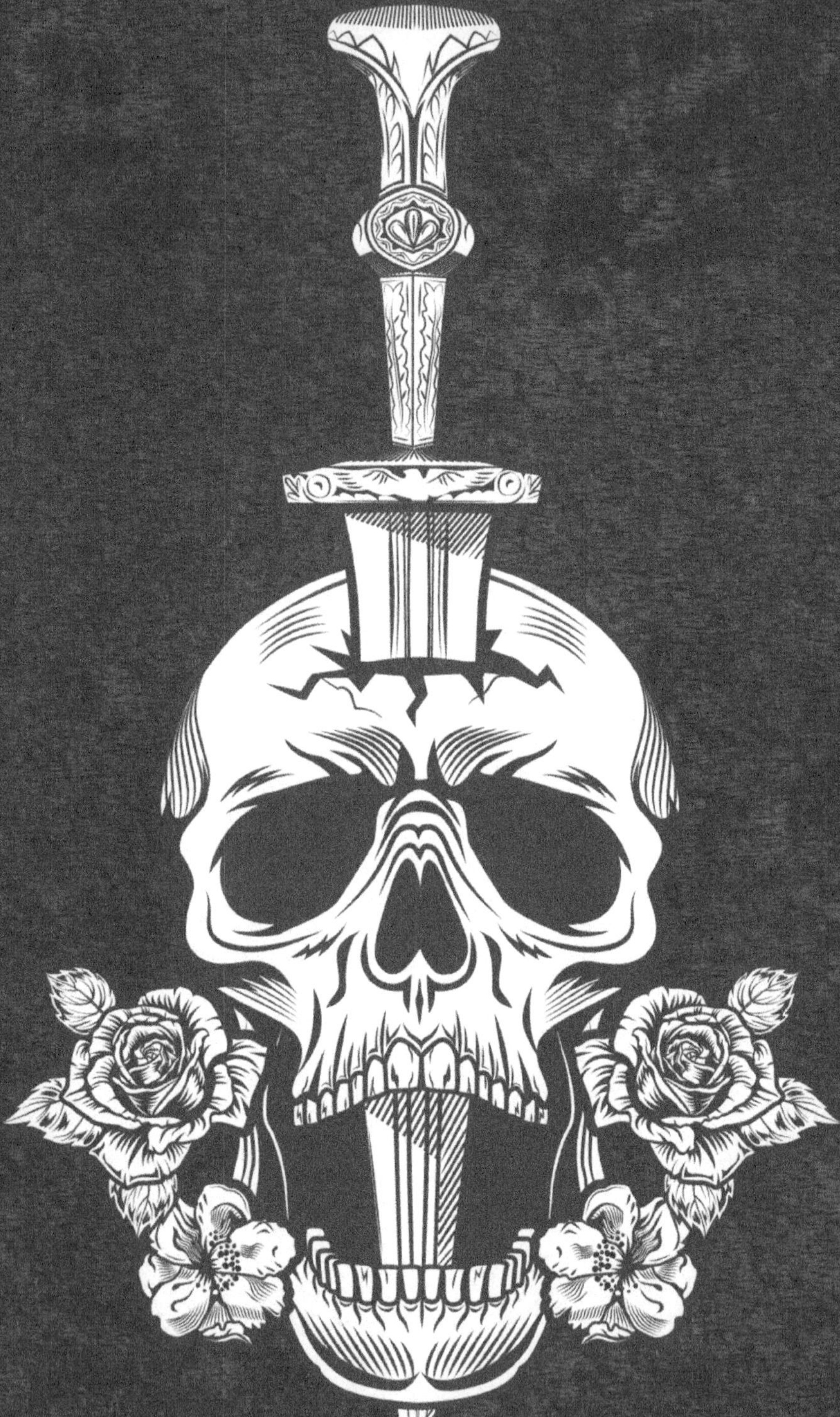

CHAPTER NINE

Arturo De Luca

*F*uck. *She's beautiful. And fierce. And sassy. And—shit, my foot is killing me! Did she have to stab me so fucking hard?*

Well, you did kind of attack her.

No, I didn't.

Yes, you did. And now you're talking to yourself like a crazy person.

Eh, what else is new?

My eyes locked on her and her beautiful body. My fingers twitched at my side, dying to touch her again. Fuck, it probably wasn't a good idea to have grabbed her like I did. To feel the heat of her pussy in my hand, to run my tongue over her skin. Now it's going to be all I can think about until I get the chance to do it again.

But it was important to check our compatibility, to make sure we could mesh well together sexually. I wasn't lying when I said I needed sex. It was something I would do every day, even if it meant a quick pow wow with one of the random women in my little black book. My life being so full of violence and adrenaline meant I needed a good outlet to unleash it all, and sex was the best one.

I was a dominant fucker in bed. Not 'Christian Grey' kinda dominant, but a different kind. The kind that craved control, liked to give orders. I knew it, the women I fucked knew it and it was important that Illayana knew it, too. Judging by her reaction to me, she didn't just know it—she liked it.

"Arturo?" Illayana's soft voice tore me from my thoughts, and I refocused on her.

"Hmm?" For what felt like the millionth time, my eyes roamed up and down her body. I couldn't stop it. It was like they had a mind of their own, and all they wanted was Illayana.

She chuckled. "I said, do you want me to treat that?" She pointed at my foot and I only just realised I had been favouring my left side.

I shook my head. "No, I'm fine. I barely felt it."

Right, that's a fucking lie. Good way to start off, Turo.

She opened her mouth, about to speak, when the sound of someone knocking on her bedroom door interrupted her.

For fuck's sake.

Her beautiful blue eyes shot to the door and irritation flashed on her face, clear as day. She didn't like being interrupted either. "What?!" she barked, her tone laced with anger.

"Don't shoot!" someone immediately yelled from the other side of the door. I had to refrain from laughing out loud. "It's just me."

Illayana immediately tensed, her body going rigid. She knew who was behind the door, but she looked...uneasy. She didn't look that way when her brothers knocked earlier. Interesting.

She moved quickly to my side, light as a feather on her feet. She crooked her finger at me and I lowered my head so she could whisper in my ear.

"You need to hide," she whispered.

Because I was dying to touch her, I gripped her hips with both hands and brought my lips to her ear. "Why? Just tell them to go away like last time."

She shook her head feverishly, her long black hair flowing over her shoulders. "That's Aleksandr out there. He won't go away like Lukyan and Nikolai did. Especially if they ran and got him, which I have a feeling they did." Her eyes narrowed at the door accusingly. "Aleksandr isn't afraid of me like they are. If I don't open that door, he'll kick it down."

"Illayanaaa," Aleksandr called out. I could hear the subtle warning in his voice. That fucker would definitely kick the door down.

"Just a second," she yelled back.

She looked at me with those ocean-coloured eyes and started moving me to the back of the room. "Hurry up," she hissed. She quickly flicked off the lamp on her bedside table, encasing her room in darkness.

"Fiiine," I groaned, moving in amongst the shadows. "I don't get what the big fucking deal is," I grumbled as I moved into position.

I picked a spot that gave me a clear, unobstructed view of the door so I could see what was going on. It was probably smarter to move so there was no chance of being spotted, but I love to live dangerously. I was there after all, wasn't I?

Illayana opened the door and, sure enough, her brother Aleksandr was standing just outside.

Man, he really was a big motherfucker. And he had to be just as tall as me, if not a smidgen more (just a smidgen, though). His bright blue eyes landed on Illayana, scrutinising every detail. Then his gaze swept the room behind her. His eyes moved over me in the shadows and I tensed.

"Everything okay, Illayana?" he asked, looking back at her.

"*Da.* Why?" She tilted her head to the side, like she was confused why he was even asking.

I saw her other brothers pop out from behind Aleksandr's large frame. One was on the left side, the other on the right. They looked like they were using his big, overgrown body as a shield. Man, they looked terrified.

Well, she did throw a knife and shoot at them, all within a thirty-second period. I'd say their fear is warranted.

"Just...making sure," he replied, his eyes sweeping the room once more. Just as his gaze fell on me, his eyes narrowed.

Fuck.

I didn't realise my hand was moving until I felt the hilt of Illayana's knife in my palm.

No! I couldn't kill her brother...could I?

No. Just no.

Aleksandr continued to talk with Illayana, yet his eyes never left mine in the shadows. "Illayana," his voice was like ice, and she tensed. "Are you sure you're okay? Do you need any...help?" By the way he was talking, I could guess he knew I was in the room.

Clever, observant son of a bitch, aren't you?

All of the tension seemed to dissipate instantly, her body relaxing. She took a step forward and placed a hand on his cheek.

"*Rodnoy brat.*" *Brother.* His eyes moved to her. "I promise, I'm fine. You should know if I ever need you, I'd come to you."

His gaze found mine again amongst the shadows and he scowled. "If you're sure," he grumbled.

"I am," she chuckled. "Now move." She flicked her wrist, signalling him to move to the side.

The edge of his lips curved into an evil smirk, the first sign of true emotion I'd seen from the guy yet. His big body moved gracefully, revealing her two older brothers.

Fuck. They breed them big in The Bratva.

All of them seemed to be around the same height (give or take a few inches). It was clear Aleksandr was the oldest, though. Even if you ignored the dude's gargantuan size, he had a certain air about him. The way he held himself, his mere presence demanded respect and authority. Like mine. I was super curious to see how the man fought. Maybe one day I'd find out. I was giddy at the idea.

Based on the information Vin gathered on the Volkov family, the one with shoulder-length brown hair and blue eyes was Lukyan. He wasn't as muscular as Aleksandr (more lean than packed overboard with muscle). That made the other guy Nikolai. He had short black hair, a neatly trimmed beard and bright blue eyes. He seemed to be in the middle of his two siblings, body wise. Not as muscular as Aleksandr, but not as lean as his other brother.

Their eyes widened when they realised their big brother wasn't planning on protecting them from their sister. She took a menacing step in their direction and they both took a step back.

"Now, Illayana," Lukyan began to say, his voice shaky. He had his hands up in front of him, like was surrendering.

"You tattled," she tsked, disappointed.

"No. No, no, no," Lukan replied, his head shaking. He elbowed his brother in the gut and scowled at him. "Nikolai?"

Nikolai straightened his body and looked at Illayana. He didn't seem *as* frightened as Lukyan did, but he definitely looked uneasy, like he had no idea what was going to happen.

"*Sestra. Sister.* We were worried about you. You haven't tried to kill us in years. We thought you were in trouble," his voice was laced with a thick Russian accent.

Illayana stayed quiet for a few seconds. "Lies," she said, her voice strong.

"What?" Nikolai asked, confused.

"You're lying. If you really thought I was in trouble, you wouldn't have left. You would have kicked that door in, guns blazing."

Nikolai and Lukyan exchanged a look with each other.

Huh, she was right.

"You both knew I would open the door for Aleksandr, so you went and got him. Why?"

"It's not what you think, Illayana," Nikolai began.

"We didn't tattle," Lukyan continued.

"You threw a knife at Lukyan and shot at us. You only do that kind of shit when you're either one: pissed at us. Or two: hiding something." Lukyan nodded along enthusiastically. "Since we haven't done anything to piss you off for a few months, we knew you were hiding something."

"We just wanted to see what got you all 'kill crazy', that's all," Lukyan said, looking into the room. "And we knew you would open up for Aleksandr, because he would have kicked it in otherwise," he chuckled.

Aleksandr shrugged a shoulder, seeming unfazed by the whole thing.

"You wanted to see what got me all 'kill crazy'?" Illayana asked, her head tilting to the side.

Lukyan nodded fast, whereas Nikolai just arched an eyebrow, eyeing her suspiciously.

She placed her hands behind her back and crooked her finger, signalling for me to come out.

I slunk out of the shadows and moved towards her.

Nikolai and Lukyan instantly reacted, pulling their guns from their holsters and aiming at me. Aleksandr didn't move a muscle, but he tracked my approach with his eyes.

"Who the fuck is that?" Nikolai cocked his gun, Lukyan following suit.

I stopped directly behind Illayana. I was tall enough to see straight over her head without her having to bend. Their faces were tense, jaws clenched, scowling at me like I was the devil.

"You don't recognise him, *rodnoy brat? Brother?*" her voice was laced with mischief.

Nikolai narrowed his eyes on me. He focused on my face before realisation lit his features. "What the fuck is a De Luca doing here? Better yet, how did he get in here?" He kept his gun locked on me.

"De Luca?" Lukyan repeated, moving his head between myself and Nikolai. His gun still stayed pointed at me, too.

Such a welcoming family.

Aleksandr still hadn't moved. The only acknowledgement of my presence was the scowl he aimed my way.

"Aleksandr, Nikolai, Lukyan," Illayana began, her voice strong and clear. "I'd like to introduce you to Arturo De Luca, my fiancé," she reached back and grabbed my arm, moving me to stand beside her.

Aleksandr tilted his head up and sighed, like he knew this was going to happen, but he wasn't thrilled about it. Nikolai and Lukyan both dropped their mouths open wide, their brows hiked up in complete surprise.

I wrapped an arm around her shoulders and looked at my three new brothers-in-law. "Hiya, boys."

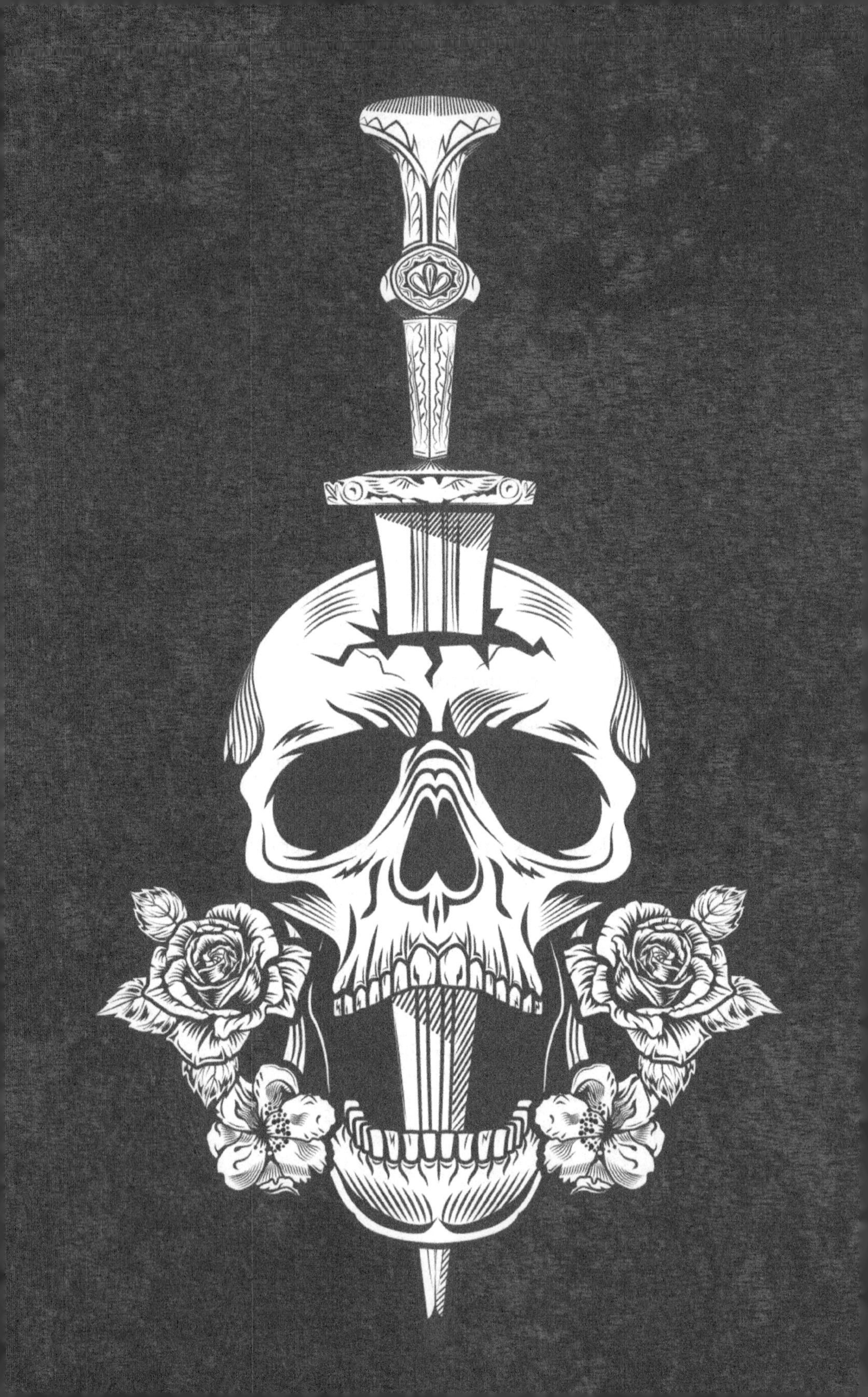

CHAPTER TEN

Illayana Volkov

"What in the fresh hell is this?!" Lukyan shrieked. He slowly lowered his gun as his eyes jumped between Arturo and I.

It took every bit of self control I had not to laugh at the expressions on their faces.

"Zander?" Nikolai arched an eyebrow, facing him.

Aleksandr sighed. "Let's all go downstairs. Might as well fill you both in."

"I don't want to go downstairs," Lukyan said, narrowing his eyes on Arturo. "I want to know what this dude is doing in my fucking house, and in your goddamn bedroom, Illayana! He's Cosa Nostra!"

Arturo tensed at my side, his big body going rigid. He glared those gorgeous blue-green eyes at Lukyan, grinding his teeth together. "Watch it," he sneered. "I don't give a fuck if this is your house, you will not speak to her like that."

Nikolai and Aleksandr both groaned. It was probably the worst thing you could say to Lukyan, and we all knew it.

Lukyan stood up straighter, puffing out his chest. "I can talk to her anyway I damn well please! She's *my* sister!" he snapped.

"Guys, come on," I said, trying to defuse the situation.

Arturo's arm tightened around my shoulders briefly before he growled and stepped towards Lukyan, "Not anymore, you can't."

"Oh yeah? And what the fuck are you going to do about it?" Lukyan mocked. He took a step forward, copying Arturo, closing the empty space between them entirely.

They stood toe to toe, neither one backing down. I looked to Aleksandr, who was standing next to Nikolai, off to the side. They had both moved out of the danger zone when shit started to get heated. He didn't seem fazed by the new turn of events though. Nope, not at all. Actually, if I didn't know better, I'd say the fucker was excited.

I guess I shouldn't be surprised. Aleksandr did always love a good brawl. The bloodier the better, according to him.

"Shouldn't we stop this?" I hissed at them.

They both just shrugged their shoulders.

Argh. Fucking useless.

"If you weren't Illayana's brother, and killing you wouldn't incite a war, I'd slit your fucking throat," Arturo growled.

Lukyan took a step backward, his eyes flashing with excitement. He had a broad smile on his face as he reached into his pocket and pulled out a blade.

"Well, let's ignore all that then, shall we? Right now, I'm just a man who wants you to get the fuck out of my house." He twirled the blade around his fingers, something he always did when he was excited. "Come on, big boy, let's dance."

"Lukyan. Enough," a deep voice commanded. I didn't even need to look to know my father had joined us.

Lukyan stiffened, sensing the dark presence my father exuded as he came up behind him. He cursed in Russian as he put his knife back in its sheath. He did not look happy to have been interrupted, but then again, he'd always been that way. You tell the kid not to do something, and it's all he wants to do.

My father stepped up to my side, wearing plain grey sweatpants and a dark t-shirt. The only time you'd see him out of a suit was right before bed. His black hair was still damp from his shower, and the pronounced lines on his face showed how exhausted he was.

He flicked his eyes over Arturo briefly before pinning his gaze on Lukyan. "Go on, get out of here. I'll explain everything tomorrow."

"But—"

"No buts, Lukyan!" Father snapped. "Go, and go now. You two as well." He flicked his wrist at Aleksandr and Nikolai. They all bowed slightly before making their exit.

Lukyan scowled at Arturo, giving him the middle finger as he walked away.

Arturo chuckled. "I like him," he whispered in my ear, sending shivers down my spine. "He reminds me of Vincenzo. Brothers. You love them, but you can't help but want to beat the shit out of them at the same time."

"Lukyan has that effect on people," I replied, laughing.

"Oh, I can tell."

He turned to face my father full on, eyeing him curiously. "I have to say, you're taking my presence here quite well. I thought you would have had me shot the second you found out I was here." His eyes lit up with excitement, like he found the idea entertaining.

Crazy. So fucking crazy. But my kinda crazy.

My father shook his head, chuckling softly, something he would do when a child said something amusing. "Do you really think you were able to get in here without my knowledge?"

Arturo's face dropped instantly, his smile disappearing.

"You were good, very good," Father continued. "But one thing you'll come to realise eventually is that there's always someone out there better than you. That just happens to be me in this circumstance."

"How? How did you know I was here?" Arturo asked, narrowing his eyes.

Father tsked. "Maybe one day I'll tell you. For right now, it is late and I don't trust you enough to let you stay in my home. Say goodbye, Illayana. Arturo is leaving."

"But there's things we need to discuss, Father. Details about what's to happen next," I replied, my brows wrinkling in confusion.

"All plans will be made shortly and swiftly, but not now. Say goodbye, Illayana. I will be escorting Arturo to the front gate in thirty seconds." Father clicked his fingers and two of his soldiers moved to stand next to him, one on each side.

I narrowed my eyes but didn't argue. I knew better than that.

I turned to Arturo, and when our eyes locked I felt that now-all-too-familiar feeling of my stomach fluttering. "I guess I'll talk to you later?"

His lips curved up into that trademark smirk of his as he spoke his final word in Italian.

"Presto." Soon.

"Tell me everything!" Tatiana said excitedly, holding her cup of coffee in one hand and a biscotti in the other. She dunked the biscotti in her drink and slurped it into her mouth as I took a sip of my own coffee.

After Arturo left last night, I called her and asked her to meet me at our go-to café. She was all too eager. She was the first person I called when I needed someone to talk to, someone to help me sort through the chaotic thoughts flowing through my mind. She always gave me her brutally honest opinion, no matter how rude or bitchy it might come across. If she thought you were wrong, she told you. If she thought you were acting crazy, she told you. If she thought you weren't acting crazy enough, she told you. And she didn't care if she offended you in the process. She didn't have a filter, was unceremoniously blunt and always spoke her mind. I loved it.

Excitement flashed across her heart-shaped face, her dark brown eyes watching me over the rim of her cup. Her long, platinum blonde hair hung in ringlets down her back, and she was wearing a simple blue sundress that fell to her knees. She looked like a delicate little angel, but anyone who knew her knew she was the complete opposite.

"What were they like? Were they as hot as they look online? Come on, tell me everything!"

I shook my head, laughing softly. "If I didn't know any better, I'd say you were obsessed with them."

"Oh, I am. I wanna spread my legs and have their babies." She took a chunk out of her biscotti, crunching on it loudly.

One of the elderly women at the next table gasped and stared at Tatiana in shock. She didn't even notice.

"Which one?" I asked curiously. The last thing I wanted was my best friend crushing on my fiancé.

Tatiana placed her elbow on the table and rested her chin in her hand, staring off into the distance with a dreamy expression. "The younger one. Vincenzo. He's gorgeous. I'd let him fuck me any way he liked, and wouldn't even care if he didn't call me back the next day."

"Well, who knows, maybe you'll get your wish. You'll see him at the wedding."

Tatiana sat up straight, her entire attention on me. "Wedding? Whose wedding?"

I smirked into my cup. "Mine."

"What?!" she yelled, gaining the attention of the entire café. "You're getting married?! To who?!"

"Who do you think?"

"A De Luca?" she breathed in reverence.

I tapped my nose and put my coffee back on the table. I picked up my BLT and took a bite, laughing silently at the look of complete bewilderment on my best friend's face.

She raised a hand and shook her head. "Hold up, hold up, hold up. How did this happen? Aren't they Cosa Nostra? Don't they have some deep-seated tradition in the *famiglia* about only marrying other Italians?"

"They do, but Arturo doesn't care. They need my father's guns to help fight off the Outfit. In exchange they are offering access to their territory, as well as Chicago when the Outfit is out of the picture."

"Alright, I'm following so far. How did the topic of marriage come up? That's a pretty big leap in the opposite direction."

I nodded, taking another bite. "We're officially entering into an alliance with them. One of the ways to solidify that is through marriage. Alessandro's only daughter is ten years old, so she's out. That leaves me."

"Wow. So is this like, against your will?"

Scoffing, I wiped my mouth with a napkin, taking another sip of my coffee. "You think I'd ever do something I don't wanna do?"

"True," Tatiana exhaled. "Holy moly, this is insane! When's the big day?"

"Less than a week."

Once my father heard my decision to marry Arturo, he immediately sent word out that a union between the Bratva and La Cosa Nostra was taking place. He gave me a week to plan the wedding, which was fine with me because I only wanted something small.

For the second time in the span of five minutes, Tatiana yelled at the top of her lungs. "What?! You can't plan a wedding in seven days! Are you crazy?"

Pushing my plate away, I leant back in my chair. "Yes, I can. You know me. I don't need—or want—a big, flashy wedding. I'll be fine with something small and to the point."

"Oh my god, you're gonna give me an aneurysm," she muttered, rubbing her temples. "You're the *Pakhan's* only daughter. You can't have a mediocre wedding. I won't allow it."

I frowned. "What's that supposed to mean?"

"It means I'm going to plan it, dumbass. And it's going to be grander than Meghan and Harry's royal wedding." She nodded slightly, like she'd made up her mind, and finished off her biscotti.

Groaning, I ran my hands down my face. If she was planning my wedding, it meant it was going to be beyond over the top. Her extravagance knew no bounds.

"We've got so much to do, and so little time to do it in." She pulled out her phone. "We need to plan the menu, pick the flowers, locate a venue, choose the bridesmaid dresses, send out invitations, find a wedding dress for yo—"

"Alright, stop," I barked. "No, no, and hell no. This is exactly what I didn't want. I don't want to plan it. Thinking about it gives me a headache. If you wanna do it, fine. But I don't want to be involved."

Tatiana stared at me like I was losing my mind. "You don't want to plan your own wedding?"

"No. I don't care about any of that stuff, T. The only thing I care about is wearing my mother's wedding dress. Everything else is inconsequential."

A flash of sadness streaked across her face and then she locked it away. She knew I didn't like to talk about my mother or her death. It was a no-go subject for me. "Okay. Do I have full reign over the wedding?"

I sighed. "Yes. Do what you want, just don't make it tacky."

She glared at me. "Tacky? Bitch, do you even know me?"

I laughed and finished off the rest of my coffee. Tatiana had impeccable taste and had a real knack for interior design. If anyone could make my wedding a spectacular extravaganza, it was her (not that I wanted something big like that, but there was no way she'd let me have something small).

"You'll have to coordinate with Nikolai. He'll most likely be in charge of security for the event."

Tatiana pursed her lips. "Do I have to?"

I shook my head, chuckling softly. "Yes. Something as big as a wedding between two mafia families has to have some top-notch security. That's Nikolai's department. You can't plan it without running everything through him."

She grumbled under her breath.

"Unless you just wanna skip the whole big wedding thing and do something small?" I asked hopefully.

"No," she said quickly, sighing. "I'll sort it out."

The bell over the café door dinged, announcing the arrival of a new patron. Heavy footsteps thudded in the small space. The familiar hint of my brother's cologne hit my nostrils a second before a shadow loomed over our table. I looked up and saw Nikolai.

Speak of the devil.

"Nik, hey. What are you doing here?"

Tatiana stiffened slightly and looked up from her phone, glaring at my brother. Nikolai locked eyes with her and sexual tension crackled in the air between them. I rolled my eyes. Neither one wanted to admit they wanted the other. Instead, they played this ridiculous game of pretending that they didn't like each other. But anyone who spent more than a second in their presence knew they were hot for each other. Everyone except themselves.

They both looked away at the same time.

"Father wants you. I'm here to take you home," Nik said, eyes on me.

"Uh, why? What's going on?"

"He didn't say, just told me to come get you."

"But I drove my car."

"Leave it. We'll get it later."

I frowned. That was weird, but I knew better than to ignore a direct order from my father. I shrugged and packed up my things, putting my keys, phone and wallet back into my purse and slinging it over my shoulder.

"Sorry, T. I'll talk to you later?"

Tatiana smiled. "No worries, girl. I'll call you after my run later tonight."

Nikolai scowled at her. "You shouldn't be running at night. It's dangerous."

Tatiana smiled brightly but it looked forced, fake. "And?"

"What do you mean 'and'? It's not safe, so don't do it."

"You're not the boss of me, big guy. I'll do what I want." She waved us off and focused on her phone, effectively ending the conversation. "Off ya go, before daddy gets mad."

Nikolai growled deeply, his jaw clenched and teeth grinding against each other. "Tatiana—"

"Aw, leave it alone, Nik. The more you tell her not to do it, the more she wants to. You're just making it worse. Come on, let's go. Catch ya later, T."

"Bye," she called out, eyes still glued on her phone.

I dragged Nikolai out of the café and over to his car.

"Why'd you do that? You think it's alright for her to go running late at night on her own?" Nik grunted, opening the driver's side door.

"I think it's none of your business what she does," I said, walking around the car to the passenger's side. I arched an eyebrow. "Why do you care, anyway?"

He didn't answer, just grumbled under his breath and got into the car.

When we got home, I went straight to my father's office. Nikolai left to do his own thing. I knocked on the door and stepped inside after he bellowed, "Enter."

As usual, my father was planted behind his big mahogany desk in his classic three-piece Armani suit. There were two other men in the room along with him. I knew one of them. Adrian Alexeev, my father's main bodyguard. He was tall (pushing 6'5, I'd say) and built like a pro football player. He had short black hair and deep brown eyes. He had a scar that started a few inches above his left eyebrow, running down to just underneath his eye. It gave off a real 'Scar' from *The Lion King* vibe. He was dressed in a plain black suit with no tie.

The other man I had never met before, and I was sure of it. He was a bit shorter than Adrian, but he looked just as deadly. He had neatly styled blonde hair and blue eyes. His nose was slightly crooked, like it had been broken several times. He was dressed similarly to Adrian: black pants, black dress shirt.

"Father," I said, coming to a stop in front of his desk. "You needed to see me?"

He placed the papers he was reading down on the desk and looked at me. "These are your new bodyguards." He nodded to the two men in the room. "They're to go everywhere you go. You know Adrian, and this is Lorenzo from the Cosa Nostra. Arturo sent him to be your other guard."

Lorenzo bowed his head slightly, making sure to maintain his posture beside my father's desk.

I frowned. "Guard? Since when do I need a guard?" I asked, confused.

"Since we announced your engagement to Arturo. The merging of our families has brought forth some...problems." Father reached for his glass, half-filled with vodka, and took a swig. Adrian and Lorenzo stayed unmoving, hands clasped behind their backs, the epitome of professionalism. "It's nothing we didn't expect. Just people unhappy with you marrying outside the Bratva, especially when there are plenty of eligible Russian men available for you to marry. But I would be a fool not to take precautions, and I am no fool."

"Father, you know I don't need a guard. I can take care of myself."

"Nevertheless, you will have them. And I'll hear nothing else on the matter, understood?" He narrowed his eyes at me, his voice deep as he issued his command.

I clenched my teeth to refrain from lashing out. "Understood," I growled.

He nodded and motioned towards the door. "Good. Now go, I have work to do."

I turned and walked out of his office, accompanied by my new guards. I definitely wasn't happy about this situation. My father taught me how to protect myself. Taught me how to use a gun, use a knife. Taught me hand to hand combat. For years I trained every day, honing those skills until I became just as good as my brothers. If my brothers could walk around without any guards, I didn't see why I needed them. Not when I'm completely capable of taking care of myself. But I knew better than to balk at my father's orders.

When we left my father's office, I turned left, heading down the long corridor towards the kitchen, my new guards in tow. "This is ridiculous," I grumbled under my breath, aggravation gnawing at my bones.

Adrian chuckled. "You know it's only because he cares about you, Illayana."

"I know that. Doesn't mean I have to like it." I stopped and looked at Lorenzo. "Arturo sent you?"

"Yes ma'am," he nodded.

I winced. "Please don't call me ma'am. I'm twenty-one, not sixty."

"Apologies, Miss Volkov."

"Illayana is fine."

"Miss Volkov," Lorenzo repeated, not willing to refer to me with such familiarity.

I shrugged my shoulders and continued on my way to the kitchen. "Whatever works for you."

Lukyan was at the kitchen table, leaning back in his chair with his feet kicked up on the table. He had his hands clasped behind his head as he balanced on the two back legs of the chair with ease. He was wearing a sharp grey suit with a black tie, and his long hair was tied at the nape of his neck.

When I entered the kitchen, he scowled at me. He dropped the two front legs of the chair back to the ground with a loud *thud*, picked up his coffee on the table and turned around, giving me his back.

Okay, so he's still a little upset.

When Lukyan realised I had accepted Arturo's proposal and would be moving to New York, he had been in a perpetually sour mood, but only towards me. In a way, I could understand. Out of all my brothers, I was closest to Lukyan. For the first fifteen years of our lives, we were basically inseparable. We did everything together. We terrorised the place with our pranks and crazy personalities. He was finding it hard to accept the fact that I would be leaving. I guess he thought I would always be here. I did too.

I sighed and moved to stand next to him. He didn't acknowledge my presence, just continued sipping his coffee.

"Lukyan."

Nothing. Fucking crickets.

"Lukyan," I said, a little harder this time.

Still the fucker stayed silent.

"Come on, Lukyan, we both know you can't keep this shit up forever. I'm going to go out and do some shopping. Wanna come? I'll get you a donut from The Grind. I know how much you love their donuts."

"I don't want a fucking donut," he grumbled, glaring at his coffee cup.

Yeah fucking right. The kid lived for anything sweet. I swear, sometimes he was like a child stuck in a grown ass man's body. He would choose lollies and chocolate over a decent meal any day.

"Fine. I'll be back later then." I turned and started walking away. Just before I left the kitchen, I heard Lukyan's voice.

"What kind of donut?"

I kept my back to him, hiding the smirk on my face. I knew he couldn't resist. "Any kind you want."

He stayed silent for a few seconds, and then I heard the sound of his chair sliding across the marble floor. The scent of alcohol and cigars hit me like a title wave as he moved to my side.

"This doesn't mean I forgive you for leaving," he said, nose in the air. "I just want a fucking donut."

"Uh-huh," I smirked as I made my way out of the kitchen, heading towards the front door.

"What's with the shadows?" he asked, referring to Adrian and Lorenzo following behind us.

I groaned. "Father's stuck me with guards."

"Ha! Seriously? Suck shit," he laughed.

"Shut up," I grunted, elbowing him in the ribs.

He pranced forward and turned, walking backwards down the corridor. "So you drew the short straw, huh, Adrian? Went from guarding the big boss to his precious little flower? Sucks to be you."

"I am not a precious little flower!" I blasted, leering at him.

Adrian just shook his head. "It's an honour to watch over Illayana," he replied to Lukyan, not rising to the bait.

Lukyan scoffed. "Yeah, right." His eyes flicked to Lorenzo. "And who are you?"

"I'm Lorenzo," he replied, not bothering to say anything else.

"Right. And?"

"And nothing, Lukyan, would you just shut up?" I growled.

"Temper, temper," Lukyan smiled, turning back around.

Once we stepped outside, Lorenzo moved to the black Range Rover parked in the driveway and opened the door to the backseat.

"Thank you, Lorenzo." I jumped in, taking a seat, Lukyan joining me. Adrian took to the driver's side while Lorenzo sat in the passenger seat.

"Where to first, Illayana?" Adrian asked, his voice laced with his thick Russian accent. He manoeuvred the car with ease down the driveway and onto the road.

"We'll go to The Grind first, please, Adrian, so we can get my stupid brother his donuts."

He chuckled, his hands moving effortlessly over the steering wheel as we made our way to the city. "Didn't you just buy a pack of twenty-four yesterday?" he asked Lukyan, glancing in the rear-view mirror.

"Yeah. *Yesterday*," Lukyan scoffed, rolling his eyes.

"Seriously, with all the crap you eat how are you not severely overweight?" I chuckled. The kid ate more than everyone in the house combined, and it was mainly junk food.

Lukyan shrugged his shoulders, a smile on his face.

After twenty minutes, we pulled into the street The Grind was located on. As per usual, there was nowhere to park. Parking in Las Vegas was a total nightmare. We usually had to park a couple blocks away and walk, which I never minded.

Adrian managed to find a park only a block away. As soon as the car stopped, Lorenzo was out and opening my car door. I stepped out and smiled at him.

"You know you don't have to do that, right? I can open my own door."

"I know, Miss Volkov," he replied.

Adrian walked in front of me, his big body shielding me from anything and everything while Lorenzo stayed behind me. Lukyan was at my side, trying hard not to run ahead as we walked down the street.

The footpath up ahead was blocked, several workers milling around, laying a new round of cement. Lukyan groaned, annoyed at the hold up. He looked left and signalled for us to follow him. He stepped into an alleyway littered with rubbish and garbage bins.

"We'll go around." Lukyan moved further into the alley, with me at his side and my guards behind me.

"Well, well, well. What do we have here?" A man stepped out from behind a dumpster, followed by four more men.

I instantly tensed, my hand moving to grip the knife at my waist. *Why the fuck didn't I bring my gun? I'm usually always strapped.*

Lukyan immediately stood taller, his big body looking every bit as lethal as I knew it was, his face laced with menace and hands moving to grasp the gun strapped to his chest holster.

I looked behind me to see another five men coming from where we'd just entered. They were the workers from the main street.

Fuck. It was an ambush.

Lorenzo and Adrian pulled their guns, taking aim at the five new arrivals, their backs pressing tightly to mine.

Shit, this isn't good. We were outnumbered.

All of them had masks on and were dressed in black pants and long black shirts. The only part of their bodies you could see were their eyes. The fuckers were even wearing gloves.

I tried to control my heartbeat and breathing, making sure to keep a level head. I watched Lukyan in my peripheral vision. His eyes were roaming over the men in front of us, looking for weaknesses.

The man who spoke stepped ahead of the others, standing a few feet in front of me.

"Well, if it isn't the Russian whore," he spat. I could hear the faint traces of a Spanish accent under his words. *The Los Zetas?*

Lukyan tensed at my side and growled lowly in his throat, moving to stand in front of me protectively. I patted his chest, stopping him, and he halted.

"Are you sure you want to do this?" I asked calmly.

Even from where I stood, I could see the man's lips curve up into a smile underneath his mask.

I felt Lorenzo and Adrian at my back, and a part of me was so fucking thankful that my father had pushed for me to have guards (not that I'd ever admit it. I was stubborn like that).

The man's eyes stayed glued on me as he addressed his men. He spoke in Spanish, clearly assuming we couldn't understand. "Take the girl alive. Kill the rest."

My eyes flicked to Lukyan and he nodded slightly, signalling he heard and understood what was said. I wasn't sure if Adrian or Lorenzo could speak Spanish, and I didn't want to risk that they couldn't. I kept my eyes on the man in front of me as I spoke. *"Sii pronto. Hanno sparato per uccidere gli ordini." Be ready. They have shoot-to-kill orders.* I said to Lorenzo in Italian. Lukyan spoke to Adrian in Russian. *"Oni planiruut ubit nas yi vzyat illayanu. gotovsya." They plan to kill us and take Illayana. Get ready.*

All at once the men sprang forward, attacking. I didn't have time to think about anything else but the situation in front of me. I could only hope that Adrian and Lorenzo could hold their own. I couldn't worry about the other five men behind me *and* the five in front of me.

Four men jumped for Lukyan while the man who spoke walked slowly towards me, taking his sweet fucking time. They thought I wasn't a threat, that much was painfully obvious. The fact that they stuck four on Lukyan and only one on me clearly showed that. Well, they'd see soon enough.

Gunshots rang through the small alleyway and sounds of fighting reached my ears, but I blocked it out. I blocked it all out and focused on the fucker who thought he could take me down. I didn't have the time or luxury to screw around. Lukyan had four guys coming at him. I needed to get rid of this guy quickly so I could help him. Knowing Lukyan, he'd take all four of them head on without using his gun, because the fucker liked to fight with his hands. It wouldn't be the first time. He only used his gun in dire circumstances. He was a knife man.

The second the man stepped within my reach, I attacked. I struck my hand out, delivering a solid palm strike to his nose. His head whipped back and I heard his nose break, but I didn't give him a chance to retaliate. I swiftly followed with a punch to his sternum, a blow to his kidneys, a kick to the kneecap and finished off with a solid uppercut—all in under five seconds.

He grunted as I delivered each blow, pain rippling through his body. Without losing momentum, I dealt him a solid roundhouse kick right to the chest, sending his body flying back and sprawling to the ground. The sound of more gunshots came from all around me, but I didn't have time to stop and look. I needed to finish off my opponent before he recovered.

He was lying on the ground, eyes closed and groaning in pain. I nudged him with my heel and his eyes shot open. *"Quien es la puta ahora?" Who's the whore now?* I said in Spanish, my lips curving into a smile.

Before he could respond, I picked up my foot and drove my spiked heel deep into his throat. He choked, a painful gurgling sound slipping past his lips as blood poured out of his mouth. Blood spurted out everywhere as I pulled my heel out. His hands wrapped around his throat, his eyes wide open with fear. I wish I could have stayed to watch the life drain from his eyes, but there wasn't time.

I turned and ran to Lukyan. He had already taken out one of those fuckers, leaving three left. He was holding off two of them, blocking their attacks while the third was circling him, trying to find an opening to attack. I pulled a knife out and jumped onto his back, wrapping my legs tightly around his torso. Before he could react, I pulled his head back and used the blade in my hand to cut his throat swiftly.

As his body fell, I leapt forward, flipping in the air and landing solidly on my feet. I turned around just in time to see Lukyan drive his knife deep into a man's heart. He kicked his body, pulling the knife free at the same time. The last man remaining ran forward, trying to catch Lukyan off guard.

Not on my fucking watch.

I threw my knife hard, aiming for the fucker. It flew through the air and struck him in the head, directly between the eyes. Knife throwing was one of my best skills.

We both immediately moved to help Adrian and Lorenzo. They had each taken down one man, leaving three left. They were both covered in blood, holding a knife in each hand. The ground was littered with guns, obviously having been knocked aside during the fight. Lukyan jumped to help Adrian, who was squaring off with two men, while I moved to Lorenzo.

The man was distracted, his focus stuck firmly on Lorenzo. He didn't even see me coming. I dealt a swift kick to his legs, bringing him to his knees. I quickly pulled another blade from my waist and drove it deep into his back, severing his spinal cord. He screamed in agony as I twisted the knife deeper and deeper until it couldn't go any further. I kicked him in the back and he fell to the ground face-first.

I went to move onto the next when I realised there was no one left. Adrian and Lukyan stood side by side breathing heavily, blood dripping from the knives in their hands. Bodies were lying everywhere, pools of blood beginning to form.

A painful groan came from behind me. Lukyan's eyes snapped to where the sound was coming from and he moved swiftly to the man's side. He picked up the back of his head and was about to slit his throat when I spoke.

"Wait," I said, breathless.

"Why?" Lukyan growled, looking at me, the rage from the fight still burning in his eyes.

"Don't you think Father is going to want to speak with him?"

A sinister smile spread across his face as he pulled my knife from the man's back and flipped him over. The man groaned again, his face contorted in pain. Lukyan gripped his chin roughly, forcing the man to look at him.

"You're going to wish I had killed you. My father will have no mercy,"

Lukyan spat.

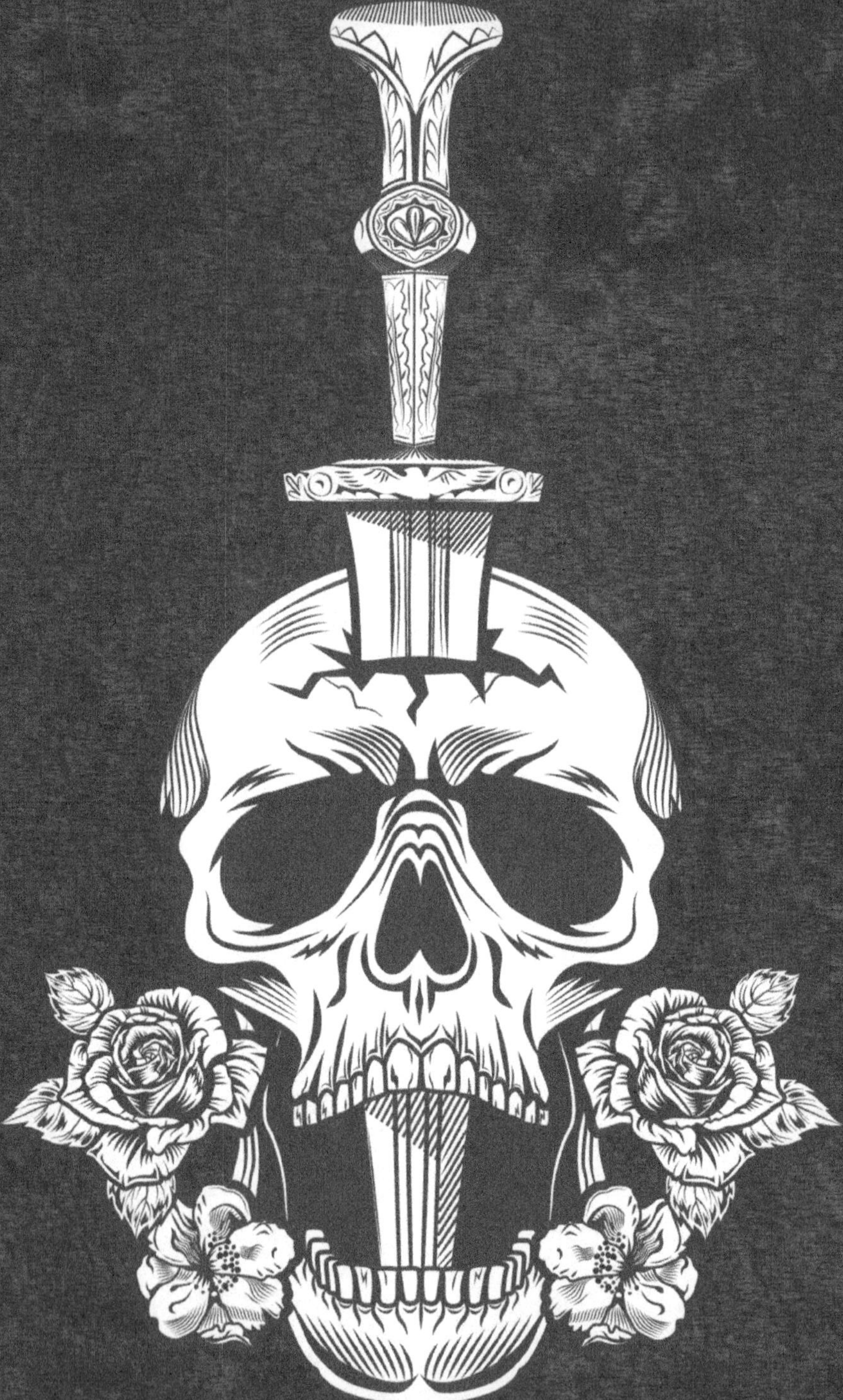

CHAPTER ELEVEN

Arturo De Luca

The sound of my office door opening made me look up from the screen I was glaring at, filled with so many numbers it was giving me a fucking headache. Vincenzo was standing directly in front of me, his dark hair (for once) styled neatly, wearing a light grey suit with a black tie.

"What do you want?" I asked, looking back at the iPad in front of me. I didn't have the time to talk right now, not unless it was important.

As underboss, I oversaw all our capos, making sure they were doing their job and keeping our soldiers in line. There was a certain hierarchy to the Cosa Nostra. As Don, my father was in charge of everyone and everything, but he delegated certain tasks to others. Vin was our enforcer, responsible for dealing out punishments to those who deserved it, and he was usually brutal about it. I not only dealt with our capos and lower-ranking soldiers, but also kept the books for our businesses, making sure everything matched up.

We owned several different companies as well as a few small-time businesses, all of which required daily monitoring. We also had our not-so-legal enterprises. We owned the drug trade here in New York. If you wanted a little something, it came from us. Coke, meth, heroin, weed. You name it, we had it. And we were the *only* ones to sell it.

If we caught anyone else selling shit in our territory, we made an example out of them, making sure it was crystal fucking clear what happened when you sold on our streets. Right now, I was sifting through our accounts, running the numbers on our latest drop. Something wasn't adding up. We were missing money, and I had no idea why. Over $50,000 just...gone. Into thin fucking air.

Vin took a seat, leaning his big body back in the chair, and kicked his boots up onto my desk. "You don't look so good, big brother. Tired?" he smirked.

I scowled at him and knocked his feet back to the ground. "Don't put your shoes on my desk, you little shit. What's so important you had to come in here and bug me?"

Vin straightened and his green eyes connected with mine, all sense of humour vanishing from his face. "What's going on? That's your 'I'm going to kill someone' voice."

I rolled my eyes. "I don't have a voice like that."

"Uh, ya, you do. Now spill."

I cracked my neck, trying to relieve some of the tension in my body, and handed him the iPad. "We're missing money."

His eyes flew over the screen as his fingers scrolled through the figures. "Shit," he breathed. "That's, wha—"

"$51,365," I growled, my anger soaring.

"Fuck. Does Dad know?"

"Not yet." I took the iPad back and placed it on the desk. "Who's responsible for handling the cash at the drop houses?"

"Marco's in charge of the houses north of the city, and Diego's responsible for the south."

We had five drop houses altogether, spread throughout the area. They were where we stored all our cash until it could be laundered safely through our businesses and into our accounts. The houses were small and inconspicuous so as not to attract attention. They weren't even in our names (on the off chance they got raided, we didn't want the money traced back to us). Anyone with access was now a suspect.

I kept meticulous records of everything, from how many of our drugs have hit the streets to how much money we should have for said drugs. Once a week, I visited every drop house to confirm the cash on hand matched what we had on file. This was the first time that it didn't. It meant someone was skimming off the top, taking a little bit of cash here and there and hoping we wouldn't notice.

"I want a list of everyone who has access to the drop houses, from the handlers to the soldiers guarding the place. I want everyone."

"On it," Vin pulled out his phone, running the names down.

I was going to find out who was responsible, who had the gall to steal from us, and I was going to flay them alive and dump their body in the fucking street so everyone could see what happened when they fucked with us. With me.

"In the meantime, we're going to pay a visit to Marco and Diego, find out what they have to say about this shit."

Vin looked up from his phone and smiled, a truly dark and evil smile. "Sounds good to me. Oh, by the way, did you tell Gabriella yet? That you're no longer planning to marry her?"

I winced. No, I hadn't. I wasn't looking forward to that conversation. Gabriella and I had known each other since childhood. It was never written in stone, but it was always assumed we would marry. Ever since she turned eighteen, my father had pushed me to wed her. She was now twenty-four and had waited the last six years for me to propose.

She was a beautiful woman and came from a good, strong Italian family. She was well behaved, never fought with anyone, never argued. She was always polite and spoke appropriately. The perfect little stepford wife who lived for pleasing a husband and doing whatever he commanded.

I always thought that was what I wanted in a wife; someone who listened unconditionally and wouldn't question me. Then the hurricane that is Illayana Volkov swept into my life and blew all that out of the water. I realised after meeting her that I didn't want a weak, docile wife. I wanted a fighter, a queen.

When my father first told me he was stepping down as Don, he told me I had to marry before he would allow me to take his place. He suggested I finally bite the bullet and marry Gabriella. I didn't want to, but I would have if I hadn't met Illayana.

When Gabriella found out I was marrying someone else instead—someone who wasn't even Italian—she was going to lose it. She could have married three times over by now if she wasn't waiting on me.

"I'm going to take that look on your face as a no," Vin chuckled. "What are you going to do?"

"What do you think?" I asked sarcastically. I picked up my phone. After a short conversation, I hung up.

There was a knock at my office door a few minutes later. I leant back in my chair and told them to come in.

Enzo walked in, his face hard and body tight. He was tall and lean, with thick, dark hair and even darker eyes, eyes that showed he had been through a lot in his life, and he was scarred because of it. He was one of our most loyal and devoted capos. He was also Gabriella's father.

He came to a stop in front of my desk and bowed slightly. "Boss."

"Enzo, thank you for coming."

He nodded and widened his stance, arms clasped behind his body, waiting to find out why I had called him into my office.

"I wanted to discuss something with you. As you know, we recently had a meeting with the Bratva to establish an alliance and gain some new weaponry against our fight with Nero Gambino."

"Yes, Boss. Did you manage to get what you were after?"

"Oh, he did alright," Vin whispered under his breath. I glared in warning.

"We did. A case of high-powered machine guns will be delivered within the week," I answered.

"That's great, Boss." He looked around the room uncertainly. "What, uh, did you need from me?"

I sighed and looked him in the eye. "To strengthen the bond of our alliance, a marriage was proposed."

He stiffened, nostrils flaring, not saying a word.

"Please apologise to your daughter on my behalf, but our engagement will not be going forward. I will be marrying a Bratva woman."

Anger flashed across Enzo's face. He licked his lips and glanced between Vin and I. "Is this a joke, Boss?"

I arched an eyebrow. "Do I seem like a joking man, Enzo?"

"It doesn't make sense otherwise, sir. For the past six years, it has been discussed that you would marry my daughter and now, now it's no longer happening? You can't do this."

I narrowed my eyes. "I'm going to allow that brief lapse in etiquette because I know how confusing this must seem to you. But that is all I'm going to allow. Do you understand?" I asked darkly, letting my voice drop. "I want you to take notice of the fact that you said 'discussed', not arranged. I never said I would marry her. Yes, there were discussions of it over the years, but that's all they were. Discussions. I have made my decision, and this is how it's going to be. Understood?"

He stared at me, shock and anger radiating from him. He nodded stiffly. "Understood. Was there anything else?"

I waved him away and he left, his feet stomping loudly on my Italian marble flooring.

Vin blew out a breath. "That went well," he chuckled sarcastically.

I grunted and stood, buttoning my suit jacket. One problem down, another to go. "Get your shit, we're going to see Diego and Marco."

My phone rang and I pulled it out of my pocket, glancing at the screen. *Illayana.*

Vin groaned. Loudly. "I know that look. We don't have time for you to have phone sex with your girlfriend right now. We've got shit to deal with."

"She's my fiancé, not my girlfriend. And you'll wait," I commanded as I accepted the call. *"Kotenok, chto ya mogu sdelat' dlya vas?" Kitten, what can I do for you?* I asked in flawless Russian.

"Don't freak out," her voice came through strained, like she was tired.

The hair on the back of my neck immediately went up and my body became rigid. Her tone of voice didn't sound distressed, but her words had me concerned. Vin gave me a confused look as I slowly sat back down. I had a feeling I should be sitting when she spoke next.

"There's been an. . .incident."

My hand gripped the phone tighter. "What kind of incident?"

"Arturo, you need to be calm. I can hear the anger in your voice already and I've barely spoken."

"I'm not angry. I'm fine," I said a little too quickly. "What happened?"

She took a deep breath in and exhaled, like she was preparing herself.

"Illayana," I growled, my frustration growing the longer she remained silent. "What. Happened?" "We were ambushed. Ten thugs cornered and attacked Lukyan and I. I can't be sure, but they might have been Los Zetas. One of them spoke Spanish."

My anger spiked all over again. Rage pounded into me like a drumbeat. That stupid motherfucker Nero. I didn't anticipate him going for Illayana, though I should have. He would do anything to hurt us, and going after my future wife was a good fucking way to do it. He didn't have the balls to go after us directly anymore. We came out on top every time. Instead he played stupid little games, hitting our trade routes and stealing our drugs, trying to fuck up our business and cut us off. Since the Los Zetas joined the fight, he's grown more ballsy, encroaching more and more into our territory and then pulling back before we had a chance to strike back.

Now he'd gone after Illayana.

I closed my eyes and took a deep breath in, trying to calm myself like she said. It didn't work. No one touched what was mine.

"Fuckers!" I yelled, slamming my fist on the desk. The wood splintered from the impact. "Are you okay? Where the fuck was Lorenzo?"

"Arturo. Calm," she soothed. "I'm fine. I wasn't hurt, and Lorenzo was with me."

"He was there? He protected you?"

She laughed. I had no idea what the fuck was so funny.

"I don't need protection, Arturo, but yes. He was there. As well as Adrian, my other bodyguard."

Vin was still watching me intently. He could tell something was up and he was smart enough to keep his mouth shut.

"I'm sending another guard to you. Two's not enough, especially if they're sending that many men after you. Where are you now?"

I balanced the phone between my ear and shoulder as I scribbled a note on a piece of paper and handed it to Vin. He took it without question and read it. He gave me a quick nod and typed something into his phone, putting it to his ear as he walked out of the room.

"On my way home. I'm covered in blood and in desperate need of a shower."

"Blood?!" I roared. "You said you weren't hurt!"

"It's not mine, Arturo."

I breathed a sigh of relief. "Good. That's good. Look, when you get home, I want you to stay there. Don't leave. I'm coming."

"No, there's no need. I'm honestly fine. My father has gone into overprotective mode and I couldn't be safer at the moment."

"I don't give a fuck! The jet is being prepped and will be ready in a few hours. I'm coming, Illayana. I'll be there by tonight. End of discussion," I snapped.

She sighed, but didn't argue any further. "Fine then. Would you like to hear some good news?" Her tone of voice instantly changed from strained to downright giddy.

"Sure. I could use some good news right about now." Vin came back into the room and took a seat. He gave me a subtle nod to inform me the jet was being prepared, but other than that remained silent.

"We have a prisoner."

I immediately sat up straight, a smile spreading across my face and excitement bubbling through me. "A prisoner, you say?"

She giggled. "Yes. My father plans to have a few words with him."

"I bet he does. I want to talk to him too."

"Hold on." She started speaking to someone, though I couldn't hear exactly what was being said. The voices started to get louder and more pronounced until finally she returned. "My father's agreed to wait until you get here to question him. But if you take too long, he'll start without you."

"That's fair enough," I replied, leaning back in my chair. "Are you sure you're okay?"

"I promise, I'm fine. You worry too much," she chuckled. "I have to go. We're pulling up to the house."

"Okay. I'll be there later tonight, Illayana. And I'm gonna make that fucker pay."

"You're gonna have to get in line. There's a lot of people who want to have words with him."

"I'm at the top of the line. Everyone else can have what's left over."

"So bossy," she chuckled. "I'll see you later, Arturo"

"Ciao, gattina. Stai attento." Goodbye, kitten. Be safe. I said in Italian.

"Anche tu." You too.

I swear, whenever she spoke Italian, I got goosebumps. I hung up the phone and looked at Vin.

"Bad news, I take it?" he asked, tilting his head to the side.

"You've got no fucking idea," I grumbled as I got to my feet. "Come on. Let's go see Marco and Diego. I'll explain everything on the way."

We pulled up in front of *Bare Essentials*, one of the many buildings we own located in downtown New York. At night, it was a high-end strip club, but during the day it was where we packed and distributed our drugs.

Both Marco and Diego were meant to be there, but whether or not they were doing their jobs or getting their dicks sucked by the girls was anyone's guess.

I stepped out of my Mercedes, buttoning up my suit jacket. I was wearing an all-black suit with a black tie and black shoes. I looked dark, evil. Just the way I liked it. Vin stepped up and walked beside me as we made our way to the entrance. A black SUV pulled up behind my car and four of my men got out, moving to take up position behind us.

"I can't believe those fuckers sent ten guys after them," Vin said, shaking his head. "How the hell were they able to hold off that many? It was just the four of them?"

I had no idea. Ten was a lot for four to handle. I knew the Bratva were skilled in their training, and I knew Illayana was capable of fighting. She proved that the night I broke into her house. But still, how *did* they manage to beat that many? Not that I was complaining.

"Got no clue," I grumbled. "As far as I know, it was just Lukyan, Illayana and her two bodyguards." I was still pissed that she'd been attacked to start with, and I was itching to get my hands on the prisoner they had.

"You gotta admit, that's pretty badass though."

"I don't have to admit shit," I hissed. "She shouldn't have been attacked in the first place."

"Calm your farm. I highly doubt it's the first time she's been attacked. She's the daughter of the *Pakhan*. She's probably attacked weekly."

I glared at him and his hands shot up in a defensive gesture, his palms facing outwards.

"Whoa, I was just sayin'."

"Just shut your mouth, how about that?"

"Righto, Cujo."

Two men were stationed outside the strip club, guarding the front door. As we made our approach, they both nodded. One of the men turned and opened the door, allowing us to step inside. The place was completely empty apart from the stages, tables and stripper poles distributed throughout the room.

"Did you tell them we were coming?" I asked Vin as we made our way over to the office at the back of the building.

"Nope," he replied, popping the 'p'.

"Good."

I opened the office door and wasted no time making my way over to the bookcase. I searched through the books until I found *The Art of War* and tilted it back. The bookcase shook as it opened wide, revealing a hidden passage. We followed the staircase down into the basement until we came to a large steel door. A keypad was on the wall on the right-hand side of the door. I quickly put in my personal eight-digit code. The red light above the keypad turned green and the door swung open.

The room was filled with half-naked people, all working to cut, clean and package our drugs. Most were women, dressed in just their bras and underwear. The few men in the room were guards, stationed along the walls and monitoring the floor. No one acknowledged us as we moved throughout the room, which was exactly the way I preferred it. I was paying these people to do a job and mind their own business.

I flicked my wrist at two of the men, who came inside with me—Christian and Luca. They were identical twins who had been at my side for years. They were both big guys, packed with muscle, incredible fighters. Dark-haired and blue-eyed beasts.

"You two, stay out here and monitor the work. I want to know if anything is amiss," I commanded as I continued to the back office.

"Yes, Boss," they both said at the exact same time.

Fuck, I hated it when they did that. It was creepy as fuck.

Vin and my remaining two guards, Stefano and Thomas, stayed close by my side as I stood in front of the door. I turned to Vin and he gave me a cheeky smile. He was way too excited for this.

I raised my leg and kicked in the door.

"Knock, knock," I sang as I stepped in.

I was greeted with a high-pitched shriek of terror and Marco's bare, white ass. *Lovely.* A red-haired woman was on her knees in front of Marco, her hair dishevelled and lipstick smudged. All she had on was a skimpy lace outfit and what had to be at least six-inch hooker heels.

"What the fuck?!" Marco screamed as he pushed the woman to the side and turned to face us, grabbing a gun.

The second he saw it was me, his smile dropped. He was a short, stumpy guy, about 5'6 with short brown hair. His eyes were frozen wide open in fear, the gun in his hand trembling.

"Mr-Mr De Luca," he stuttered. "What a surprise."

"Ah, so you do know who I am." Vin moved from my side, walking menacingly around the room. He took a knife out of his sheath and started spinning the blade between his fingers—his go-to scare tactic.

"Of course, sir."

"So why the fuck are you still pointing a gun at me?" I growled.

He paled and immediately lowered his gun. "I'm sorry, sir."

I pointed at the redhead cowering in the corner. "You. Out."

She got to her feet instantly and ran from the room at full speed. Marco's lips twitched like he wanted to say something, but luckily for him, he stayed quiet. I moved to the large wooden desk in the centre of the room and sat behind it, leaning back comfortably in the black leather chair. It was a classic power play. I wanted him to see that even if it was his office, his desk, I owned it all.

Marco frowned. "I wasn't expecting you, sir."

"I bet you weren't. Nevertheless, I'm here. And we have an issue to discuss." I narrowed my eyes and felt an odd sense of satisfaction as he squirmed underneath my gaze.

"Is-issue, sir?"

"Stop stuttering," I snapped. "Where's Diego?"

"Diego? I don't know, sir."

"You don't? He's meant to be here with you, isn't he?"

"Well, yes, but he called earlier to say he couldn't make it in. He's sick."

"Sick?" I repeated, my voice dropping low.

Marco gulped. "Yes-yes, sir."

"You'll have to do then. Remind me what your job is, Marco?"

He glanced uneasily around the room. "M-my job is to oversee the distribution of the coke and meth, and deliver the cash to the drop houses."

I smiled and kicked my feet up onto the desk, crossing them at the ankles. "Correct. And if a problem were to arise—say, a large sum of money went missing—who would be responsible for that?"

Fear flashed across his face as he turned white as a sheet. "Missing, sir?"

"Missing. Poof. Gone, like magic."

"Is" —he licked his lips nervously— "is this hypothetical, sir?"

"I don't know, Marco, is it?" I whispered darkly.

He shifted from one foot to the other, avoiding eye contact. Vin continued to circle him, his knife flipping through the air. "Sir, I don't know what's going o—"

Enough games.

I grabbed a pen and, with blinding speed, jumped over the desk and jammed it into his neck. He screamed and tried to back away, but Vin placed his hands on his shoulders, holding him in place. I kept my hand around the pen as I pushed it further in.

"Now, I just punched a hole in your carotid artery. That means you have about sixty seconds before you pass out," I drove the pen a little further in, enjoying his screams of agony. "Talk. Now," I growled.

"Sir, please! I have no idea what's going on!" he gurgled.

"You don't? Are you sure you don't know a little something about where my money went?"

"No! I swear!" His body shook, blood pouring freely down his neck, drenching his clothes.

"Well, someone has to know something, Marco. *You're* in charge of the money. You and Diego. So if it's not you, then it has to be Diego. Is that what you're telling me?"

"Yes! Yes, it has to be Diego. Please sir, don't kill me."

I eyed him suspiciously. I couldn't tell if he was telling the truth or not. I've come across some magnificent liars in my time. He could have been one.

"Well, don't worry, Marco. We're going to get this matter straightened out right away. We'll find out who's taken my money." I ripped the pen out of his neck and he screamed, dropping to his knees. I pulled a silk handkerchief from my pocket and held it to the wound, applying pressure.

I crouched and locked eyes with him. "And when we do, they're going to pray for a swift death. I promise you that."

I rose to my full height and looked at Vin, nodding at Marco sobbing on his knees. "Patch him up and take him to the dungeon. We'll continue this when we find Diego."

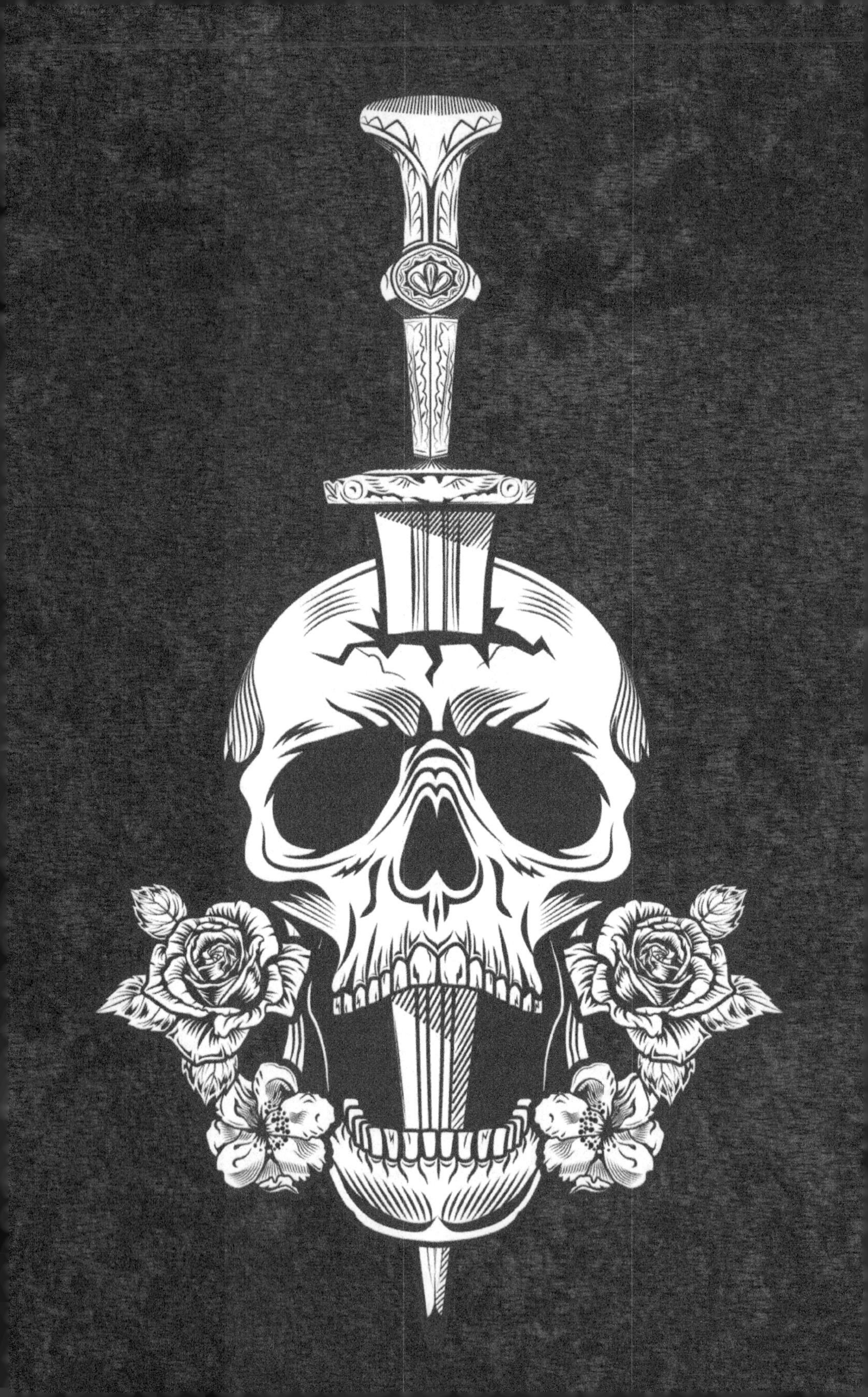

CHAPTER TWELVE

Arturo De Luca

*K*nock, knock.

"I'll get it!" A soft voice yelled from inside the house.

Illayana.

After dragging Marco's ass to the dungeon located beneath our house, I left immediately for Las Vegas. Vin was going to call me the second he found Diego, and then we were going to torture them together. One of them would talk eventually. It was their job to monitor the money coming in and out of the drop houses. Even if they weren't directly responsible for the theft, they failed in protecting the money, and they would pay the price for it. They could no longer be trusted with anything of importance. The missing $50,000 proved that.

The front door swung open and, instead of Illayana, I was greeted by Lukyan.

Fucking delightful.

"What the fuck are you doing here?" he sneered. "And who the fuck are they?" He waved his hands at the twins standing behind me.

"Where is she?" I asked, ignoring his questions.

"Not home." He started closing the door and I wedged my foot in the entryway to keep it open.

"Now, see, why don't I believe you?" I barged through the door just in time to see Illayana quickly running down the stairs.

She was wearing a pair of black sweatpants and a long-sleeved white t-shirt. Her long black hair was tied up in a ponytail, swaying from side to side as she walked.

I shoulder-barged past Lukyan and made my way over to her, meeting her in the middle of the foyer.

"Hey!" Lukyan exclaimed, almost losing his balance.

My eyes roamed up and down her body, looking for any sign of injuries. "You okay?"

"Yes, I told you I was fine. You really didn't have to come all this way."

"I agree," Lukyan cut in. "So why don't you just leave? Nobody wants you here," he said, holding the door wide open.

"Lukyan! Shut up," Illayana snapped.

"You shut up," he barked back.

I rolled my eyes. Lukyan was so much like Vin, it was actually a little scary.

Illayana looked over my shoulder as the twins walked through the front door and stood behind me.

"Who are they?" she frowned, her face scrunching up in confusion.

I moved to stand beside her, sweeping my hand out in front of me. "This is Christian and Luca D'Arco. They'll be shadowing you from now on."

Christian and Luca took a step forward and bowed slightly. "Ma'am," they said at the same time in that creepy way of theirs.

They were both dressed in identical black suits, making it even more difficult for people to tell them apart (not that I ever had that issue. I've always been able to tell them apart).

"She doesn't like being called 'Ma'am'," Lorenzo's stony voice called out as he stepped into the foyer. He moved quickly to stand beside Luca, dressed in his usual all-black attire.

"Boss," he said, tilting his head in greeting.

"If she doesn't like being called 'Ma'am'—" Christian began.

"Then what do we call her?" Luca finished, cocking his head to the side, studying Illayana. They had a tendency to finish each other's sentences like that.

Lorenzo shook his head and gave a sigh of exasperation. "How about her name, *idiotas?*" Idiots?

Christian and Luca exchanged a look with one another, "Rigggght. Her name," they said in unison, their brows drawn together in concentration.

I shook my head and chuckled slightly. They were great fighters, loyal to the bone. But common sense sometimes eluded those two.

"No offense to you guys, but I've already got bodyguards. I don't need any more. I'm fine with Lorenzo and Adrian."

"It's non-negotiable," I stated firmly. "You'll take them and I'll hear no more on the matter."

She turned and pinned me with an icy glare, her anger slowly starting to surface. "Arturo, four guards is excessive. Not to mention the fact that they don't exactly blend in," she said, waving a hand through the air in front of the twins.

Okay, she did kind of have a point. They were big blokes. And I wasn't too insecure to admit they were handsome dudes, too. They gathered quite a bit of attention when we walked on the streets. Men and women ogled them constantly, like they had never seen identical twins before (not that they ever seemed to mind). Still, I trusted them with my life, and I knew if the situation ever called for it, they would die to protect me. Just like I knew they would do the same for Illayana.

"I don't care. You'll do what I say. You don't go anywhere without Christian, Luca and Lorenzo. Do you understand me?"

Lukyan laughed. A full-blown, top-of-the-lungs, shrieking-like-a-damn-monkey laugh. We all turned to look at him, confused as fuck. Well, everyone except Illayana. She was giving me a mean death glare, her brows drawn together and her face turning red. I could feel the heat of that gaze burning a hole in the side of my face.

Lukyan continued to laugh, hunched over and slapping his hands on his thighs like he just heard the world's funniest joke.

Christian looked at Luca, his face contorted in confusion, and mouthed "*what the fuck?*"

Luca shrugged.

Suddenly, Illayana turned and speed-walked out of the foyer without so much as a glance at me.

"Illayana!" I called out, but she continued walking.

The twins and Lorenzo exchanged an awkward glance with one another while Lukyan continued to laugh. My temper spiked. I felt a flash of irritation flow through my body.

"What the fuck are you laughing at?!" I snapped, pinning my anger on Lukyan. Seemed like the perfect outlet to me.

Lukyan's eyes sparkled with amusement as he straightened and looked at me, his body still shaking with laughter. "There's only one man...one man in this world who can tell my sister what to do. And you ain't him."

I narrowed my eyes. "And who is that?"

Lukyan inclined his head behind me and I turned to find Dimitri striding towards me. He was dressed in a tailored light blue suit (weird for one o'clock in the morning, but alright) and black tie. Aleksandr and Nikolai were at his side, stony expressions on their faces.

"You're not even here for five minutes and you've already pissed her off. Not a smart move," Dimitri said, stopping in front of me.

He ran his light blue eyes over Christian and Luca. They both stood up straighter and puffed out their chests as Dimitri examined them. It was clear he was assessing them, determining their worth. They may have looked young, but they were deadly. And I'd never come across a set of people who worked so well together.

After he scrutinised them for a few more seconds, he gave a subtle nod of approval. "I'll make sure she accepts them, but she won't be happy about it. She's never needed guards before. I taught her how to protect herself, so she'd never have to rely on anyone."

Christian scratched the back of his head, his brows pulled together in a frown. He leant over and whispered into Luca's ear.

"Something to say, boy?" Dimitri asked, arching an eyebrow.

The twins immediately separated, standing up as straight as they could. "No, sir."

Dimitri tsked, shaking his head in disappointment. "I don't like liars. Care to try that again?"

Christian and Luca looked at each other intently. To anyone else, it would look like they were having a staring competition, but I knew better. They had this uncanny ability to be able to communicate without using actual words, like they could read exactly what the other was thinking by just looking at their face. It's what made them so lethal in a fight.

Luca grabbed Christian by the arm and shoved him forward.

"Uhm, we—"

Luca kicked him in the shin.

"Ow, fuck!" Christian scowled at his brother, rubbing his leg. "I mean, I was just a little confused about something you said, that's all."

"Let me guess," Lukyan interjected, "you don't believe she can protect herself?"

Christian looked down at the ground, not answering.

"Show them," Dimitri commanded.

Nikolai moved instantly, heading down the long corridor and disappearing into a room. Aleksandr motioned for us to follow him as he made his way through the house. He led us to the kitchen and took a seat at the large wooden table in the middle of the room, gesturing to the empty seats.

Lukyan plopped down next to him, kicking his feet up onto the table. The twins, Lorenzo and I all exchanged looks with one another before slowly sitting down on the opposite side of the table. Dimitri stayed standing.

"Want some advice?" Lukyan asked, leaning back casually in his chair and humming softly.

"Not really, but I have a feeling you're going to give it to me anyway," I replied.

"She's fucking crazy. Get out while you can."

Aleksandr slapped him on the back of the head. Lukyan grunted and scowled at his older brother, massaging his head.

Christian and Luca snickered.

Nikolai came back into the room carrying a laptop, his square jaw clenched and eyes narrowed in concentration as he typed away. He placed it down in the centre of the table. "The alleyway Illayana and Lukyan were attacked in had surveillance. The owner of the convenience store on that block installed a camera after his staff got attacked while taking out the trash one night. I hacked into the CCTV system and deleted the whole thing, but not before I made a copy."

He clicked a button on the laptop and took the empty seat next to Aleksandr. Christian, Luca and I leant forward, watching as a video started to play. The quality wasn't very good, the video grainy and heavily pixelated. But the second Illayana and Lukyan stepped into view, I forgot all about it. Adrian and Lorenzo were following close behind, right on their tails.

Suddenly, five men sprung out from behind a dumpster and stood in front of them. One of the men stepped forward and started talking. There was no fucking sound though. Of course. Cheap ass camera.

Another five men came from where they entered from, essentially boxing them in. Raw anger shot straight through me at the events unfolding before my eyes. Even though I knew she was okay and wasn't hurt, it was still difficult to just sit there and watch.

In an instant, the men pounced. Four on Lukyan, three on Adrian, two on Lorenzo and one walking slowly towards Illayana. Rage pulsed through my veins as I watched him slowly descend on her.

Oh, god, what the fuck is going to happen?

My eyes flicked quickly to Lukyan, who had a broad smile on his face.

Is that a good sign or bad sign?

Just as the man got within reach of Illayana, she attacked. She moved quick, so fucking quick. And she didn't hold back. She dealt out blow after blow, the man stumbling back as each shot connected with his body. She finished with a solid roundhouse kick, sending him sprawling to the ground.

"Holy shit," Christian and Luca whispered, their eyes never leaving the screen.

"Oh, oh, watch this part. Ready?" Lukyan asked in a cheery voice.

Illayana walked over to the man on the ground and, after a few seconds, she pulled her foot up and slammed her heel into his throat.

Jesus fucking Christ.

Quick as a cat, she spun around and ran towards Lukyan. Without hesitating, she jumped onto the back of one of the men, wrapping her legs around his body like a goddamn spider monkey. She brought a knife to his throat and swiftly cut his throat.

"Daaaaaaaamn!" one of the twins cheered. I had no idea which one. All of my focus was on Illayana.

She's fucking amazing.

Lukyan and Illayana moved as one towards Adrian and Lorenzo. She jumped into the chaos with ease, swiftly striking out at one of the men's legs, bringing him to his knees. She jammed her knife deep into the man's back and kicked him to the ground. And then it was over. All that was left was the ground, littered with bodies and blood.

"As you can see, my daughter doesn't need your protection. She can protect herself. That's how I raised her." Dimitri looked me straight in the eye as he spoke. "However, I find myself agreeing with you, and not her. Strange," he said, voice low. "Even though this altercation ended in our favour, I can't help but think about what could have happened if she didn't have back up."

I nodded. "Me too."

"She will have guards from this point forward. She will go nowhere without them. That, I can guarantee you. Once she's in New York, it'll be your responsibility to make sure she doesn't slip them."

"Slip them?" I asked, frowning.

Dimitri chuckled. "Believe me, she'll try it." He leant over the table and paused the video on the man that Illayana stabbed in the back. "This gentleman is the guest we have waiting for us in the pit. Shall we go see him?" he asked, a wrathful smirk on his face.

I smiled broadly and rose to my feet. "I would love to."

Dimitri held a hand up in the air, halting me. "I suggest you talk with your fiancé first, Arturo. It is never a good idea for a woman to go to bed angry. Especially a Volkov woman."

Aleksandr, Nikolai and Lukyan all started nodding enthusiastically, like they had firsthand experience with an angry Volkov woman. Hell, they were probably fucking experts.

"Good idea."

"Dining room, third door on the left." He pointed a finger down the corridor. "Be quick. I've waited long enough for you." With that said, he turned and started walking further into the house.

Aleksandr got to his feet and walked around the table, his bulky body moving effortlessly. "I'll meet you here in five minutes and I'll take you to the pit. Take any longer and my father really will start without you."

I nodded and looked at Christian and Luca. "You two, stay here. Don't fuck with anything," I said, narrowing my eyes in warning.

"We won't," they said together.

As I made my way out of the kitchen, I heard Lukyan's voice address the twins. "So, you guys wanna see something cool?"

Oh, lord. Please don't let them break anything.

Once I reached the dining room, I quickly opened the door and stepped inside. Illayana was seated at the table, her feet up, leaning back casually in the chair. Her blue eyes connected with mine as soon as I entered.

Okay, she doesn't look too angry. That's good.

As I walked further into the room, she picked up a knife that was on the table and started twirling it between her fingers. It was freaky how much that move reminded me of Vincenzo. She kept her eyes on me as the blade moved effortlessly through her fingers.

"I warned you, Arturo," she said menacingly.

I froze. "Warned me about what?"

"I told you from the get-go that I hate being told what to do, and I hate being disrespected."

I cocked my head and arched an eyebrow. "Okay, I'll concede to the whole telling you what to do thing, but I've never disrespected you."

"The way you spoke to me out there. Your tone of voice, the words you used, the way you just dismissed what I was saying...*that* was disrespectful. Especially in the presence of others. I'm your fiancé, soon-to-be wife. Not one of your goddamn soldiers you order around," she scowled.

I groaned, rubbing a hand down my face. "I'm not going to apologise for that. Your safety is, and always will be, my number one concern. You can be pissed about that. I don't care. But I will keep you safe, even if you don't want me to."

I could see her anger spiking, her fist clenching tightly around the hilt of her knife.

Fuck. Of course I'm making it worse. Comforting women wasn't exactly my strong suit. If they got upset, I'd just leave. Never had to give a shit before.

"I'll admit, I shouldn't have spoken to you so abruptly in front of others, so I will apologise for that. Next time, we'll disagree in private. How does that sound?" I asked, giving her the smirk I knew she loved so much.

Her grip loosened slightly on her knife and her face started to soften. "I understand why you want me to have extra guards. I do. And I'm willing to concede. Just don't talk to me like you own me."

I gave her a wicked smile as I walked slowly towards her. I ran my eyes up and down her sexy body, stopping a little too long on her breasts and enjoying the way colour rose to her cheeks at my perusal.

"But I do own you, *kotenok,*" I said seductively as I moved behind her. I lowered my lips to her ear, loving the fact that her breath hitched as I slowly ran my tongue over her earlobe. "I own every single inch of you." I ran a finger down her arm, watching as goosebumps rose all over her skin. "And soon, everyone will know it."

She moaned as she unconsciously started moving closer to me. "Why do you keep calling me 'kitten'?" she asked breathlessly.

I tilted the chair back so it balanced on two legs and spun it around so she faced me. I picked her up by her hips, shoving the chair aside so I could plop her right on the edge of the table. She gasped in surprise. "Because that's what you are. A vicious little kitten that will claw my eyes out the second I piss you off," I whispered over her lips. "And I fucking love it."

"Do you?" she purred, wrapping her legs around my waist and arms around my neck.

I gripped her chin roughly and kissed her. Devoured her. Smothered her with my mouth and tongue as I held her completely still, my finger and thumb digging into her skin. She moaned and gripped my hair tightly, pulling me closer as she ground against my cock unashamedly.

I was already hard—rock-fucking-hard—and her movements made pleasure shoot down my spine. I grunted as she picked up speed, moving faster and faster, dry humping the fuck out of me like her life depended on it as her lips moved against mine, fighting for dominance, for control. Her body shuddered as she chased her pleasure, and I knew by the way her breathing became rapid that she was close to achieving it.

I ripped her fingers from my hair and shoved her back until she smacked into the table, pinning her hands above her head. She mewled exactly like a fucking kitten and fought my hold, trying to reach out to me, to touch me, but I held her in place firmly.

"Uh, uh, uh," I taunted, squeezing her wrists. "Something you need to learn early, *kotenok*," I murmured, staring down at her, "I'm in control here, not you. You'll get your pleasure, but only when I allow it."

Her eyes turned to ice and she glared at me. "Are you fucking serious?" she hissed, like the angry little kitten she was.

I smirked and slowly trailed a hand down her body, keeping her wrists firmly secured in my other hand. I cupped her pussy roughly, grounding my palm against her clit. "This, here, is mine now, which means your pleasure is mine too. You come when I say you can come, not a moment sooner."

"Then tell me to come."

I chuckled and licked her cheek slowly, dragging my tongue over her skin. "You've got to earn that first."

"How the fuck do I do that?!" she snapped angrily.

"By being a good girl."

"Oh, you son of a—"

I slapped her pussy, hard. She jolted, yelping in surprise. Lust burned in her eyes.

"Name calling isn't being a 'good girl', is it, *kotenok?*" I whispered against her skin.

"No," she groaned, squirming under the weight of my body.

I pressed her deeper into the table and bit her neck lightly, just enough for her to feel the slight sting of my teeth. "It's important that you understand exactly what kind of man I am in the bedroom, Illayana. That's the one place I will not accept disobedience. But don't worry, you've got plenty of time to learn what's expected of you." I gave one more quick nip and then pulled back completely, removing my body from hers and stepping back. "Now, I have an appointment with a guest you have in the house."

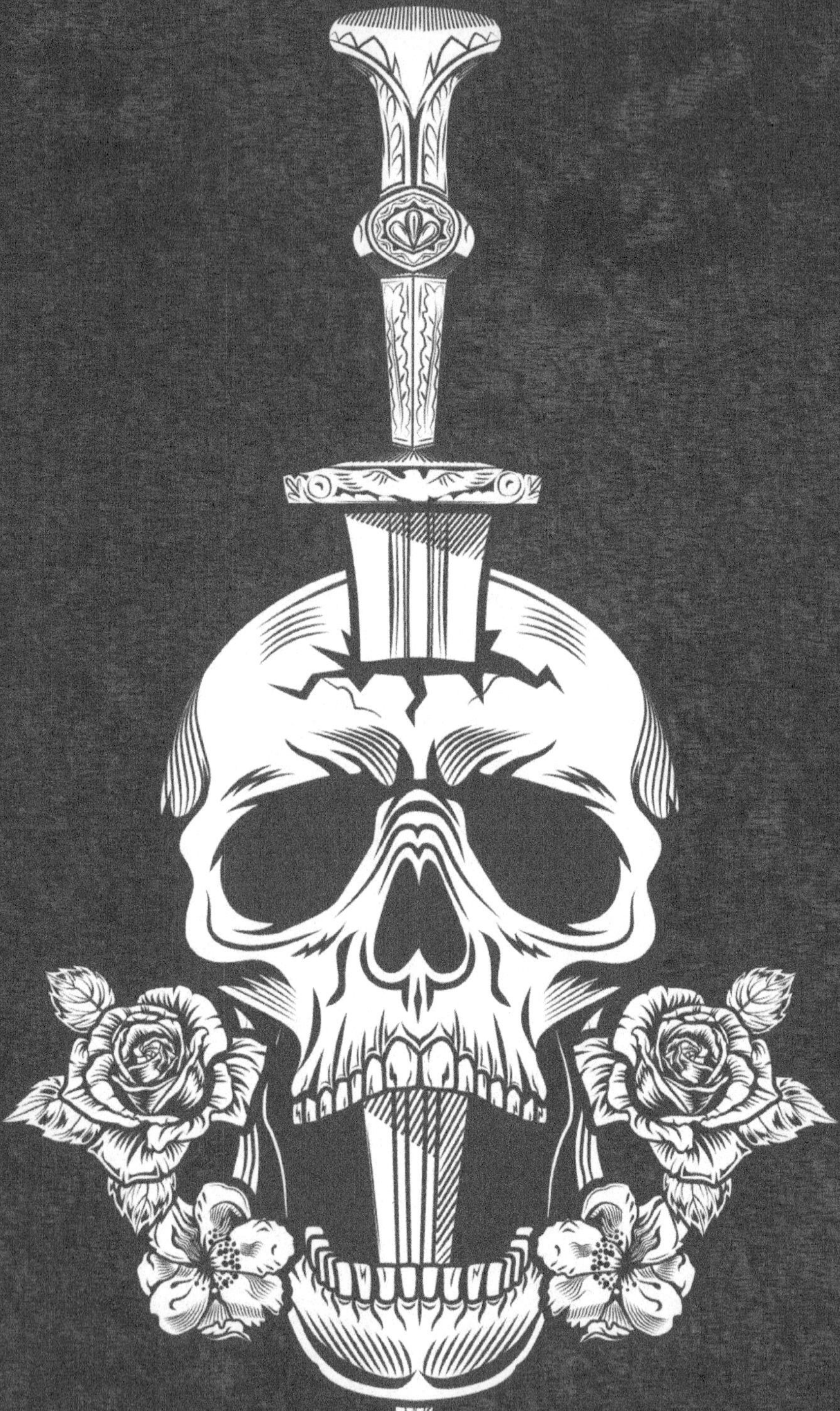

CHAPTER THIRTEEN

Arturo De Luca

True to his word, Aleksandr was waiting in the kitchen for me when I left the dining room. Leaving Illayana like that, all hot and heavy, was for me one of the hardest things I've ever done in my fucking life. I wanted nothing more than to completely annihilate her, fuck her until the only thing she could think about was me. But unfortunately, there was another matter that required my attention.

Christian and Luca were nowhere to be seen. I could only assume they were off gallivanting with Lukyan.

Alessandro always did like to criticise me about those two. Granted, they were young (at twenty-two, they were practically babies in the Mafia world), and at times they could both be extremely childish. But none of that deterred me from their greatest quality: loyalty.

"She alright?" Aleksandr asked as I made my way over to him.

"She's fine."

Aleksandr nodded and turned, leading me through the house in silence. It was something I'd come to notice about the giant. He didn't speak unless he had to, and when he did, it was always straight to the point. No screwing around, no unnecessary words. It made me wonder if he'd ever had any fun in his life.

Once we got outside, we took a short walk until we came across a large warehouse. It looked like any other normal warehouse, aside from the fact that it was located on residential property instead of an industrial area. However, appearances can often be deceiving. It may have looked like your everyday garden variety warehouse, but inside it was a completely different story.

The entire floor was covered in every single piece of gym equipment known to man. Leg press, arm curls, leg extensions, chest press, squat rack. You name it, they fucking had it. They even had their own boxing ring! And it looked state of the art too. I was impressed, to say the least. The warehouse seemed to stretch on for miles, with doors blocking off access to other areas. It made me curious about what else was in the place.

Without losing stride, Aleksandr manoeuvred his way around the endless amount of machines with ease until we reached a large steel door. After placing his finger on the scanner, the door slowly started to open, creaking as it went.

"Before we continue, I feel like I should warn you," Aleksandr's deep voice was laced with his thick Russian accent.

"Yes?"

His bright blue eyes connected with my mismatched ones as he spoke. "My father can be quite…particular when it comes to his interrogations."

I frowned but remained silent, allowing him to continue.

"No matter what, do not speak unless he calls on you."

At that, I scowled, my lips turning up in distaste. Did he seriously just tell me, Arturo De Luca, Don of The Cosa Nostra (soon, anyway), not to speak unless I was spoken to? Anger flowed through my veins at his lack of respect. I felt a flare of disappointment rise up within me, too. I was actually starting to like the big behemoth.

Aleksandr sensed my anger and immediately raised his palms in front of him in a placating gesture. "I meant no disrespect. As I said, my father is particular about his interrogations. He doesn't like it when *anyone* speaks while he's questioning a prisoner. Not even me."

My body relaxed slightly and the anger started to slowly dissipate. If that was truly the case, then in a way I could understand. It was clear Dimitri had some sort of routine he liked to do when interrogating someone, and obviously he didn't like to be interrupted.

"I understand."

Aleksandr eyed me suspiciously like he didn't believe me, before nodding slightly and beginning his descent down the steps into the darkness.

A burst of bright white light filled the room as Aleksandr flicked a switch on the wall. He led me down a long corridor. We walked past several doors, both on the left right sides, and my curiosity peaked.

What exactly is down here?

He turned a corner at the end of the hall and I followed close behind, the sound of someone groaning in pain getting louder and louder the further we went.

We eventually came to a stop in front of a door that was being guarded by one of Dimitri's men. The heavily tattooed, muscular man nodded at Aleksandr and opened the door. We stepped inside.

It was a small space, no bigger than your average bedroom. It was mostly bare, apart from a few chairs spread throughout the room and a table littered with torture implements in the far corner. The walls and floor were stained red with blood, some of it old, like it had been there for years, and other spots that looked fresh. Really fresh. There was a single drain located in the middle of the room, where I'm assuming the blood flowed to.

Slouching with his head hanging forward was a man. He was bound to a chair bolted to the floor in the centre of the room. Rage nearly consumed me as the video from the attack came to the forefront of my mind. This fucker was there. He was responsible (partly, anyway), and I couldn't wait to make the bastard pay.

The man started to slowly raise his head, groaning as his eyes moved around the room, dazed and confused. A scream tore through his throat as he fully regained consciousness and his mind was finally able to process the amount of pain flowing through his body. Brown orbs locked onto me before moving to Aleksandr. Confusion, followed by anger flowed across his square face as he swivelled his head from side to side, trying to figure out where he was. He had short brown hair that looked like it hadn't been washed in years. His bruised skin was covered in ink, some clearly gang-related.

Even though his hands were bound behind his back, I could see he was struggling, trying to get himself free. Panic, pain and fear overtook his face as he spoke for the first time in Spanish.

"¿Por què no puedo sentir mis piernas?" *Why can't I feel my legs?*

"Eso es porque mi encantadora hija te cortó la médula espinal." *That's because my lovely daughter severed your spinal cord.*

Dimitri entered the room, his big, imposing body coming to a stop beside me as he replied to the man in perfect Spanish. His blue eyes locked onto his target and a vile smirk spread across his lips.

The man growled in anger. Even though he couldn't move his legs, he still attempted to get free. His arms struggled against the bindings as he continued to pull and pull, his face contorted in pain and anger.

Dimitri just stood there and watched the man try his hardest to escape, amusement plastered all over his face. After what felt like an eternity, the man slouched forward, his body clearly drained of energy.

"Now that that's over with," Dimitri said, moving and picking up a chair from the far corner. He plopped it directly in front of the man, taking a seat. He leant back casually, resting his ankle on his knee as he studied the man. He cocked his head to the side, his blue eyes staring the man down. "Do you know who I am?" He spoke softly but clearly.

"No hablo ingles." I don't speak English.

Dimitri tsked, shaking his head. "Now, Miguel, I know for a fact that you're lying."

Miguel tensed, his body going rigid at the mention of his name.

Dimitri smiled. "Oh, yes. I know who you are. I know where you live, who your family is, what you like to eat for breakfast. . .everything. I even know your goddamn blood type," Dimitri chuckled. "But let me tell you something about myself, Miguel. You see, I absolutely despise liars. So, let's try this again. Do you know who I am?" Dimitri repeated his question, this time speaking slower, with more venom in his voice than I'd heard the first time.

Miguel's eyes darted around the room one more time, desperately looking for an escape.

"Dimitri Volkov?" Miguel asked, his voice trembling just slightly.

"Net." No. Dimitri shook his head. "I asked if you know who I am, not what my name is."

Miguel looked between Aleksandr and I with confusion. Granted, I could understand why. The two questions seemed one in the same to me, but I kept my mouth shut.

Dimitri slammed his foot back to the ground and leant forward in his chair, clearly losing patience. Miguel flinched and shook his head.

"Aleksandr," Dimitri barked.

"The Bratva Butcher," Aleksandr replied automatically.

My eyes widened. *The Bratva Butcher?* That was him? I had first heard of The Bratva Butcher years ago, but I had no idea it was Dimitri. I'd assumed it was some mercenary or assassin, not the actual leader of the goddamn Bratva. The Bratva Butcher was rumoured to be the cruelest, most ruthless motherfucker of all time. I heard he slaughtered an entire family line. Just wiped them off the face of the earth. Women, children…no one was safe from him.

"Da." Yes. Dimitri's eyes gleamed with pride at Aleksandr's words. "And do you know why they call me The Bratva Butcher, Miguel?"

Miguel shook his head again slowly, like he was afraid of the answer.

A genuine smile crossed Dimitri's face as he raised his hand in the air and clicked his fingers. I'd only met the man three times and I could already tell he loved to pull that move.

A door off to the left that I hadn't noticed before swung open, revealing Lukyan and Nikolai. And they weren't alone.

"No," Miguel whispered in shock as they dragged in four people from the other room.

Connected by a thick, metal chain were three adults—two women and a man—and a child, no older than ten. The women and child were crying hysterically, gripping onto each other for dear life. Their tear-stricken faces took in their new surroundings and one of the women let out an ear-piercing shriek at the sight of Miguel tied to the chair.

"Miguel!" she cried, trying to run towards him, but the chain connecting them all together locked her in place. They all looked quite similar in appearance. Brown eyes, brown hair and the same olive skin. If I had to guess, I'd say they were all related. Possibly siblings.

"You bastard! Let them go!" Miguel roared, desperately trying to get free. His wrists were bleeding from how hard he was pulling against his bindings.

"Do you know why they call me The Bratva Butcher?" Dimitri asked again, ignoring his outburst.

"Because you butcher people, you sick fuck!"

Dimitri laughed, his big body shaking in his chair. "*Da*," he nodded his head. "I do, but there's a little more to it than that. You see, I have a bit of an anger problem. My wife used to say I was like a raging bull, ready to attack at the slightest provocation. When people threaten my family, all I see is red. All I feel is rage. All I want is vengeance. They call me The Bratva Butcher because I'll not only butcher you, I'll butcher your entire goddamn fucking family. I'll rip them all to shreds for the sins of another, and I'll have no problem with it. Because like I said, when my family is threatened, all I see. Is. Red."

Dimitri stood gracefully, buttoning up his suit jacket. He moved and stood directly in front of the child. A little girl. She shivered and tried to squirm away as Dimitri raised his hand and started slowly stroking her hair.

"Don't touch her!" Miguel growled. "Let her go! She has nothing to do with this!" Miguel pulled harder against his restraints, desperate to escape.

Dimitri's head snapped to Miguel, his blue eyes lit with fire. "Oh, but she does," Dimitri hissed, continuing to stroke her hair as he spoke to Miguel. "Did you seriously think you could come after my only daughter, my own flesh and blood, and there wouldn't be any consequences?" he scoffed

"You fucker!" Again Miguel tried to break free, but it was no use. "Let her go!"

"Why? You tried to do much worse to my daughter. Why should I spare your daughter pain when you weren't going to do the same for mine?"

"Because she's just a child!" Miguel begged.

"Illayana is a child! MY CHILD!" Dimitri roared, trembling with rage. "It doesn't matter if she's ten or 100. She will *always* be **my child**! And you tried to take her from me, tried to hurt her! Had she not had protection, you may have succeeded."

The little girl started sobbing uncontrollably.

Miguel looked frantically around the room, his brown eyes jumping from person to person, looking for something—anything—that might help him.

Aleksandr, Nikolai and Lukyan all stood with their hands clasped behind their backs, their faces impassive. If he was looking for help from them, he wasn't getting it.

Miguel lowered his head in defeat. "What do you want?"

Dimitri smiled and moved away from the girl. She immediately buried herself into the women next to her, trying to hide. He sat back down in his seat across from Miguel, his eyes sparkling with excitement.

"You have two choices. First choice: you tell me everything you know. I want everything. Why you tried to kidnap Illayana, what you planned to do with her once you got her. Every goddamn thing. Do that, and I'll give your family a quick and painless death."

Huh? Usually when people cooperated, their reward wasn't death. Unless death was the better option?

Miguel frowned. "Why would their death be an incentive for me to tell you what you want to know?"

A malicious smile crossed Dimitri's face. "Because of your second option. If you don't talk, I'll sell your sisters to sex slavers." Miguel paled, all the colour draining from his face. "I'll keep you alive, so you can live every day knowing that men are defiling the ones you love. Your brother, I'll chuck in the fighting pits. Perhaps he can make me some money," Dimitri shrugged. "And then, when you can't bear to live any longer, I'll sell you too, so your body will be just as broken as your mind."

Holy fucking shit. This man was fucking ruthless! *Note to self: never hurt Illayana.*

"I personally am not involved in the skin trade," Dimitri continued. "However, Illayana's godfather is. You may have heard of him. . .Mikhail Vasolv."

If it was even possible, Miguel's face turned even whiter, and I couldn't blame him. The Cosa Nostra aren't involved in the skin trade either, but we knew all the key players.

Mikhail Vasolv was a man of horror, the type of man people have nightmares about.

Tears burst from Miguel's eyes as he looked at his family. "Please," he begged. "Just let them go, and I'll tell you anything you want to know. I swear it."

"*Net*," Dimitri shook his head. "There is no scenario here where your family lives. You went after my family. Now I go after yours." The women started to sob loudly at Dimitri's words. "The only choice you get to make is whether your family dies quickly, or slow and painfully. And I can guarantee you, Mikhail will make it painful."

Miguel slumped forward, all the fight in him evaporating. His eyes ran over his family, filled with so much regret and sorrow. I knew 100% what I would do in his situation. There's no way I'd let Illayana be sold to a sex slaver.

Dimitri started tapping his foot, his patience wearing thin. "Decide. Now," he snapped, narrowing his eyes.

"Option one," Miguel said, his voice barely above a whisper.

Dimitri smiled, flicking his wrist. Lukyan and Nikolai grabbed the chains holding the prisoners together and started leading them out the way they came. Miguel watched as they left the room, his face filled with sadness.

Dimitri leant forward, resting his elbows on his knees as he looked at Miguel. "Why did you try to kidnap Illayana?"

"Because Nero ordered us to."

I fucking knew it. That old shitfuck of a Gambino tried to steal my fiancé! It took everything in me not to leap across the room and pummel him for more information. I clenched my fists at my side, determined to stay in place and exert my self control.

Dimitri narrowed his eyes. "Why? Why did he want her?"

"To keep you from interfering."

"Interfering in what?"

"His crusade against the De Lucas. He doesn't want you helping them, arming them with your guns. He wants you to butt the fuck out and mind your own business. He planned to keep her and threaten her life if you got involved."

"That was a big mistake. By making a move against her, he's made himself another enemy."

"You were already an enemy. The second you agreed to merge your family with the De Lucas, you became his enemy."

Dimitri pursed his lips and tapped a finger on his leg. His brows lowered in thought as he processed Miguel's words. "Why are The Los Zetas helping him? Is your boss his new bitch?"

Miguel narrowed his eyes and clenched his jaw. "My boss is nobody's bitch," he snapped.

Dimitri backhanded him. Miguel's head whipped to the side with the force of it. "Watch your tone. Answer my question."

Miguel ran his tongue across his bleeding lips, his eyes burning with rage. "I don't know."

"You don't know?" Dimitri repeated slowly.

"No, I don't. Our second, Juan, just told us we had to follow Nero's orders."

"And you didn't think to ask why?"

Miguel gave him an 'are you serious?' look. "You don't question orders from Juan. He tells you to do something and you do it. You ask questions, you get shot."

Dimitri pursed his lips as he studied him.

"Why does Nero have such a hard-on for my family? I highly doubt all this shit is happening because my father stole his girl nearly thirty years ago."

Dimitri stiffened. Aleksandr cursed and narrowed his eyes at me.

Whoops. Forgot about his little bit of advice. Oh well.

"How the fuck should I know? I'm just a grunt. I don't get told about anything substantial. They tell me to go somewhere and kidnap some bitch, and I do it. You wanna know more? Kidnap one of his men."

"You *are* one of his men," I scowled.

"No, I'm not. I'm cartel, through and through. Just because I take orders from that Italian scum doesn't mean I'm one of his men."

Confusion flared through me. There was clearly no love lost between the Cartel and the Outfit, so why the fuck where they taking orders from Nero? The whole thing wasn't making any fucking sense, and it was driving me crazy.

Dimitri rose to his feet and walked over to his son. He held his palm out facing upwards and Lukyan stepped forward, placing a pad and pencil in his hand. Dimitri walked over to Miguel and released his bindings, setting him free. Miguel instinctively touched each wrist (something everyone seemed to do after they'd been cuffed).

Dimitri laid the pad and pencil in Miguel's lap and pointed a finger at him. "I want the names of every fucker in your organisation, addresses for every safe house you've got and any more information you have on Nero and what he plans to do."

Dimitri pinned me with his gaze and tilted his head towards the door. "A word, Arturo."

Without waiting for a response, he headed out the door.

I scowled at Miguel, pissed that I wasn't getting my pound of flesh that second, and moved to follow Dimitri. Aleksandr and Nikolai both gave me nods of encouragement while Lukyan stuck his tongue out and gave me the finger.

I shook my head and chuckled as I walked out of the room, shutting the door behind me. Dimitri was waiting just outside, arms crossed over his chest and his brows drawn down in a scowl. I arched an eyebrow at his aggressive stance.

"Get your father on the phone. We need to discuss how to handle this situation."

I bristled at the clear command and glared. "Don't bark at me like I'm one of your soldiers, Dimitri."

He may be *Pakhan* of the Bratva, but that didn't mean he could talk to me like I was his bitch. There was no way I was going to take that shit.

Dimitri arched an eyebrow in surprise. I don't think he was used to anyone speaking up to him like that.

Well, he better get fucking used to it.

"You might as well know now. My father is stepping down as Don the moment this shit with Nero is handled. He's put me in charge of dealing with this, so if you need someone to talk to about what to do next, you talk to me."

Shock flashed across Dimitri's face. It was the first time I had ever seen him at a loss for words. He looked me up and down, assessing me. "Are you ready?"

I didn't hesitate. "Yes." I was ready. I was born for this.

He nodded. "We need to discuss the next course of action to take, then."

"After," I barked, turning around and placing my hand on the doorknob.

Before I could open the door, Dimitri spoke. "After what?"

I glanced over my shoulder and raised my chin in the air. "After I cut Miguel to pieces." I walked back into the room, shrugging off my suit jacket and hanging it up by the door. *Oh, this is going to be fun.*

Aleksandr gave me a slight nod before gliding past me and back out to his father. My feet froze when I caught his next words. "Same as usual?"

Curiosity got the better of me and I lingered, stretching out my ears to try and hear their conversation.

"*Da,*" Dimitri replied. "Find the little girl's closest living relative and drop her there. If you can't find anyone, send her to Blue Haven Orphanage. They're the only organisation I trust that don't harm the children."

Huh. So the Butcher wasn't as evil as everyone thought.

"Yes, Father. And the women?"

"Where they involved?"

"They were driving the getaway car."

"Kill them. Make it quick and painless."

Aleksandr nodded once. "That story about Mikhail always works, doesn't it?" he laughed.

Story?

Dimitri scoffed. "Reputation is everything. You carve out a vicious enough one and people will cower the second they hear your name. We both know Mikhail isn't involved in the skin trade, but other people don't. And *that's* what gets them to talk."

Interesting. This family is full of surprises.

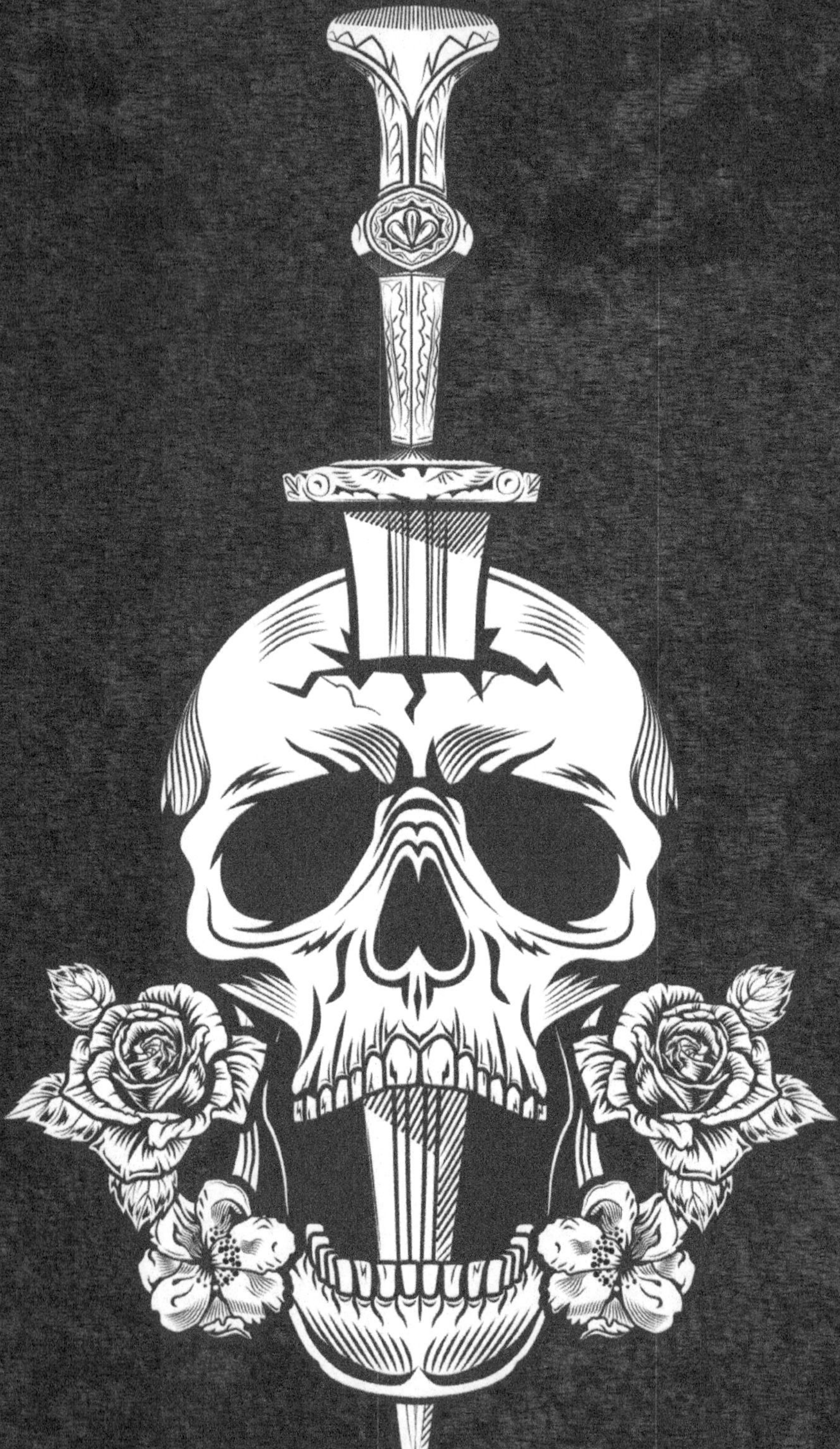

CHAPTER FOURTEEN

Illayana Volkov

I woke enveloped in warmth, strong arms embracing me against a bare chest. I instinctively leant back and sighed in content. I closed my eyes and tried to drift back off to sleep, but it was too late. My mind and body were now wide awake, painfully aware of the fact that Arturo was spooning me, his entire body encasing me like a cocoon.

He gripped me tight and pulled me closer to his body, nuzzling my neck. He took a deep breath in and sighed, relaxing.

I slowly lifted my head, my eyes squinting from the sunlight beaming into the room.

What time is it?

I turned to look at Arturo, his beautifully sculpted face relaxed in his sleep. Part of me wanted to wake him so I could look into those gorgeous multi-coloured eyes, but I knew he needed his sleep. He had only come to bed a few hours ago, so I knew he was exhausted. I actually couldn't believe my father allowed him to stay the night, especially in my room with me.

I slowly untangled his limbs from my body, being extra careful not to disturb his peaceful sleep. His arms tightened around me as I tried to move, like even in his sleep he didn't want to let me go.

As the bed shifted, he turned to lie on his back, mumbling something incoherent in Italian. I took the time to appreciate his muscular, toned body. His chest was completely bare, giving me an unobstructed view.

His tattoos encompassed the entire length of his upper torso; from his wrists up to his shoulders, fanning out over his chest, down his abdomen and wrapping around his back. His gorgeous, tan skin was as smooth as silk (which was hard to believe, considering the tough life he lived).

Of course he had a set of perfectly sculpted abs…six-pack from the looks of it. No, wait—eight. My fingers twitched at the sight of him lying in my bed, his dark hair fanned out over my pillow. I ached to run my hands down that immaculate body, but I was too afraid to wake him. He deserved his sleep.

I rose to my feet and stretched out my body. I had no idea what he had planned for the day, whether he was hanging around Vegas or flying home. Either way, I knew he'd be hungry when he woke up, so I quickly chucked on a pair of sweats and a t-shirt and made my way downstairs to the kitchen to make him breakfast.

When I walked in, Lukyan was seated at the kitchen table, leaning back casually in his chair with his legs kicked up on the table, as per fucking usual. Mum used to hate it when he did that, and I knew if she were here right now, she'd be having a fit.

Don't worry, Mum. I gotcha covered.

As I walked closer I noticed he had his eyes shut, like he was sleeping. I slowly snuck up from behind, being careful not to make a sound. Before he sensed my presence, I lashed out, kicking the legs of his chair and sending him sprawling to the ground.

His big body hit the floor with a solid thud as he mumbled a curse in Russian. He immediately pulled out his gun and had it aimed at my chest in under a second.

I couldn't help it. I laughed. "If you had reacted that quickly earlier, you wouldn't be sprawled out on your ass right now."

He narrowed his eyes and cocked his gun. "I could still shoot you. Nothing wrong with a little flesh wound," he smirked.

"You could, but we both know you won't."

He grunted and lowered his gun.

"You deserved it anyway. You know Mum hated it when you did shit like that."

His face softened, the mention of our mother bringing out his softer side. He sat up and crossed his legs, for some reason deciding to stay on the ground.

"You miss her," he stated, cocking his head to the side.

I moved to the kitchen and started preparing Arturo's breakfast. "Don't you?"

"Of course I do, but I try not to think about it. About...her."

I could understand that, but it was a little harder for me. With my wedding mere days away, it was even more painfully obvious she wasn't here. This was something I had always envisioned her being a part of, right up until the day she died.

No—until she was murdered.

Just the thought of her not being here to see me get married, to meet Arturo, made my heart ache with so much sadness it felt like it would break me.

"I wish I could do that," I whispered as I cracked a few eggs into a frying pan.

The sound of the eggs sizzling and popping as they cooked helped distract me from the conversation I wished to God we weren't having.

Lukyan seemed to sense I needed a distraction, so he changed the subject.

"Where's your fiancé?" he sneered, making a face.

I chuckled and flipped the eggs. "What's your deal with him? Why do you hate him so much? I don't get it, what'd he do to you?"

He shrugged his shoulders and grumbled, "I don't hate him. Just don't like his face."

I laughed out loud, transferring the eggs to a plate and putting on a few more. "It's because he's prettier than you, isn't it?"

With his long, dark hair, his deep brown eyes, high cheekbones and chiselled jaw, Lukyan's always been known as the 'pretty boy' of the family. My guess? He didn't like having someone steal his thunder.

Fuck, he can be so childish sometimes. But I guess I shouldn't be surprised. Being the youngest boy, Mum used to spoil him rotten when he was a kid.

"No," he snapped, "and I'm not pretty, I'm handsome. Men don't like being called pretty," he scoffed.

"Uh-huh," I chuckled.

I put the remaining eggs on the plate and started cooking some bacon, mushrooms and tomatoes. The smells enveloped me, making my stomach rumble and my mouth water.

"Since when do you make breakfast? Usually you get the maids to do it."

True. I hardly ever cooked my own food anymore. Why do it when you have people to do it for you? That's my opinion, anyway. But this time, I wanted to do it myself. I wanted to be the one to cook Arturo's breakfast.

"Since now."

Lukyan got to his feet and took a seat back in his chair just as Christian and Luca walked into the kitchen. My new bodyguards. Part of me was still a little ticked off about having them, but my father insisted it was a good idea, and I've never once known him to be wrong.

They were gorgeous men, both with dark hair and blue eyes. They stood at about 6'4 with broad shoulders and muscular builds. The fact that they were identical twins was pretty cool.

I transferred the bacon, mushrooms and tomatoes to a plate as Christian and Luca made their way over to me. They both bowed slightly.

"Ma'am," one of them said, and I had to repress my wince.

I knew he was only being polite, but I hated being called 'Ma'am'. It made me feel old. The other twin (the one who didn't speak) tried to subtly kick the other in the shin, but it couldn't have been any more obvious.

"I mean, Miss Volkov," the first twin corrected, and I chuckled.

"Good morning, Christian, Luca. Would you like some breakfast?" I moved around the kitchen, putting a few slices of bread into the toaster.

They gave me a look of surprise, their mouths dropping open slightly.

"Yes, thank you, Ma'a—Miss Volkov," the first twin quickly corrected.

I pointed to the kitchen table and both men moved to take a seat next to Lukyan.

"I'd like some breakfast," Lukyan said, raising his hand like he was in bloody kindergarten or something.

I arched an eyebrow. "And when was the last time you made me breakfast?"

Fucking never.

He lowered his hand and scowled.

That's what I thought.

I removed the bread from the toaster and put two on each plate, as well as the eggs, bacon, mushrooms and tomatoes. I moved to the table and put a plate in front of each twin.

"Thank you," they both said at the exact same time. I wondered if that was something that just happened, or if it was intentional.

I nodded and pointed to the twin on the left. "Which one are you?"

They both laughed.

"I'm Luca," he said, pointing at his chest.

I removed one of the sparkly red bracelets from around my wrist and put it on him. He raised his arm into the air and stared at it with disgust. His blue eyes shot to me and he raised his brows in question.

"So I can tell you two apart," I elaborated.

Luca grumbled something under his breath, not happy with his new accessory.

"Dude, that's totally gonna salt your game," Christian laughed while he shovelled food into his mouth.

Luca narrowed his eyes and flung some eggs at his twin brother. "Shut up," he growled.

"If you guys weren't wearing the exact same outfit, and didn't have the same damn hairstyle, I would be able to tell the two of you apart."

Christian and Luca both looked down at their clothes. Dressed in black slacks, a black shirt and black boots, it was like they didn't want people to be able to tell them apart. They both looked at each other and shrugged.

"I can tell them apart," Lukyan smirked, leaning back in his chair and running his eyes over the twins.

I moved back to the kitchen and started making Arturo's breakfast again, which was the entire damn reason I went down there in the first place.

"You can not," I chided.

"Can too."

I turned around and pointed my spatula at him. "You so can not. They look exactly the fucking same!"

Christian and Luca continued to eat like this was an everyday occurrence for them. It probably was. They looked between Lukyan and I, listening with amusement.

"Wanna bet?" Lukyan winked.

Oh, this fucker. He knew I never backed down from a bet. It's in my Russian blood.

"Stakes?" I asked, flipping the eggs.

"I want your Wather Q5," he said, his lips curving into an evil smile.

I groaned. Of course he fucking did. He'd been eyeing that gun ever since I got it as a gift from my godfather. The semi-automatic was quickly becoming one of my favourite pieces. It looked a bit other-worldly with its machined frame, like something out of a futurist Sci-Fi movie. It had a Quick Defence Trigger and weighed around two kilograms. The Q5 recoiled fast, allowing the user to shoot with blazing speed and precision. Truth be told, I didn't want to bet it, just in case he could actually tell them apart. But I couldn't help it. I loved betting.

I piled all the food onto a plate and placed it on the kitchen counter.

"Fine. But if you can't tell them apart, you have to apologise to Arturo for being a dick. And you have to be nice to him from now on."

Lukyan scowled at me. "No. Pick something else."

"Nope. You want my Q5, I want you two to get along. Take it or leave it."

Lukyan growled, his face scrunching up in displeasure. He looked at the twins, sizing up his odds at being able to tell the two identical men apart.

After a few seconds, he nodded. "Deal."

I smiled and moved to stand next to the twins. Despite the fact that their mouths were overflowing with food, they continued trying to shovel more in, like they were afraid I was going to take it away from them.

I twirled my finger in the air, signalling for Lukyan to turn around. After giving us his back, I motioned for the twins to stand. Luca did immediately, his fork clinking onto his plate as he rose to his feet. Christian took a little longer, making sure to shove another forkful of food into his mouth first before standing.

"Does Arturo not feed you two or something?" I chuckled.

Christian looked at me, his eyes lit with amusement, but it was Luca who spoke. "He does, but his cooking sucks compared to yours."

I started shuffling the twins around, like a magician does a deck of cards. I made sure to keep an eye on Lukyan as I moved. He was a notorious cheater when it came to any games we played, and I wouldn't put it past him to do something sly. One time when we were playing monopoly, I made the mistake of letting him be banker. Every time I looked away, he would grab cash from the bank and add it to his pile. We were halfway through the game before I realised something was off, that he had way more cash than he should have.

Once I was satisfied, I took my sparkly bracelet off Luca and stepped back.

"Okay, you can turn around now."

Lukyan turned on his heels, quick as a cat. He narrowed his eyes first before taking a step forward. The twins stood tall under his scrutiny, hands clasped behind their backs, faces impassive. He slowly circled them, his eyes running up and down their bodies. He stepped towards Christian and sniffed him.

"What are you doing?" I groaned.

"Shhh. I'm concentrating." He moved to Luca and sniffed him as well. He grabbed his arm and lifted it, moving it around in the air before going back to Christian and repeating the movement.

"Seriously, Lukyan, what the fuck are you doing? You can't tell them apart by sniffing them and moving them around."

"You don't know my process," he said without taking his eyes off the twins.

I slapped a palm to my forehead in exasperation. "You're infuriating."

"No, you are."

"What are you, five?" I snapped.

His eyes twinkled with mischief. "No, you are."

I growled. "Don't, Lukyan. Don't you dare. We're too old for this shit."

Growing up, Lukyan and I always loved to piss each other off, usually by deliberately doing things we knew the other detested. He hated whenever I mimicked him, touched his PlayStation or went into his bedroom. I hated whenever he ate my food, stole my guns or just said "No, you are" back to everything I would bloody say. Even if it didn't make any fucking sense, he said it. I hated it all when I was a kid, and I fucking hated it now.

Lukyan smiled. "No, you—"

That's as far as he got. I pounced, shoving the plates on the table to the ground as I leapt over the kitchen table. I jumped into the air, trying to wrap my legs around his neck and bring him to the ground. Unfortunately, he knew exactly what I was going to do (one of the many disadvantages of fighting someone familiar with your moves).

With a smirk on his face, he gripped my legs in mid-air and spun, using the momentum of his body to bring me down to the ground hard. He tried to climb on top of me, but I was quick and pissed off.

Before he could get a stable position, I struck out, delivering a solid blow to his solar plexus. He groaned, his hands moving to grip at his chest as pain radiated through his torso. I pushed at his chest, knocking him to the ground, quickly scrambling for the dominant position.

"You're such a little shit, Lukyan," I grunted as I tried to land a few shots to his abdomen, but he managed to block each one with ease.

"No... you... are," he smirked, poking his tongue out.

Arghhhh! He was purposely antagonising me—and it was working. I would love to say I had more restraint than that, but truth be told, I didn't. I had an extremely short temper and not a lot of reasoning skills (hence why I was trying to beat the shit out of my brother for simply saying something annoying). Maybe I really was crazy. Oh well.

I pulled my arm back, preparing for a punch right to his stupid, smug face when an arm of steel wrapped around my waist and pulled me to my feet. I lashed out, shouting profanities and trying to kick free, enraged someone was meddling. Then I got a whiff of Arturo's intoxicating scent. I felt myself relax instantly at the feel of his warmth against my body, but the anger was definitely still there.

"Be calm, *kotenok*," his deep, seductive voice whispered in my ear.

Lukyan raised his head from his position on the floor, the rest of his body staying firmly on the ground, and gave me a sly smile. "That's Luca," he said, pointing to one of the twins.

They had both moved off to the side at the start of our little squabble, mixing up the positions they were originally in. I had no idea if Lukyan was right or not, but based on the look the twins gave me, he fucking was.

I growled and tried to get to Lukyan again, but Arturo had a solid grip on me.

"Will someone tell me what the fuck is going on?" Arturo snapped, looking around the room. I hadn't even noticed Aleksandr and Nikolai had joined our little party until right at that moment. They stood in the corner, both munching on a packet of potato chips and watching on with amusement.

"They made a bet. Lukyan said he could tell us apart, Miss Volkov said he couldn't," Christian replied.

"What were the stakes?"

"If Miss Volkov won, Lukyan had to apologise and be nice to you."

Arturo scoffed. "And if she lost?"

"I get her new favourite gun," Lukyan rose gracefully to his feet, wiping down the front of his clothes and smiling.

I heard Aleksandr and Nikolai start talking amongst themselves in Russian, but I was too far gone to really pay attention.

"You swindled me!" I growled. "You knew which one was which."

"I told you I could tell them apart. Not my fault you didn't believe me," he shrugged.

I tried to move towards him again, stretching my arms out to wrap my hands around his throat, but Arturo was like a rock, not budging the slightest.

"How?" Arturo questioned.

"How what?" Lukyan snapped.

"How did you tell them apart? I've had people working for me for years—people who have known *them* for years—who can't tell. So, how is it that someone who has literally just met them is able to tell who is who?"

Lukyan shrugged and moved to Luca's side. He gripped his forearm and slowly lifted it into the air. He pointed to a small, thin scar on the inside of his wrist.

"Noticed Luca had this scar on his wrist last night, my guess from a knife fight." He moved to Christian. "Christian wears the same cologne as I do, and Luca wears something downright dreadful." He scrunched up his nose. "No offence, bro," he said, winking at Luca.

"That's why you were sniffing them," I said, putting the pieces together about his crazy behaviour.

Arturo slowly loosened his grip on me but stayed close. "Hmmm," was all he said as he stared at Lukyan.

"Impressive, huh?" Lukyan grinned.

Great. Just what he needed. An ego boost.

My father stepped into the kitchen a moment later, looked at the broken dishes and food all over the kitchen floor and shook his head. "Someone better clean that shit up," he grunted.

"Not it!" Lukyan yelled, running out of the room.

I glanced at the mess on the floor and winced. I totally ruined Christian and Luca's breakfast. "Sorry guys," I said, looking at the twins.

They both smiled and said at the same time, "No sweat."

"I'll clean it up, Miss Volkov," Flora said, stepping into the kitchen and grabbing her cleaning supplies.

"No, no, it's okay. It's my mess, I'll clean it."

Everybody began clearing out of the room as I started cleaning up the broken dishes and food from the floor. Everyone except Arturo. He leant his elbows against the kitchen counter, watching me intently. I pointed to the plate of food next to him. "That's for you."

He glanced at the plate and raised his brows. "You made me breakfast?"

"Yep," I said, popping the 'p'. I scraped all the broken glass and food into the dustpan and placed it in the bin. Grabbing a bottle of multi-purpose spray and a cloth, I wiped the floor down, cleaning up every bit of leftover food and dirt.

"Thank you." He picked up the plate and moved to the table, taking a seat.

I was slightly nervous. I wasn't the best cook in the world. I could do the basics, that's about it. Hopefully it would be good enough for him.

"How'd last night go? Did the guy talk?" I asked, washing my hands and making my way over to the table. I took a seat opposite him.

"Oh, he talked alright," Arturo said, shoving a forkful of food into his mouth. "Your father can be quite motivating, if the situation calls for it."

I laughed. "Did he pull the whole 'I'm the Bratva Butcher' bit?"

Arturo smirked. "Does that a lot, huh?"

"Oh yeah. It's his go-to interrogation technique. Most people have heard of the Bratva Butcher, so it seems to work."

"It definitely works. Miguel squealed like a pig and told us everything he knew. Nero was the one who told them to kidnap you. He wanted leverage against your father."

I frowned. "Leverage? For what?"

"Nero wants him to butt out of our feud. He figured the best way to get your father under his thumb was to take his only daughter."

Smart. Would have totally worked if he'd succeeded, too. Nothing was more important to my father than family, his children.

"One thing I just can't figure out is why the Los Zetas are doing Nero's dirty work," Arturo said, frowning.

"Miguel didn't say?"

"Claimed he didn't know. Not sure if I believe him, though." He took another bite of his food, his brows lowered in thought.

"Maybe they've got an alliance, like we do?" I suggested.

Arturo shook his head. "Would your father and his men run off to do our bidding if we ordered it?"

I scoffed.

"Exactly. This was different. The Los Zetas are a brutal Mexican Cartel. It makes no sense that they would run around and do whatever Nero told them to."

"Unless Nero has leverage over them, too? Like he tried to get with my father?"

Arturo stopped eating and sat up straight. "That must be it. Nero's got something over the Zetas. He has to."

"What do you think it could be?"

"I don't know, it could be anything."

"We should try and find out what he's got and where he has it stashed. If we can take his leverage away, he loses control of the Los Zetas."

Something flashed across his face, an emotion I couldn't quite place. "Good idea."

It was silent for a few moments, only the sounds of cutlery hitting the plate as Arturo ate his breakfast. Until I spoke.

"Tell me about your first kill," I blurted out of nowhere. I was curious about him, about his life and what he'd experienced. There was still so much I didn't know about him, and I wanted to know everything there was to know.

He chuckled. "Nothing really to tell. It wasn't really a fair fight. I was nine. I'd been shadowing Alessandro for years, learning the ins and outs of the Cosa Nostra. As his successor, it was important for me to get familiar with death and violence at an early age. Being in this life, with a near constant stream of danger around every corner, there isn't any room for weakness. One day, he took me down to the dungeon and sitting in a chair, bolted to the floor, was a scrawny little guy. Early twenties, with track marks all over his arm. He jumped one of our dealers and took off with the whole stash—over $10,000 worth of drugs. Alessandro tracked him down and originally planned to make an example out of him. Until he decided it was the perfect opportunity for me to get my first kill out of the way. Looking back, I always thought it was kind of cheating. The dude was strapped to a chair and couldn't fight back, so like I said, it wasn't really fair. I stabbed him in the throat and then threw up afterwards." He shook his head, chuckling slightly. "Alessandro was *not* happy about that. Any time we had someone down there, he got me to kill them until I could do it without throwing up. Took a few tries, but eventually I got there." He looked at me. "How about you?"

"I was seven," I began, staring off into space. "A group of thieves had broken in. They saw the guards at the front gate, the big, beautiful mansion and figured it was a good score. They weren't your garden variety thieves, they were the real deal. Smart, professional, well prepared. They managed to get over the fence and into the house without anyone noticing. It was a real testament to their skills, considering the grounds were patrolled twenty-four hours a day. One of the men was a closet paedophile."

Arturo stiffened, his fork frozen in the air. I kept going.

"He crept into my room and when he saw me, jumped into my bed. I tried to scream, but he put his hand over my mouth and pressed his body on top of me. I remember how heavy he felt, the stench of alcohol and smoke on his breath. I thought I'd vomit. When he reached down to take my clothes off, something snapped in me. I had been practicing with knives for years, and always kept one under my pillow. It was my favourite one, and Lukyan liked to steal my things, so I thought by keeping it under my pillow, he could never steal it. I grabbed it and stabbed him in the throat. His blood poured over me like a waterfall, drenching my clothes, and when his hand left my mouth I screamed as loud as I could. My father and brothers came in and hell broke loose after that."

Arturo's eyes were soft. "I'm sorry that happened to you," he whispered, leaning forward to run his fingers over the top of my hand.

I shrugged. It was traumatic, for sure. I had nightmares afterwards. I was terrified someone was going to sneak into my room again, and I used to cry myself to sleep until Aleksandr came and slept on my bedroom floor. He promised to watch over me during the night and not let anyone hurt me. For months, he slept on a crappy air mattress at the foot of my bed until I was better. But I would never tell Arturo that.

"How's the food?" I asked, looking at his near-empty plate.

"Great, thank you," he said, pulling his hand back. He took a few more bites, finishing it off. He pushed the empty plate forward and leant back in his chair. He studied me for a moment. "You didn't tell me your father was the Bratva Butcher."

I shrugged. "You didn't ask."

"Hmmm," was his only reply.

I picked his plate up and took it to the sink, washing it and putting it in the dish rack.

I gasped in surprise when Arturo's hands gripped the kitchen bench in front of me, his arms boxing me in. I didn't even hear him move. One second he was at the table, the next he was standing behind me, his chest pushing into my back as he crowded me, invading my space. His scent surrounded me and I wanted to bathe in it. He smelt so fucking good.

"Is there anything else you need to tell me?" he whispered in my ear, making me shiver.

"Not that I know of," I breathed, pushing my ass into his cock. I couldn't help it. Whenever I was around him I just wanted to touch him, to feel him. His body was all hard, toned muscles. The body of a man who worked hard, fought harder and lived a rough, dangerous life.

He flexed his hips and pushed me forward, pinning me into the kitchen bench with his body. "You sure, *kotenok?* No more surprises?"

"Oh, I've got plenty of surprises. You'll just have to wait to find those out, though. I'm not spoiling the fun."

He kissed the side of my neck softly—just a light touch of his lips against my skin—and it gave me goosebumps. And then he bit down, hard.

I moaned and reached back, wrapping my hand around his nape and holding him to my neck, wanting—needing—more.

He sucked my skin into his mouth and let it go with a pop. "I can't wait to find out, then," he murmured.

His phone started ringing. He gave me one more quick kiss and then stepped back, pulling his phone out of his pocket and answering it.

"What?" he barked.

I turned around and propped my ass against the kitchen bench, running my hands over his chest. His muscles strained against the fabric of his shirt and I loved the feel of all that hard, powerful muscle beneath my fingertips. The firmness and sculpted definition of his body made me so wet, I soaked through my fucking underwear.

Arturo stiffened. "What the fuck do you mean you haven't found him yet, Vin?" he snapped into the phone. Tension rolled off him, his anger increasing as he listened intently. "I don't give a fuck what you have to do, find him! I'll be back soon, and I want him in the dungeon next to Marco by the time I get back."

He hung up and exhaled heavily.

"Something wrong?" I asked, my tone light.

"Just business. Nothing to concern yourself with."

I frowned. "Maybe I can help?"

"You can't. I have to go."

He turned and began walking away. He was dismissing me.

Oh, hell fucking no.

My anger spiked. I picked up a butcher knife from the dishrack and flung it towards him, making sure to aim wide so it didn't actually hit him. The blade embedded deeply into the wall in front of him.

He stopped dead in his tracks and glanced over his shoulder, a dark look in his eyes.

"Don't walk away from me when we're in the middle of a conversation," I hissed. "And don't think for one fucking second that you can put me on the sidelines. For as long as I can remember, I've been involved in my father's business. I'm not new to this life. As your future wife, I expect you to include me in your shit."

Narrowing his eyes, he marched over to me. I didn't move, didn't back down as he got right up in my space so we were nose to nose. His presence smothered the air around me with menace, making it hard for me to breathe. He watched me for a moment, his stunning blue-green eyes trailing over my face. "Alright," he said.

"Alright?" I repeated, eyeing him suspiciously.

He nodded slightly. "Alright, I'll include you. But, *kotenok*, the next time you throw a knife at me, I'm going to tie you to the bed and fuck you until you can't take it anymore. Until you're begging me to stop."

My breath hitched. "Is that supposed to be a punishment? Because it doesn't sound like it."

"You say that now, but after you've been denied your orgasm time and time again, you'll think differently." He backed away and I felt like I could finally breathe again. He pulled the knife from the wall and placed it on the kitchen counter. "Someone stole from me."

"Stole from you? How much?" I asked, watching him carefully. There was tension in his body, his face hard and eyes dark. He was beyond angry. He was furious.

"Over $50,000."

I gasped. "Shit. Do you have any idea who?"

"There's two men responsible for handling the cash at our drop houses. Marco and Diego. Marco's too much of a pussy to go against the family, but that doesn't mean he wasn't somehow involved. He could have easily given the right information to someone else, and they took the cash."

"And the other guy? Diego?"

His lips thinned. "He's missing. I've sent Vin to find him, but so far he's having no luck."

I nodded. "You need to go back, sort it out and find who took your money. Something like this is bad for organisations like ours. If word gets out, people will think it's okay to steal from you. To cross you."

"I know." He ran the back of his fingers across my cheek. "I wanted to stay a bit longer, get to know you a bit more."

When his fingers got near my mouth, I nipped them lightly. "We've got plenty of time for that."

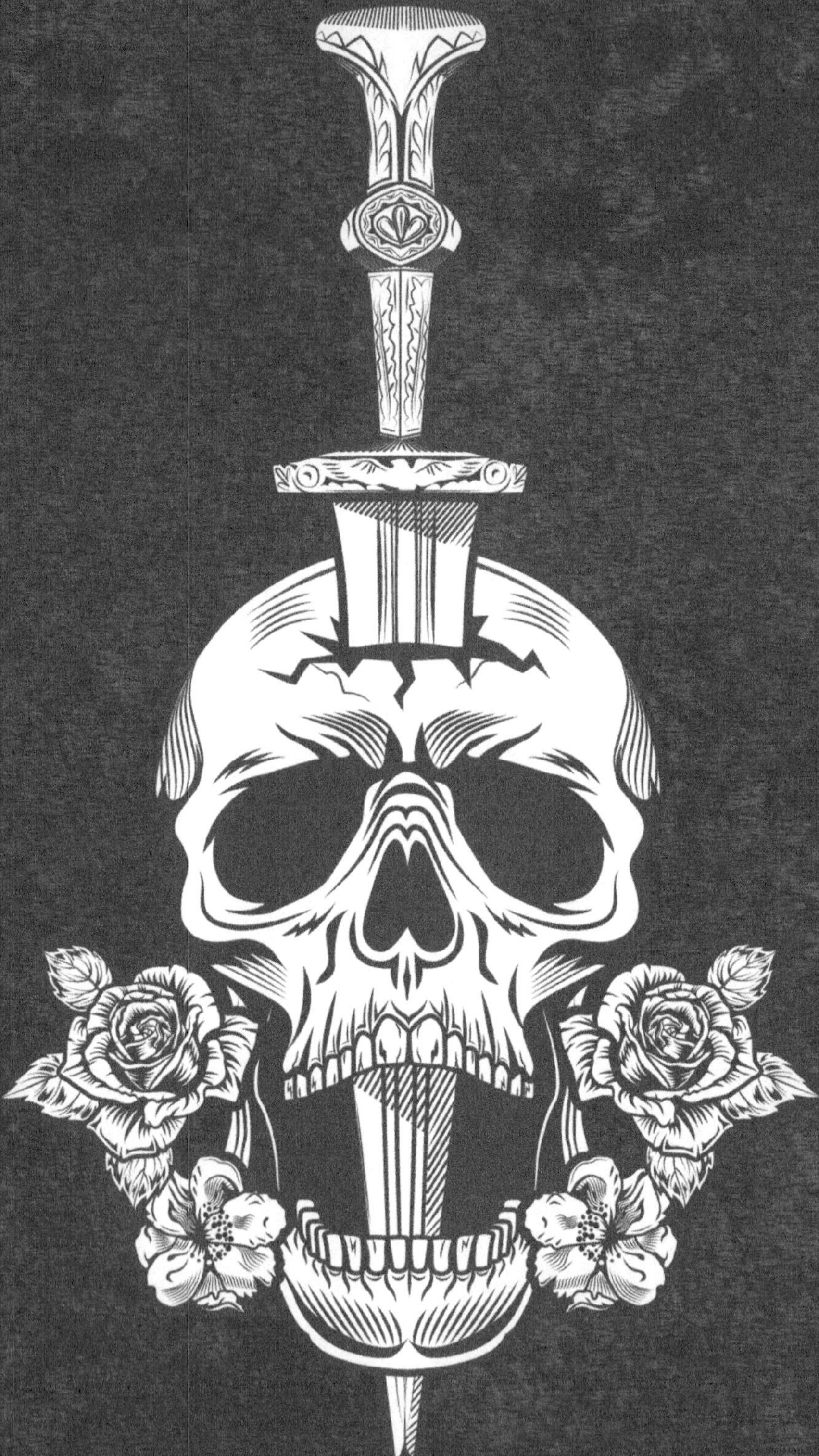

CHAPTER FIFTEEN

Illayana Volkov

I was watching *The Witcher* in the lounge room when a commotion at the front door made me frown, pausing the TV. Voices fluttered to me and I instantly recognised that high-pitched, squealy voice.

Tatiana.

"Move it, Lukyan!" she snapped. I rolled my eyes. Only she would have the audacity to order someone of Lukyan's stature around.

Tatiana rounded the corner and stepped into the lounge room looking as regal as ever in a stylish green dress and gold, strappy sandals that travelled all the way up to her calves. Lukyan followed a moment later, grumbling loudly and hands overfilled with so many binders he could barely see where he was going.

"Ah, there she is! The bride-to-be!" Tatiana said excitedly, clapping her hands.

I got to my feet and gave her a hug. I stared at the binders. "What's all this?"

"These, my dear best friend, are the plans for your wedding!" She clicked her fingers repeatedly. "Come on, Lukyan, over here," she said, pointing to the couch (not that he could see it).

Lukyan growled and dropped the binders to the ground where he stood.

Tatiana gasped. "What are you doing?!" she screeched, dropping to her knees to reorganise everything.

"I'm not your damn slave," Lukyan grunted. "And I'm not doing anything to help this wedding. It's a bad idea."

I rolled my eyes and helped Tatiana pick everything up, placing some of the binders on the couch. "You need to get over it. I'm marrying Arturo, whether you like it or not. You'll just have to deal with it."

"Fine, but don't come crying to me when he cheats on you with some tall, skinny bitch in the *famiglia*. 'Cause you know he will." He turned and stomped away.

"Oh my god, is that a possibility?" Tatiana asked, juggling the rest of her binders and coming over to the couch, taking a seat.

"Not if he wants to live, no," I replied, 100% serious. I would fucking kill him if he did something like that.

Tatiana laughed. "Of course. Look who I'm talking to here." She shook her head. "Alright! Let's get planning!"

I groaned and plopped down next to her. "I told you I didn't want any part in the planning. I'm fine with getting married at City Hall or some shit."

"You are *not* getting married at City Hall. Over my dead body. Come on, I need you to make some decisions."

Sighing loudly, I hunkered down and prepared for the worst time of my life. The 'decisions' she needed me to make were so insignificant I couldn't even fake being interested. Whenever she gave me options on something—flowers, linen, silverware—I just chose at random, not giving a flying shit. Because I didn't. I wasn't that type of woman. I liked weapons, fighting. Doing dangerous, reckless shit. Not frilly dresses and fucking centrepieces. It all gave me a headache, and by the second hour I couldn't even pretend to give a shit anymore.

I shook my head, slamming the binder filled with different colour combinations shut with a growl. "I'm done! No more. For the love of God. Please, no more."

Tatiana sighed and took the binder from me. "I'm surprised you lasted that long, to be honest. I was expecting you to chuck in the towel within ten minutes." She placed all the binders to the side, stacking them on top of one another. "At least I got you to pick some things. Better than nothing."

Yes, it was.

"You hungry? Want something to eat?"

"Yes fucking please."

We stood and made our way to the kitchen. Flora and a few of the maids were preparing lunch, slicing food and putting it in the large pots sitting on the stove.

"What can I do for you girls?" Flora asked, adding a bunch of onions into the boiling water.

"Got anything to munch on?" I asked, leaning on the kitchen bench.

She pursed her lips. "You'll ruin your appetite for lunch."

"It's for T," I said, nodding towards my best friend.

"There's some leftover pizza in the fridge from last night, but I think it's your brother's."

"Which brother?" If it was Aleksandr's, it was a big no-no. He'd lose his fucking mind if someone ate his pizza. He was a territorial motherfucker when it came to his food, just like me.

"Nikolai," Flora responded.

"Oh, goody." Tatiana opened the fridge and took the box of pizza, opening it and taking a slice out of the box. "Don't mind if I do." She bit into it, moaning in delight.

"Gimme a piece," I whispered, and she subtly handed me a thick piece loaded with chicken and cheese.

"Illayana!" Flora shouted in disappointment.

I laughed and ran out of the kitchen, Tatiana hot on my heels. We went back to the lounge room, kicked up our feet and sat back, enjoying the pizza.

"So, what's been going on with you lately?" I asked, taking a big bite out of my slice.

She shrugged. "Nothing really. Dad's been a real tight-ass. He doesn't want me going to college next year."

"Why not?"

"He's worried about my safety." She rolled her eyes. "He doesn't get that I can't just sit on my ass anymore and do nothing. I already deferred for a few years because he wasn't comfortable with me leaving home. I want to do something with my life. Study. Travel. Anything. Right now, the most exciting thing happening in my life is your wedding. How depressing is that?"

I looked at my best friend and the sadness flickering across her face made my heart clench. Tatiana might be a little crazy, but she had the sweetest soul. There was nothing she wouldn't do for the people she cared about, the people she loved. She was always the first person there to comfort me whenever something shitty happened in my life, with a bottle of vodka in one hand and a joint in the other, ready to help drown my sorrows.

"Would your dad be willing to compromise?"

Hope flashed in her eyes. "Compromise how?"

"Instead of you going off to college, what if we signed you up for some online classes? Nowadays you can study a range of things online from the comfort of your home, and you've only got to go into campus a few times a week."

She gnawed on her bottom lip. "Maybe. It's worth a try."

I nodded. "Give it a go. If he's still being a jackass about it, tell me and I'll handle it."

"Uh-oh. I don't like the sound of that. Handle it how?"

I winked. "Leave that with me."

The front door opened and slammed shut, making us jump. Nikolai strolled through the foyer and glanced into the lounge room. He froze when he saw us.

"Whose pizza is that?" he asked, his baritone voice hard enough to cut glass.

Tatiana picked up a slice, wrapped her tongue around the cooked dough and bit down hard, ripping a piece off. "Not sure, found it in the fridge," she said, a teasing smile on her face.

Aggression wafted off him, his fists clenched at his side and jaw locked in anger. "That was mine."

Tatiana shrugged and took another bite. "Now it's mine."

Nikolai growled and took a threatening step into the lounge room.

Fuck. An angry Nikolai was a very bad thing. It took a lot to ruffle his feathers. Out of all three of my brothers, he was always the calm, composed one. But whenever it came to Tatiana, that seemed to fly out the fucking window.

I jumped up and stood in front of him, palming his chest. "Hey, Nik, Flora's making lunch. Carbonaro, your fav. Why don't you go see if she's finished?" I asked, trying to distract him from my idiot best friend who insisted on antagonising him.

He hesitated briefly and then glared daggers at Tatiana before stomping to the kitchen.

I blew out a breath and turned to my best friend. "You know, one of these days, he's gonna kill you."

She just smiled and said, "Let him try."

The next few days flew by in a complete blur. My time was divided between trying to fend off Tatiana and helping my father handle business. Her crazy insistence that i help plan the wedding—when I made it perfectly fucking clear I wanted nothing to do with it—was aggravating me so badly that I took out all my frustrations on the people my father sent me after.

The Devil's Sons, a local MC gang we had worked with for years, decided to short us $3,000 on their last payment for a case of guns we provided, either thinking we were too dumb to notice or that they were big enough hotshots now to get away with it.

They weren't.

My father gave me twenty men and permission to handle it any way I saw fit. I chose to walk right into their clubhouse dressed in my sexiest black pantsuit with my four-inch Louboutins, bitch-slapping their Prez right in the face. Before the shock wore off, my men shoved him onto the ground and held him down while I stood over him, digging my heel into his temple and pointing my gun right between his eyes.

Risky, I know, considering we were on their territory, but when you were at the top of the food chain, you couldn't afford to show even the slightest hint of weakness.

When I asked the Prez why they shorted us, he told me I could get the money back if I sucked his cock. I shot him in the face instead. All hell broke loose at that point. Their bunnies (that's what they called the women who belonged to the club) screamed and cried as they ran out of the room. The other MC members were ready to take us on, until they realised who we were. Their VP, who was promoted to Prez the moment I pulled the trigger, apologised on behalf of the club and gave me back the missing money plus interest for the trouble.

The Bratva had to be cutthroat in the way we handled business. We couldn't afford to be anything less.

Then there was the little fucker who thought it would be a good idea to try and rape one of our girls at *Strip*. I had a lot of fun dealing with that one. I cut his dick clean off and shoved it down his throat.

On top of all that crap, plans were being finalised to make sure the De Lucas had their gun shipment by the time of our wedding. The MP5s and M60s were easy. We basically had an endless supply of those. It was the Canadian submachine guns (the DAR7014s) that were a little tougher to get a hold of.

Large wooden crates were designed to store and transport all the weapons, each one constructed with a false bottom so the guns could be easily concealed. Since we were getting married at my father's estate, it was arranged that the guns would be shipped with us when Arturo and I flew to New York City after the wedding. Aboard our own private jet, the guns would never be found. Even if the jet were to be searched, they would never be able to find the hidden compartments throughout the aircraft.

In between dealing with all that, Tatiana was there, trying to get me to pick the furniture, decide the menu or something else completely inconsequential to me for the wedding. It was a lot to deal with in the space of a few days.

I didn't get to see Arturo again until the wedding (which was disappointing), but I understood. He was dealing with his own problems in the *famiglia* that required his absolute attention.

Suddenly, I blinked and boom—wedding day.

I woke up early Saturday morning to Tatiana and a team of beauticians standing at the foot of my bed. I had to refrain from hurling things at them, their bright and cheery faces already putting me in a sour mood.

"Happy wedding day, bitch!" Tatiana squealed, her face perfectly done with makeup and her hair pristine. "Ah! I'm so excited! Let's go, up! Up!" She yanked me out of bed by my arm and I stumbled, still half asleep.

She led me over to my en suite and pushed me inside. "You've got ten minutes. We're on a tight schedule." Then she slammed the door shut.

I shook my head, stripped and jumped in the shower. Nerves riddled through me as I washed my hair and lathered my skin. I was beyond nervous. I was a fucking wreck. It felt like only yesterday that Arturo and I met, and now I was getting ready to marry him! It was all happening so fast.

I knew arranged marriages were common in La Cosa Nostra, but for the Bratva? Not so much. Not unless it was a marriage that would significantly benefit those involved. I tried not to think about how little we still knew each other. The things I did know made me excited to be his wife, so I focused on those.

Once I finished showering, I dried myself off and put on the nice silk rob Tatiana had left for me. Sitting on the countertop was a glass of vodka and I sent a silent thank you to my best friend. I chugged it down like a shot, enjoying the slight burn as it travelled down my throat, then left the bathroom.

Tatiana walked over to me, took my arm and guided me to a seat in the middle of the room that sat in front of a large mirror with numerous lights plastered all over it. She shoved me into the chair and clicked her fingers at the army of women behind her. "Alright, fix this," she said, drawing a circle in the air around my hair. "And this." She pointed to my face next and then walked away, leaving me at the mercy of the random women poking and prodding my body.

"Uhm, T," I winced as my hair was getting brushed out rather vigorously.

"Ya, girl?" she called out, running a handheld garment steamer over the bridesmaid dresses, completely oblivious to the pain I was in.

"Can't I have breakfast first?"

She gasped, like what I said was complete blasphemy. "And risk you being bloated in your wedding dress? Absolutely not." She walked over and grabbed her purse sitting on the bed and opened it, pulling out a bag of peanuts. "Have these."

"Mmm, yum," I mumbled sarcastically.

"Hey, if you don't want them—" she reached out to take them back and I yanked them to my chest.

"I didn't say that."

She laughed and went back to steaming her dress. "Alright, so we gotta run through a couple things before we make our way downstairs."

"Like what?" I asked, crunching on the nuts. Luckily for her, they were tasty.

"Well, first I have to warn you that I didn't have any control over the guest list. Your father handled that."

"Alright?" I frowned. "Why are you warning me about that?"

"Because I saw Rayna is invited."

I sneered, the very mention of my bitch of a cousin's name making my hackles rise. Rayna and I used to be very close growing up, until her jealousy got in the way. She couldn't stand the fact that I was more important than her. That I was higher up on the social order than she was. That it was my father who was *pakhan* and not hers. Over the years her jealousy festered, morphing into hateful emotions until finally, one day, she acted on them.

Trying to get the one up on me, she convinced a now-ex-boyfriend of mine to cheat on me. I'm not going to lie, I was definitely hurt by her actions, and a little ticked off. Okay, a lot ticked off, but I never let it show. I never let her see how much it got to me, which in turn pissed her off even more.

She was superficial, the type of person who cared more about material possessions than the people in her life. She posted every little thing on social media, pretending that she lived some grand, glamorous reality when in reality she was just a basic bitch with a fake-ass life. It got to the point that I had to block her on Instagram and Tik Tok because I couldn't stand looking at all that fake bullshit.

"You're fucking kidding me," I said, looking at my best friend in disbelief.

"I tried to tell your brother that you and Rayna aren't on good terms, but they said your cousin and uncle had to be invited. It was non-negotiable."

"For fuck's sake," I hissed, shaking my head. "You know she's gonna make a move on Arturo. The bitch can't help herself."

"Don't worry about it. I'll handle her, alright?"

I closed my eyes and took a deep breath. I had no doubt she would handle her, but…"Just don't do anything too crazy. My uncle isn't the type of guy you want to cross."

"Oh, I know," she said, giving me a serious look.

"You said there were a couple of things we had to run through? What else?"

They were minor things, like the fact that the florist delivered the wrong flowers and we didn't have a vegetarian or vegan option, in case some of the guests didn't eat meat. After a while we had hashed out the last few details, and it was time to get in my wedding dress.

I stared at my reflection in awe. I couldn't believe the transformation these women managed to make. I barely recognised myself. They had spent the last few hours meticulously going over every inch of my skin, removing any blemishes they could find. They spent an inordinate amount of time on my hair and makeup, more time than I think I've ever spent on either in my entire life. But I had to admit, they did an amazing job.

My long, black hair was left to flow freely down my back, a few strands braided back so they wouldn't get in my way. My face had layers of makeup applied to it, from foundation and blush to eyeliner, mascara and my signature red lipstick. I had it all, and it looked tasteful. I didn't look like a two-cent hooker, and I guess that's all a girl can wish for on her wedding day, right? That and not getting stood up.

My wedding dress (well, my mother's wedding dress) fit perfectly. The sleeves ran all the way down to my wrists and were made of the softest lace I'd ever felt. The bodice had an intricate design that hugged my body flawlessly, showing off all my curves in a respectful manner. The open back gave the dress the perfect style for a statement-making bride like myself. The train of the dress only ran a few metres behind me, and was made of the same lace material that encompassed most of the dress.

All in all, it was beautiful. More beautiful than even I originally thought.

My white heels were only a few inches, putting me around 6'4 (thank the devil that Arturo is a tall motherfucker).

Tatiana sniffed, wiping a tear from her cheek. "Oh my god, you look so beautiful," she cried, wrapping her arms around me.

I smiled and hugged her back. "Thank you for everything you've done, T. I would be utterly lost without you."

"Oh, I know," she chuckled, pulling back. She shook herself off and gave me a bright, beaming smile. "Alright, I'm going to make sure everything is in order downstairs. Try not to freak out."

"I don't freak out."

She smirked. "Sure you don't. I'll see you out there." She opened the door and left.

For a moment I was alone with nothing but my chaotic thoughts to keep me company.

Holy fuck, I'm getting married.

My anxiety spiked. My palms started to sweat. My heart thumped so loudly I could hear it in my ears.

I can't believe I'm getting married. Me! It's fucking insane. I'm insane. Who marries a man they've only just met? Oh...me! A crazy woman. I don't think I can do this. Can I do this? No. YES! I can. I'm Illayana Rae Volkov, daughter of Dimitri Volkov, The Bratva Butcher and Pakhan of the whole motherfucking US Bratva. I can do whatever I put my mind to. Right?

The sound of someone knocking on my bedroom door pierced my thoughts.

"Illayana? *Sestra?*" Sister? Lukyan's voice was firm yet calm as he opened the door and stepped inside.

He was wearing a dark tailored tuxedo, the black dress pants and black jacket encompassing his body entirely. His long, dark hair was tied up neatly at the nape of his neck.

"Are you okay?" he asked, his brows furrowed as he made his way over to me.

I could see the concern etched on his face, yet I couldn't bring myself to acknowledge it.

"What if I'm making a terrible mistake, Lukyan? What if I can't do this?"

I looked down at my hands, only just realising they were shaking. My entire body felt like a bundle of nerves, and I couldn't remember a time in my life when I felt so...scared. I didn't like it.

He gave me a sincere look and clasped my trembling hands in his, holding them close to his chest. *"Sestra*, breathe. You can do this. There isn't anything in this world you can't do. The question isn't if you can do this, it's do you want to?"

I closed my eyes and took a deep breath in, taking comfort in his presence. I reopened my eyes to Lukyan watching me intently. "I do. I'm just nervous. Not only am I marrying a man I only just met last week, I'm packing up my entire life and moving hundreds of miles away from the only home I've ever known. From the only family I've ever known. The whole thing is...daunting," I sighed.

Lukyan nodded, giving me a sad smile. "I know. But you can take comfort in one thing."

"What's that?"

His eyes flashed with excitement as his lips curved into a broad grin. "You're not going alone."

I turned to face him fully, a smile creeping onto my face as I processed his words. "You're coming with me?"

He scoffed. "Of course I am. Did you seriously think I'd let you go without me?"

"But Father? The Bratva?"

"Will be completely fine without me," he said, the smile still on his face.

My bedroom door opened once again. This time, Aleksandr and Nikolai walked through. They were dressed in similar tuxedos to Lukyan, the only difference being the colour. Aleksandr's was dark blue with a black bow tie. Nikolai's was light grey. He chose to forgo the bow tie, preferring the open-collared look. Their eyes landed on me and they both gave me a broad smile, helping quell some of my nerves.

Aleksandr stepped forward first, stretching his arms out and embracing me in a tight hug. "You look beautiful, little sister," he whispered into my hair.

I leant my head against his massive chest and breathed in his comforting scent. Nikolai and Lukyan moved to hug me as well, all three of them encasing me in one big bear hug.

"Thank you. All of you." I raised my head and looked at my three older brothers. There truly wasn't a stronger family bond than the one between siblings. Brothers were a gift from the heart, friends to the spirit and protectors of all.

"Are you ready?" Nikolai asked as I stepped back and looked into the mirror once more.

I smiled, trying to banish the last little bit of nerves running through my body. "As ready as I'll ever be."

Aleksandr and Nikolai both offered me an arm and I looped my own through each of theirs and let them lead me out of the room, with Lukyan following close behind.

An assortment of beautiful coloured flower petals covered the ground as I made my way downstairs. An array of floral decorations adorned the house as we walked through, the entire floor devoid of any living souls but us.

With each step I took, I could feel my nerves coming back, could feel my body start to shake as sweat rolled down my back.

Relax. Breathe. You're going to be fine.

We entered the kitchen to find my father standing tall and proud next to the double glass sliding door that led to the patio outside. A large black curtain covered the entire length and width of the door, obscuring the view outside.

My father's eyes snapped to me as we walked in and he froze. For a terrifying second, I feared he was angry that I chose to wear my mother's dress. But as he walked towards me, I could see the emotion on his face, something he always tried so hard to hide.

A single tear escaped his eye and ran down his cheek as he stood in front of me. He raised a hand, softly tucking a stray piece of hair behind my ear. "You look so much like your mother," he whispered, sadness lacing his thick Russian accent.

I smiled, trying to speak, but all that came out was a whimper. "I wish she was here."

His chin trembled slightly, his eyes moistening as he looked at me. "Me too." He took a deep breath in and closed his eyes. For a moment we all stood in silence, remembering the amazing woman who influenced us all.

After a few seconds, he stepped back and cleared his throat. "Here we go. You ready, *moja doch'?*" *My daughter.* He offered me his arm and I looped my own through it, smiling.

"Ready."

Aleksandr and Nikolai moved to the glass sliding doors in unison. As Aleksandr reached for the handle, his arctic blue eyes shot to me for one last confirmation. I nodded.

He simultaneously opened the door and pulled back the curtain, revealing our large outdoor patio, filled with people. I tried to ignore them all, my eyes honing in on the handsome figure at the end of the aisle. He stood beneath a tall floral arch, with Vincenzo at his side.

The theme for my wedding was clearly floral. Flowers of all different types were decorating every piece of furniture you could see. The ground was littered with rose petals of all different colours. The beauty of it took my breath away, even though I wasn't an overly big flower girl. Tatiana did an amazing job. No wonder she kept asking me to pick fucking flowers.

A makeshift aisle was made leading directly from the door to where Arturo stood. Beautiful white chairs were placed on either side, each one occupied with a member of our families. I caught a glimpse of the twins, dressed in sharp, black suits, and Lorenzo on the groom's side. Christian and Luca both gave me a thumbs up while Lorenzo smiled reassuringly.

My father gripped my arm tightly and began leading me down the aisle.

As we got closer, I took in Arturo's appearance.

Dear God, how is one man this fucking handsome?!

He wore a stunning dark red Brioni suit with a black tie. It was tailored to fit his build perfectly, accentuating those hard-earned muscles and broad shoulders. His dark hair was kept short and styled neatly. When we locked eyes, his lips curved into that sly, sexy smirk that made me weak in the knees. His gorgeous multi-coloured eyes sparkled, his emerald green eye and electric blue eye drawing me in instantly. I couldn't look away even if

I wanted to.

My heart was beating a million miles a minute. If it wasn't for my father holding my arm, I know my legs would have given out by then.

He just looked so damn fiiiiiiiiiine. The edges of his tattoos peaked out of his suit, giving off that dangerous, bad boy vibe that made me so fucking wet. What I wouldn't have given to rip that suit off his body and fuck him right there. Turns out, being turned on helped quell my nerves. Who knew?

Arturo extended his hand, palm upwards, his eyes never leaving mine. My father leant over and kissed me on my cheek, before placing my hand in his and taking a step back. His jaw clenched slightly, so slightly I almost missed it, and I tried to give him a reassuring smile.

Arturo's warm hands clasped mine as he pulled me closer and upwards the priest standing underneath the floral arch.

He leant over and whispered into my ear, his deep, seductive voice sending shivers down my spine. *"Ora, sei mio."* *Now, you're mine.*

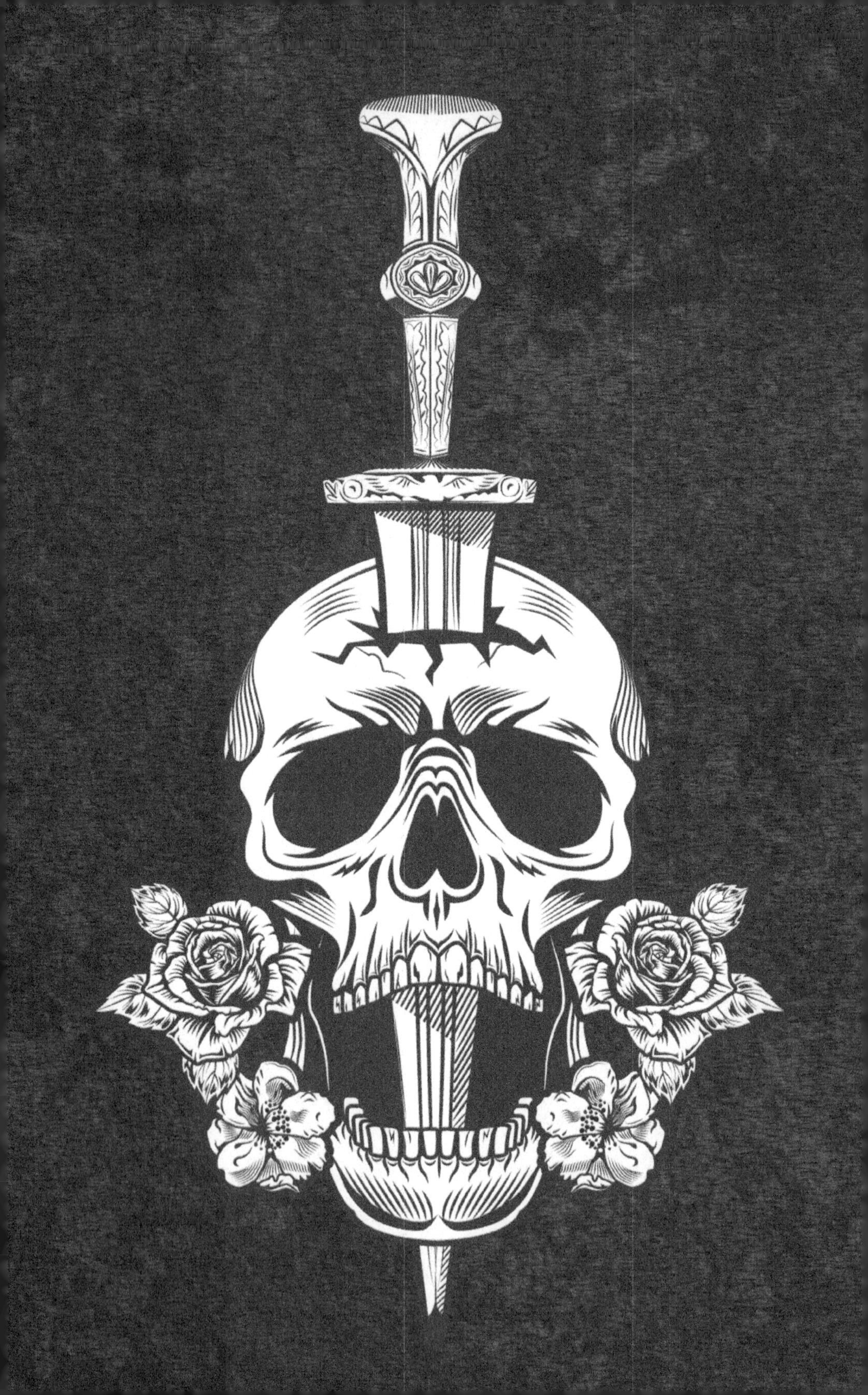

CHAPTER SIXTEEN

Arturo De Luca

"You know it's not too late to make a run for it. Get on a plane, fly to Costa Rica or some shit. I've heard marriage is a real killer."

I rolled my eyes and turned to face my younger brother, who stood by my side underneath the large floral arch. To be honest, it wasn't to my taste. Not at all. But as the husband-to-be, it wasn't my job to comment on the decorations. No. My only job was to show up on time, dressed to the nines, ready to commit myself mind, body and soul (according to Alessandro, anyway).

"We both know if anyone is going to be the death of me, it's going to be you."

Vin's green eyes lit with amusement as he shook his head and laughed. "True."

He wore a dark green three-piece suit that matched his eyes perfectly, paired with an even lighter green tie. He always loved to accentuate his eyes. He firmly believed they were his best feature.

Illayana's maid of honour, who also happened to be her best friend, wore a sleeveless dress the same shade as Vin's suit. She stood off to the left side, hands clasped in front of her body, her face a mixture of excitement and nervousness. I had spoken to her briefly before making my way to the arch. She was determined to give Illayana a beautiful, graceful wedding, even though Illayana didn't particularly want one. She seemed nice (and by the way she snapped commands at everyone around her, she had that fiery spirit a lot of the Bratva women seemed to have).

Vin was definitely interested in getting in her pants. I knew my brother. I knew all his tells. If the smirk he kept throwing her way was any indication, he was going to try something. But I wasn't sure if she was interested. I caught her gaze shifting to Nikolai frequently and then darting away before he could notice. It was...interesting.

Looking out in front of me, I took note of our surroundings. The Volkov mansion was huge, giving us plenty of room to hold the wedding here comfortably. The patio was filled with people. Some I knew, some I didn't. Most, if not all, were in some way involved with the Mafia.

My mother and father were seated in the front row talking amongst themselves while my younger brother, Lucian, and younger sister, Theodora, were chasing each other around the yard. I couldn't help but smile as I watched them duck and weave in between guests, both trying to catch the other.

In truth, I envied them. To be that young again, so carefree, not a trouble in the world. I missed that feeling. Soon Lucian would come of age and begin his transition into the *famiglia*, and that feeling would slowly start to fade for him. If it were up to Alessandro, he would already be in the thick of it, like Vin and I were at his age. But my mother was adamant about giving him at least some semblance of a childhood.

Lucian came bounding towards me and started to run circles around my body, Theodora hot on his heels. He looked adorable in his little black suit and tie, even if it was already dirty.

"Give it back, Lucian!" Theodora shrieked, her tiny face scrunched up in anger. Her pink dress was already covered in grass stains, her dark brown hair tousled with dirt and sticks. I knew my mother was going to pitch a fit when she noticed the state she was in.

"No! I want to give it to her," Lucian huffed, making sure to keep me between himself and Theo.

She went to dart around me, determined to catch him, but I crouched down and gripped her shoulders lightly, holding her in place. "Lucian," I said sternly, clicking my fingers.

His head popped out from my right side, his little hands gripping my shoulders for support. I pointed next to Theo. He dropped his head and moved to stand next to her, dragging his feet. I could hear Vin laughing behind me, but I ignored him for the moment.

"What's going on?" I asked, looking between them.

Theodora's bright green eyes connected with mine and she pointed at Lucian accusingly. "He stole the present for our new big sister, and won't give it back!"

"Liar!" Lucian yelled, stomping his little foot. "You left it on the chair. I didn't steal it."

"Yes, you did. Mum said I could give it to her."

"I want to. Why do you get to do it?"

"Because Mum said so!" she yelled.

"Enough!" I snapped. I held my palm out, facing upwards. "Give it to me, Lucian."

His shoulders sagged and he lowered his head as he reached into his little suit jacket and handed me a small purple box.

Huh. Wonder what it is.

I plucked it from his grasp and passed it to Theo. "Run along."

She beamed at me, her smile seeming brighter than the sun as she leant over and kissed my cheek.

Little vixen.

She ran off to sit with our parents.

Lucian turned to skulk off but I placed a hand on his shoulder, stopping him. I reached down and pulled out the small blade in my ankle holster. Illayana's blade. I had planned to give it back to her eventually, so why not have Lucian give it to her as a gift?

"You can give this to her as your present, okay?"

His blue eyes looked at the knife in my hand briefly before reaching forward and taking it. His little fingers curled around the hilt and he lifted it into the air.

"Do you think she'll like it?" he asked nervously.

I smiled. "I know she will. But that's a dangerous weapon, Lucian. And what does Father always say about weapons?"

He stood up straighter and puffed out his chest. "That they're not toys and should always be treated with care."

I nodded and tousled his dark hair. "Good boy. Now run along and join our sister. The ceremony will be starting any minute." I gave him a little pat on the back and nudged him towards our parents as I rose to my feet.

Vin was watching me, his green eyes studying me intently.

"What?" I snapped, straightening my tie.

He remained silent for a few moments, his eyes continuing to scrutinise me. "You'd make a great father, you know that? Some people would think handing a nine-year-old a knife is crazy, but I don't."

Stunned, I stared at him in shock.

Where the fuck did that come from?

Before I could respond, the glass sliding doors opened, the curtain was pulled back and out walked Illayana on her father's arm.

Vin let out a low whistle as she stepped into view completely and the crowd fell silent, rising to their feet. The music began to play and they started making their way down the makeshift aisle. My eyes drank in every inch of her body, from her long legs to her dark black hair. I was entranced.

Fuck. She's beautiful.

Her long dark hair was flowing down her shoulders, a few strands intricately braided up. Her ocean eyes sparkled as they landed on me and I curled my lips into that sly grin I knew she loved. My stomach tightened with each step she took, anticipation coursing through my body at what the future would bring us.

Vin's last words blared through my mind as they stopped a few paces in front of me. I wondered how she felt about children. Probably should have had the discussion earlier. Oh well.

Illayana smiled as Dimitri placed her hand in mine. Her hand was warm and steady as I led her to the priest. I leant over to whisper in her ear, loving the feeling of her body shaking at my proximity. *It's nice to know I affect you just as much as you affect me, kotenok.*

"Ora, sei mio." *Now, you're mine.*

The ceremony itself was quick and relatively painless. The usual shit was said. 'Do you, Arturo, take Illayana to be your lawfully wedded wife, to have and to hold from this day forth?' Blah, blah, blah.

A few oaths were given in Italian and Russian, both of us reciting them word for word. After exchanging rings, it was time to kiss the bride. It took every bit of self control I possessed not to throw her over my shoulder and march up to her bedroom when her lips touched mine. That brief contact was more intoxicating than any sex I'd had in my life—and then some. I could feel my cock harden as she moved to deepen the kiss, her body pressing up against mine. I groaned in frustration and regrettably pulled back, painfully aware of the fact that we weren't alone.

The crowd jumped to their feet, roaring in congratulations, cheers and whoops ringing out all around us.

Illayana looked around at our guests and blushed, embarrassed at her public display of affection for me. I wasn't, though. I picked up her hand and kissed the back of it, giving her a reassuring smile.

I led her back down the makeshift aisle, the crowd throwing confetti over us and clapping enthusiastically as we passed.

A waiter with a tray of champagne was waiting patiently for us at the end of the aisle and I grabbed two flutes, handing one to Illayana.

Instead of continuing the path back into the Volkov mansion, I turned left, leading Illayana down a few steps into the yard where the reception was being held. Soon, our guests would begin to crowd around us, ready to offer their blessings. It was a tedious tradition, but tradition nonetheless.

I took a sip of my champagne, not at all a fan of the bubbles, but meh. I turned to gaze at my wife.

Fuck. My wife.

"Any regrets?" I smirked.

Her blue eyes landed on me as she took a sip of her drink. "I don't know yet. We've only been married for thirty seconds. Ask me again in a few years," she winked.

I chuckled, drinking the rest of my champagne and handing the empty glass to one of the waiters walking past.

The first round of guests appeared before us. Dimitri, Aleksandr, Nikolai and Lukyan.

They looked large and imposing, all of them standing well over six feet tall with muscular builds and hard, sculpted faces. If I wasn't 100% sure they agreed with our union, I'd think they were about to kill me (well, try to anyway).

Dimitri hugged Illayana first, whispering something in her ear that I couldn't quite make out, then moved to stand in front of me. He extended his hand, his hard eyes locked on me as he squeezed my hand in his.

"Congratulations," he said emotionlessly.

I thanked him and went to pull my hand back when his grip tightened. Not enough to cause pain, but enough for me to see it for what it was. A warning.

He stepped forward, covering the empty space between us and whispered in my ear. *"Esli khot kak-to trones moiu doch, ya tebya zarezu."* *If you hurt my daughter in any way, I'll butcher you.*

The fact that he delivered his threat in Russian made it all the more menacing, which I think was what he was trying to achieve. As he went to step back, I tightened my own grip on his hand, halting him.

He arched an eyebrow in surprise, his eyes lit with fire.

I felt Illayana tense at my side, but I continued to stare into his eyes, refusing to back down. I've met men like Dimitri my whole life. At the slightest hint of weakness, they pounced. I couldn't show weakness. I refused to.

"Mne plevat, esli the myasnik bratvy, ugrozhay mne snova yi tebe nay ponravitsya to, chto proisoidet." *I don't care if you are the Bratva Butcher, threaten me again and you won't like what happens.*

I released his hand and wrapped an arm around Illayana's shoulders, loving the looks of shock on her brothers' faces. Clearly no one had ever spoken to their father that way. Or maybe they had, they just never lived to talk about it.

An uncomfortable silence fell over us until, eventually, Dimitri smiled. An honest to God, genuine smile. Something I only saw him do once, when he was tormenting the Mexican gang member in his basement a few days ago.

Maybe that's what he plans to do to you. That's why he's smiling like a bloody lunatic.

"I look forward to that day, Arturo," he winked, moving along.

Aleksandr, Nikolai and even Lukyan all gave me a firm handshake and their congratulations before following after their father.

"Are you insane?!" Illayana hissed as they walked away. "No one has ever—and I mean *ever*—spoken to him like that. Not even me, and he loves me."

I couldn't help grinning at her words. "I gathered as much by the looks of horror on all of your faces after I said it," I chuckled.

"If you weren't my husband, he would have gutted you."

"Maybe," I shrugged.

The next guests to give us their blessings stopped in front of us. My mother, father and younger siblings. Alessandro put a hand on my shoulder, giving me a smile of encouragement before moving to Illayana. My mother appeared next, her green eyes sparkling with moisture as she stood up on her tiptoes and kissed my cheek.

"Oh, Arturo, I feared I wouldn't live to see this day."

I rolled my eyes and patted her on the back. "You overreact, mother."

She slapped my shoulder and tsked. "I do not. My concerns were valid. You never kept a woman longer than a week."

I groaned. "Can we not have this conversation right now? Or ever?" I mumbled, flicking my gaze to Illayana, who was waiting patiently to greet my mother.

She flushed with embarrassment, her face turning red as she realised she was referring to other women on my wedding day, in front of my new wife.

"Of course. Of course." She waved a hand in the air and moved in front of Illayana. She ran her eyes up and down her body briefly before stepping forward and enveloping her in a tight hug. "My dear, you are even more beautiful than my boys described."

Illayana shifted her gaze to the floor. She always seemed to get uncomfortable whenever anyone paid her a compliment.

"Thank you, Mrs De Luca."

"Oh, please, none of that nonsense. Call me Isabella."

Illayana smiled, joy seeming to radiate off her in waves.

I felt something pull on my slacks and I looked down to see Lucian tugging on my pants, trying to gain my attention. I crouched down to his height and watched as he placed his little hands on either side of my head and turned it to the side so he could whisper in my ear.

"Can I give her the present now?" He cupped a hand around his mouth in an attempt to keep the conversation between us, but unfortunately for him, his voice didn't get that memo.

My eyes darted to Illayana, who was watching us intently. Her face was soft, filled with an emotion I couldn't quite place.

I tousled his hair and gave him a little nudge in her direction. "Go ahead."

He scowled at me and tried to fix his hair first, patting it down and smoothing it over until he was satisfied, before moving to stand in front of Illayana. She immediately lowered herself to his height, not caring at all that her dress could get dirty.

Lucian bit his lip nervously as he reached into his little suit jacket and pulled out her blade. "I'm Lucian," he whispered shyly, looking down at his feet.

Illayana gripped his chin lightly and forced him to look back up at her. She smiled broadly, her face lighting up with happiness. "Hi, Lucian. I'm Illayana. It's so nice to meet you. I've always wanted a little brother."

He smiled, showing his missing two front teeth. The nervousness seemed to fade from him as he offered her the knife. Frowning, she reached forward and took her blade. She held it up in the air, admiring it. Recognition flashed on her face.

"This is beautiful, little one. Is it for me?"

Lucian's bright blue eyes connected with mine first, as if searching for approval. I nodded in encouragement. He smiled at her, nodding enthusiastically.

"Thank you, Lucian. I love it. I'll carry it with me wherever I go." She twirled it between her fingers a few times before she took out the blade in her ankle holster and replaced it with that one. She tossed the knife into the air, the blade landing in her palm, before offering the hilt to Lucian.

"For me?" he breathed in shock.

Just before his little fingers were able to wrap around the hilt, she pulled it back slightly, out of reach. "For you, little one. But it's very sharp and could hurt someone if you don't know how to use it properly." She tilted her head to the side, studying him. "Do you?"

He stood up straighter, trying to make himself seem older than his nine years. "Yes. I can hit the target board when we practice," he said proudly.

She smiled affectionately and handed the knife over. "That's good. Maybe one day we can practice together. You can show me some moves."

"Okay!" He smiled broadly before grasping the knife and running off to show our parents. Vin gave us both a wink before chasing after him.

Theodora was nowhere to be seen. I could only guess she'd gotten herself into trouble and was in timeout, something our mother loved to do to us whenever we misbehaved. She'd stick us in a corner with a bodyguard watching over us. If we tried to move, the guard had permission to put us back in place.

"Your little brother is so fucking cute," Illayana commented.

"And he bloody knows it, too."

Another group of people made their way over to us and I stiffened.

Illayana noticed the change in me and her brows furrowed.

Shit.

Gabriella and her parents were standing in front of us. I knew they would be there, of course. Gabriella's father was one of our capos, after all. But still, I wasn't looking forward to seeing her. Her reaction when she found out I wouldn't be marrying her was quite the tantrum, or so I heard. She swore. She threw things. She screeched at the top of her lungs. Which was quite unexpected, I admit. I'll be honest, I didn't think she had that behaviour in her. But from what several of my men told me, she had a dark, venomous side that had emerged when she found out I wasn't going to marry her.

Turns out, she thought the right of being married to the future head of the Cosa Nostra was hers, considering she had put her life on hold for six years waiting for me.

"Congratulations, Arturo," she said sweetly, showing none of the venom that I heard she'd possessed. Her brown hair was done up nicely in an elegant updo, her brown eyes staring daggers at my new wife. It didn't slip past me that she was wearing a stunning white floor-length gown, either.

She leant in and kissed me on both cheeks, her lips a brush away from mine before stepping back. She turned to Illayana and smiled. "Congratulations. I'm Gabriella, one of Arturo's oldest friends. It's nice to meet you." She held out her hand.

Illayana smiled back, but I saw the anger that flashed in her eyes. She shook her hand. "Nice to meet you, too."

Gabriella looked at me, her eyes running the length of my body in an obvious show of perusal. "I always said red was your colour, didn't I?" she asked, brushing her fingers lightly over my shoulder, as if wiping away a speck of dirt.

The contact showed familiarity, and based on the way Illayana's eyes narrowed at the touch, she didn't miss it.

I smiled stiffly. "You did."

Enzo and his wife, Sofia, gave their congratulations next, Enzo's short and brisk and Sofia's quiet and respectful. Throwing one last smile my way, Gabriella and her family moved on.

I raised my finger in the air, halting the next group of people who were about to make their way over to offer their congratulations, and turned to face Illayana. Her face didn't show any trace of anger, but her eyes? Yeah, that was definitely anger sparkling in those shiny blue orbs.

"About Gabriella—"

"Not now," she said sharply, a fake smile plastered on her face.

I narrowed my eyes. "Fine, we'll discuss it later then."

"You bet your ass we will," she grumbled under her breath.

I turned back around and motioned the next group of people forward.

After a while, all the faces seemed to mash together and all I wanted was for the whole tedious ordeal to be over. We were greeted by all the key players in the Cosa Nostra and the Bratva, each one offering their heartfelt congratulations for our union. But I wasn't buying it. Nope. Half, if not all, of the people here objected to joining our families. If they all weren't so terrified of Dimitri and Alessandro, I can bet they would have objected quite vocally at the ceremony.

I shook every hand that appeared before me, even if I had no clue who the damn person was. Illayana was just as polite, smiling and engaging in small talk with everyone who offered their blessings. Yet I could see the strain on her face after what felt like the thousandth well wishes to us.

Just when I thought we were free and clear, a deep voice spoke from behind us. We both turned around to find Dimitri standing there, a woman on his arm.

Huh. A little young for you, Dimitri. But each to their own, I guess.

I was confused as to why he was coming to congratulate us again, until Illayana responded, her voice cold and emotionless.

"Uncle."

Uncle?! It took every bit of self control I had not to react to that. *Dimitri is a twin?! An identical twin? Why was I never told this? Better yet, why the fuck did none of the information I collected about the Volkov family mention it?*

Dimitri 2.0 laughed, his big body shaking with amusement as he studied Illayana. *"Akh, moya dorogaya plemyannitsa. The vsegda mog nas razlichat. Skazi mne, ditya, vie cham tvoy secret?"* *Ah, my darling niece. You've always been able to tell us apart. Tell me, child, what's your secret?*

Illayana pressed her lips firmly together, her eyes locked with his in an icy glare. It was painfully obvious she didn't care for the man.

Curiosity spiked within me. I was dying to know the story there.

"Ya znayu, kto moy otets Dominik." *I know who my father is, Dominik.*

He smouldered with resentment and scoffed. *"Overen, chto znaete. Vse znayut velikogo Dmitriya Volkova. Groznogo bratvo myasnika."* *I'm sure you do. Everyone knows the great Dimitri Volkov. The fearsome Bratva Butcher.* He sneered. His blue eyes flicked to me, his lips curling up in distaste. *"Priznayus, ya oudivelin, chto tvoy otetz pozvolil tebe zhenitsya na italiani sobake. Kazhetsya, on zabludilsya."* *I'll admit, I'm surprised your father let you marry the Italian dog. It seems he's strayed far from tradition.*

I growled in anger at his words, my fists clenching at my sides. He obviously had no idea I could understand every bloody word he said. Or maybe he did and he just didn't care. Either way, he was really starting to get on my fucking nerves.

Illayana seemed to sense my discomfort and she patted my chest lightly in an offer of support, her gaze never once leaving Dominik's. *"Naskolko ya pomnyu, dyadya, vy toze nikogda nay byli poklonnikom traditius."* If I recall, Uncle, you were never a fan of traditions either.

She arched an eyebrow, challenging him to contradict her words.

He rolled his eyes and waved a hand in the air. *"Eta malenkaya shtuchka? Dmitriy vse eshche plachet ob ethom?"* That little thing? Is Dimitri still crying about that?

What little thing?! Dimitri crying?! What the fuck was going on?!

Illayana tensed, her entire body going rigid. Anger poured off her in waves, the veins in her neck pulsing with rage. I had no clue what exactly was going on, but the fact that this dude was upsetting her was seriously pissing me off.

"Perhaps we should move along? This Italian dog is getting hungry," I smirked.

Dominik's face filled with surprise before he managed to mask it, as he realised I could understand every word that was being spoken in their native tongue. His expression turned stoic as he extended his hand to me. "Dominik Volkov, Illayana's uncle."

"I gathered as much," I replied bleakly, shaking his hand.

His jaw clenched and he squeezed my hand, hard. But I didn't react, just giving him a cocky smile.

He turned to face the young woman who had accompanied him. "This is my daughter, Rayna."

Before I could say a word, the little woman stepped forward, wrapping her arms around me in a tight hug. I stood frozen in place for a moment. *Why does this feel super fucking weird, like I shouldn't be touching her?* My question was answered when I pulled back and caught a glimpse of Illayana's face.

Oh, shit. She was pissed.

"Pleasure to meet you, Arturo. Welcome to the family," she said seductively, batting her eyelashes and biting her lip.

Seriously?

She was an attractive woman, sure. With her shoulder length brown hair and those signature bright blue eyes most of the Volkovs seemed to possess, she would please any man. Her features were soft and delicate, like a porcelain doll.

"Congratulations on your wedding, cousin." She took a step towards Illayana, preparing to hug her as she did me, but Illayana immediately raised a hand in the air, halting her.

"Rayna," she greeted coldly.

Ouch.

Rayna narrowed her eyes, taking a step back. Embarrassment flowed off her at having been dismissed in such a way.

Dominik looked between the girls and cleared his throat. "Well, it seems we've worn out our welcome already," he laughed.

"You were never welcome to begin with," Illayana replied, lifting her chin defiantly.

Dominik smirked. "Perhaps. But I'm here nonetheless." He titled his head to the side, his blue eyes dancing with mischief. "Unless you plan to have us removed?"

Illayana scowled, her gorgeous face scrunching up in displeasure. She remained silent.

Dominik chuckled, straightening his tie. "Didn't think so. Don't look so worried, my darling niece. I'm not here to cause any trouble. Now, where is that brother of mine?"

Without another glance in our direction, he strode off towards the tents set up in the backyard for the reception. Rayna winked at me before turning to face Illayana.

"I wish you nothing but happiness on your special day, my dear cousin." Her eyes darted between Illayana and I before a sly smile graced her lips. "I sure hope you don't run into any...problems."

With that, she turned and followed after her father.

"Okay. What the fuck was that?" I asked.

Illayana's eyes were glued on Rayna as she walked away, fury burning through her. "That is a long fucking story," she grumbled.

"I look forward to hearing it." I leant down and gave her a soft kiss on the cheek. She immediately melted in my arms, leaning into my embrace and taking comfort in the support I was offering.

"Later," she mumbled, tension slowing seeping out of her. "When we don't—"

A huge explosion ripped through the Volkov Estate, throwing Illayana and I into the air. I curved my body around hers, shielding her from as much of the blast as I could as we tumbled to the ground.

Screams erupted from all around us, the sounds of bullets whizzing past and men yelling in Russian and Italian filling my ears. Another explosion rocked the ground beneath me, debris raining down like confetti all around me. Blood spilled down my face and my body ached beyond belief, but I couldn't think about that right now.

"Illayana?"

I could feel my eyes beginning to close, the blood loss starting to take its toll on me. I fought the haziness as much as I could, but it was no use. The last thing I saw before my eyes closed was Illayana's unconscious body lying beside mine.

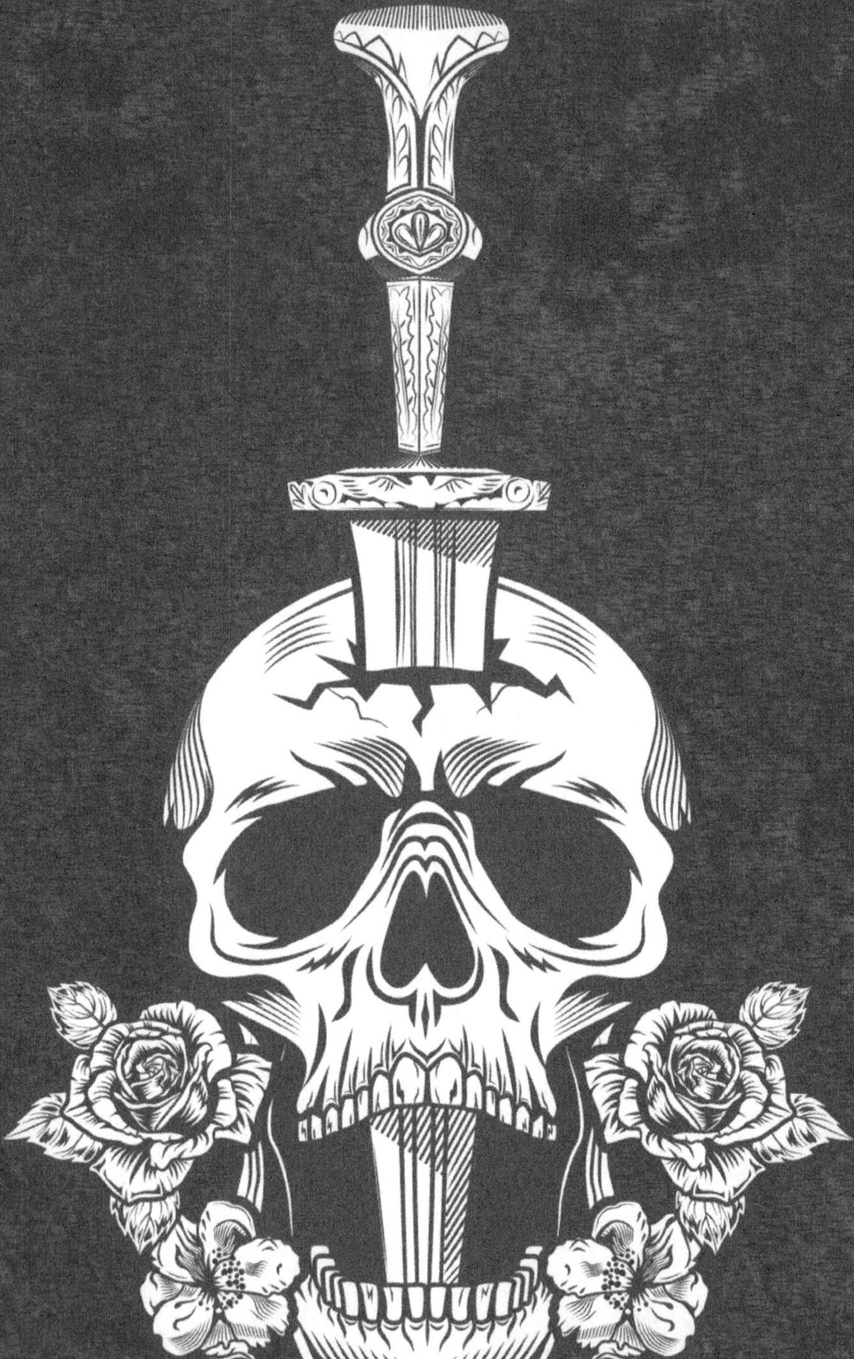

CHAPTER SEVENTEEN

Illayana De Luca

All I could feel was pain.

All I could see was smoke.

All I could hear was an incessant ringing in my ears.

I blinked, trying to get my eyes to focus, but it was like I was stuck in a haze. Nothing was coming through right. I could taste blood on my tongue and I knew that at least on some level, I had internal injuries.

Don't worry about that now. Worry about it later.

I heard someone calling my name over and over again, saw them standing over me, but my senses still weren't working properly. All I saw was a blur, all I could hear was ringing. That damn ringing.

A sharp slap to my face knocked my head to the side. That momentary sting somehow managed to snap me back to reality.

Who the fuck just slapped me?!

"Illayana!"

My eyes began to focus on the figure standing above me, the blurriness slowly starting to fade until Aleksandr's worried face came into view. I blinked rapidly, fighting the last bit of obscurity from my eyesight.

"Did you just fucking slap me?" I rasped, my voice rough and thick.

Relief flooded his face as he leant forward and wrapped me in his embrace. He sat me up, squeezing my body tightly.

"Can't...breathe," I choked.

His hold immediately loosened, but he kept his arms around me as he leant back to study my face. "Don't do that again. You scared the fucking shit out of me."

I scanned my surroundings, taking in all the destruction and chaos around me. Smoke and the scent of blood tainted the air, nearly overcoming all my senses. Bodies littered the ground, their limbs grotesquely contoured from being hurled into the air by the blast.

Bile rose in my throat from the sight and stench of all those bodies, and I had to work hard to keep it all down. People I knew, people I had just spoken to only moments ago, lying dead all around me. I had grown up familiar with death, had seen more dead bodies as a child than most people see in a lifetime. But this? This was fucked.

Now isn't the time to get squeamish, Illayana! Pull your shit together!

Fire blazed from our house, the entire front section crumbling as Cosa Nostra and Bratva men worked together to try and put it out while others fought against masked invaders.

I looked around, panic setting in when I couldn't find my father, brothers or Arturo.

"Where are they?" My eyes darted rapidly around my surroundings, searching for them.

Oh, God, please let them be okay.

The longer I went without seeing them, the worse my panic got. My heart started to beat faster and faster, my breathing becoming erratic.

"*Sestra,*" Aleksandr said sternly, gripping my shoulders and shaking me lightly. "Snap the fuck out of it before I slap it out of you again."

I narrowed my eyes and wretched my body out of his grasp. "Do it and you'll be fucking sorry," I snarled.

His eyes twinkled. "Ahhh, there she is. You had me scared there for a minute. Thought you were turning into one of those useless, hysterical women."

"Where...are...they?" I spat.

"They're fine, jeez." He rolled his eyes. "We turned the warehouse into a makeshift infirmary. Anybody with injuries is being put there for now. Arturo is one of them. He's fine!" he interjected. "Just a little banged up from shielding you from the blast. Lukyan and Nikolai are in charge of guarding the warehouse, making sure no one gets to it. We've called in every doc who's on our payroll within a thirty-mile radius to come and treat them."

"And Father?"

He gave me a stern look. "Where do you think he is?"

If I knew my father, he'd be in the thick of the chaos. And he'd be in a rage.

"What the fuck happened?"

"We were hit with some high-powered explosive device. Father sent me to find you immediately after the explosion and get you to safety. I have no idea how many we're up against here."

I could see a few of our soldiers fighting the attackers, but the majority of our men were working on getting the fire under control before it spread any further.

A rage unlike anything I had ever felt before blasted through me as I watched one of the assailants knife an Italian soldier.

Who the fuck do these people think they are?!

I rose to my feet, my body aching with protest. I ignored it, ignored the pain and just focused on all the rage building inside me.

"Whoa, whoa, whoa. Hold it." Aleksandr gripped my arms, holding me in place. "Where do you think you're going?"

I scowled, shaking him off. "Where do you think?! There's still enemies on our grounds. I'm not just gonna sit here and watch our men die!"

I grabbed the knife from my ankle holster and used it to cut the bottom half of my dress off. A twinge of guilt hit me right in the gut as the fabric fell to the blood-stained grass, but I couldn't think about that. There was no way I would have the manoeuvrability I needed to take down those fuckers with a skin-tight, floor length dress on.

"Nuh-uh. No fucking way. Father told me to get you out of here. If this is Nero, there's a good chance they're here for you."

I scoffed. "Let them fucking come," I growled, plucking my heels from my feet and snapping the heel off each one. The last thing I needed was sinking into the damn grass when I was fighting.

Aleksandr watched as I slipped them back onto my feet, his face set in a mask of disapproval.

I went to move, but he placed a hand on my shoulder, stopping me. "I swear to the damn devil, Aleksandr, if you don't let go of me right now, you'll be the one on the receiving end of all this rage I have inside me right now."

He arched an eyebrow.

I growled in frustration. I was almost at the point where I wanted to rip out my bloody hair. "If you're so fucking worried, then come with me! Cover my back."

He opened his mouth to respond when an ear-piercing scream had us both turning around. A few metres ahead of us, Lucian was being dragged away by his hair, kicking and screaming.

No!

I didn't hesitate. I couldn't. I bolted for him, shoving Aleksandr to the side and pushing my legs as hard as they could go. Lucian was fighting hard, thrashing his little limbs and screaming at the top of his lungs. He managed to get out of the attacker's grip, and I yelled for him.

"Lucian!"

His head snapped to me, relief and fear all over his face as he started running towards me, his attacker a mere inch behind him. I steadied my grip on my knife and prepared to throw.

"Down!" I yelled, pulling my arm back and taking aim.

Lucian dropped to the ground without hesitation. As soon as he was clear, I hurled my knife at the attacker, the blade piercing the man's chest with blazing speed.

He screamed in agony as he fell to the ground, his hands grasping at the knife in his chest before he went still.

Lucian tried to get to his feet, his legs shaking so badly he would have tumbled back down if Aleksandr hadn't been there to catch him.

"Lucian...Lucian." I ran my hands over his tiny body, looking for any sign of injury. "Are you okay?"

He nodded his head. "I'm f-fine," he stuttered.

Anger pulsed through me at the look of fear on his face, at the sight of blood on him.

"We need to get him out of here!" I hissed, looking at Aleksandr.

He scanned the area, looking for the best route out of the chaos. I saw Alessandro and Vincenzo fending off several assailants, their bodies placed firmly in front of Isabella, protecting her. Alessandro saw us, saw Lucian in Aleksandr's arms and tried moving towards us, but his attackers kept preventing him from advancing.

"There," I pointed to them. "Give him to me. You're better to defend."

He nodded, handing Lucian over. I grunted and adjusted his weight evenly. He sure was heavy for a nine-year-old. He wrapped his arms around my neck and legs around my torso as Aleksandr took point.

"Stay close."

I hugged Lucian closer to my body, determined to do everything I could to protect him. People ran all around us, some just trying to find a safe place to hold up until it was all over and some trying to fight our attackers. The pure mayhem was indescribable.

Relief flashed over Alessandro's face when he caught sight of Lucian and I slowly making our way over to him.

Everything's going to be okay, Lucian. I won't let anything happen to you.

We stayed low, manoeuvring around the broken furniture and dead bodies as quickly as we could.

Suddenly, we were falling. Everything happened so quickly. Too quickly. My brain was slow to process what was going on as Lucian and I fell to the ground. At the very last second, I managed to twist my body so I took the brunt of the fall, with Lucian landing on top of me.

Something squeezed my ankle and I looked down to see a man I had presumed dead gripping my ankle ferociously.

Fuck!

He started scrambling up my body and before I could even think about what I was doing, I gripped Lucian and flung his body over my head and out of the way just before the man climbed on top of me completely.

His hands wrapped around my throat instantly, applying an unbelievable amount of pressure.

I struggled, punching him as hard as I could in the abdomen, but he barely flinched. My vision started to blur, darkness slowly creeping in as I pounded at his chest over and over again. But it was no use. He was too big, too strong. He had caught me by surprise, and now I was paying the price.

My head spun as I tried gasping for breath, my fingers uselessly clawing at his hands.

This is it. This is how I'm going to die.

My eyes started to droop, life literally draining out of me, and all I could do was lie there and take it. Triumph flashed in his dark eyes when he realised I had given up, that there was no fight left in me.

I was so far gone my brain barely registered Lucian's war cry as he came running towards us, knife raised in the air. My attacker was too interested in watching the life drain from my eyes to notice. By the time he did, it was too late.

Lucian rammed the knife into the man's throat with a grunt, blood spurting out of the wound and all over his little suit. Lucian growled, baring his teeth like an animal as he shoved the blade in deeper.

The man's wide eyes shifted to Lucian, bewildered as he let go of my throat and gripped his own. A rush of air entered my lungs and I took a deep breath in, savouring the ability to fucking breathe again.

Lucian used the full force of his body to ram into my attacker, pushing him off me. The man tumbled to the ground, gurgling and choking on his own blood before he went completely still.

I breathed a sigh of relief as I watched his eyes close forever. Lucian put his little hands on mine and tried to help me stand.

"Are you okay, new big sister?" he asked, his hands and voice trembling.

Without hesitating, I threw my arms around him and wrapped him up into a tight bear hug. "Thank you, thank you, thank you!" I peppered his face with kisses, loving the sound of his laughter as he tried to squirm away from my affection.

My eyes found Aleksandr just as he snapped a man's neck and the body fell lifelessly to the ground. He stood still, taking several deep breaths, his eyes burning with rage before making his way over to Lucian and I. Five bodies lay at his feet, each one as dead and broken as the next.

So that's why he didn't come to my rescue. The fuckers had thrown five men at him, and they still lost.

His suit was torn, blood dripping down his face from a cut on his forehead but other than that he seemed relatively fine.

"Are you alright?" he asked, concerned.

I smiled and gave Lucian another big smooch on the cheek. "I am, thanks to this superstar."

Alessandro, Isabella and Vincenzo ran towards us the first chance they got, scooping Lucian up and hugging him tightly.

"*Ragazzo mio. Stai bene? Sei ferito? Dov'è la tua guardia? Dov'è Tomasso.*" *My boy. Are you okay? Are you hurt? Where's your guard? Where's Tomasso?* Alessandro spoke fast, the words flying from his mouth as he held his son.

"*Morto. La mia nuova sorella maggiore mi ha salvato. Dead. My new big sister saved me.*"

They all turned to look at me, gratitude radiating from them.

"Actually, he saved me." I pointed at the dead man with the knife sticking out of his throat.

"*Oh, ragazzo mio! Mio prezioso figlio!*" *Oh, my boy! My precious child!* Isabella shrieked, pulling Lucian from Alessandro's grip and wrapping him tightly in her own embrace.

"*Madre, sto.*" *Mother, stop.* Lucian whined, trying to escape his mother's clutches. His face turned bright red, embarrassed at the level of affection being displayed.

Alessandro stared at his son, pride wafting off him in waves. He smiled, tousling his hair. "*Ben fatto, figlio mio.*" *Well done, my son.* He looked around, scanning our surroundings and furrowed his brows. "Where's Theodora?"

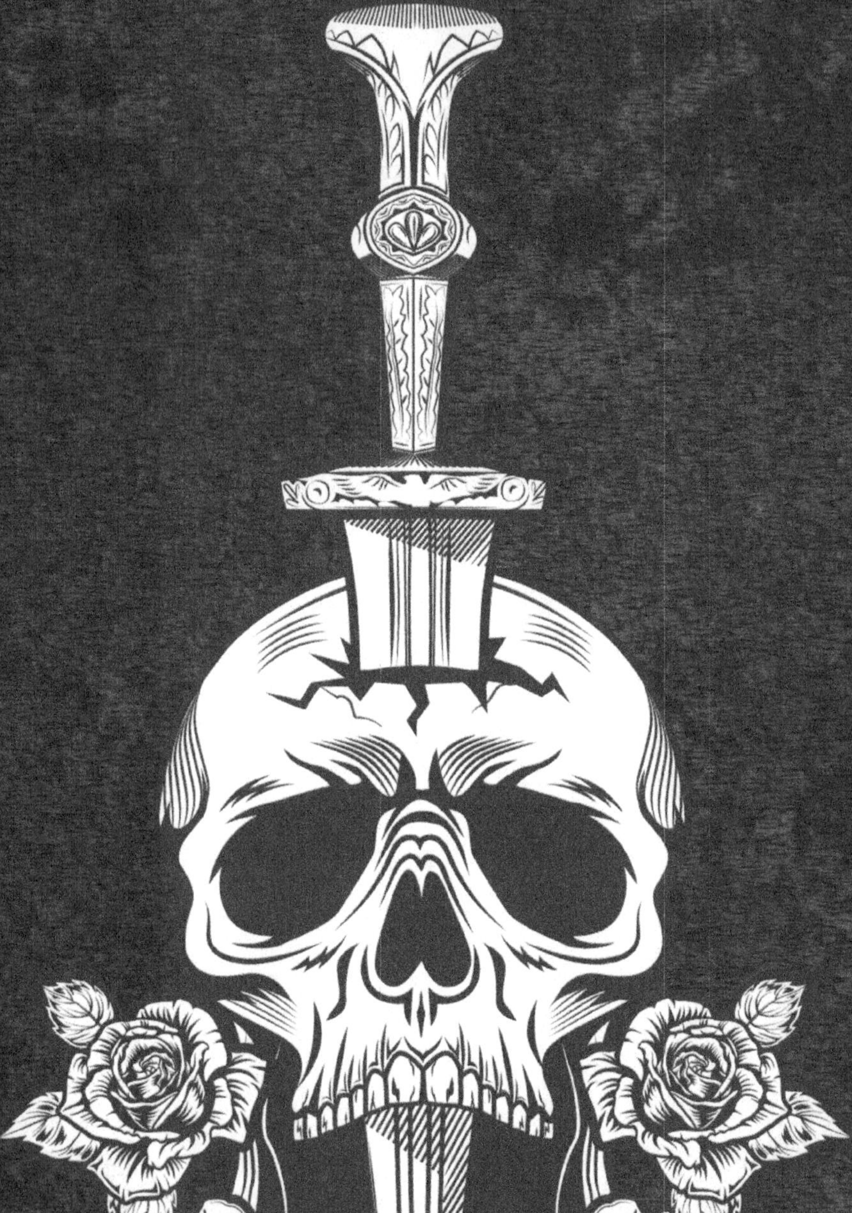

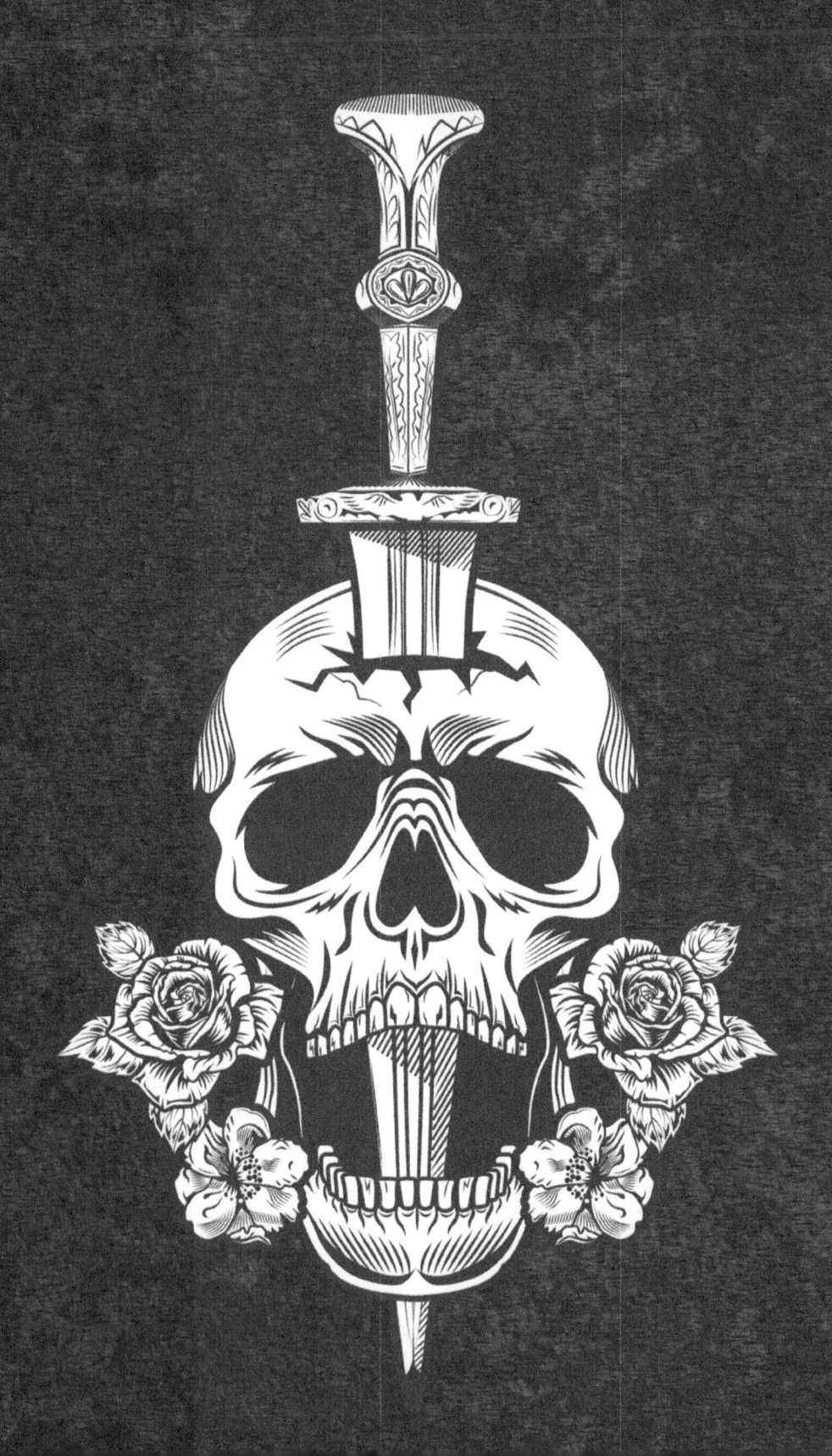

CHAPTER EIGHTEEN

Illayana De Luca

"What the fuck happened?!" My father yelled, staring into the eyes of the men before him.

We were all crammed into his office. Alessandro, his *consigliere*, Gabriel Dattoli—a tall, well-built gentleman with brown hair and dark eyes—and one of his *capos*, Stefano Fragola—a middle aged bald man with a slim build—were sitting on the couch on the far side of the room. Vincenzo stood at his father's side.

At the opposite end stood my father's new *Sovietnik*, Vladimir Turgenev, and his *Brigadier*, Andrei Petrov—the man responsible for recruiting and training our soldiers.

Vladimir was an attractive man with deep brown eyes, short black hair and a sculpted face. I'd only met him once since he took over for Maxim. From what I could tell, he deeply respected my father and was ecstatic about his rise in the ranks of the Bratva.

I had known Andrei since I was a kid. He was in his early sixties, but still kept himself in incredible shape. He was around 6'2 with an athletic build and strong, sharp features.

My father sat at his large mahogany desk, tapping his fingers impatiently as he looked around the room. My brothers stood like sentries behind him;

feet planted firmly on the ground, hands clasped behind their backs, faces hard and stoic.

I perched myself on the edge of my father's desk, legs crossed at the ankles, arms folded across my chest, my mind a jumbled mess. Before we had all crowded in there, I spent what felt like forever searching for Tatiana. Fear gripped me hard when I couldn't find her. That was, until Nikolai told me he had gotten her to safety after the first round of explosions. I was so fucking thankful she hadn't been hurt, but the thought that she might have been was enough to fuck with my emotions.

I tried to put it at the back of my mind and focus on the matter at hand.

The air was thick with tension as we all stared at one another in silence. Even though my father didn't address anyone directly, he was still expecting someone to answer his question. So, when he was greeted with nothing but that eerie silence and scathing looks, it only served to anger him more.

"I said, what the ***fuck*** happened?!" he roared, slamming his fists onto the desk. His blue eyes lit with rage as he stared menacingly at Vladimir and Andrei, but it was Nikolai who responded.

He stepped forward, moving in front of my father's desk. "At 9:18 a.m., two black SUVs rammed through our gates, both exploding simultaneously metres out from the house. Two teams of twenty then infiltrated the grounds, killing the guards posted at the gates, Ivan and Donat. One team moved inside while the other stayed outside confronting our men."

Father growled in anger, gritting his teeth as Nikolai grabbed his laptop and played the surveillance footage. It showed exactly what he described: two cars ramming the gates and exploding only seconds later.

"Secondary explosives were placed around the patio—three or four, I'd guess—which suggests an inside job. I've got Koyla searching through the footage to try and find who laid the charges."

"What were they after?" Father asked, leaning back in his leather chair.

"Ya ne znayu, Otets." I don't know, Father. "Their motive for the attack is still unclear. I'm inclined to believe they were attempting to stop the wedding, stop us from forming an alliance. But I cannot be sure."

It made sense, but why go to all the trouble of attacking us, only to be too late to actually stop the wedding? Unless that wasn't their ultimate goal. I mean, sure, it could have been a contributing factor, but part of me had this feeling I was missing something vital. I felt like the answer was on the tip of my tongue, that it was staring me straight in the face, yet I couldn't see it properly. It was driving me crazy.

"Round up their dead and bring them here. I want to see who we're up against." Father flicked his wrist towards the door as he issued his command. Vladimir gave a small bow before leaving the room.

"We're wasting time!" Alessandro snapped.

It was the first time I'd heard him speak since Theodora was taken. I was terrified of what Arturo's reaction would be when he found out. He was still unconscious from the initial attack after suffering a serious blow to the head. As soon as I was finished, I planned to be at his side, taking care of him.

What a way to spend your wedding night, huh?

"My daughter is out there somewhere, with these filthy men doing God knows what to her while we sit here talking!" Anger pulsed through him, enough to make even me a little uneasy.

Father watched him intently, his face softening the slightest bit. He rose from his chair and strode across the room. He lowered to his hunches, placing a comforting hand on his shoulder. *"Mio amico,"* My friend, "I promise you, we will find her. We will find the men who took her, get her back and make them pay."

Interesting.

I've never seen my father comfort someone like that before. Except for my brothers and I, and only when the situation absolutely called for it. He obviously had some deep history with Alessandro, more so than I'd originally thought.

A faint tapping sound had me looking around the room in confusion.

What is that?

Aleksandr watched me closely, his brows furrowed as I slowly walked around the room, hunting for the sound.

Tap.

Tap.

Tap.

There it was again!

I shoved Aleksandr and Lukyan to the side and got down on my hands and knees. I tapped on the hidden trap door behind my father's desk.

Not a lot of people knew about it. Just my father's most trusted soldiers, and obviously my brothers and I.

When I got a response of three more taps, I knew without a shadow of a doubt that someone was in there. But who? Who else knew about it apart from the people in this room?

I grabbed the latch and opened the trap door, completely taken by surprise by who was on the other end.

Nadia Petrov, Andrei's daughter.

We were close growing up. Our mothers were best friends, so in a way we were too. Until that dreadful day, ten years ago. It wasn't only my mother who was killed, but Nadia's too.

You would have thought something like that would have brought us closer together, that we would have leant on each other for comfort and support during such a difficult time. But no. It was the opposite.

Nadia blamed me, blamed my family for the death of her mother. And in a way, she had a right to. It was us the Voznesenskys wanted dead, and unfortunately Nadia's mother was collateral damage to them. After their deaths we fell apart, only speaking when the occasion called for it. Like now. I was surprised she was even at my wedding. Her father must have dragged her there.

"Nadia." I tried to mask all those repressed feelings wafting through me at having seen her and reached down, offering her a hand.

She hesitated for only a few seconds before accepting it and climbing out.

"Nadia?" Andrei's deep voice came from behind me." What are you doing in there? I thought you left after the ceremony!" He moved to her side, his eyes scanning over her, looking for injuries.

Nadia's chocolate brown eyes found her father's and she smiled reassuringly. "I was on my way out when the explosion happened." —she flicked her auburn hair over her shoulder as she bent down to the trap door again— "I found this little one being dragged outside by a few of those fuckers. I had no clue who she was, who her parents were, so I hid her in here until it all blew over."

Theodora's beautiful face popped out from the trap door, her emerald eyes glistening with tears and her face red from crying.

The second Alessandro spotted her, he jumped off the couch and ran for her, wrapping her into a tight embrace. *"La mia bambina! Stai bene? Sei ferita? Ero così preoccupato per te, principessa!" My little girl! Are you okay? Are you hurt? I was so worried about you, princess!*

"*Padre!" Father!* Theodora cried. She buried her face into the crook of his neck, wrapping her limbs around his body like a spider monkey.

Alessandro ran a hand up and down her back comfortingly, kissing her hair and whispering soothing words in Italian.

Vincenzo came over and plucked her from Alessandro's grip, despite his father's

protest. He squeezed her tightly, kissing her on the forehead and closing his eyes. "*Per Dio, non farlo, Theodora. Ero così spaventata per te.*" *By God, don't do that, Theodora. I was so scared for you.*

Something I had noticed about the De Lucas was that whenever anything stressful happened, they all seemed to revert back to their native tongue. It was a good thing that I was fluent in Italian, otherwise I would never know what they were bloody saying.

Alessandro leant over, his face full of love and affection as he kissed her on the cheek. "Take her to your mother. Now. Don't let her or Lucian out of your sight, do you hear me? They were both targeted during this attack. I'm not risking anything else happening," Alessandro told Vincenzo, his eyes hard.

"*Si, Padre.*" *Yes, Father.*

Vincenzo immediately turned on his heels, leaving the room in a hurry. Alessandro turned to Nadia, extending his hand. "I can't thank you enough for saving my daughter, for keeping her safe. If you ever need anything, the De Luca family will be there for you." He bowed respectfully, bringing her hand to his lips and kissing the back of it.

Nadia blushed, her olive skin turning beet red. I couldn't blame her.

Despite his age, Alessandro was in great shape, and he was one of the most handsome men I'd ever met. Clearly, good genes ran in their family.

"It was really nothing. I'm sure anyone else would have done the same thing in my position."

Alessandro's lips twitched. "I doubt it."

The door to my father's office opened and several men came piling in, carrying the dead bodies of our enemies. Twenty-seven in total. Not bad, considering we were taken completely by surprise. Father pointed to the empty space in the middle of the room and the bodies were dropped carelessly in the spot he indicated.

They were all dressed in identical clothing: black long-sleeved shirts, black pants, black boots, black gloves and black balaclavas over their heads.

"Strip them," Father commanded.

The men stripped them down to nothing but their boxers.

Once stripped, it was easy to tell which nationality they were. The ink on their skin was very foretelling. They were a mixture of Mexican and Italian descent, meaning it had to be Nero behind the attack.

My father growled in anger, clearly coming to the same conclusion I did. He kicked one of the bodies in frustration. "Reach out to our contacts in the LVPD and get them to run their prints through the database. I want names, addresses, everything you can get on these fuckers. Dispose of their bodies discreetly afterwards."

My father's men moved as one, picking up the lifeless bodies and heading towards the door. But something still wasn't right. Something was gnawing at me, at my mind. And if I didn't figure it out soon, it was going to make me crazy.

Well, crazier.

I moved to the pile of blood-stained clothes that had come from our attackers and started sifting through it.

"Is this it?" I asked no one in particular.

"Is what it?" Aleksandr moved to my side, studying the pile of clothes.

"Is this all they had on them? Where are their weapons?"

"Weapons?" Stefano scoffed. "What weapons? All I saw were knives and a few mediocre handguns."

Everyone in the room nodded in agreement, which only served to confuse me more. I furrowed my brows as my mind continued to work. My father sensed my confusion and moved to join Aleksandr and I.

"What is it, *moya doch?" My daughter?*

I tried to get my thoughts under control. What *was* it? Something. Something wasn't right. I was missing...something.

"If you were planning to attack not only one of your enemies, but two, would you send your men into the fight with nothing but a bunch of knives and some shitty handguns?"

Father narrowed his eyes. "Of course not."

"No, you wouldn't. You'd send them in with the best of the best, ensuring their victory."

Father nodded like it was an obvious statement.

"So...why didn't Nero?"

The room fell silent, my question left hanging in the air. Why would Nero send his men to attack when they were seriously outgunned? It made no fucking sense.

"Maybe Nero's just an idiot?" Lukyan asked, shrugging his shoulders.

"Nero may be an idiot, but even he wouldn't send his men into battle without appropriate weaponry," Alessandro interjected.

"And yet, that's exactly what he's done. Unless..."

"Unless what?" Nikolai asked.

And then it clicked into place. "Unless...he didn't have a choice."

My father and Aleksandr both frowned, processing my words. Right at that moment, standing side by side with a near identical look on their faces, they were the epitome of father and son.

My father's brows shot up to his hairline, a look of surprise on his face that quickly morphed into anger. "Check the shipment," he barked.

Aleksandr moved instantly, wasting no time leaving the room. He returned a few minutes later and it was evident by the look on his face that we weren't going to like what he had to say.

"It's gone. Everything we had packed and ready for the De Lucas—gone." He shook his head, his lips drawn back in a snarl. "The fuckers even cleaned out our armoury."

My father stared at him, pure rage rolling off of him in waves. Anger flooded his veins, making him clench his fists and grit his teeth. He cracked his neck left, then right, then rolled his shoulders back.

Oh, no.

He roared at the top of his lungs, slamming his fists onto his desk once, twice, three times. The timber cracked under the relentless pressure, which only seemed to anger him further. He placed his hands underneath the desk and flipped it into the air, sending it flying across the room in his fit of rage. People scrambled out of the way to avoid being hit by what was left of his (very expensive) desk.

"Podozhdi poka ya ikh ne dostanu!" Wait until I get my fucking hands on them! he growled in Russian.

"Wait, they took everything?" I asked Aleksandr.

His crystal blue eyes watched our father briefly, concern etched all over his face, before he looked at me and nodded.

"Even the AK-47s and P-90s?"

My father had a new contract with a local MC Gang here in Vegas. We had never worked with them before, but they needed some serious hardware for a turf war going on with a rival gang—and they offered us double. Two cases of AK-47s and P-90s were set to be delivered in a matter of days.

Lukyan stepped forward, his eyes flashing with excitement. "Illayana, you're a fucking genius."

"What?" Andrei asked, looking between Lukyan and I.

"My father can be quite...paranoid." My eyes flicked to him and he shrugged in response. "When he makes an arrangement with people we've never worked with before, he places a tracking device in with the shipment. On the slim chance they decide to double cross us and take off with the guns without paying, we have a way of tracking them down."

"Activate it. Find out where they are," my father snapped.

Nikolai started doing his usual techy shit. After a couple of minutes, he turned his laptop to face us, a wicked grin on his face. "Got 'em. They're a couple hours away, in a town called San Bernardino."

My father smiled, a truly evil and vindictive smile.

"They must be driving back to Chicago. This is the perfect opportunity to get our guns back."

My father nodded. "We'll leave at nightfall. They have our weapons, so we're already at a disadvantage. We'll need the cover of darkness to help even the odds."

"How are we going to take them on? We're seriously outgunned here," I asked.

"I think it's time I make a call to your godfather," he smirked. "Andrei, I want twenty of our best soldiers here, ready to go by dark."

Andrei bowed and left the room, Nadia in tow.

My father faced Alessandro. "Will you be joining us?"

Alessandro scoffed. "Do you even have to ask?" He pulled out his cell phone and put it to his ear, his eyes sparkling with anticipation. "Vincenzo, round up the men. We're going hunting."

"Good. Because I'm ready to fucking kill something."

We all turned at the sound of a new voice. Arturo stood at the door, bloody and bandaged, his multi-coloured eyes blazing with anger as he stared into the room.

My heart immediately started beating faster at the sight of him. Even beaten and bloody, he was still the most beautiful man I'd ever laid eyes on.

"Arturo," I breathed, moving to him.

His eyes scanned my body, relief flashing on his face at seeing me unharmed. *"Ciao, moglie."* Hello, wife.

Before I even had a chance to respond, his lips were on mine. He kissed me like he hadn't seen me in days, with a fervour and passion I had never seen before, never experienced. I felt my body heat up as he pulled me closer to him, my blood boiling with desire. His tongue dipped into my mouth, his taste overwhelming all my thoughts, all my senses.

I moaned in pleasure, my hands moving to grip his thick, muscular shoulders for support. I deepened the kiss, our tongues dancing together in unrefined passion. It was the most intoxicating sensation I had ever experienced. And then, too soon, it was over.

Arturo stepped back and gave me that sly motherfucking grin that always made me hot. His eyes snapped to Alessandro and my father, both standing in the centre of the room.

"When do we leave?"

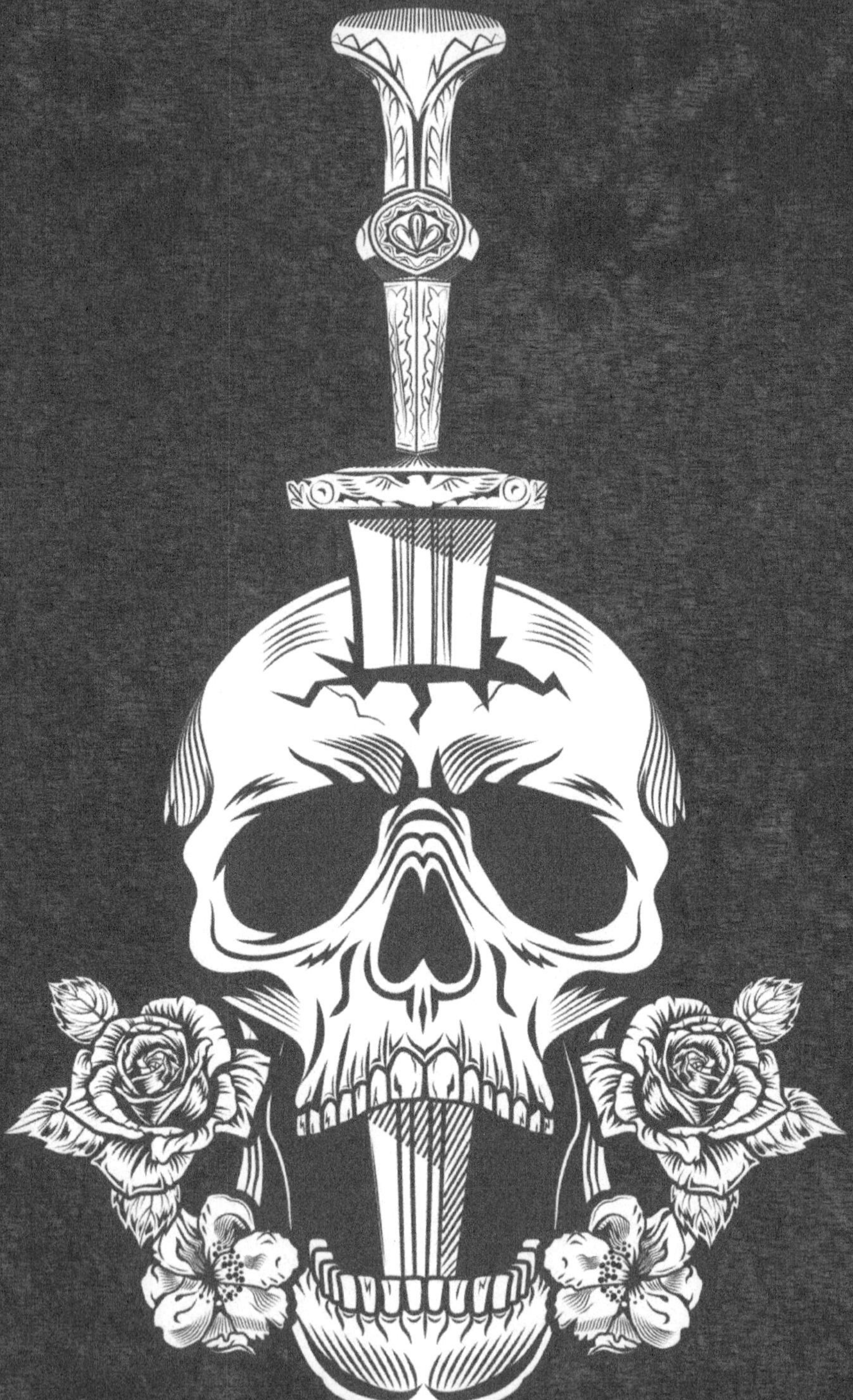

Chapter Nineteen

Arturo De Luca

"I really don't think it's a good idea." Illayana pursed her lips as she watched me with disapproval.

We had been arguing for the better part of an hour, and we still weren't making any progress. I wanted to join the hunting party that was going out to get our guns that night. She wanted me to stay here and rest, to let my body heal itself from the injuries I sustained in the explosion.

I could see her point, could see she was just concerned for me. But that was something she'd just have to get used to. I'd be head of the Cosa Nostra soon, which meant my life was going to be in constant danger. Better she get familiar with that feeling now, as opposed to later.

"I understand," I said, slowly unwrapping the bandage from around my torso.

I sat comfortably on the edge of her bed, Illayana sitting with her legs crossed on the floor directly in front of me. Her long, dark hair was up in a high ponytail and she was wearing a pair of black tights and a loose fitting top. She looked just as beautiful as she had walking down the aisle.

Fuck, it's my wedding night.

"I don't think you do. Your body has just gone through a major trauma. The last thing you need to do is more fighting."

I groaned and had to refrain from rolling my eyes. Even I knew that rolling your eyes at a woman was just asking for trouble. "I know. You've said all this."

I tossed the used bandage to the side and began applying more antiseptic cream to my wounds. In truth, I wasn't that badly injured. Just some grazing and pretty intense bruising. My body ached whenever I moved (not that I'd tell Illayana that) and I had a mild headache, but that was it. It looked a lot worse than it actually was (which was why I think she was so determined to keep me there).

"Then maybe you should fucking listen," she snapped.

I arched an eyebrow, secretly enjoying that sassy attitude more than I cared to admit. "Looks like someone put their cranky pants on this morning," I mumbled, wrapping a new round of bandages around my torso.

She scoffed, stretching her long legs out in front of her. "If you think this is me cranky, you're in for a fucking surprise."

Okay, that didn't sound good.

The safest thing I could think of to do was change the subject. It was clear we weren't going to solve this problem any time soon, unless she decided to finally listen to me.

Fucking doubtful.

We still had a couple of hours to kill before we were scheduled to leave. Nikolai and Lorenzo were monitoring the GPS feed, in case they moved positions and we needed to readjust our plan.

I pushed off the bed, slinking down to the ground in front of Illayana, and leant back against the mattress. She watched me cautiously, her arctic blue eyes scanning my body for any sign of pain or discomfort.

Nice try, kotenok. I'm not going to make it that easy for you.

"Tell me about Dominik. I know there's an interesting story there."

She laughed, her face lighting up with amusement. "That's an understatement. It's also an incredibly long story."

I shrugged. "So what? We've got the time."

She pursed her lips and frowned. I could tell she didn't really want to get into it right then, but I couldn't help myself. I was dying to know. She took a deep breath in and sighed. "Fine. But stop looking at me like I just killed your damn dog."

I gave her a wide grin, flashing my teeth. She shook her head and chuckled, amusement dancing in her eyes.

"It really is a long story, so I'll just give you the short version." She took another deep breath before continuing. "As I'm sure you've figured out, my father is a twin. An identical twin. Usually, the role of the next *Pakhan* went to the first-born son. And even though Dominik was born two minutes before my father, my grandfather decided he wanted them to compete for the position. So, while they were growing up, he pitted them against each other, made them compete over anything and everything. My grandfather only wanted the best to walk in his footsteps. Over the years, it became clear who the superior twin was."

"Your father?"

She nodded, pride shining in her eyes. "He was better at everything. Planning, strategizing, fighting. You name it. The better my father was, the more Dominik hated him. He held years of resentment towards him. He felt that the role of *Pakhan* was his birth right since he was born first, even if it was only by a few minutes. He hated the fact that he had to compete for what he viewed was rightfully his. One day, my grandfather decided he wanted to expand into the States, but he also didn't want to leave the safe confines of Russia. So, he decided to send my father to establish territory and begin the Volkov reign here in America. My uncle didn't have a good reaction to that."

"Oh, I bet he didn't," I interjected, immersed in the story.

"He felt like he was being cheated out of what was his. A few nights before we were all set to leave, Dominik tried to kill my father. He figured the best way to show who was better once and for all was a fight to the death. He snuck into my father's room late at night and tried to slit his throat, but my father had always been a light sleeper. He woke just before the blade pierced his skin, and once he was awake, all hell broke loose. My father was so enraged by the fact that his own brother tried to kill him that he beat Dominik within an inch of his life. We moved to Vegas the next day and didn't speak a word to Dominik until he came to America years later."

Daaaaamn. That really was an interesting story.

I couldn't believe that, for one, Dominik tried to kill his own brother. And two, that Dimitri had let him live. He always struck me as an eye for an eye type of guy. So, the fact that his own brother tried to murder him and he just let it slide was quite strange to me.

"My turn," she said, adjusting her position and stretching out her legs. "Gabriella. I want to know what's going on between the two of you."

I frowned. "There's nothing going on."

"Didn't look like it earlier." She arched an eyebrow and I sighed.

"We've known each other our whole lives."

"Uh-huh. And?"

"And that's it. Everyone thought we'd get married. They actually kind of pushed for it. But we didn't."

"They?"

"My parents, her parents, a few of the other high-ranking families in the *famiglia.*" I shrugged. "I wouldn't go as far as to say we're friends, but we're familiar with each other."

"Did you guys fuck?"

I winced. I was hoping to avoid that question. "Yes."

"A lot?"

"Define a lot."

She bit her lip, thinking it over. The action made me want to lean over and pull her lip from her teeth so I could take its place. "Once a week?"

"No." I was really hoping she'd just drop the subject, but of course she didn't.

"Once a month?"

"I don't know the exact number," I said, avoiding the question.

"It's simple. Did you stick your dick in her at least once a month?" she snapped.

I narrowed my eyes. "Yes."

"For how long?"

Groaning, I ran my hand down my face. "Can we just drop it? I mean, this is a fucking stupid topic to talk about."

"If you want, we can talk about you going off on the hunt later tonight instead?"

"I'd rather not, to be honest. What about your cousin? Dominik's daughter? What's the story there?"

To be honest, I couldn't give a rat's ass about that slutty cousin of hers, but the subject change seemed to have distracted her from the argument we were having.

Anger flashed in her blue eyes. She scowled, her face scrunching up in displeasure. "I don't want to talk about her."

"Aw, come on. I bet you're just dying to bitch about her."

She shook her head, her ponytail swaying in the air around her. "Nuh-uh. I know what you're trying to do, and it's not going to work."

"And what is it that I'm trying to do?" I asked innocently.

She slapped me playfully on the chest, her smile lighting up the room. "Distract me. And like I said, it won't work. I grew up with three brothers. I've seen all the tricks."

I smirked. She hadn't seen *my* tricks.

I slowly ran my fingers down her arm, enjoying the goose bumps that arose from my touch. She took a sharp intake of breath, her eyes blazing with fire and lust. Any thought of Gabriella vanished from her mind as I slowly trailed my hand lower, skimming across her stomach and stopping just above the waistband of her pants.

I watched her closely and all I saw on her face was a burning need. I dipped my hand down the front of her pants and the first thing I felt was lace.

I groaned, my eyes almost rolling into the back of my head. "Do you have any idea how long I've been dying to touch you like this?" I whispered seductively, pulling her body closer.

She moaned, her head falling back as I cocooned her in a tight embrace.

"So fucking long. Since that first moment I laid eyes on you," I breathed into the crook of her neck, sending shivers down her spine. "And now...now I'm going to fucking have you—"

Knock, Knock

"Apologies, Miss Illayana. Master Lukyan has sent for you," a soft, feminine voice said from the other side of the door.

I growled in frustration, burying my forehead in her shoulder. "You've got to be fucking kidding me," I growled.

She chuckled and ran her fingers through my hair soothingly, that one act causing shivers to run down my spine. I was a sucker for head scratches.

"Let me see what she has to say, otherwise Lukyan could come himself."

Oh, fuck no.

I gave her a little tap on the butt as she stood and made her way to the door.

"Hurry."

She tossed a seductive look over her shoulder, biting her lower lip and winking at me. It wasn't helping the massive hard-on I was sporting. I quickly grabbed a pillow from her bed and used it to cover myself just as the door opened.

The tiny woman on the other side kept her head down and hands clasped behind her back. "Apologies for disturbing you, Miss Illayana. Master Lukyan sent me. He requests your presence in the warehouse."

"No, thanks!" I yelled from my position on the floor. "Tell him she's busy."

The woman's head rose slightly, her brown eyes flicking to me, then Illayana. "Miss?"

"What does he want?" she asked, her head tilting to the side.

No way. This kid was going to cockblock me and he wasn't even in the fucking room.

"I'm not sure, Miss Illayana. He was sparring with a Cosa Nostra man when he asked."

Illayana nodded. "Okay, thank you."

She closed the door and turned to look at me, excitement brimming all over her face. "I've just thought of the perfect solution to our problem."

I arched an eyebrow. "I didn't realise we had a problem?"

"You want to go on this revenge hunt tonight, I want you to stay home and recover. Neither one of us is going to back down. Hence the problem."

"I don't need to recover. I told you, I'm fine."

She raised her chin defiantly and narrowed her eyes. "Prove it then. Spar with me."

I raised my brows in surprise, not at all prepared for that statement. "Spar...with you?" I asked incredulously.

She glared at me, her usually soft, delicate features turning hard and stoic. "Yes. With me."

I suddenly felt very uncomfortable. "No, I can't."

"Why not?"

Fuck. I could see the anger flowing through her like lava, her lip curling up into a very unladylike snarl.

"Be reasonable. I don't want to hurt you." I softened my voice in an attempt to calm her down, but it seemed to have the opposite effect.

Her fists clenched at her side, her entire body going rigid. Her face started to turn red, steam basically coming out of her ears.

Oh, fuck. That can't be a good sign.

"I see," she said sternly, gritting her teeth.

Without another word, she spun around and walked out of the room.

"Illayana?" I called out after her, but she ignored me.

I sighed, dragging a hand down my face and cursing before following her.

I'm way too old for this shit.

"Illayana!" I tried again, but she continued to walk on as if she hadn't heard me at all.

By the time I reached the stairs, she was already halfway down. The air around her seemed to vibrate angrily with each step she took.

"I'm not chasing after you!" I yelled down to her.

She ignored me. Again.

Okay, now I'm getting pissed off.

"Illayana!" I snapped.

She reached the bottom of the stairs and moved out of my field of vision without so much as a glance back in my direction.

Fine. If she doesn't want to be around me, why should I care? She'll be back. They always come back.

And yet, the longer I stood at the top of the stairs, waiting for the wretched woman to come to her senses, the more uneasy I began to feel.

"If you think she's going to come crawling back to you, you're going to be waiting there a long time," a deep voice spoke from the shadows.

I turned to see one of Dimitri's men move into the light and stand right in front of me.

I shrugged and peered over the railing. "I don't care if she comes back." But even as the words left my mouth, I knew they were a crock of shit.

The man chuckled, shaking his head. "Right. Of course."

He went to slink back into the shadows, our conversation seemingly coming to an end, but I couldn't help asking one question.

"Just out of curiosity, if I was interested in finding out where she was—and I'm not saying I am—but if I *was*...where would she be?"

I kept my gaze forward, refusing to look at the man. But even in my peripheral vision, I could see the smirk on his face. I wanted to slap it right off him.

"Where she always goes when someone pisses her off."

When he didn't continue, I pinned him with a hard glare, arching an eyebrow. I didn't care if he was a Bratva man. If he didn't hurry up and talk, I really would slap it out of him.

"The warehouse."

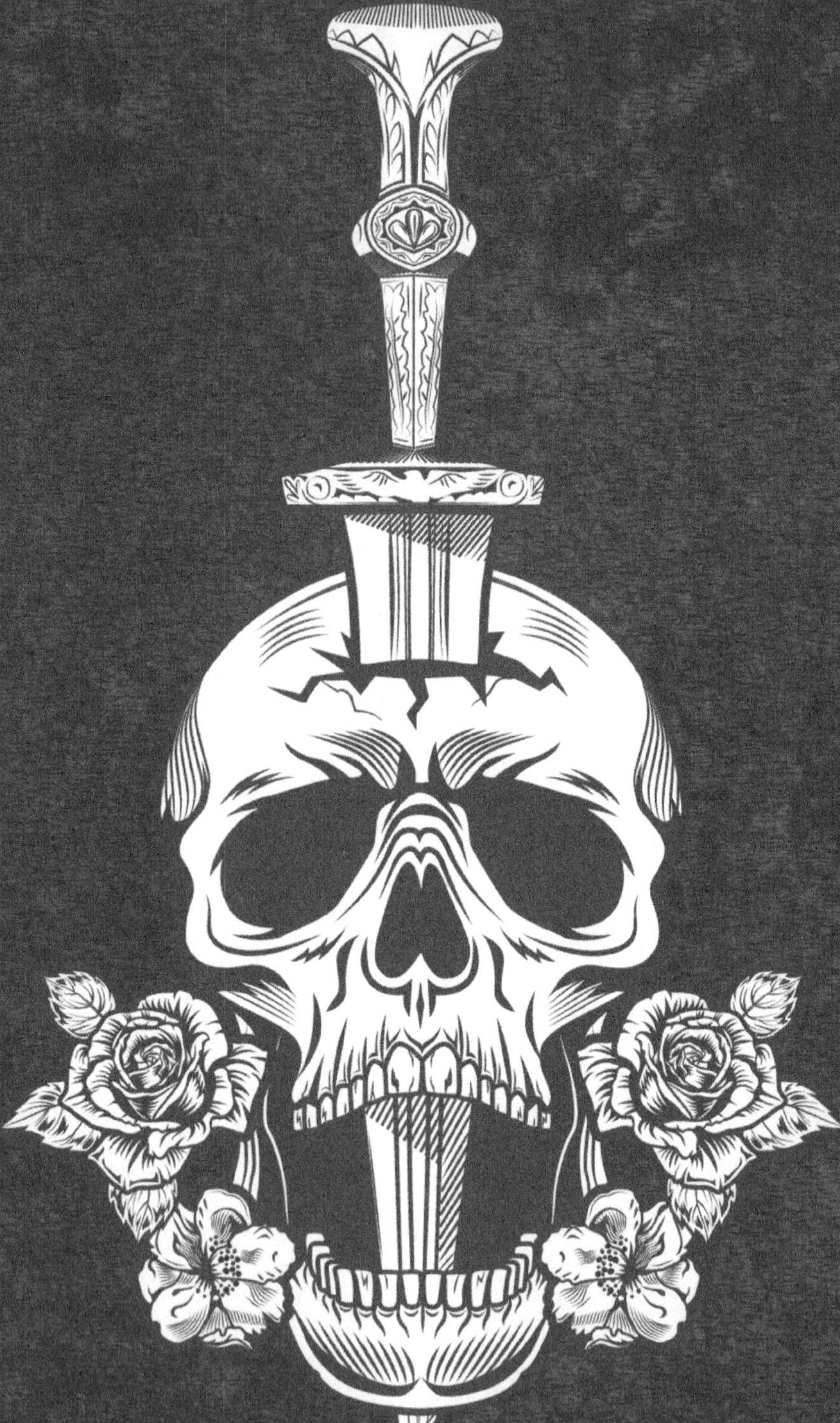

CHAPTER TWENTY

Arturo De Luca

I'm not going to do it.

Nope. Nuh-uh. No fucking way.

I'm Arturo Giovanni De Luca. I chase after no woman, not even my wife.

Okay, if that was even remotely true, then why are you halfway to the warehouse right now?

Sometimes I wish I could bitch-slap my own damn brain.

This was unfamiliar territory for me. Usually, when I had an argument with a woman, all I'd have to do is click my fingers and they'd come running back.

But not Illayana.

What pissed me off the most was that I kinda liked it. I liked that I couldn't control her. I liked that I had no clue what she was going to do next. It was...refreshing.

When I walked into the warehouse, the atmosphere was electric. You couldn't tell that mere hours ago, a devastating event occurred on these grounds.

Excitement buzzed in the air as people crowded around the boxing ring, cheering for more bloodshed. All the people injured during the attack had been moved to another room in the building, freeing up the space that allowed our soldiers to blow off some much-needed steam.

Illayana sat between Lorenzo and Luca, legs crossed underneath her and face smiling. I bristled at the closeness of their bodies and glared hard at my men.

Christian and Lukyan were in the ring, trading blows. Nothing too serious, that much I could tell. Just a friendly sparring match.

The crowd went wild, everyone jumping to their feet and clapping hard when Christian struck hard, his fist connecting with Lukyan's face. His head snapped to the side, blood trailing from his now-split lip and down his chin.

Lukyan turned his head back to face Christian, and the fucker smiled.

A feminine voice called my name and I turned. Gabriella strode towards me, her eyes red from crying and still wearing her white ball gown from earlier. Except now, it was covered in dirt and blood. She hugged me tightly, laying her head on my chest as she cried hysterically.

"Oh my god, Arturo. Mum's still unconscious. She hasn't woken up yet. I can't believe this is happening."

I hugged her back stiffly. "She'll be alright."

"But what if she's not? What if she dies?" she hiccupped, burying her face deeper into my chest.

"She won't." I pulled out of her arms and took a step back, putting some distance between us. Her face dropped for a second and then she covered it with a small smile.

She glanced around the warehouse. "This is a little crazy, isn't it? Can you believe they're this barbaric? Fighting each other while people place bets and cheer them on?" she asked, shaking her head in disgust.

"I think it's pretty awesome, actually."

She threw her head back in laughter. "Of course you would." She took a step towards me and brushed her fingers over a small bruise that had formed just under my eye from the impact of the blast that threw me into the air. "Poor baby, you're hurt."

Illayana's gaze found mine over the crowd and the smile on her face vanished, her eyes narrowing into slits.

Fuck.

Before I even had the chance to back away from Gabriella, she rose to her feet. We stared at each other for what felt like bloody hours, but I knew it had been barely ten seconds. I quickly stepped away from Gabriella, but the damage was done.

She broke eye contact first, moving with determination towards the ring. Lorenzo and Luca immediately stood, following close behind her. Once she reached the ring, she slapped her palm twice on the hard floor to get her brother's attention.

Lukyan straightened from his defensive position and moved to the edge of the ring, bending down and sticking his head between the ropes so Illayana could whisper something in his ear. After a few seconds, his eyes locked onto me from across the room and he smiled. He gave a single nod before rising to his full height and making his way over to Christian.

Illayana moved quickly to a wall on the far side of the building that housed a variety of different weapons. Knives, daggers, swords, axes, fighting sticks, staffs, batons. The list went on and on. The whole thing was actually pretty damn impressive.

She picked up a pair of fighting sticks and a long wooden staff, making her way back to the ring.

Christian had already jumped down, joining his brother and Lorenzo in the crowd. Lukyan stood shirtless in the centre of the ring, blood and sweat dripping down his torso. He wrapped his long hair up into a high bun to help keep it out of his face and lightly jumped up and down on the spot, keeping the adrenaline pumping through him.

I could hear Gabriella's shrill voice still talking to me, but I wasn't processing a single word she was saying. My eyes were glued to the scene playing out in front of me.

Illayana threw the staff like a javelin and Lukyan caught it with ease, twirling it around his body effortlessly before landing in a fighting stance, facing Illayana. She had a fighting stick in each hand and a look of determination on her face as she stopped directly in front of the ring.

Oh, fuck off.

I took a step forward, intent on locking this shit down right fucking now, when a strong hand gripped my shoulder. I turned my head slightly, curious to see who the fuck thought it was okay to stop me, when I saw Dimitri standing at my side.

He glared at Gabriella and she shrunk back, cowering. He flicked his head to the side, signalling for her to go away. She did, running back to the infirmary room where her mother was.

He eyed his children curiously. "You said something to piss her off, didn't you?" he asked.

I was a little irritated that he figured out I was responsible for her bad mood so quickly.

"Anything I say makes that woman mad."

Dimitri chuckled. "True. She is quite temperamental, just like her mother. Word of advice?"

I grunted.

"She's getting up there to prove a point to you, and only you. Pay attention."

I narrowed my eyes. "That sounds an awful lot like a command, Dimitri," I sneered, my anger rising. I wasn't in the fucking mood to be spoken to like I was one of his goddamn soldiers.

"That's because it is. Trust me when I say she'll be even more pissed off if she has to do this shit again just to prove her point to you."

Illayana jumped into the ring and my focus snapped to her. She twirled her fighting sticks around her body a few times before crouching into a position similar to Lukyan's.

The emotions in the room were a mixture of excitement, confusion and worry. The Bratva men were talking to each other fast in Russian, placing bets on who would win and passing money around. The Cosa Nostra men—*my men*—were looking at my new wife in bewilderment.

Bodies facing one another, Illayana and Lukyan both turned their heads towards their father. After a few tense seconds, Dimitri's deep voice could be heard throughout the entire warehouse.

"*Nachat.*" Begin.

Lukyan lunged, bringing his staff down hard and fast, aiming for Illayana's head. Illayana didn't falter, didn't hesitate. She brought her fighting sticks up high over her head in an X formation, blocking his attack. She shoved forward, pushing Lukyan back a couple steps, and went on the offensive.

She struck quickly. Left, right, high, low, alternating between both hands. But Lukyan blocked each strike, matching her stride. Lukyan swiped his staff at her head and she ducked underneath it. In a move almost too fast to track, she jumped, pressed her foot into his thigh and pushed off, spinning in the air and kicking him straight in the face. Lukyan's head snapped back, the crowd cheered and Illayana landed on her feet with a cheeky smirk.

Damn, that was sexy.

My eyes were glued on the fight, on *her*. She was unlike any woman I'd ever met in my life. I couldn't tear my eyes from her even if I wanted to.

Illayana didn't give him a chance to retaliate. She ran at him, jumping into the air. She brought her fighting sticks together and struck hard, using her momentum and gravity to deliver a harder blow.

Lukyan brought his staff up quickly to defend, but the power of Illayana's attack broke his staff in two, forcing him to stumble back.

Lukyan looked down at his hands, each filled with a piece of his broken staff, and then looked back at Illayana. They stared at each other for a few seconds before they both chucked their weapons to the side.

They ran at one another, meeting in the centre of the ring. Lukyan swung a brawny arm, Illayana ducked and delivered a solid punch to his abdomen. Quick as a cat, she followed with an uppercut to his chin. Then she spun on the balls of her feet, planting a kick to his chest and sending him flying back.

She pounced on him, wrapping her long legs around his arm and locking him into an arm bar. Lukyan struggled, his grunts of frustration loud enough for all to hear, but Illayana's hold was airtight. He wasn't getting out of it. She increased the pressure and he shouted out in pain.

Everyone was on their feet, clapping and cheering at the fight taking place.

"Don't be a fucking idiot, Lukyan," Illayana grunted. "Tap. I've got you."

Even from where I stood, I could see the smirk on Lukyan's face. "Never," he growled. Just one word, yet it was laced in pain.

Illayana hissed, increasing the pressure yet again, and I knew she was only seconds away from breaking his arm.

"Illayana," Dimitri called out. *"Nay slomay emu ruku." Do not break his arm.*

Illayana growled in frustration but relented, loosening her hold on her brother. She brought her leg down hard and fast, using the heel of her foot to strike him in the chest. She rolled backwards, crouching on her haunches.

Lukyan gripped his chest, his face contorted in pain as he slowly got to his feet. He rubbed his sternum, eyes narrowed in anger at his younger sister.

In the blink of an eye, he moved. One second, he was a few feet from her, the next he was directly in front of her, a hand wrapped around her throat. He lifted her a few feet off the ground, snarled in her face and then hurled her to the floor.

I didn't even realise I was moving towards the ring until a set of hands gripped my arms, holding me in place.

"Wait," Dimitri said, eyes still on his children.

I gritted my teeth and clenched my fists, fighting everything inside me not to run over there and kick that little shit's head in. Lukyan was crouched over Illayana, his hand still on her throat. All I wanted to do was march over there and kick him in the face.

Moving like some sort of professional acrobat, Illayana flung her legs back towards her chest and then wrapped them around his torso like a spider monkey. With more force than I think even Lukyan was prepared for, she used her legs to fling him off her.

Illayana quickly scrambled to her feet and started blocking the tirade of blows Lukyan unleashed. Her lip was split and there was a nasty bruise starting to surface under her left eye, but at least Lukyan looked just as bad.

They were locked in a grapple, each trying to rise to the dominant position. Then, Illayana hooked her foot behind Lukyan's leg and pushed.

He went down hard, his big body crashing to the ground with a solid *thud* like a stack of dominos. Illayana let him rise halfway off the floor before she pounced on his back, wrapping her legs around his torso and arms around his neck, locking him into a chokehold. The crowd went wild. Everybody screamed over one another, cheering them both on. The whole atmosphere was insane. Electric. Addictive.

Illayana squeezed, trying hard to make Lukyan either tap or pass out. He rammed his elbow into her side a few times, but Illayana wasn't giving up. From the looks of it, neither of them would.

Through sheer force of will and determination, Lukyan slowly got to his feet, with Illayana clinging to his back.

Dread coursed through me when I realised what he planned to do. *"Lascialo stare! Ora!"* Get off his back! Now! I yelled in Italian.

Illayana must have heard me, because mere seconds before Lukyan hurled himself backwards, she jumped off, rolled a few feet and landed on one knee. She pivoted, facing Lukyan as he got to his feet.

Just as they started running at each other to start all over again, Dimitri spoke in Russian. *"Dostatochno."* Enough.

Despite the adrenaline coursing through them, they both froze instantly, fists raised in the air, eyes locked on one another, blood and sweat dripping from their bodies. You could tell they wanted to keep going, that they weren't even close to being done, but it seemed they were both willing to let it go and listen to their father (at least, so I thought).

Illayana straightened, a lethal smile on her face as she approached her brother. She stuck her hand out for him to shake. He eyed it suspiciously for a few seconds before extending his own and giving a firm shake.

With a smile still plastered on her face, she punched him in the stomach and kicked his legs out from under him. Before he could retaliate, she quickly ran out of the ring.

"I win!" she yelled, weaving her way through the crowd and heading towards Dimitri and I.

I didn't know if she was still pissed at me, and quite frankly, I didn't care. She fought just as good as any of my men would have, and it was clear that I'd been underestimating her the whole time.

No more.

Illayana jumped and I caught her midair, holding her tight as she wrapped her long legs around my body. She stared deep into my eyes, a serious expression taking over her face quickly. "If Gabriella touches you again, I'll kill her."

Yep. And I had no doubt that she could do it, too.

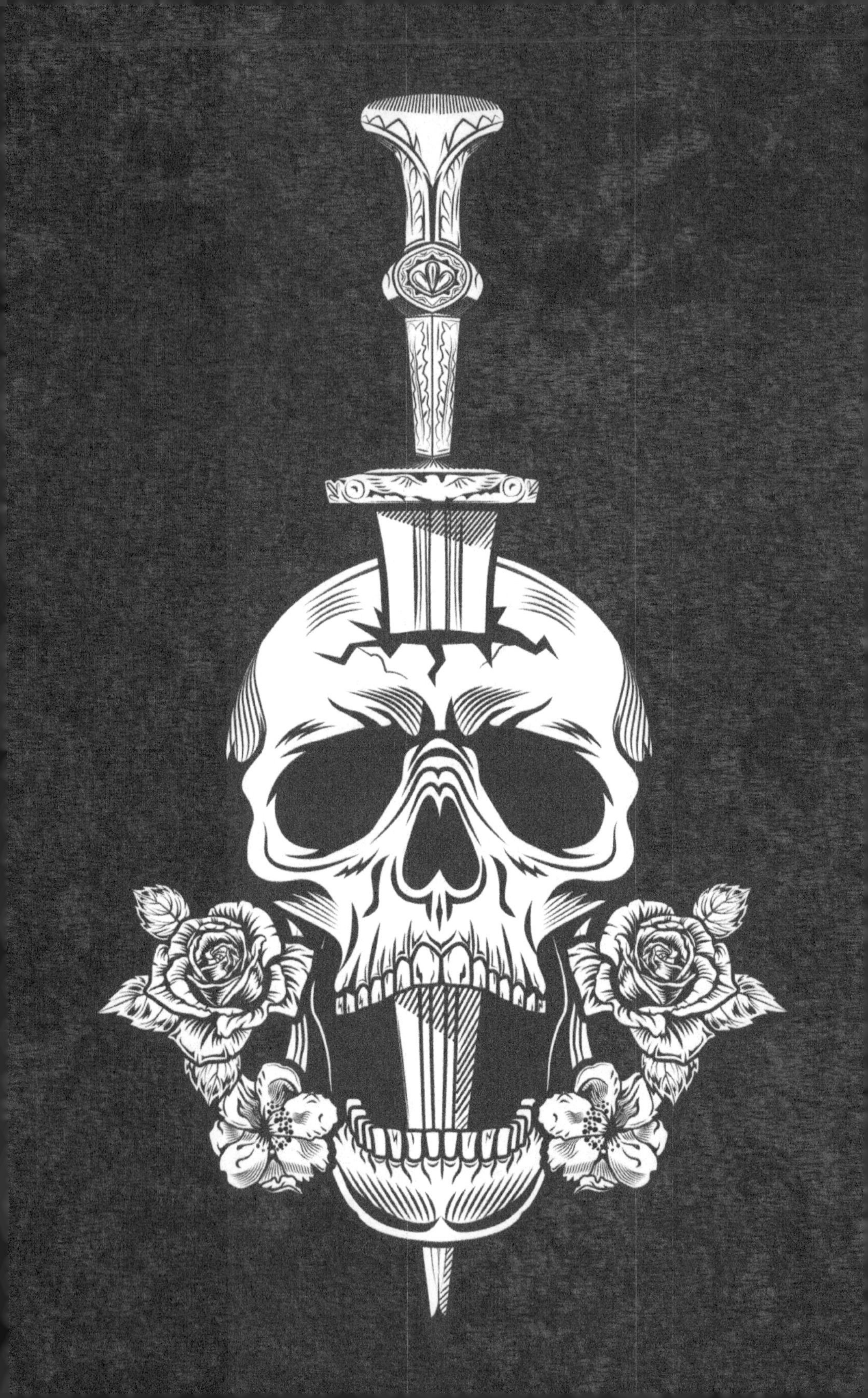

CHAPTER TWENTY-ONE

Illayana De Luca

My back slammed against the wall as Arturo's tongue dove into my mouth, excitement zinging through my entire body, making me moan. My legs locked around his waist, my nails digging into his shoulders as I tried to deepen the kiss, fighting for control. But he didn't give it, didn't let me take charge. He pressed his hard, muscular body into mine, pinning me to the wall as his hands gripped my hair tightly, holding me in place, refusing to allow me to move even an inch from where he wanted me.

I fucking loved it. I wanted more, craved more.

My stomach tightened with anticipation. Pure lust curled down my spine and my whole fucking body tingled. My pussy clenched, desperate to be filled, and I squeezed my thighs tightly, grinding down on him and making him grunt.

"You were so fucking hot," Arturo breathed, trailing kisses down my neck. His teeth latched onto my pulse and I gasped, loving the sting of the bite. "I could have fucking killed him for a laying a hand on you, slit his throat for making you bleed."

"It was just a friendly sparring match."

"I don't give a fuck. I have half a mind to beat his fucking ass."

I trailed my hands down his chest, going further and further south until

I reached the waistband of his pants. "Can we not talk about my shithead of a brother right now?" I whispered, tracing his thick lips with my tongue. "I can think of better things to do with our mouths than talking."

Arturo grabbed my hands before I could touch his goods and pinned them above my head. "Can you now?" He ground his pelvis into me, showing me exactly how excited he was. "Sometimes talking can be half the fun."

He transferred both my hands to one of his and used the other one to collar my throat. "Don't you wanna hear how badly I want to fuck you right now? How, ever since I met you, I've wanted you like this? At my mercy?"

I moaned and tried to lean forward to kiss him, but he held me back with a slight squeeze of his hand.

"Oh, you like the sound of that, don't you, *kotenok*? You want to hear about all of the filthy things I've thought about doing to you."

"Yes," I whined, my blood getting hotter and hotter, my body aching for his touch, his closeness, the huskiness of his seductive voice.

Arturo gave my wrists a tight squeeze, then trailed his hand down my arm slowly, leaving goosebumps in his wake. My breath hitched as he gripped my shirt in both hands and tore it straight off my body.

Oh, fuck.

His hands cupped my breasts roughly, his lips hot on my neck. "I've been dying to find out how you taste, how your body feels writhing beneath mine, what sounds you make when you come." He nipped my collarbone and I shivered. "It's about time I found out."

He kissed me hard, consumed my mouth like it was his to own, his to use. He gripped my ass tightly and carried me to the bed as his tongue ravished me. Licking, biting, dragging moan after moan from me.

He was *so* fucking good with his tongue that my mind instantly thought of what it would feel like to have it somewhere else.

He dropped me onto the bed and stared down at me, eyes blazing with lust. "Strip."

You don't gotta tell me twice.

I ripped off what was left of my tattered shirt, tugged down my black tights and kicked them off as fast as I could. And all the while Arturo stood over me, tall and powerful, jaw clenched and breathing hard.

His beautiful mismatched eyes roamed over my body, satisfaction flashing on his face. "Everything. I want everything off."

I reached behind me and unclasped my bra, letting it fall away from my body. I hooked my fingers into my underwear and pulled them down, baring myself entirely.

Some women might have been self conscious in a position like this, lying completely naked in front of someone, but that wasn't me. I wasn't model material, not by a long shot. But what I lacked in sexual appeal, I made up for in confidence.

A confident woman could be just as sexy than a drop dead gorgeous woman, if not more so. And luckily for me, I had a bucketful of confidence.

Arturo's eyes locked onto my pussy and he licked his lips.

"Well? What are you waiting for? Taste me," I breathed, anticipation filling my bones.

He arched an eyebrow. "And what makes you think you're in charge here?"

Slowly, methodically, he started to undress, first kicking off his shoes, then undoing his belt, drawing it free at a leisurely pace, his eyes never leaving mine. The belt clanged loudly when he dropped it to the ground. He reached behind him and fisted his shirt, pulling it over his head and off his body.

My breath hitched. My pulse skyrocketed. He was just...so...fucking...*hot*! All that muscle, all those tattoos. He was like every woman's sexual fantasy. Over six-and-a-half feet of pure, masculine strength and energy. And it was all mine.

I went to sit up, to touch him, to run my hands over that immaculate body, but he pushed me back down.

"Did I say you could get up?"

Oh, Lord have mercy.

His voice was deep, rough. The huskiness of it was making me even hotter. Not to mention the fact I had a serious weakness for dominant men. Men who weren't afraid to take control.

Arturo gripped my ankles and yanked me to the end of the bed. "Answer me," he whispered huskily.

Heat coursed through my veins at his command, my body throbbing with need. "No, you didn't."

"That's right. You're going to do everything I tell you to do, aren't you, *kotenok?*"

"Yes," I answered instantly, because I seriously fucking was.

I might have had a problem with it if we weren't in bed, but like I said before...serious weakness for dominant men.

He spread my thighs and stared down at my dripping pussy. My heart nearly stopped at the look in his eyes, the heat blazing down at me.

I squirmed, eager to have his mouth on me. Aching for his touch, his tongue. He pushed my legs back until the heel of my foot touched my ass.

"Hands above your head. Interlock your fingers. Don't move them until I say."

My body rippled with tingles, desire igniting my soul. God, I was so hyped up I could barely think straight as I did what he said. My chest heaved. My breath quickened.

"You're shaking," he rumbled, dropping to his knees.

"I wonder why? I've got a sexy as fuck dude in between my legs, staring at my pussy like he's about to ravish me."

Arturo smirked. "Oh, I'm definitely going to ravish you. But I'm going to take my time doing it."

The heat of his lips hit my inner thigh and I gasped. He kissed, nibbled and teased as he travelled up and up, so close to where I wanted him to be, and yet so far away. It was killing me.

"Arturo," I whined, my body trembling.

I felt the wetness of his tongue as he dragged it over my skin and finally clamped his mouth over my clit.

I jolted and moaned as he swirled his tongue over that sensitive bundle of nerves, a wave of pleasure crashing through me. "Oh, sweet baby Jesus."

I arched into his mouth, my hips gyrating as he amped up the speed and pressure of his tongue. His hands clamped on my waist, holding me still while he licked, sucked and utterly consumed me.

He hummed and the vibrations made me jolt again.

"You taste even better than I thought you would," he rumbled, nails digging into my skin. "So fucking sweet."

His tongue was unbearably soft, his movements drawing moan after moan from my lips.

"Fuck, fuck, fuck," I chanted, writhing against him.

He laid open-mouthed kisses all over my pussy, his tongue gliding through my slick folds until he reached my entrance, and then he speared his tongue inside me.

"Oh my god!" I squealed.

"Mmmm, you're so tight."

My hands gripped his head tightly, holding him against my pussy. I couldn't help it. The combination of his tongue and that deep, gravelly voice made it impossible for me to keep my hands off him.

He moved so quickly that I barely registered it. He pinned my wrists above my head, eyes blazing with fire and lips glistening wet. "I told you not to move."

"I can't help it," I whined, aching for him. "I want to touch you."

"You'll get your turn. Right now, it's my turn." He ran his tongue up the side of my neck and sucked my earlobe into his mouth. "Now, do you want to come?"

"Mmhmm."

He slapped my ass. "Words, Illayana. I want the words."

"Yes, I want to fucking come!"

He bit into my shoulder and I yelped in surprise. "Watch that attitude, or you won't get to come at all."

That motherfuck— "You wouldn't."

He leant back and smirked down at me. "Wanna risk it?"

No, I fucking don't. I shook my head.

"Didn't think so." He traced my lips with his tongue and then moved lower, trailing kisses down my neck and over my chest. He latched onto my nipple and sucked hard.

"Oh, fuck!" I arched into his mouth, desperate to touch him, but I knew if I moved my hands again, he'd stop.

Releasing my nipple with a wet *plop*, he moved onto the other one. "Such perfect, gorgeous tits." He swirled his tongue around the taut bud before lightly biting down. "I want to come all over them."

"Mmm, you should."

"Next time," he whispered, nipping the underside of my breast.

He wedged himself between my legs, placing them on his shoulders as he spread my folds with his thumbs. The flat of his tongue travelled from the opening of my clit in one long, giant lick and he groaned, his eyes rolling back. "So fucking good. I could lick you all day."

His glorious tongue swirled over my clit achingly slowly, and it only increased the pleasure shooting through my body. He moved his mouth like he was kissing me, his lips and tongue touching me everywhere, roving over every inch of my pussy.

White-hot pleasure shot through me, that blessed tongue driving me higher and higher as he flicked, lapped and thrust inside me.

I moaned, my fists clenching so hard that my nails dug into my palms, my legs shaking so badly that he had to hold me down.

"Arturoooo," I groaned, bucking into his mouth. "I'm gonna come."

"Fucking come for me then, *kotenok*. Give it to me."

He speared two fingers inside me and my pussy clamped down, a blazing hot orgasm rippling through me. My back bowed, a choked cry falling from my lips as the most intense pleasure I'd ever felt tore through my body, lighting up every nerve.

"Mmmm." Arturo lapped at my pussy, licking up all my juices at a slow, leisurely pace. He curled his fingers and gave one more quick pump before pulling them out, his digits glistening wet. He sucked them into his mouth and closed his eyes. "Best thing I've ever tasted. I just want to feast on you all over again."

Even though I just came, my body started to wind up all over again, that look of pure male satisfaction making my arousal skyrocket.

He got to his feet, the bulge in his pants snagging my attention straight away. He stared down at me. "Up," he barked, breathing hard. "On your knees."

Excitement blasted through me. Despite the fact that my limbs felt like jello from the mind-blowing orgasm he just gave me, I scurried off the bed, eager to get my hands on that beautiful body. Arturo took a step back, giving me room to sink to my knees in front of him.

"Take my pants off," he ordered, voice gruff and thick with desire.

My hands flew to his waist and I unbuttoned his pants, tugging them down his thick, muscular thighs.

Good lord. He wasn't wearing any underwear.

His cock stood tall, hard as steel and long enough to make me curious about whether or not he'd fit. The head wept with precum as it throbbed against his rock-hard abs.

I knew he was big. I had felt it against my leg. But seeing it up close and personal, bopping in front of me, made me realise exactly how big he was. And he was fucking huge.

Arturo fisted his cock and pumped it twice, staring down at me with lust-filled eyes. He slipped his other hand into my hair and tilted my head the way he wanted. "Open your mouth."

I smirked, my mischievous mind running wild. I slowly ran my tongue over my lips, teasing him. I flicked the soft, smooth head of his shaft and he stiffened, his jaw clenching so hard that I thought he'd shatter his teeth.

"Illayana," he warned, tapping his cock against my lips. "Open."

My body hummed with the need to follow his command, and I couldn't hold off any longer. It was teasing me just as much as it was teasing him.

I opened my mouth and he surged forward, thrusting far enough to hit the back of my throat. He groaned and his hold on my hair tightened to the point of pain.

Fuck...I loved a little pain with my pleasure.

I sucked him in further, hollowing my cheeks. He pumped his hips faster, both of his hands gripping my face tightly as he held me in place, using me for his own pleasure.

I fucking loved it. I loved every second of it.

I moaned, saliva pooling in my mouth. I moved my tongue over the underside of his cock and he cursed, his movements turning erratic, thrusting in and out so fast his balls slapped my chin.

"Fuck...yeah...take it all, *kotenok*. Every fucking inch."

He didn't relent, didn't slow his pace. Even when he pushed so far down my throat that I gagged. I just sucked harder, more determined to make him lose control entirely and take me even rougher. Use me. Fucking consume me.

In one quick manoeuvre, he pulled out of my mouth, picked me up and threw me onto the bed. The weight of his muscular body landed on me a second later, his mouth latching onto mine in a ravishingly devastating kiss.

"No more teasing. I need you now," he growled, biting my lower lip.

He spread my thighs roughly, nails digging into my skin, and speared me with his cock.

The hot bite of pain mixed with the unbelievable pleasure of finally having my pussy filled with his rock-hard length made me scream out in shock. A deep, guttural moan passed my lips as he rutted into me, pinning my thighs wide open for his assault.

"So. Fucking. Tight," he grunted, pounding so hard, the bed whacked against the wall over and over again. "Your pussy is all mine, isn't it, *kotenok?*"

I arched into him, bucking against his thrusts. My mind was hazy with all the pleasure sailing through me, yet I wanted more. I wanted to test him, make his control snap altogether and take me so hard that it left bruises on my body.

"Mmm, maybe."

His hand snapped around my throat and he glared down at me with fire in his eyes. "What was that?" he whispered darkly, daring me to repeat it.

Because I loved to test the limit, to see how far I could push him, I said it again, curving my lips.

He pulled out and slapped my pussy, hard.

I yelped in surprise. Warmth engulfed me, heat curling down my spine.

"Make no mistake, Illayana. This pussy *is* mine. Mine to use. Mine to fuck. Mine to mark." He speared three fingers inside me, squeezing my throat at the same time. "Do I make myself clear?"

"Yes," I rasped, ecstasy flowing through my bones. I was drunk on his dominance, the power and masculinity he exerted.

He flipped me onto my stomach, yanked my hips into the air and pinned me down with a hand to my nape. He slammed into me so roughly that I squealed.

"I planned to take you for the first time staring into your eyes, showing you how much I wanted you. How much I craved you." He pounded hard, his thick, glorious cock hitting me so deep, I swear I could feel it in my womb. "But since you decided to get smart with me, I'm going to punish you, fuck you like a whore instead."

I moaned loudly, fisting the bedsheets, holding on for dear life as he rode me. My pussy rippled, the pleasure so good, so intense that I knew I was a heartbeat away from coming.

He gripped my hair and yanked my head back, pulling me up until my back smacked into his chest. He ran his tongue up my neck. "Oh, you like that," he chuckled. "You want me to fuck you like a whore, don't you, my beautiful wife?"

"Yessss," I whimpered. "Yes, oh God. Please, Arturo, don't stop."

He swivelled his hips, keeping one hand in my hair as the other came up to collar my throat. Driving forward, he powered into me, our bodies slick with sweat, our groans echoing all around us, accompanied by the slap of his hips hitting my skin.

"You want my cum, *kotenok?* You want to feel me shooting inside you?"

His rough voice and dirty words pushed me over the edge. My insides raged. My pussy clenched. My body spiralled out of control as pure ecstasy consumed me. Waves and waves of pleasure trailed over every inch of me and I screamed, shaking uncontrollably as my orgasm ripped through me.

Wet lips traced over my skin. Teeth latched onto my shoulder. Arturo's thrusts turned chaotic, his grunts and growls filling the space of the room. Pound after pound, deeper and deeper he hit against me. "Oh, fuck..." He lurched forward with one final, powerful snap of his hips and a deep guttural moan left his lips. His cock pulsed inside me, wet hot cum overflowing down my thighs.

His muscular, toned body draped over mine and he placed a soft kiss on the side of my neck. "Don't fall asleep," he panted in my ear. "I'll be taking you again."

My arousal shot straight up all over again.

Oh, fuck, I think he might kill me. With his dick.

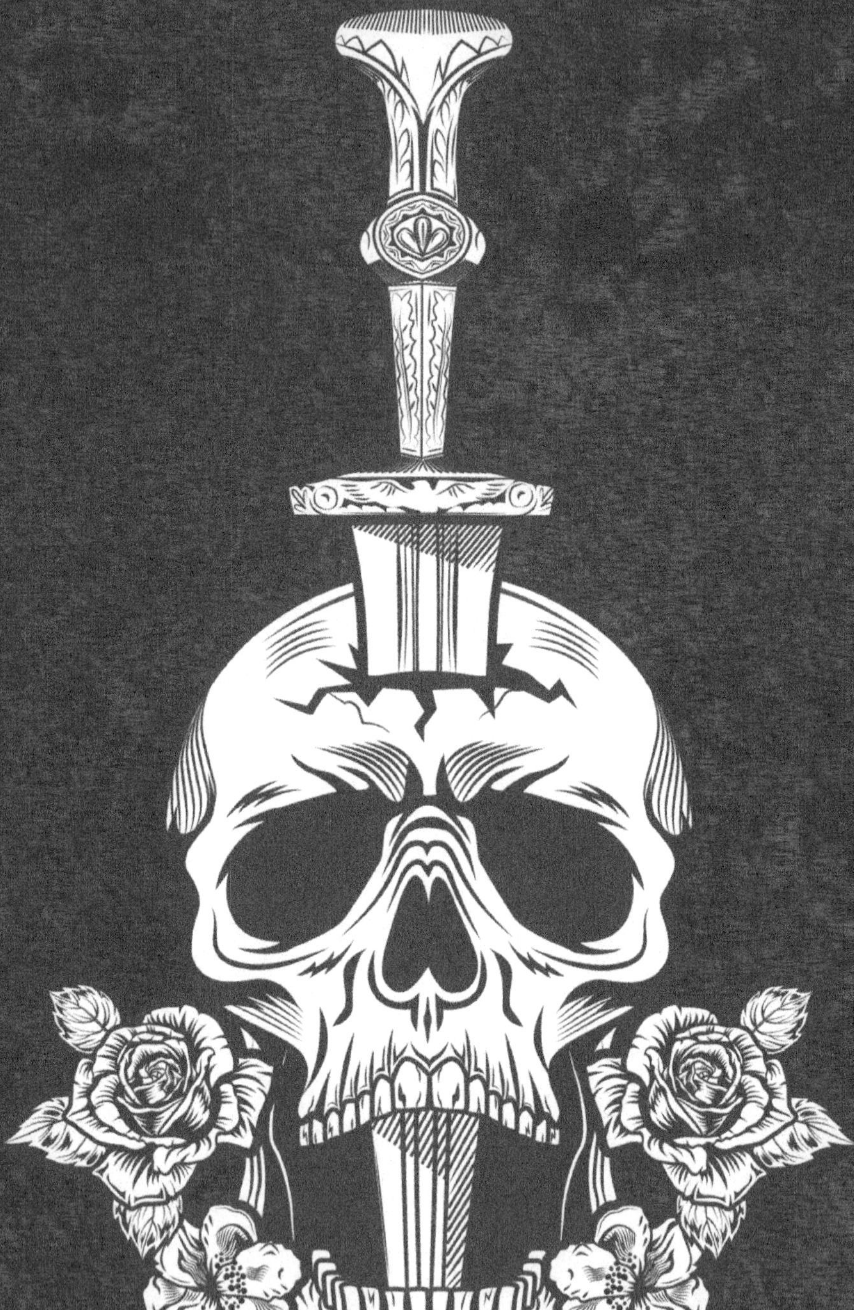

CHAPTER TWENTY-TWO

Arturo De Luca

"Everybody in place?" I asked, speaking into my earpiece as I glared at the cheap-ass motel from the shadows.

Despite how much Illayana wanted me to stay out of this fight, I couldn't. Oh, she had tried tempting me into staying, tried keeping me home with her instead of going out. After finally fucking her, being able to sink my cock deep into that tight, wet pussy, I could barely think of anything else. And she damn well knew it.

She flaunted that delectable body around me as I got ready, bending down with her ass in the air and pushing her chest out so her tits caught my attention. I nearly stabbed myself with my own damn knife, she was so distracting.

Even though I wanted nothing more than to bite into that soft, smooth skin—to hold her body tight and fuck her until she couldn't think of anything else but me and the pleasure I brought her—I couldn't.

These fuckers attacked us. Killed my men. Tried to kidnap Lucian and Theodora. I wasn't going to let that shit slide. They were going to pay in blood.

The motel was small, located just off the highway in the middle of bum-fuck nowhere. It looked like it was one small breeze away from crumbling to pieces, with holes in the roof and patches of paint and plaster missing from the walls.

After some research, we found out each room had two entry points (a front door and a back door), which meant we needed to cover both to ensure nobody escaped.

We worked out that the best plan of attack was to come at them from all sides. Box those fuckers in so they had nowhere to run, nowhere to hide.

The Bratva were going to come in from the back while, simultaneously, the Cosa Nostra came from the front. They wouldn't know what hit 'em.

"*Da,*" Dimitri's rough voice responded. "We are in position."

I looked to my left. Vin smiled wickedly, danger glinting in his eyes.

"You ready, *fratello?*" Brother? I asked, reaching into my jacket and pulling out my gun.

Vin smirked. "I was born ready."

I rolled my eyes and looked to my right. My father's steely gaze was plastered on the building in front of him, his anger like a thick cloud all around us.

"*Padre? Pronto?*" Father? Ready?

He cocked his gun and growled.

Oh, he's ready.

Fifteen of our best men crouched behind us, ready to move on our command. I knew each of them by name. I trusted them all to have my back.

Ideally, in this situation I would have Christian and Luca here. They were fucking deadly in a fight. But Illayana's safety was more important.

Thanks to Mikhail (Illayana's twisted godfather), we were armed to the tee. We each had a P-90 strapped to our backs and two handguns at our waists. Dimitri had to call in a favour with the dude after his supply was cleaned out. I thought P-90s were a bit extravagant, but the Russians never did shit in halves.

Excitement blasted through me as I made my way up to the motel door, followed closely by Vin, my father and our men.

"On my count," I whispered into my earpiece, cocking my gun. "Three...two...one...*go.*"

I raised my foot and kicked down the door, ripping it straight off the hinges just as the same thing happened to the back door, the Bratva piling in with Dimitri and Aleksandr leading the charge, locked and loaded.

I scanned the room quickly, my eyes taking in everything in under a second.

Two single beds, a man sitting at the end of each one, a woman stripping in front of them. Another man in the corner near the window, smoking a cigarette while a blonde woman sucked him off. Five men sitting on the couch huddled over a bag filled to the brim with guns.

Dimitri's guns.

A multitude of things happened all at once. The two men on the beds reached for their guns on the bedside tables. The man near the window cursed and pushed the blonde away, trying to get to his weapon. And the men crowded around the bag of guns tripped over one another as they each tried to pull a gun out and take aim.

"Vin!" I signalled for him to take the two on the bed. He put a bullet in each of their backs before they reached their guns.

I fired a few warning shots into the wall, skimming a man's ear and making him cry out in pain. "Move again and I'll take you all out," I vowed as Father came to my side, aiming his gun at the crowd of men.

As much as I wanted to kill them all right then and there, make them suffer for what they did, we agreed to take as many as we could alive. We had an example to set and a plan in motion to accomplish it—a plan that required prisoners.

The man near the window tried to make a run for it, and he ran smack into Aleksandr's big body, bounding off it like a bouncy ball and landing flat on his ass.

Aleksandr gripped him by the throat and squeezed, pulling him up and dragging him closer. He headbutted him in the face and broke his nose, blood pouring out all over the place. With a kick to the chest, Aleksandr sent him flying across the room.

Gotta love the dude's style.

"Lukyan," Aleksandr barked, pointing at the man bleeding on the floor.

Illayana's youngest brother pounced on him, holding a knife to his throat. "Go ahead," he purred, digging the knife further in and drawing blood. "Give me a reason to gut you."

The man wisely stayed still.

Lukyan pouted. "Pity."

Feminine screams echoed all around the room and irritation flowed through me. I couldn't stand that shit; weak women.

If your life is in danger, you don't scream, you don't cower. You fucking fight.

"Shut up!" I yelled, pointing my gun at the three women huddled in the corner. "Or I'll put a bullet in between your fucking eyes."

They shut up real fucking quick.

One thing our intel didn't tell us was that this was an adjoining room. All the ruckus, the gunfire and the screaming made the group of men in the next room come barrelling in, guns drawn.

It turned into a bloodbath. Bullets flew in every direction. Blood sprayed all over the walls. Everybody ran and ducked for cover. Glass shattered. Plaster rained down like confetti.

I fired round after round, taking down as many of the bastards as I could. Fuck taking them alive, it was time to fuck their shit up. We could still make an example of them by stringing their bodies up for the world to fucking see.

I flipped the couch over and took cover behind it, reloading my gun.

Lukyan scurried over and crouched at my side, a crazy smile on his face. "Isn't this fun?!" he yelled over the gunfire, laughing maniacally.

He's fucking crazy!

Lukyan jumped to his feet and used the couch as an anchor as he fired his P-90, releasing a fuck ton of bullets. "Oh, yeah! How do you like that, bitches?!"

A big boot landed next to me. I knew instantly it was not a friend; it was an enemy. Before he took another step, I pulled my knife out and slammed it into his foot.

He screamed and hunched over at the waist, trying to yank it out quickly. Pulling another blade from my waist, I rammed it into his cheek. Blood spurted out, splattering all over my face.

I leapt over his body, keeping low to the floor as I scurried across the ground. Another enemy stepped into my path, trying to kick me in the face and knock me down. I brought my arm up and blocked him. I pulled a gun from my waist, placed it under his chin and fired.

His head snapped back, the bullet going straight through his skull and into the roof.

Spinning on my knees, I fired again, blowing a hole in a man's head just as he reached Vin.

Vin growled, kicking the lifeless body in the ribs. His eyes snapped to me. "I had that!" he yelled as he flung a knife into a man's chest, halfway across the room.

I stood, glaring. "I think what you meant to say was, 'thank you', *testa di cazzo.*" *Dickhead.*

Pivoting to the left, Vin dodged an attack from behind, light as a feather on his feet. He took aim and fired, shooting the man in the back. "I've got no reason to thank you. I had it covered, *stronzo.*" *Asshole.*

Annoyance flared through me. "You little—"

"Basta voi due!" Enough, you two! Father barked, snapping a man's neck with a sharp twist and letting him fall to the ground. "I swear, it's like you guys are teenagers again."

"He started it," Vin mumbled, wiping blood from his brow.

"Fuck off I did."

My spidey senses tingled, the hair on the back of my neck standing up and I spun, bringing my forearms up in an X formation to block a knife before it could pierce my skin. I rammed my knee into the man's ribs and, with a little manoeuvring, gripped his wrist, ducked under his arm and flung him onto his back, all in one fluid motion.

Plucking the knife from his hands, I held it under his chin and straddled his chest.

"Tut, tut, tut. Too slow," I laughed, enjoying the way the fucker trembled beneath me.

Anger flashed on his face and he bucked, kicking his legs out. "Get the fuck off me, you Italian scum!"

"Hey, Vin!" I yelled, digging the knife in a little deeper, making him hiss. "We need another prisoner, or are we set?"

At my cleverly veiled threat, the man ceased his struggles, freezing instantly.

Vin looked around. "I think we got enough."

I smiled. "Wonderful." I rammed my knife under his chin right to the hilt, glimpsing the blade inside his open month, drenched in blood. I got to my feet and wiped my bloody hands on my clothes.

Groans echoed all around me as the sounds of gunshots died down and I blinked, coming out of my bloodlust haze.

In an attempt to save himself, a grubby man with blood, sweat and tears dripping down his face gripped one of the hysterical women by her hair, holding a gun to her temple. "Everyone freeze. No-nobody move, or I'll blow her head off!"

Vin and I shared a confused look with one another.

Uhh, are we supposed to give a fuck?

Dimitri stepped over numerous dead bodies as he made his way over, his Armani suit torn in several places. He was drenched head to toe in blood.

"St-stop! I'll do it! I'll fucking kill her!" the man screamed, his hand trembling.

"Why does he think we care?" Vin whispered to me, and I shrugged.

I had no fucking idea. She wasn't one of our girls (at least, I didn't think she was. Truth was, we had so many girls in our strip clubs, they all started to look the same to me).

Let's be honest. Even if she was one of ours, she didn't matter enough for us to care about her death. Harsh, but true.

Dimitri stopped in front of them, raised his gun to the woman's forehead and fired, unflinching.

Alrighty. Looks like he doesn't care about her either.

"Kelly! No!" one of the women cried, her body quaking with fear.

The man reared back in surprise and fumbled over a dead body, landing on the ground hard. His hands flew up in surrender as Dimitri pointed his gun right at his chest.

"Wait! Wait! I-I have information! Spare my life and I'll tell you everything I know! Please!"

I shook my head in disgust. Did loyalty mean nothing to these fuckers? I couldn't stand disloyalty. I'd carve him up for that offence alone.

An evil smirk tainted Dimitri's lips. "You'll tell me regardless."

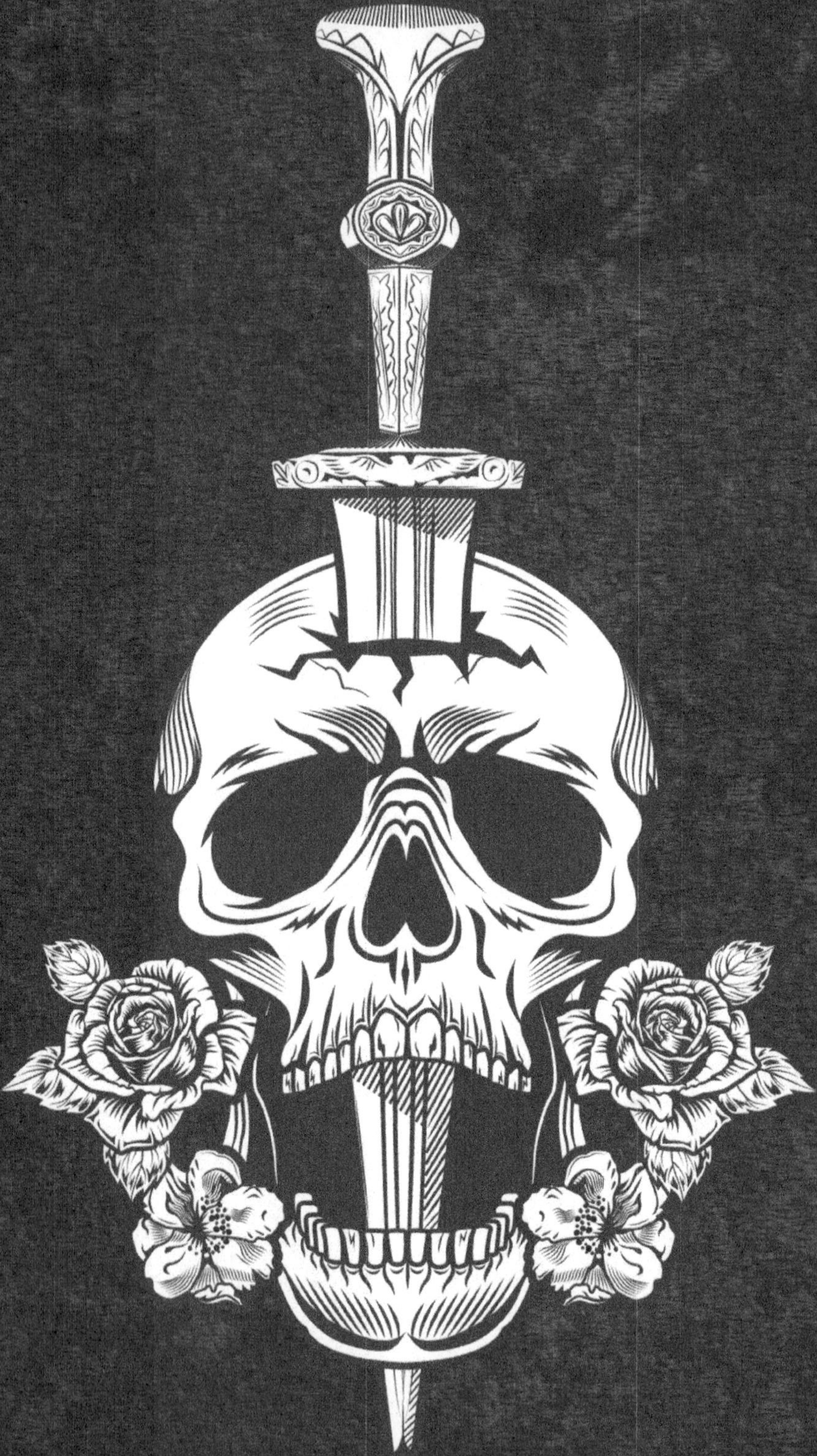

CHAPTER TWENTY-THREE

Illayana De Luca

"Have you ever wondered what makes your skin stay on?"

I blinked, looking at Christian in shock.

What kind of fucking question is that?

"Uh, what?"

"Your skin." He inclined his head to my bare arm, as if I didn't know what skin was and he was pointing it out to me. "Have you ever wondered what makes it stay on?"

"No, I haven't. Because I'm fucking normal." I adjusted my position on the couch, eyeing my bodyguard suspiciously.

Christian smirked. "It's a legitimate question. I'm sure I'm not the first person to ever wonder about it."

"Ignore him, Illayana. He asks stupid shit like this all the time," Luca said, glaring at his brother.

Christian looked offended. "Hey, my questions are awesome."

Luca chucked a piece of bread smothered in jelly, and it hit Christian square in the face.

He blinked in shock and then shrugged, pulling it off his cheek and stuffing it into his mouth. "Mmm, thanks," he mumbled, chewing loudly.

I laughed softly, turning my attention back to the TV. I watched as

Henry Cavill fought some fugly-ass monster on the screen. Christian and Luca's voices pitched higher as they argued in the background.

"Guys," I scolded. They were interrupting my ogling of a shirtless Henry, and it was seriously pissing me off. "This episode is almost over, just chill out."

Instead they got in each other's faces, pushing and shoving one another. Something smashed.

"Goddamnit! Now look at what you've done, you idiot!" Luca yelled.

"That was your fault! You pushed me!" Christian screamed back.

"You pushed me first!"

"Because you got in my face!"

"I'll show you getting in your face," Luca growled. He got Christian in a headlock, wrapping his arm firmly around Christian's head, squeezing tightly.

"Get off me, you asshole!" Christian grunted, trying to punch Luca in the ribs.

"Guyssssssss," I ground out, my temper spiking.

Their bodies twisted and turned, ramming into my father's thousand-dollar mahogany coffee table, knocking glass figurines to the ground. They smashed into the wall next, grunting and snarling at each other.

Christian bit Luca's arm. Luca pulled Christian's hair. They were like a pair of teenage girls fighting dirty, biting and scratching one another.

I'd had enough.

I got to my feet, grabbed a gun, pointed it up at the ceiling and fired twice. "Enough!" I bellowed.

They both froze in shock; Christian with his teeth latched onto Luca's arm like a dog, and Luca with a hand gripped in Christian's hair.

I pointed at Luca. "You, over there," I snapped, pointing to one side of the room. "And you, over there," I growled at Christian, pointing to the other side of the room so they were far away from each other.

I channelled my mother, her demeanour, the voice she used when she had to break up fights between my brothers and I. Fights exactly like this. "Now," I whispered menacingly.

They separated instantly, scurrying to opposite ends of the room.

Seconds later, men burst into the lounge room from all directions, guns drawn and ready for action—including my two other bodyguards, Lorenzo and Adrian.

I waved them away. "Everything's fine. It was just me."

Adrian assessed me, his eyes drifting up to the bullet holes in the roof and back down to me. He lowered his weapon. "Again, Illayana? You keep going like this and there won't be anything of this house left."

I scoffed and pointed to the front section of the house—the part that was burnt to a crisp, thanks to those fuckers who bombed my wedding. "Really? Like there's shit all left of it, anyway."

If my mother was still alive, she'd be heartbroken. The house was like her fifth child. She loved it. Seeing it so broken, so destroyed, would have killed her.

Adrian shook his head and signalled for the men to return to their posts. "What happened?" he asked, studying the twins at opposite ends of the room, glaring at each other.

"You wanna know what happened?" I asked, my pent-up frustration reaching its limit. "Arturo left me with two overgrown toddlers who fight like little bitches."

Christian gasped, his hand flying to his chest. "How dare you."

Luca winced. "We're sorry, Illayana. Sometimes we can get a bit out of control."

A deep, throaty laugh echoed in the room. I narrowed my eyes on the culprit. "What the fuck is so funny, Adrian?"

His shoulders shook from laughter, pure amusement flashing on his face. "You have no idea how much you look like your father right now. He had the exact same look on his face whenever you and your brothers used to fight."

"We were nowhere near as bad as them," I scowled, pointing at the twins.

"No, you were probably worse," he chuckled, walking out of the room.

That dick.

If anyone would know, it would be him. He'd been in my life for as long as I can remember, always at my father's side, protecting him. He was like an honorary uncle.

Annoyed, I turned off the TV. The vibe was ruined. I was no longer in the mood to pant over the gloriousness that was Henry Cavill.

"Come on, we're going out," I said, tucking my gun back into my holster and heading for the front door. When Christian and Luca didn't move, I turned around, frowning at them. "Uh, hello?" I sang, snapping my fingers. "Earth to the twinsies."

They exchanged a look with one another and awkwardly glanced my way.

I sighed. "What is it?"

"Arturo...he, uh—"

"He what?"

"He—" Luca bit his lip, afraid to talk.

"Just spit it out," I ordered, my patience snapping.

"He said we had to stay here, that we weren't to leave the house."

"Alright, works for me. You guys stay here. I'll be back later." I didn't want guards anyway, so if they didn't want to come with, it was better for me.

I walked back towards the door and the twins moved fast, Christian slamming his body against the door and Luca jumping in front of me, palms out.

"That's not what Arturo meant."

"Then what did he mean, Luca? Because surely you're not about to tell me that my husband has ordered you to keep me here?"

Luca bit his lip and glanced to the side, avoiding my eyes.

That motherfucker.

"He's just worried about your safety," Christian interjected. "He doesn't want anything to happen to you."

"So he plans to keep me locked up at home every time he leaves?"

Christian gulped. "I...uh, don't know?"

I glared, wrapping my fingers around my gun and pulling it out again. "Let's get something straight, you two. I don't give a fuck what Arturo has told you. You try to stop me from leaving this house and I'll put a bullet in both your asses. Got it?"

Christian stuttered. "Illayana—"

I pushed the barrel under his chin, tilting his head up as I pulled back the hammer and cocked the gun. "Got. It?"

Fear flashed in his eyes. He nodded fast. "Gotcha."

Adrian walked into the foyer, eyes on his phone. He glanced up, frowned, then sighed. "What now?"

I smiled brightly, holstering my weapon. "Nothing. We're heading out for a bit. We'll be back soon."

"Alright. Give me a few minutes to get Lorenzo."

"Nah, it's all good. Don't worry about it. I've got these guys. That's enough."

Adrian tucked his phone into his pocket and crossed his arms over his chest, his expression hard. "Illayana, what did your father say?"

"Depends what you're referring to. He says a lot of shit," I replied evasively.

His brows snapped together. "You know what I'm talking about, young lady."

"Don't 'young lady' me, Adrian. I'm not a kid anymore."

"Sorry, *malen'kly. Little one.* You'll always be a kid in my eyes. And we both know that if you leave this house without *all* of your bodyguards, you'll find yourself in the ring with your father."

I winced. *Fuck.* He was right. My father would *definitely* punish me for that. The last time I was in the ring with him, he broke my nose. I wasn't keen on reliving that experience.

"Fiiiiine. We'll meet you in the car. Keys?" I held out my hand and Adrian eyed me suspiciously. "I swear I'll wait. Cross my heart."

"You better." He reached into his pocket and pulled out his keys, dropping them in my hand. "Or I'll kick your ass, too."

Yeah, he probably would.

I gave him a salute. "Aye, aye, Captain." I turned and opened the door, heading outside.

"Aw, get fucked!" I cursed, slamming my hands on the steering wheel. I glared at the screen in front of me, the words *YOU LOSE* taunting me like a motherfucker.

Christian sat beside me in his own car arcade machine, a smug smile on his face. "Told ya. Women can't drive."

I scowled and got to my feet, storming off.

"Oh, come on! Don't be cranky. No one likes a sore loser!" Christian yelled, following me.

I couldn't help it. I *was* a sore loser.

Adrian, Lorenzo and Luca surrounded me, boxing me in as I moved around the arcade, looking for a new game to play.

I needed a distraction, something to keep me occupied while my husband and family were out on this mission. At first that distraction was Henry Cavill, until the two idiots behind me ruined that. The next best thing was the arcade.

"Air hockey?" I asked Adrian, turning to face him.

He scanned the surroundings, his eyes sweeping over everything. "I'm here to guard you, Illayana, not play games."

"Can't you do both?"

The other patrons in the arcade eyed Adrian, Lorenzo, Christian and

Luca warily, keeping a wide berth from them all as they went to play their own games. I couldn't blame them. To anyone else, they'd look scary, dangerous. Four six-foot somethin' men standing around glaring at anyone who even came close to me. Well, everyone except for Christian. He was the only one willing to play games with me. But so far, he'd beaten me at everything. And I was sick of fucking losing.

I played a few more games—basketball, Time Crisis (a pretty intense shooting game that I totally kicked ass at) and Dance Revolution—before I finally decided to take pity on my guards and leave.

As we left the arcade, I almost ran smack into—

"Rayna," I sneered, managing to catch myself before I made contact with her.

"Cousin!" She smiled brightly, but I didn't believe it for a second. She hated me just as much as I hated her, so her fake-ass smile wasn't fooling me. "I've been looking for you. Oh, I can't believe what happened at your wedding. It was just awful. Dreadful."

She turned to the three women behind her—her bimbo posse, who followed her everywhere she went, waiting on her hand and foot. A tall, lean man stood a few paces behind her, giving off the same dangerous vibe as my own bodyguards.

"My poor cousin had a major catastrophe at her wedding earlier today. I mean, wow, I've never seen a wedding *bomb* out like that before."

That little bitch.

I narrowed my eyes, her snicker grating on my nerves. Bimbos One, Two and Three cackled on cue like a bunch of little old witches. I felt like strangling them.

"Yeah, it was a bit of a clusterfuck. Remind me, Rayna, what happened at your wedding again? Oh, wait..." I raised my eyebrows and gave a condescending smirk.

Rayna sneered. "At least when I get married, it won't be a total fucking disaster."

"*If* you get married."

She closed her eyes and took a deep breath, nostrils flaring. A few tense seconds passed before she opened her eyes and stared at me. "I apologise for what I said. It was rude of me."

Okay, that was a complete one-eighty.

"Do you mind if we have a word?" —her eyes darted to the four hulking figures behind me— "In private?"

Suspicion coursed through my bones, but also...curiosity.

"That's not going to happen," Adrian barked, voice hard.

Rayna glared. "I didn't realise the help was in charge. Is that how your father runs things, Illayana?"

Anger throbbed through me at her insolence. "Don't think because we're in public and you've got your bimbo posse, that I won't put you in your place," I whispered darkly. "Because I will."

Unease flitted across her face and she lowered her eyes to the ground. "I'm sorry. Please, Illayana. I really need to speak to you. It's important."

"If it's so important, why can't you just talk about it here, now?"

"Because—and I mean no offence when I say this—I don't trust your men. I've come across vital information that's for your ears only. It concerns the family. I stopped by your house to talk to you about it but you weren't there, so I tracked you down here."

I was sceptical as hell. Rayna wasn't to be trusted. *At all*. But if there was a threat to the family, I needed to know.

"Alright. Fine."

Rayna smiled, and for once, it seemed genuine. "Thank you."

"Illayana." Adrian gave me a look that conveyed he wasn't happy about this, but I just shook my head.

Even if Rayna tried something, I was confident I could take her.

"Let's go over here." I motioned for her to follow me. "You guys wait here. I'll be back in a second."

Adrian gripped my arm, stopping me. "I really don't think this is a good idea."

"Relax, Adrian. It's fine."

"Illayana—"

"Adrian," I raised my voice, demanding his obedience. "I said it's fine. Now step back."

He clenched his jaw, eyes burning in anger, but he relented, letting me go. "Fine. If you insist on doing something this idiotic, then you stay in my line of sight. You hear me? You're not the only one your father will punish if something happens to you."

I nodded. I was willing to compromise.

Lorenzo, Christian and Luca all looked as if they were going to protest too, but I gave them the Volkov stare: chin up, shoulders back, eyes hard, jaw clenched, stance strong and powerful.

They backed down.

"Come on, Rayna. Let's make this quick."

She followed behind me as I led the way to the front of the mall, stepping outside but staying within Adrian's line of sight. The night was cold and dark, the moon shining brightly amongst the stars.

"Alright, you got me alone. Now, cut the crap and tell me what you wanted to tell me."

Rayna smiled again and I shook my head.

"Quit the nice girl routine. You're not fooling me, and quite frankly, it just doesn't suit you."

"What? I'm genuinely happy that you're letting me grace your all-mighty presence and talk with you."

I rolled my eyes. "If you're not gonna tell me anything substantial, then I'm leaving."

I turned to head back into the mall when she gripped my arm. "Wait. Okay, sorry. I just can't help antagonising you sometimes."

"The feeling is mutual."

"Can we sit?" she gestured to a seat a few steps away. It put me out of Adrian's view.

"No. Talk here, now. Or I walk."

She pursed her lips, but nodded. "Look, this might sound crazy, but I think there's a rat in the family."

My brows slammed down in a frown. "Why would you say that?"

"Your wedding. I overheard a group of people talking about—"

Gunfire, followed by a loud, ear-piercing scream cut through the air, coming from inside the mall. I spun around, my hand flying to the gun at my waist. There was a sharp prick in the side of my neck and I hissed, my hand slapping my skin on reflex.

I swayed, my body suddenly feeling unbearably light, my mind turning hazy, foggy, like I couldn't get a solid picture. My knees buckled and I fell backwards, crashing into something hard. A wall of solid muscle.

"Hurry up. Take her. Her guards won't be distracted forever."

Rayna's voice echoed in my head, her words repeating over and over again. I tried to cuss her out, but all I managed was a low groan.

My body was weightless, big beefy arms circling me and lifting me off my feet.

I tried to fight, to punch, kick, claw—fucking anything—but it was like my limbs wouldn't listen to me. They were like jello, floppy and completely fucking useless.

Rayna's face blurred in front of me, her face distorted, yet I could still make out the bright as fuck smile on her stupid, ugly face.

She betrayed me. She actually fucking betrayed me, and now she was giving me over to God knows who.

"I wish I could be there when they kill you, to watch you die, but the knowledge of it will have to be enough," she said, looking into my eyes. She glanced over my shoulder. "Okay, I'm ready. Make it look real."

As I was being carried away, I watched Rayna get punched square in the face by a big, hulking figure. I was so out of it that I couldn't even enjoy it properly.

My eyes suddenly felt droopy, sleep creeping up on me like a stalker in the night. I tried to stay awake, to fight the blackness quickly overtaking my vision, but it was no use.

I fell into a deep slumber. I could only hope that when I woke up, I could get myself out of this bad situation.

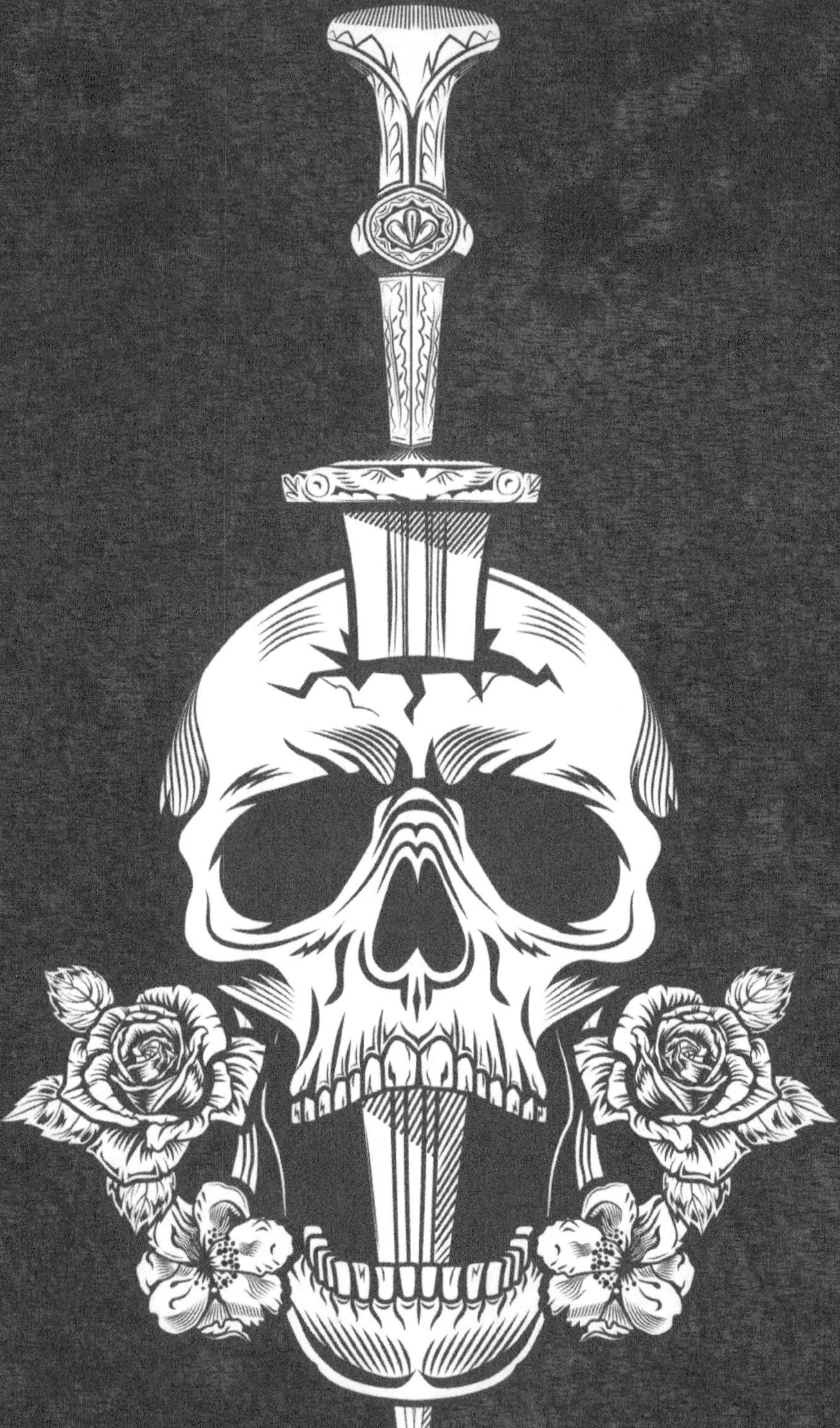

CHAPTER TWENTY-FOUR

Illayana De Luca

Ice-cold water splashed into my face, jolting me awake. I coughed uncontrollably, my body shaking violently as I tried to catch my breath and get air into my lungs. My vision was blurred, my limbs riddled with pins and needles and achingly sore. Voices spun around the room—too many to count—and it was giving me a fucking headache.

I tried to get my bearings. Hazy memories soared through my mind like flashbacks in a movie. The mall. The arcade. Rayna. That sharp prick of a needle in my neck.

That fucking bitch drugged me.

Another bucketful of water hit my face and I gasped, coughing again.

"Time to wake up, princess," a deep voice taunted, ripping me from my memories.

I wiped the water from my face, surprised to be able to move my arms at all. They didn't restrain me.

Stupid.

My eyes travelled around the room, taking in my surroundings. It was a small space; four solid walls, no windows and one door, where a group of heavily tattooed men stood, blocking the exit.

This doesn't look good.

I slowly got to my feet, my legs shaking (I was working hard to hide it). I was already at a disadvantage. I couldn't afford to show weakness. I looked down at my body. *Alright. Clothes still in place, boots on, nothing out of place. Reassuring.*

A well built man stepped forward, dressed in a pair of black slacks and a white button-up shirt (which he left undone, revealing a tanned, toned chest). He was definitely attractive, with baby blue eyes, sharp features and a neatly trimmed beard.

His stance screamed intimidation; his spine straight, shoulders back. But he wasn't fooling me. It was a façade. Even though he was twice my size, I saw the fragility in his eyes, the exhaustion on his face. He wasn't cut out to lead, and it was clearly taking its toll on him. Oh, he was trying to hide it, trying to use his massive body to intimate me. But it wasn't working. When you grew up as the daughter of the head of the Bratva, you knew what *real* intimidation was. And this man did not have it.

This had to be Nero.

The men at his back were a mixture of Mexican and Italian descent, in various shapes of build, ranging from short and stumpy to tall and muscly. How the fuck a man like Nero could gain control of the Los Zetas was beyond me. And not only gain control, but keep it.

"My name is Nero." He smiled, trying to go for friendliness, but I could tell it was forced. "It's such a pleasure to finally meet you."

"Wish I could say the same."

I studied everyone in the room. Twelve men, including Nero, all looking at me like I was their next meal.

Wonderful.

"Aw, I think you'll like me once you get to know me." He winked and waved a hand.

One of his lackeys—a bald guy with a huge gap tooth—pulled out a phone and started recording. "Smile for the camera, Pretty," he said, a sick, twisted smirk on his face.

I smiled brightly, flashing my teeth, and he faltered, the smirk slipping from his lips.

I bet he expected me to cower, to cry. To beg them not to hurt me and let me go. That's what any normal, rational woman would do in my position, I'm sure. But I'm far from normal. Or rational. I'd probably end up antagonising them further.

"My bitch of a cousin set this up, didn't she?"

Nero smiled and walked about the room, hands behind his back like some general in the army. "I'll admit, I was sceptical when she first approached me. I thought it was some sort of ploy you guys were trying to pull off. But one look at her face and I could see the hatred pouring off of her," he laughed. "Never seen a chick that hot look so crazy. I swear, I was a heartbeat away from fucking her 'til she bled."

I scrunched up my face. "Lovely. What exactly did she tell you?"

"Oh, lots of things. She was quite the Chatty Cathy once she got started."

"Don't believe everything ya hear. She's a compulsive liar."

"Funny. She said the same thing about you."

I rolled my eyes. "Of course she did. Was she the one who planted the bombs at my wedding for you, too?"

"For me?" Nero shook his head, laughing. "Oh, she didn't do that for me. She did it for her. You see, it was her idea to hit the wedding. I thought it was idiotic, considering the place was going to be full of Bratva and Cosa

Nostra men. But when she mentioned the arsenal you guys kept in that house, I couldn't say no. She suggested planting a few bombs near your reception and timing them to go off at the same time as my men crashed the gates, to increase the chaos. Then baddabing, baddaboom. The rest is history."

"My uncle. He a part of this crap too?"

"Maybe, maybe not. In all honesty, it doesn't really matter. You're here for my agenda, not theirs."

"And what *is* your agenda?"

He flicked his eyes to the phone and back to me. "To show your father and the Cosa Nostra exactly what happens when they cross me. Once they see the pain I put you through, they'll be willing to do whatever I fucking want to get me to stop."

"You overestimate my value to the De Lucas. You think they'd give a shit that you have me? All you've done is make yourself an enemy of the Bratva. And trust me, they're a worse enemy to have than the Cosa Nostra."

"As wife of the future head of the Cosa Nostra, you're definitely important to them. And the second your father got involved with them, he made an enemy out of *me*. I not only want Alessandro to see his son suffer the same way I suffered when he stole *my* wife from me. No, I also want others to see what happens when they align themselves with the Cosa Nostra."

"Fiancé," I corrected. "She was your fiancé, not your wife."

"Same shit, different name. She was *mine*, regardless of her status."

"Clearly not, since she ditched you to marry Alessandro. From what I hear, she couldn't get away from you fast enough."

Nero backhanded me. No harsh words, no build up of anger. Just a straight slap to the face with the back of his hand. My head whipped to the side, a sharp sting radiating over my cheek.

I turned back to face him, shifting my jaw from side to side. I wiped the small amount of blood trailing from my mouth to my chin with a finger, my tongue running over the bottom of my lip.

I exhaled in disappointment. "Well, that was uncalled for."

"You've got a smart mouth on you."

"So I've been told. I think it's one of my best qualities, to be honest. What about Lucian and Theodora? Why try to kidnap them?"

"Why not? They were there, the opportunity to hurt Alessandro even more right at my fingertips. If my men had succeeded, I would have sent them back to him in pieces."

Anger tore through me at the mere thought of it. There was no way Nero could be allowed to live after this. He had to die, otherwise the danger to them would never end.

Nero took the phone from Gap Tooth and pointed it at me. "Do you know what I love about technology? It's always changing, evolving. The things phones can do these days boggles my mind."

Quite the subject change, but okay. I'll roll with it.

"Suuure," I dragged out. "I can see why it might fascinate a Baby Boomer like you."

One of his men choked on a laugh and Nero snapped his eyes to the culprit: a lanky man wearing ripped jeans and no shirt, a thick, bushy beard covering half his face.

"What?" Nero snapped at him.

The man shifted his feet awkwardly. "She thinks you're, like, seventy. A Baby Boomer is someone born between 1946 and 1964."

"I know what a fucking Baby Boomer is," Nero barked, cutting him a filthy look. He looked back at me. "Like I was saying, technology. Amazing stuff. For example, did you know that you can record videos and people can watch them in real time?"

"Ya, it's called live streaming, Old Timer."

Nero narrowed his eyes, but didn't rise to the bait.

Disappointing.

I tried to ignore the uneasiness slowly rising within me. The fact that he was referring to live streaming could only mean he intended to do it then and there (if he wasn't already). I stared at the camera lens, wondering who was on the other side. Arturo? My father? My brothers?

"It's going to kill Arturo to watch as we all have a taste of your sweet, young pussy. What makes it even better is he's going to watch it as it happens." He waved the phone back and forth. "Say hi to your husband, princess, while you can still form coherent thoughts. Because believe me when I say that once we're done with you, all you'll be able to think about is wanting to die, begging for the pain to finally be over. You won't be able to think of anything else."

He handed the phone back to Gap Tooth and moved to stand in front of a dark-skinned man with deep brown eyes and a slim build. "Diego here likes to hold his women down and fuck them with his gun. I don't think his dick works anymore, but he's found his own way to compensate for that." Nero moved to the next guy. "Angelo likes to carve his name into his victim's stomach before taking them up the ass. He's an ass man."

I should be scared, terrified, freaked the fuck out at what he was saying, but I wasn't. There was no way I was going to let any of that shit happen. Or my father, for that matter. He was coming for me. I was 100% sure of it.

"Diego? You wouldn't happen to be a Cosa Nostra man, would you?"

Nero smiled and answered for him. "*Ex* Cosa Nostra."

Something clicked in my brain. "You're the one who got him to steal the $50,000."

Tapping his nose, he winked at me. "Such a smart one. It's really too bad I have to break you." He studied me, my posture, the lack of fear on my face and my cool, easy demeanour. "My, aren't you a brave little one," he chuckled. "I like it. But don't worry, after the first few rounds, that fiery spirit will be crushed."

I adjusted my footing, staring him down. I wasn't going to let him intimate me, get in my head and try to fuck with my emotions. Keeping a clear head would be my only saving grace until my father got there.

"Now, we're a civilised lot, aren't we boys? We have rules, order. So here's what we're going to do. We're going to hold a little lottery, see who gets you first. And then, once we've all had a taste of you, we'll start all over again. Sound good?"

He talked as if he was discussing something pleasant, not a fucking gang rape.

The fact that they were planning to try and take me one at a time worked in my favour, though. If they all rushed me at once, I wouldn't stand a chance. But individually, it was anyone's game.

My skin tingled with anticipation, my body buzzing with so much adrenaline I clenched my fists to stop them from shaking. Staring hard, I channelled my father. The big, bad Bratva boss. The Bratva Butcher. All the strength and power he exuded.

The training he taught me since I was a child, preparing me for situations just like this, flashed through my mind like scenes in a movie. I cherished it.

Pushing all thoughts out of my mind, I focused on the men in front of me. Reaching down, I pulled a blade from the inside of my boot and smiled. "Alright, so who's first? Is it you, Nero? Or maybe you, Gap Tooth? Or how about the lil' shorty in the back?"

Nero laughed, eyeing the knife. "Rawrrrr, this kitty has claws."

I wasn't overly surprised to discover they missed my weapons. I figured it out when I could still feel the weight of them on my body. Nero might be in control of the Los Zetas, but he was Outfit through and through. They kept women out of the business side of things just as much as the Cosa Nostra did. They didn't think women were a threat. That would be their downfall.

"Okie dokie, boys, who's got number one?" Nero asked, pulling a piece of paper from his pocket.

A black-haired guy with a face only a mother could love raised his hand, licking his lips. He was short (about 5'4) and a little on the chubby side. He stepped forward and I watched him, studying how he moved, the way he swung his arms, the way he walked. Everything, filing it all away to use against him if I could.

"Oh, ho, ho, Felix!" Nero clapped him on the shoulder. "Now, make sure to leave enough for the rest of us, okay?"

"No promises," Felix said gruffly, wiping snot from his nose with the back of his hand. He stepped away from the group and locked those leery eyes on me.

"Don't forget to look at the camera, Pretty." Gap Tooth shook the phone in his hand. "Don't want your husband to miss the tears in your eyes."

I scoffed. As if I'd ever give them the satisfaction of me crying.

With a gesture of my fingers, I beckoned Felix forward. "Let's go then, Short Stuff. Don't got all day."

The bravado was somewhat fake. I was confident I could take him. Easily. But even I could see the precarious situation I was in. Eventually, my luck would run out. I just had to hope that my father could get there before then.

Felix flexed his muscles and strode towards me, confident as a lion hunting a gazelle. I zoned everyone else out and focused on him, waiting for him to get close enough. I flipped my knife and held it in a reverse grip, the blade pointing outwards.

When he got within reach, I stepped forward quickly, swiping my knife across his throat in a deadly, clean cut. I kept walking as Felix dropped to his knees behind me, a gurgled cry slipping from his lips before he fell face-forward to the ground. The kill took less than a second.

I smirked, enjoying the way the smiles dropped from all of their faces at the unexpected kill. Well, everyone except Nero. He was smiling.

"The fuck?!" Gap Tooth hissed.

"What? You expected me to just sit back and take it?" I swished my finger from side to side. "Tut, tut, tut," I taunted, walking backwards, keeping my eyes on them as I side-stepped Felix's lifeless body until I was back in the centre of the room again.

Nero eyed me excitedly. "Impressive. I guess what Rayna said was true. You *can* fight. How about we even the odds a little this time round? Who's got numbers two and three?"

Diego and a guy with a goatee walked forward, a little more apprehensive than before, but still reeking with that oh-so-fake alpha male confidence.

I backed up a step, getting back in the zone. I pulled another knife—this time from my other boot—and spread my arms wide at my side, letting the crazy take over. "Oooo, I do love a good double team."

I flipped both the blades so I held them in a reverse grip (my preferred hold), and strengthened my stance.

They attacked together. Diego came up on my left, swinging high with a big brawny arm, and Goatee kicked low. I blocked Diego's attack with my forearm while simultaneously twisting my body out of Goatee's path. I lashed out with a kick of my own, hitting Goatee right in the face.

"Fuck!" He landed flat on his ass while Diego swung again.

I reared back, avoiding the swing effortlessly. He was slow, his technique sloppy. We locked into a battle of blows. Diego struck again and again and, even though his attacks held power, they were clumsy. Lacked finesse. Were easy to dodge, block.

Goatee rejoined the fight, striking out with the same ferocity as Diego. I blocked attacks from them both as they worked together to try and take me down, Diego coming at me from one side while Goatee came from the other, punching and kicking in unison.

I could not be any more fucking grateful that my father would make me train by fighting all my brothers at the same time. It truly prepared me for this exact moment, taking on more than one opponent at a time.

I ducked under a powerful swing and stabbed Diego in the thigh. I pulled my knife out just as quick and rounded behind him. I kicked him in the back, sending him sprawling to the ground.

Goatee pivoted on his feet and we circled each other. "You think you're tough shit, don't you? But you're just a dirty little slut."

I laughed. "Oh, I definitely am. But only for one guy." I looked directly into the camera lens and winked for Arturo.

I could picture him, screaming at me to take this seriously, to stop fucking around. I probably should have listened.

"I'm going to enjoy putting you in your place. Showing you who's boss," Goatee hissed.

"We both know you ain't the boss. Run it straight. Let's see what you got."

Goatee snarled and ran at me hard, trying to tackle me. I dug my feet into the ground for stability and met him head on, twisting out of the way at the last second. I turned, and using my long, limber legs, side-kicked him straight in the back, at the base of his spine. He arched forward with a cry and slammed into Diego as he was struggling to a stand, and they both toppled to the ground, tripping over each other.

I wasn't sure how much time I had left, whether these dickheads behind me would finally realise I was more trouble than I was worth and take me down together, instead of this stupid lottery shit. I needed to end this now, and quickly. The less I had to fight at one time, the better.

As they both got to their feet, Diego favouring his injured leg and Goatee hunching over at the waist like an old man with a bad back, I sprinted forward and went on the offensive, alternating my strikes between both hands.

A punch directly in the face for Diego, a punch in the gut for Goatee. An uppercut to Diego's chin, a knee strike to Goatee's face. A spinning hook kick to Diego's head.

Every blow made them grunt in pain, pushing them further and further back as I attacked.

I didn't give them a moment of reprieve. I struck hard and fast, using my blades to cut into their skin as I moved with all the speed I possessed, slicing their flesh over and over again while trying to dodge their attempts to hit me. Gymnastics gave me an unbelievable amount of flexibility, allowing me to bend my body in awkward ways to avoid their strikes, like an acrobat doing flips and turns in a circus.

Goatee managed to land a hard hit to my shoulder and I stumbled, the force of the blow shocking the hell out of me and making me lose my footing.

Fuuuuuck. That's gonna bruise.

Diego capitalised on it and pushed forward, ramming me with his body and lifting me up into the air in a running tackle. I dug both my knives into his shoulder blades and he roared, trying to throw me off.

I held on tight and spun around his body until I was hanging onto his back like a piggyback ride. I ripped one of my blades out of his shoulder and rammed it into the base of his neck. He screamed and flailed, but I held on until he dropped to his knees. Then I stabbed him again and again, over and over, until I was completely drenched in his blood.

I finally let him go and Diego fell forward with a splat, blood oozing out all around him. Panting, I raised my head and locked eyes with Nero. I flung my knife to the side and hit Goatee in the middle of the forehead as he ran towards me, killing him instantly.

My lungs burned. My shoulder throbbed and my body ached. I could feel the bruises already beginning to form on my skin from their attacks. Adrenaline coursed through me like the blood pumping in my veins, making my heart thump so loudly I could hear it in my ears, feel it beating in my chest.

I inhaled deeply to centre my breathing, and got to my feet.

Unlike last time, Nero wasn't smiling. With narrowed eyes and a clenched jaw, it was clear he was pissed about the fact that I killed another two of his men. He wasn't expecting me to win.

"You wanna know what your problem is, Nero? Where you went wrong?" I asked, pulling my other blade from Diego's shoulder and wiping the blood on his shirt. "You made the mistake of assuming I was just Arturo's woman. I mean, don't get me wrong, I most definitely am Arturo's woman, through and through. 100%. But that's not *all* I am. I'm also the daughter of The Bratva Butcher."

One of his men gasped in shock, and I smiled.

"You've heard of The Bratva Butcher, haven't you? But I bet you didn't know he was my father."

Not a lot of people knew the identity of The Bratva Butcher unless they were actually in the Bratva themselves, but rumours of my father's mercilessness spread far and wide the day he annihilated an entire family line.

Whispers echoed all around the room, their voices hushed yet filled with so much fear. I revelled in it.

Good. They should be scared.

"One thing you need to know about my father is that he's *incredibly* protective. Paranoid too. Like, I'm talking an *insane* amount. You see, after my mother was kidnapped and murdered, he's held his children on a bit of a tight leash. The only way he would even let us leave the house was if we agreed to let him put a tracking device in us." With the tip of my knife, I pointed to the back of my neck. "Since I was ten years old, I've had a little microchip embedded just beneath the surface of my skin. One that, once activated, broadcasts my location to my father."

Nero's eyes widened in shock just as a huge explosion rocked the building, making the ground shake beneath our feet.

I smiled. "And here he is now."

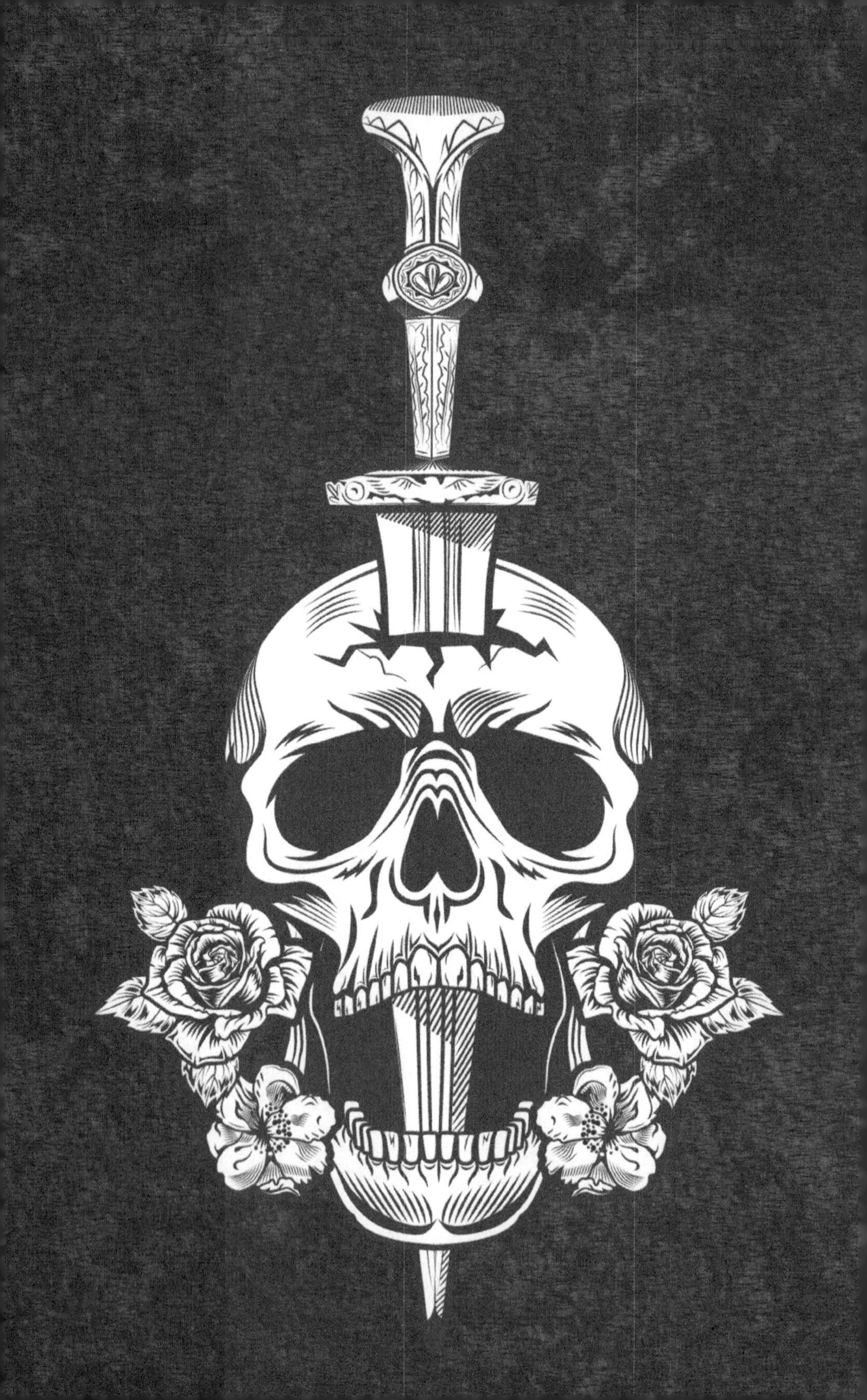

CHAPTER TWENTY-FIVE

Arturo De Luca

"That was so much fun!" Lukyan yelled, a bright, beaming smile on his face as we walked into the house.

Their large Victorian-style mansion was well underway to being repaired, with dozens of men working hard to restore the house to its former glory. Builders, carpenters and electricians all worked around the clock to fix the damage Nero caused, cleaning up the rubble, fixing the walls and applying new plaster and paint.

The Bratva sure did work fast, and they wasted no time.

"I mean, fuck, did you see how much blood and guts where on the floor by the time we left? They're gonna have to rip that carpet out. There's *no way* they're gonna get all those blood stains out," Lukyan continued, heading towards the kitchen.

"I know right! It was so fucking awesome. What about that one fucker who pissed his pants?" Vin laughed, following behind Lukyan like a little puppy dog.

I knew the second those fools met, they'd bond like crazy. They were too much alike not to. I shook my head and sighed, trailing after them. They talked loudly, chatting about their kills and how much fun they had just had. Lukyan handed out shots of vodka to everyone. They were like a bunch of teenage girls talking about their latest crushes, voices all high and excited.

"Oh my god, yes! That was hilarious. Fucking pussy." Lukyan tossed back his shot and poured another. "Illayana is going to be so pissed she missed it. She hates missing out on all the fun."

Speaking of, where is my wife?

I'd noticed her absence immediately, but just assumed she was upstairs somewhere. This place had four fucking floors. She could be on any one of them, but surely she would have come downstairs when she heard us come back?

I went to leave the kitchen when Vin spoke.

"Turo, where the fuck are you going? Let's celebrate! We got all the guns back, got a few prisoners *and* we didn't lose a single man. Win, win, fucking *win*."

All valid points to celebrate, but...

"I'm going to find my wife."

"Don't bother. She'll just be killjoy, ruin our buzz." Lukyan shrugged out of his bloody suit jacket and hung it over a chair.

Aleksandr slapped him over the head. "Don't talk about her like that."

"What?! I'm just being honest," he whined, massaging his head. "Watch. The second she comes down here, she'll whine and bitch about how she wasn't allowed to come."

I left them to argue and went to find her. After checking upstairs and the rest of the house that wasn't being repaired, I was irritated as fuck when I still couldn't find her.

Where the fuck is she? She better not have left the house. I gave very specific instructions to Christian, Luca and Lorenzo. They better have fucking listened, or there'd be hell to pay.

When I stepped back into the kitchen alone, Aleksandr frowned. "Where's Illayana?"

A sinking feeling churned in my stomach. "I don't know. I couldn't find her."

"Relax. She's probably in the warehouse or something, punching out her frustrations," Lukyan said, taking another shot, not at all bothered by the fact that his sister wasn't there.

Aleksandr walked over to the glass sliding door and pulled back the curtain, peering outside. "There's no lights on in the warehouse. She isn't in there." He walked back to the kitchen bench and knocked back a shot, the frown still on his face.

The sinking feeling grew, spreading throughout my body, and I clenched my fists.

Oh, I'm going to kill them. They fucking left.

I pulled out my phone and just as I went to dial one of her idiot bodyguards, it rang, the name CHRISTIAN flashing on the screen. I answered quickly.

"You better have a damn good fucking reason as to why you aren't here," I growled.

"I'm sorry, Boss. Fuck, I'm so fucking sorry."

I stiffened, my whole body going rigid. "Put her on the phone."

"Boss—"

"Put. Her. On. The. Phone," I repeated slowly, my voice deepening with every word.

Christian spoke fast. "I-I can't. Listen, Boss, it was a mistake. A stupid fucking mistake that we shouldn't have made, but she wanted to go out and she wouldn't take no for an answer. And then we ran into her cousin who wanted to talk to her alone, and then I seriously don't know what happened. We got gassed or some shit, I dunno. When we came to, she wasn't there anymore. Fuck, I don't even—"

"Enough!" I yelled. "Where is she, Christian?"

"I'm sorry, Boss, I don't know. She was taken."

Taken.

Time slowed down, everything around me grinding to a halt as those words sank in. She was gone. Someone had kidnapped her, taken her from me.

Rage blasted through me. I roared, screaming at the top of my lungs. I lashed out, kicking furniture over and cursing him three ways to Sunday, calling him every filthy name I could think of. I was no longer speaking English. Everything came out in a rush of Italian.

I punched the wall, every curse word accompanied by my fist punching through plaster. I kicked in the China cabinet filled with expensive antiques, bashed the shit out of everything in my reach until my knuckles bled.

Aleksandr stepped towards me (to do what, I had no idea), but Vin got in his path, shaking his head. He knew the best thing to do was stay the fuck out of my way when I was like that.

Christian didn't say a word the entire time, but I knew he was still on the phone.

"Get your asses back here. Now," I snarled, hanging up.

They were all going to pay for disobeying my orders.

The room was silent, Aleksandr, Nikolai and even Lukyan staring at me with intense eyes. They looked at the destruction I'd caused and said nothing. I didn't feel guilty about it. I'd pay to replace everything later.

"What's happened?" Aleksandr asked, his body tight with tension.

I didn't even want to say the words. "Illayana's gone."

"Gone? What do you mean, 'gone'?" Lukyan snapped.

"Someone's kidnapped her."

Suddenly the room sprang to life, Illayana's brothers moving like the house was on fire. Aleksandr barked orders, Nikolai grabbed his laptop, typing away furiously while Lukyan ran out of the room, a few Bratva men hot on his heels.

My mind swirled. All I could think about was Illayana, about what could be happening to her and who could be doing it. My thoughts turned savage, the idea of her being hurt making me want to burn the whole fucking world to a crisp. I had no idea what I was going to do, but I had to do something. I had to find her.

"Vin, call Derek. See if he can track her phone. If it hasn't been ditched, we might be able to find her."

"There's no need." Dimitri stomped into the room, anger in every step, hair wet from a shower and dressed in a fresh Armani suit. Bratva men trailed behind him, concern wafting off them as they ran to do as he commanded, gathering weapons and supplies.

My father stepped into the room a second later, coming over to me. "Is it true, son? She's been taken?" He placed a hand on my shoulder, offering support.

"Yes. And I'm about to lose my fucking mind." I shrugged off his touch and went to Dimitri. We had to find her, get moving *now*. "What did you mean, there's no need to track her phone? You know where she is?"

Dimitri's blue eyes shone with menace as he barked, "Nikolai," effectively ignoring me.

His son jogged over, laptop in hand.

"Dimitri!" I snapped, my patience nonexistent. "Why wouldn't I need to track her phone?"

His gaze snapped to me and I could see the fire burning in his eyes, the anger radiating from him, but I wasn't deterred. He didn't fucking scare me, even if he was The Bratva Butcher.

"We can glare at each other later. Right now, you need to talk to me or you and I are finally going to go at it."

A chorus of gasps echoed in the kitchen. Silence reigned over the room, but I couldn't let it last. We didn't have the fucking time to waste. Every second we stood there staring at each other, she could be getting hurt.

Fed up, I reached into the holster strapped to my chest and gripped my gun, ready to start threatening if he didn't start fucking talking. Just as I was about to pull it out, my father bodychecked me, ramming his chest into mine and pushing me back a step. Aleksandr jumped protectively in front of his father, a scowl on his face.

"*Figliolo, tranquillo. Respirare,*" *Son, calm. Breathe,* he whispered in my ear.

"*Lo sono calma, cazzo,*" *I am fucking calm,* I growled, shoving him away.

Alessandro stayed in front of me, blocking me from Dimitri in case I lost my temper again. "Dimitri, I'm sure you have a plan. Please, share it."

My father, always the fucking peace maker.

Dimitri pushed his son to the side and stepped forward, glaring at me. "You and I are going to have a few words when this is all over, Arturo—"

"Looking forward to it," I snapped, interrupting him. "But right now, we've got more important shit to deal with."

"I agree. It's the only reason you're still breathing right now. But make no mistake, this matter will be dealt with." Dimitri took the laptop from Nikolai and turned it to face me.

I stared at the screen, seeing a map of a small town in the middle of nowhere and a bright red dot. "What the fuck am I looking at?"

Dimitri narrowed his eyes, irritation wafting off him. "That's Illayana. Her location. I'm assembling my men now. I suggest you do the same. We leave in three minutes."

"You bugged her phone?"

"Not exactly."

"What does that mean?"

"It means we can waste time while I explain it to you, or you can move your ass so we can get going."

I glared, but luckily for him, he had a point. No reason to waste even more time than we already had.

"Fine. Vin, gather the men. Get them armed and loaded back into the car. We're going to get my wife back."

"Tell me how your father knows exactly where Illayana is," I demanded, casting my eyes to Lukyan, who sat in the passenger seat of the SUV.

I was surprised he chose to ride with us, and not his own family. He had even fought Vin for the front seat, literally pushing him to the ground when Vin opened the passenger-side door.

Vin now sat in the back seat next to Father, glaring daggers at the back of Lukyan's head. If looks could kill...

"Did he bug her phone or something?" I asked, following the other SUV in front of me as we merged onto the highway.

I wasn't 100% sure where we were going, just that the location was somewhere outside a small town on the outskirts of Las Vegas.

"Or something." Lukyan turned and tapped the back of his neck.

The fuck?

"He bugged *her?*" I asked incredulously.

"Calm down, it's not like she doesn't know about it. We've all got 'em."

"Got what exactly?"

"It's like a little microchip. It's implanted just beneath the skin. No big deal."

Vin poked his head into the front section of the car, a frown on his face. "Like what cats and dogs have and shit?"

"Yeah, kinda. It's a safety measure, in case one of us gets lifted."

"Lifted?" Father questioned, confused.

"Kidnapped," Lukyan clarified.

Father sighed and grumbled, "Young kids and their stupid slang."

I wouldn't really call Lukyan 'young', but whatever. I switched the car into cruise control and leant back. "So, you're telling me you all have trackers in the backs of your necks that broadcast your location to your father?"

"You make him sound crazy," Lukyan laughed. "He's just a bit protective, that's all. He got a bit paranoid after our mother was kidnapped. He wasn't able to find her before she was raped and killed. He decided he wasn't going to go through that shit again, hence the tracker."

I didn't know how I felt about that. I mean, in the moment it was coming in handy, but I wasn't comfortable with Illayana having a microchip in her like she was a fucking animal.

My phone chimed. I picked it up and glanced at it quickly, making sure to keep one eye on the road.

A text message:

Unknown: Your wife sure is a pretty little thing.

Rage poured through me like hot, boiling lava and I ground my teeth, squeezing the steering wheel until my knuckles turned white. Another text message came through. It was a link to a website.

My stomach dropped. What would I find when I clicked it?

"What is it? You've got a real murdery look on your face right now," Lukyan said, and I glared. He inched away from me. "Yeah, that look."

"Take the wheel." I climbed over the centre console, moving to the back seat.

"Aye, what the fuck?!" Panic flashed across Lukyan's face as he jumped to grab the steering wheel before we veered off the road.

"Move," I barked, shoving Vin over so he squished up against the window.

"Ow, Turo! You fucking prick."

"Shut up, before I shut you up," I snapped, opening the message.

"Your road safety awareness is a bloody joke," Lukyan squawked, eyes flicking to me in the rear-view mirror before returning to the road.

I ignored him and focused on my phone. "Someone sent me a link."

"To what?" Vin asked, climbing into the passenger seat.

Lukyan tapped on the breaks and Vin flew forward, smashing into the dashboard. Vin shrieked and groaned in pain.

"Whoops," Lukyan chuckled.

"Will you stop fucking around? This is not a fucking game, Lukyan! Your goddamn sister is being held captive, and you're playing around like there's nothing fucking wrong. What the fuck is the matter with you?"

Hurt flashed in his eyes and he stared at the road, jaw clenched. "People cope in different ways, Arturo. I'm choosing not to dwell on something I can't change, and instead try and relax before I walk into a situation that has the potential to shatter my heart. I love my sister. Out of all my siblings, she's the one I'm closest to. And if we get there too late…if she's dead…" he choked, his words dying off.

I blinked, momentarily taken aback. I definitely wasn't expecting something so….deep, so meaningful, to come out of his mouth. It was like a whole other side of him.

My father gave me a deathly glare. "Arturo." That one word held a magnitude of reprimand. "That was uncalled for. I understand how you're feeling, but you can't lash out at everyone around you."

He was using his 'Dad' voice. I sighed and looked up from my phone. "Sorry, Lukyan." I wasn't really, but I didn't want to continue the conversation.

I clicked on the link and it took me to a website that was live streaming a video.

Illayana stood in the centre of the room, hair wet like she'd been dunked in a bucketful of water, her clothes covered in dirt. I stiffened at the sight of her, my blood running cold.

The grip on my phone tightened and a dark growl slipped from my lips as a man backhanded her across the face.

Nero.

He walked towards the camera and took it, pointing it towards Illayana as he spoke, his words echoing in the car.

He talked of the benefits of live streaming, of how excited he was to know that I would be watching as he defiled my wife, as his men took what wasn't theirs to have.

My body grew tight, my anger skyrocketing as I was forced to sit there and listen to that sadistic asshole talk about how his men planned to have her, what they were going to do to her.

Lukyan cursed and beat his fists against the steering wheel. He slammed his foot down on the accelerator and we sped forward, overtaking the car we were following with his father and brothers in it, taking the lead.

His phone rang and he answered in Russian, his words harsh as he explained to whoever was on the other line what was going on.

I didn't know how far away we were, but I prayed we were fucking close. I had the stomach to deal with a lot of things. I've gutted men from throat to pelvis. I've ripped organs from their bodies and then eaten a turkey sandwich while I stood in a pool of their blood. But this? Watching Illayana being hurt? Brutalised? *That* I couldn't stomach.

The camera panned out to the men in the room—a dozen at least—and I tried to commit every one of them to memory. I would hunt them all down and inflict twice the amount of pain and suffering they caused Illayana.

I squinted at the screen.

Wait a second, is that Diego?

It was! Standing amongst the men waiting to defile my wife was that little shit stain, his eyes lit with excitement.

Motherfucker.

One of the men walked forward, heading towards my wife. My gut churned.

Oh, God. I don't think I can watch.

Father stared at the screen, a worried but thoughtful expression on his face. "She doesn't look scared."

I zeroed in on her face. My father was right. She didn't look scared at all. If anything, she looked excited. Eager.

"What's happening?" Lukyan demanded, one hand on the steering wheel and the other holding the phone to his ear. His eyes darted to me impatiently.

"She's about to fight some guy one-on-one."

I described the scene for Lukyan as he drove, never taking my eyes off Illayana. I honestly felt like my heart was going to burst out of my chest at any moment, like my body was going to shut down from all the stress and anxiety flowing through me.

Within a second, Illayana slit the man's throat with one quick manoeuvre, and I breathed a sigh of relief. That was, until Diego and another man stepped forward. Then my heart sped up all over again. I could have sworn that I was going to end up having a fucking heart attack.

This fight lasted longer. It was more hands on, more brutal. Every time I saw those fuckers swing at her, I wanted to wrap my hands around their throats and choke the life out of them.

"How far away are we?" I shouted, my grip on my temper and sanity at breaking point. I was going to snap.

My father tried to comfort me, whispering supportive things in Italian, but it wasn't any good. Nothing could comfort me except having her in front of me, unharmed.

"Not far," Lukyan gritted out, focused on the road as he weaved in and out of traffic. He jerked off the highway and we sped down a long, dark road, driving further and further away from civilisation and deeper into the sticks.

Illayana stabbed Diego in the leg and kicked him away. She and the other man circled each other, then she looked directly at the camera and winked.

She. Fucking. Winked.

"For fuck's sake, Illayana," I hissed, grinding my teeth.

When I got my hands on her, I was going to punish the fuck out of her for that. For playing around when her fucking life was at stake.

The car came to a screeching halt and I finally looked away from the screen. A large house sat a few miles away, surrounded by mountains of dirt and an abundance of cars and motorbikes.

A knock at my window had me reaching for my gun. Dimitri stood outside the car, face hard and expression as dark and deadly as the devil himself. He stepped back as I opened the door, giving me room to slide out.

"She in there?" I asked, pulling out my gun and checking the chamber. Ready to go.

"*Da*. Lukyan said you were sent a video? I want to see it."

"Trust me when I say there isn't time for that. We need to go, and we need to go *now*."

T J MAGUIRE

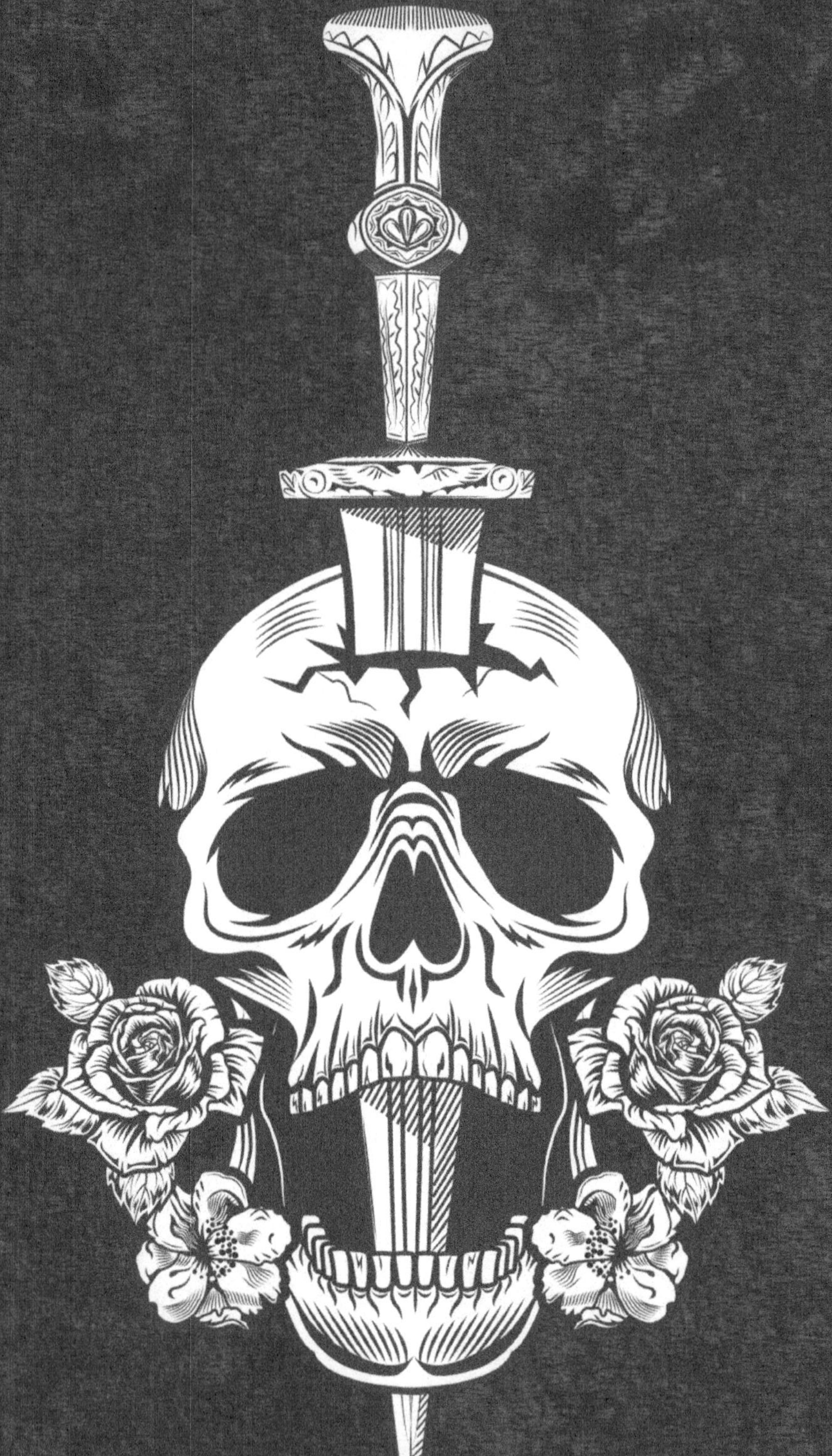

CHAPTER TWENTY-SIX

Illayana De Luca

Nero shook off the surprise of the explosion quickly, clicking his fingers repeatedly at his men. "Go check it out," he barked, and half of them bolted out of the room.

The other half who remained exchanged looks of confusion, fear and worry.

I strengthened my stance and stared them down with the air of the Bratva warrior I was. "If you leave now, you've got a chance of making it out of here alive. But I can guarantee you, anyone still in this room when my father gets here will experience the most excruciating death he can think of. And my father has a very vivid imagination." I smiled, the thought bringing me joy.

"Don't listen to her," Nero thundered, fists clenched at his side. "Even if that's your father out there, there's no way he'll make it past my men. No fucking way. We've got all his guns. What's he gonna do, come at us with sticks and batons?"

Gunfire echoed outside the door, followed quickly by screams of pain and cries for help.

"Did you really think my father wouldn't get his guns back?" I laughed at his idiocy. "You really should have done your research before you fucked with us."

Nero glanced nervously around the room. "My men will kill them all. The Bratva is no match for them."

"Even you don't really believe that."

Nero pulled out a gun and aimed it right at my head. "What's to stop me from killing you right here, right now, huh? Splattering your brains all over the goddamn walls?"

"Absolutely fucking nothing," I shrugged. "But we both know if you do that, my father will make you regret it." I tilted my head, Wanda Maximoff-style. "I'm curious, could you handle years of torture, Nero? Because that's what my father will do to you. He won't kill you. He'll keep you alive, so he can make you suffer day after day after day. My brothers will get in on the fun, too. And then, of course, there's Arturo. Granted, I haven't seen him in action yet, but based on what I know about him, I think he'll be just as creative about making you suffer as my father. Maybe even more so."

His hand shook slightly and terror filled his eyes. The action made his men shuffle their feet, as if they wanted to bolt from the room and get as far away as they could. He was losing his men, and their confidence in him.

"They're gonna do that shit regardless."

That was the worst thing for him to say. If his men hadn't lost faith in him before, they sure as shit did then.

More gunfire rained inside the house, followed by grunts and groans, screams and cries loud enough for all to hear. Almost all at once, Nero's men scurried, running for the exit. But it was too late.

The door was kicked in with such powerful, brute force that it ripped off the hinges and smacked one of them in the face, knocking him down.

And then there he was. My husband, a look of pure menace on his face. Darkness vibrated from him, tainting the air with a promise of violence, death and destruction. There was something different about him, something I'd never seen in him before: an evil lurking behind those beautiful multi-coloured eyes. An evil that demanded retribution.

He was glorious, a Greek God in human form. Blood dripped down his face, on his clothes, his knuckles, over nearly every inch of him. He looked...terrifying, like the devil in a Brioni suit.

The fact that I was insanely turned on by just the sight of him made me realise I was a lot more fucked up in the head than I thought.

Oh well.

Nero moved fast, faster than I ever thought he was capable of. He spun, wrapping an arm around my throat and putting his gun to my head, right against my temple. "Nobody fucking move."

Arturo froze, Nikolai and Lukyan behind him doing the same, their guns aimed directly at us. Nero's men moved towards them, either to try and escape or take their weapons. Who knows. In unison, my brothers diverted their aim to them, warning them not to move while Arturo kept his gun pointed at Nero, hiding behind me like the little bitch he was.

My eyes locked with Arturo's. "Hi, husband," I said sweetly, giving him a smile. I was happy to see him, even if I did have a gun digging into my temple.

He narrowed his eyes, his glare promising punishment. "You didn't stay at home like I told you to, *kotenok*."

"Wellllll, if we're being technical, you didn't tell *me*. You told Christian and Luca."

Nero jostled me so hard that my head whipped back and forth, making me wince. "Shut up! All of you! Here's what's going to happen. You're all gonna back up now, nice and slow, and let me pass. Otherwise, I'll blow her head clean off."

Arturo sneered, his rage palpable. "No." And then he fired, shooting Nero directly in the head. There was no hesitation, no second-guessing his decision. No indication that he was even going to take the shot. He just fired. It was a skilled shot, one that showed exactly how good he was with that gun.

Blood splattered on my cheek and Nero fell away, his lifeless body hitting the ground with a solid *thud*.

Arturo swerved, aiming his gun at Nero's men. "On the ground."

They didn't hesitate. One of them even had the courage to speak as he went down to his knees.

"Listen, we didn't want any part in this." His words held the traces of a Spanish accent. A Los Zeta. "This was all Nero's idea, his revenge. It had nothing to do with us."

"*Kotenok,* come here," Arturo ordered, never taking his eyes off the group of men, his gun steady in the air.

I walked to his side and looked up at him. "Yes, husband?" I was placating him, trying to smooth over the shitstorm I knew was coming my way at having ignored his *request* for me to stay home. My hope was that if I didn't fight him too much, he would go easy on me.

Doubtful.

Staring directly at the men on their knees, he gripped my chin with his free hand and dragged my face to his, lifting me to my tippy toes. His lips crashed into mine, his tongue licking into my mouth in a searing hot kiss, one that sent tingles straight to my clit.

It was a fiercely dominating kiss, one that screamed possessiveness. Claiming. He was showing these men that I was his, and he wouldn't let their actions go unpunished. He wanted them to see, to watch the control he exerted over me, to know that he owned me.

I moaned and tried to move into him, desperate to feel the hard lines of his body against me, but he kept me in place with the strong grip he had on my chin, not allowing me an inch of movement. It was like I was his puppet, only free to move if—and when—he wished it.

He bit my bottom lip hard enough to sting, and I yelped in surprise. "I'm going to bend you over my knee and spank your ass for leaving the house when you knew you weren't meant to."

Pulling back, he smirked down at me, the desire I felt for him evident in my rapid breathing and flushed cheeks.

Lukyan gagged. "Dude. I so did not need to hear that."

"Yeah, too much information," Nikolai grunted.

Arturo nipped my bottom lip once more before finally releasing me. I stumbled, breathless, my legs like jello at his intoxicating touch. My skin was hot, my belly was on fire and I desperately wanted to get him alone in a room and let him do wicked, depraved things to me.

"You say it had nothing to do with you, yet you would have tried to have your way with my woman. Take what doesn't belong to you," Arturo growled, glaring hard at the man who spoke.

"No, man. Seriously. We wanted no part in this. Honest. *Tienes que creerme. No fuimos nosotros, todo fue Nero.*" *You've got to believe me. It wasn't us, it was all Nero,* he rushed in Spanish.

They all nodded eagerly, and that's when I realised the only men left in the room were Los Zetas.

My father strolled in, his Kevlar vest strapped to his chest and a P-90 in his hands. Alessandro was a step behind him, sweat on his brow and blood in his hair.

"Moya doch'." He pushed his way to me and wrapped me in a tight embrace. His body shook (with fear or adrenaline, I had no idea), but when I stepped back he hugged me tighter, not letting me go.

"Otets, ya v poryadke," Father, I'm fine. I whispered reassuringly, but he just squeezed me tighter. I sighed, letting him nearly squish me to death.

Finally, he let me go, the briefest glimpse of tears in his eyes before he schooled his features and blinked them away. His ferocious gaze scanned the room and he locked onto Nero's lifeless body.

"Why is that fucker dead?" he growled. "I wanted him alive."

"He did it." Lukyan pointed to Arturo and I rolled my eyes.

Fucking tattle tale.

Arturo stood tall, not shrinking under my father's intense stare. "It was him or her. I chose Illayana."

Father sighed. "Fair enough." He tilted his head to the men on their knees. "These guys will have to do. Take them."

My brothers and a few Bratva men moved to follow his command.

"Wait! Just listen!" The guy who spoke before shouted as he was dragged to his feet. "We weren't going to touch her! I swear!"

"You honestly expect me to believe that?" Arturo scoffed. He held up his phone. "I watched you fuckers."

"That wasn't us! Please, just hear me out!"

"Take them away," my father grunted, not interested in hearing a single word.

But I was.

"Wait," I called out, moving towards them.

Arturo blocked my path. "No," he growled. "You're not going near them."

"Just chill out, I wanna ask them something."

"They were going to rape you, Illayana, while I sat there watching it happen, knowing there wasn't a damn thing I could do about it. You're. Not. Going. Near. Them."

I sighed. "Fine. I can ask from here, then."

The other men had been taken away, but the guy who spoke—the only one who had the nerve to—stared at me with pleading eyes. Lukyan stood in the doorway, one hand wrapped around the dude's arm, waiting for me.

"Why are the Los Zetas taking orders from Nero?"

The man glanced away, licking his lips nervously. "I can't tell you."

"You do realise this is your only chance to save yourself? My father's not going to give you another chance to tell your story. This is it. I'd take advantage of it."

He sighed. "He has something that belongs to us."

"What?"

His lips slammed shut and he shook his head. The message was clear. He wasn't going to say anything more.

"Take him away," my father ordered, and Lukyan obeyed.

I blew out a breath, mentally and physically exhausted. I was definitely ready to get the hell out of there.

"Put me down! *¡Hijo de puta! ¡Te mataré!*" *You son of a bitch! I'll kill you!* A feminine voice screeched in Spanish.

I frowned and walked further into the house. Marching towards me, Aleksandr had a petite, dark-haired woman flung over his shoulder like a sack of potatoes, kicking and screaming as she beat her fists against his back, cursing him in Spanish.

My brows shot up in surprise.

"Glad to see you, brat," Aleksandr grunted, moving past me and out the front door.

I pointed after him. "Uh, who is that?"

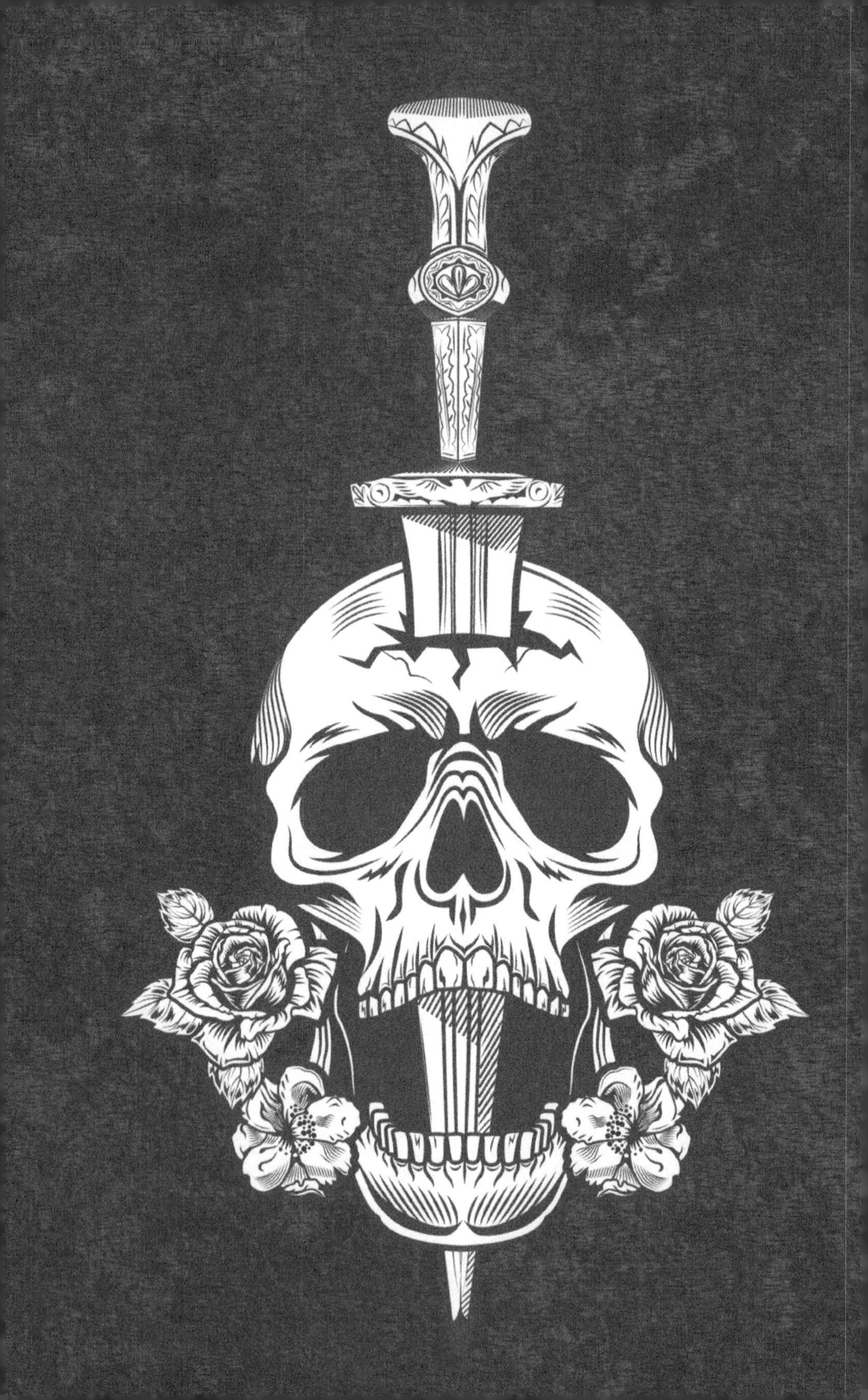

CHAPTER TWENTY-SEVEN

Illayana De Luca

"Arturo, please," I whined, begging for mercy. For the better part of an hour he'd been teasing me, keeping me on the edge of orgasm before taking it away. He was punishing me for leaving the house, for disobeying him. Torturing me with pleasure and then taking it away. Controlling everything, only letting me feel what he wanted me to feel. It was the most exquisite torture I'd ever experienced. And he was doing it all without laying a single finger on me.

My hands were bound to the headboard, my legs spread wide open and shackled to the bed posts. Shivers racked my naked body. Goosebumps pebbled my skin. Heat coursed through my veins, and I literally cried when Arturo shut off the vibrator before I could come. *Again.*

"No!" I thrashed wildly, desperate to get free.

Arturo sat comfortably in a chair in the corner of the room, wearing nothing but his black slacks, his tattooed, muscular chest on full display. In his hands was the vibrator's remote.

"Have you learnt your lesson yet?" His voice was rough, thick with want and arousal, his taunting words making me even angrier.

"Argh! You're a fucking bastard!"

"Guess not." He flicked the vibrator to full power and I cried out, my back bowing. He turned it off a moment later and I slumped back onto the bed, panting hard.

"Okay, okay, okay. I've learnt my lesson."

He stood gracefully, his long, limber body unfolding from the chair, and walked to the end of the bed, staring down at me. "Well? What was the lesson, *kotenok?*"

I breathed hard, my chest rising and falling. "To listen when you tell me to do something."

Even he knew I wouldn't really do that. I had a fiery spirit, a free mind. I did what I wanted, when I wanted to do it, and he knew it. It was what he liked most about me. He was used to getting his way all the time, and I was the only one who challenged him. But in the bedroom? Yeah, I could definitely listen there.

His entrancing blue-green eyes roved over every inch of my body, the path his gaze travelled searing my skin. "You've got no idea what seeing you tied up like this, completely at my mercy, does to a man like me."

I squirmed, wriggling my hips to try and entice him to touch me. "Arturo, please, stop teasing me. I can't take it anymore."

"You can," he said dismissively. "You'll take whatever I give you, and you want to know why? Because you want to please me." He pulled the vibrator out of my pussy and placed it on the bed.

I whimpered at the loss of it, my pussy throbbing with the need to be filled.

Achingly slowly, he undid the bonds around my wrists and ankles, stepping back. "Let's see how well you learnt your lesson." He sat back in his chair and spread his legs wide. "Crawl to me." His deep, throaty voice made me shiver, and my body zinged with a desperate need to obey him.

On my hands and knees, I crawled to him, my breasts swaying as I moved. Arturo tapped his knee with his index finger, watching me, his lust-filled eyes staring into mine.

"Such a beautiful little *kotenok*," he murmured.

When I stopped in front of him, he placed a finger under my chin and tilted my head up until I was staring into his eyes. "Very good. Up."

On shaky legs I stood, my pussy directly in his line of sight. He leant forward and ran his tongue from my stomach to my breast in one long, languid lick. He sealed his lips around my nipple and sucked hard. I moaned and arched into him, my fingers sifting through his hair as I held him against me.

He gripped my hips and lifted me easily, like I weighed nothing at all, and sat me on his lap. "Shall we see how wet you are for me?" He delved into my slick folds and sunk a finger knuckle deep in my pussy. "You're soaking," he rumbled against my skin.

My head fell back on a moan as I rode his finger, pleasure shooting through me like the world's best drug was coursing through my veins. He nipped my throat, leaving little love bites over my flesh as he kissed and nibbled my hot skin.

Arturo wrapped his arm around my waist and stood. My legs coiled around his torso as he continued to pump me with his finger. He walked me over to the bed and dropped me hard enough to make me bounce.

"You want my cock, *kotenok?*" He unbuttoned his pants and pulled them down his thick, muscular thighs.

I nodded, licking my lips at the sight of his rock-hard length standing tall.

He fisted his cock and pumped it slowly, dragging his hand up and down leisurely.

It was the hottest thing I'd ever seen.

"Tell me what you want," he whispered darkly.

"I wan—need you. Always you."

Without wasting another second, he drove into me in one quick, powerful thrust. I gasped, my pleasure soaring at the feel of his thick, heavy cock finally filling me.

He rode me hard, pounding into me with such ferocity that I knew I was going to be feeling it the next day (which I'm sure was what he wanted).

"So hot. So tight. And all fucking mine," he grunted, punctuating each word with a rough thrust of his hips.

"More, Arturo. More," I begged, and he gave it.

He pulled out, flipped me over and slammed back into me all in one clean move.

My eyes rolled into the back of my head. Glorious, mind-blowing pleasure.

He slapped my ass. "Clench. Squeeze my cock."

I did as he commanded and was rewarded with a deep, guttural groan, the sound pushing me closer and closer to orgasm.

The weight of his body pressed against mine, pushing me deeper into the mattress with every thrust, was like ecstasy. I loved every moment of it.

"Do you want to come?" he breathed huskily in my ear.

"Yes," I groaned, long and loud, pushing back, meeting him thrust for thrust.

"Beg me."

"Please, Arturo. Please, for the love of God, let me come!"

"Not God, *kotenok*." Relentless and unforgiving, he hammered into me over and over, not giving me an ounce of relief. He licked up my spine. "I'm the fucking devil." His movements turned feral. Ferocious. Chaotic.

I moaned, relishing in the intensity of every stroke, in the feel of his cock completely filling me.

"Fuck," he snarled, latching onto my shoulder and biting hard enough to leave a bruise as he rutted like a man consumed.

His cock was so hard, so thick, that it hurt.

Pain and pleasure gripped me hard, working together to drive me higher and higher until I felt like I could touch the sky.

My core tightened and I came, shaking violently.

I screamed.

My pussy pulsed.

Stars exploded behind my eyes.

Arturo was right there with me. He roared, the sound loud and deafening, like a wild animal in the jungle. His grip on me tightened, nails digging deep into my skin as his hips pistoned sporadically while he emptied himself inside me. His cum overflowed, running down my thighs.

"Fucking hell," he rasped, collapsing on top of me.

My breath whooshed out of me and I wheezed, trying to elbow him off me. "Arturo, can't...breathe."

He groaned and finally rolled off of me, panting with exertion.

"I'm fucking dead," I moaned, flipping over onto my back.

Chuckling, Arturo turned onto his side and walked his fingers through my breasts, down my stomach to my pussy.

Whimpering, I shook my head. "Arturo, no. I can't go again."

"I'll give you two minutes," he whispered, slipping his fingers into my entrance. "And then I'll have you again."

Despite my languid body, pleasure shot through me and I groaned, spreading my legs wide. "Your cock is going to kill me one day," I panted.

He chuckled and climbed back on top of me. "And what a way to go that would be."

"Do you seriously need all those shoes?" Lukyan asked from his position on my bed, feet crossed at the ankles and hands behind his head.

I was in the middle of packing my things for the move to New York. It had been a week since I was kidnapped by Nero, and I was still in Las Vegas (much to Arturo's dismay). The first few days were hectic. Chaotic. My father tried all his usual torture techniques, but nothing worked on the Los Zetas we had captured, and they died with their secrets untold.

We still didn't know why they were taking orders from Nero. It was very unusual for a Mexican cartel to take orders from the Italian Mafia. It wasn't like the alliance between the Bratva and the Cosa Nostra. The Zetas were literally following Nero's every command like little bitches, and we didn't understand why.

But no matter how much Father tortured them, inflicting more pain than anyone could bear, they didn't talk. Not even when Arturo cut off their dicks and let them bleed out. They stayed loyal to the very end, to whatever agenda they had.

I'll admit, the entire thing was pissing me off. The not knowing. Especially when it felt like the answer was right under my nose.

"I mean, shit, how many pairs of shoes does one chick need?" Lukyan reached over and grabbed a bouncy ball from the side table and started throwing it up in the air. Throwing and catching, throwing and catching. "It's ridiculous."

"You seem awfully concerned about my shoes, Lukyan. Do you want to borrow some to prance around in?"

He scowled and threw the bouncy ball at me. I dodged it. "Dude, three times that happened. And I was nine. Stop bringing it up all the time."

Tatiana burst into laughter, her eyes glued to the full-length mirror as she held one of my dresses to her body. "Oh my god, I remember the first time you told me that. I don't think I stopped laughing for a week."

Lukyan turned beet red. "Stop mentioning it!"

With a twirl, Tatiana put down the sleek black dress and picked up a skintight red one that showed a bit too much cleavage. She looked at Lukyan through the mirror and poked her tongue at him. "Ya big baby." She held the dress to her body again, trying to imagine what it would look like on her, decided she didn't like it and threw it back to where she got it from.

She huffed and made her way over to me, taking a seat on the floor and crossing her legs. She watched me struggle to zip up my suitcase. "I can't believe you're abandoning me."

I laughed. "What did you think was gonna happen after I married Arturo?"

"I dunno. Not this," she pouted.

"Think of this as a good thing. Now you've got a good reason to get out of Las Vegas and check out New York. And your dad can't say no because you'll be coming to visit me," I winked.

Her face lit up. "You're right!" she squealed. "Come on, let's hurry up and get you packed!"

I laughed and tried to zip up my suitcase again, but it was too full. "Shit. Come help me with this, will ya, Lukyan?" I grunted.

Groaning, he rose from the bed and came to my side. He pushed down on top of the suitcase while I tried to zip it up.

"You've got too much crap," he grunted, sitting down on top of it.

"Just shut up and help me."

"I'm trying," he snapped.

After a few more attempts, we finally managed to zip it shut. We sat it next to my other suitcases at the door.

I blew out a breath. I was excited to finally be joining Arturo in New York. For the first few days after the kidnapping, Arturo had stayed here in Vegas with me while his father flew home and handled transferring the leadership of the Cosa Nostra over to him.

Even though I told him repeatedly it wasn't their fault, he decided to use our boxing ring to punish Christian, Luca and Lorenzo for failing to keep me in the house. He fought them all one-on-one, taking the time to hurt them all in excruciatingly slow detail. By the time he was done, Christian had a broken nose and three broken ribs, Luca was bruised from head to toe and had a dislocated shoulder and Lorenzo had a shattered femur.

I felt fucking horrible. It was all my fault, but no matter how much I begged Arturo, he didn't stop hurting them until he was sure his point was made. That his orders were to be followed without hesitation. All three of them ended up going back with him when he left for New York. He left another three men here to guard me until they were all back on their feet.

I wasn't meant to be there for as long as I was, but it was hard for me to leave when things were up in the air like that. We started a war with the Chicago Outfit when we took Nero out, and their new don would need to set an example, start out strong by avenging their former leader.

There were rumours that Nero's younger brother, Franco, stepped up after his death, and that he was ten times better fitted for the position. He had already mobilised the men and cemented his leadership by taking out an entire MC gang that had encroached on their territory during the transition.

Then, of course, there were the Los Zetas. There were still a large number of them spread throughout New York and Chicago, and their reasons for following Nero's commands were still up in the air. Would they also look to avenge his death?

Surveillance on them was needed to find out exactly what was going on. The entire thing was worrisome, and it made me hesitant to leave my family behind when they might need my help. But the same went for Arturo.

He was my husband now. I couldn't just stay in Vegas and leave him to face his troubles alone in New York. I had to make a decision, even if it broke my heart to choose between them.

"Any more news about the woman Aleksandr took?" I asked, wiping sweat from my brow.

"Whoa, hold up. Aleksandr *took* a woman?" Tatiana asked, her nose scrunching up. "I never pegged him for the kidnapping type."

"She was at the house Nero kept me in when they came to rescue me. I think he's trying to find out what she was doing there."

Lukyan nodded. "Yeah, but she still isn't talking."

"Seriously? He losing his touch or something?"

"Ha, as if. More like he's gone soft."

I scoffed. "Aleksandr? Soft? No way."

"No, seriously. When I offered to help, he got all pissy and told me not to go near her. It was super weird." He picked up the bouncy ball again and started bouncing it against the wall. "Even threatened to break my fingers if I touched her."

Frowning, I grabbed the ball before it bounced back to him. "You're kidding."

"I swear! Got all grouchy and growly, more so than usual."

"Wonder why."

"Maybe he has a crush," Tatiana sang, her lips curving into a smirk.

Lukyan and I looked at each other and then burst out laughing. "Aleksandr? Crush?" I shook my head, my body still shaking with laughter. "No way." A devious plan formed in my mind. "Should we go see her?"

Tatiana nodded excitedly, already getting to her feet, and Lukyan looked uneasy. "I dunno—"

"Aw, come on! Don't be such a wuss!" I slipped on my converse and tied my hair up to get it out of the way.

"That's easy for you to say! You're his favourite. He wouldn't dare hurt you. He'll fucking castrate me."

"Oh, grow a pair." I dragged my suitcases out of my bedroom door and left them in the hallway.

Tatiana followed behind me, just as eager as I was to talk to this woman, when her phone rang. Frowning, she pulled it out and sighed.

"Fuck, I gotta go. Dad wants me home."

I shook my head. "You've got to start standing up for yourself, T. You're twenty-two. He can't control you anymore."

"I know, I know," she sighed, giving me a hug. "Text me as soon as you get to New York, okay?"

"I will." I went to pull back and she hugged me harder.

"I'm going to miss you," she said sadly, and I smiled, squeezing her tight.

"I'll miss you, too. Don't worry, I'll come back every now and then. And you can come visit me anytime you like."

She scoffed and stepped back. "Yeah, if the Grinch ever lets me." She kissed my cheek. "Later, girl. Bye, Lukyan," she called out as she went down the stairs and out of sight.

I sighed. I was really going to miss her. Turning to Lukyan, I smirked. "Come on, let's go see that woman. If we're quick, we can be in and out in no time."

Aleksandr rounded the corner and we both froze, eyes wide. He scowled. "Why do you two look like you're up to no good?"

"No reason," Lukyan and I said at the same time.

He narrowed his eyes in disbelief. "Right." He waved at the suitcases piled at the door. "Come on, let's get your stuff and get down to the car. The plane's waiting."

Damn it.

Lukyan and I shared a look.

"Alright, seriously. What's going on with you two?" Aleksandr barked.

"I wanna talk to the girl. The one you took from Nero's," I answered quickly, before Lukyan could make up some lie.

Aleksandr growled. "No."

"But—"

"I said no, Illayana. Now get your shit and move it." He picked up suitcases by the handle in each hand and marched downstairs.

"Told ya." Lukyan grabbed a suitcase and hefted it onto his shoulder. "He's touchy about her."

I sighed, taking my last piece of luggage and following after them. When I got to the foyer, my father was there waiting. He gave me a small smile. "All packed?"

"Yep," I huffed, dragging my overpacked suitcase behind me. "Gonna miss me?"

"The house will definitely be quieter without you."

"I know. Won't it suck?" I laughed, giving him a hug.

He stiffened slightly but then relaxed, returning it for all of two seconds before he coughed awkwardly. "Alright, that's enough."

"Five more seconds."

He gave them to me.

When I pulled back, I gave him a sad smile. "I'll admit, I'm a little nervous. Here, I've never really had to make decisions, just follow orders. But there? There, I'll be—"

"Queen of La Cosa Nostra. A role you were born for."

"I don't know about that," I mumbled, riddled with self-doubt.

"I do." He placed a supportive hand on my shoulder. "You're beautiful, smart, strong and best of all, vicious. You'll have New York eating out of the palm of your hand in no time. Just believe in yourself. Be confident. And I'll always be here if you need help."

I gave him another hug. "Thank you, *Otets*." Father.

Nikolai burst into the room, panting hard. "Oh, good. I made it." He was out of breath and covered head to toe in sweat. "I was afraid I wouldn't make it back before you left."

"Where were you?" I asked, pulling out of my father's embrace.

"My daily jog. I thought I'd have enough time to do my twenty miles and be back in plenty of time, but I ran into Tatiana outside." His brows lowered into an angry frown at those last words, and I laughed.

"You do this to yourself, you know. I don't know why you let her rile you up so much."

"She's infuriating! She has no sense of personal safety, and always gets herself into trouble."

I swear, I had asked him this question a million times, but I couldn't help asking it again. "Why do you care?" I smirked.

"I don't care!" he shrieked, turning red. He took a deep breath to calm himself down. "Anyway, I made it in time to give you this." He pulled out a small box and gave it to me.

I opened it and gasped. Inside was a gorgeous antique locket. The pendant had a stunning red jewel in the centre, surrounded by an intricate pattern of swirls engraved into the silver.

"It used to be Mum's." Nikolai reached over and opened the locket. Inside was a family picture of all six of us before our mother died. "I thought you should have it."

I choked, gripped with emotion. Sadness washed over me and I cleared my throat, trying to push back tears.

"Thank you," I whispered. I took it out of the box and held it up. "Will you?"

Nikolai took the necklace and I turned around. He clipped it around my neck, the weight of it soothing and comforting as I touched it with my fingers.

My father, who had remained quiet the entire time, looked at the piece of jewellery with glassy eyes. "It suits you," he said softly.

"Is-is it okay? If I have it?"

"Of course. She would have wanted you to have it." He cleared his throat and adjusted the lapels of his jacket. "Alright, you best get going before Arturo sends out a search party. Aleksandr will drive you to the airstrip. Adrian is already in the ca—"

"Wait, Adrian?" I frowned. "Why is Adrian in the car?"

"He's going with you."

"But he's *your* guard. I thought he was just covering me until I went to New York."

My father shook his head. "He's the best fighter we have in the Bratva. I want him with you, watching your back."

"But I—"

"No buts, Illayana. This is the way it's going to be. Now, one more hug." He wrapped his big, beefy arms around me one more time and kissed my cheek. "Give 'em hell."

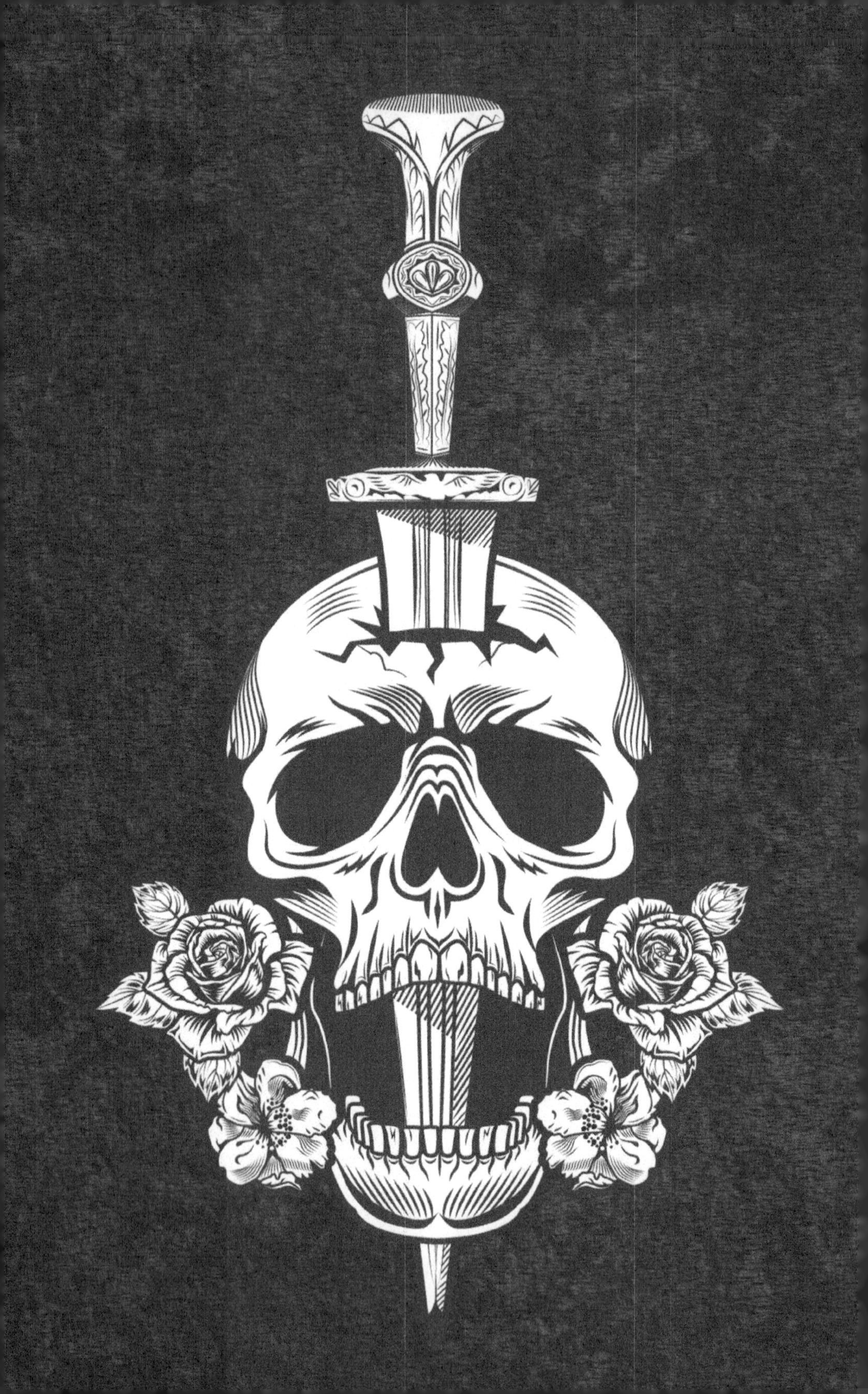

CHAPTER TWENTY-EIGHT

Arturo De Luca

"Is she here yet?" Vin asked, stepping into the basement downstairs that served as our torture dungeon.

I pummelled the fucker strapped to the chair we had bolted to the floor in the middle of the room, punching him repeatedly in the face, even though he was knocked out.

I didn't fucking care. I had anger to work out, and this guy was the perfect option.

He *was* a Cosa Nostra man…until he decided to open his stupid fucking mouth and insult my wife.

"She's on the way."

One final punch and I was done. For the moment. I grabbed a cloth sitting on the metal table off to the side of the room and wiped the blood from my knuckles.

Vin watched me with intense eyes. "Have you told her yet?"

"No, I'll tell her when she gets here."

Vin frowned. "You sure that's wise? She'll be within hitting range."

I blew out a breath. Truth be told, I wasn't sure if it was wise. And once I told her what I needed to tell her, she was going to lose it. I was sure of it.

After returning to New York, I spent days dealing with the Outfit. They were still causing us trouble, their new Don, Franco, trying to make a name for himself by stepping into our territory with his men and drugs. It was pissing me the fuck off.

Add in the fact that there was also dissension in my ranks due to me marrying outside the *famiglia*, and I was getting problems from all sides.

The Los Zetas had been quiet, but it would be stupid to count them out of the game. Whatever reason they had for following Nero's orders wouldn't keep them down.

My father had officially stepped down as head of the family, relinquishing control entirely to me. He was still somewhat in the picture (more so on an advisory level than anything else).

Vin was my number two.

Even with all the shit that happened, I was still expecting Illayana *days* ago. But she was hesitant to leave her family when so much crap was still up in the air. I understood, but that didn't mean I was fucking happy about it.

"Wise? No. Unavoidable? Yes," I said, finally answering Vin's question.

"Is she the jealous type?"

I scoffed and threw the bloody cloth back on the table. I walked up the stairs, heading back into the house. "If the way she acted when Gabriella touched me is any indication, I'd say yes."

Vin followed and slammed the steel door shut behind him. It locked immediately. When he stepped away from the door, I clicked the button underneath my desk and the bookcase moved back into place, concealing the door.

"Right. I forgot she threatened to kill her."

I started to undress, taking off my tie and unbuttoning my shirt. "I didn't think Gabriella was capable of being so manipulative. She's always seemed so—"

"Docile? Passive?"

"To say the least," I grunted, shrugging out of my shirt. "Anyway, let's talk about something else. Any news on the Zetas?" I asked, eager to change the subject.

"Nothing of merit. I've put word out on the streets to keep an eye out for them. If anything substantial comes through, I'll let you know."

"Good. Keep a close eye on it. What of Franco?"

"He's stepped back after we butchered his last round of dealers. But I have a feeling he'll be back."

I moved to the closet and pulled out a fresh shirt, placing my dirty, bloody one in the basket on the floor to be disposed of. "Me too. We'll have to hit him first, show him we're not to be fucked with."

Vin sat in my chair and kicked his feet up on my desk. "Whatcha got in mind?"

"First, kicking your ass for sitting in my fucking chair," I growled, scowling at my younger brother.

He rolled his eyes and got up. "You're like a big, overgrown baby. Tell me the plan so I can get it started."

I slipped a new shirt on, buttoning it up. "Get a couple of the men together. We'll go into his territory tonight and hit them back. Do some research first. Find out what businesses they own, and which one makes the most money. I want to know the comings and goings of their people and who sits where in the hierarchy." I strapped a holster to my chest and placed my guns in the pouches. "Now that Franco has taken over, we need to find out who his most trusted men are."

"Gotcha. You gonna try and turn them? Like Nero did to Diego?"

I growled at the mention of that fucker's name. When I watched the video of Illayana's attack and saw Diego there, fighting her, trying to be one of the men to rape her, I felt like I could burst, there was so much rage inside me. It should have occurred to me that Nero had converted Diego to his side, but it didn't. I just assumed the little bitch took my money and fled the country, not that he went running to my enemy and gave him every fucking dime.

"We can try, but if it doesn't work, we always have the option of killing them."

"True, true. Well, leave it all with me and I'll handle it." Vin gave me a thoughtful look, like there was something he wanted to ask, but he didn't want to question me.

I sighed. "What is it?"

"Illayana is due here within the next few hours, right? Do you think it's a good idea to leave her here alone on her first night in New York? If you want, I can handle this so you can stay with her."

"What makes you think I'm going to leave her here?"

Vin's eyes widened in shock, his brows shooting up. "You'r-you're gonna bring her along? Are you serious?"

I laughed at the look on his face. "Of course I am. She's going to be pissed when I tell her what I need to tell her. I'm going to need something to divert her anger. Killing our enemies and burning a few of their buildings seems like the perfect outlet to me."

I grabbed my phone and sent a few texts off in rapid fire. A few minutes later, my office door opened and Christian, Luca and Lorenzo hobbled in.

They were all still beaten and bruised, and maybe I should have felt bad about it, but I didn't. They now understood the consequences of disobeying me, and I highly doubted they would do it again. They stopped in front of my desk and bowed slightly.

"Boss," Luca said, wincing slightly at the pain shooting through his shoulder.

"Illayana is due here in a matter of hours. I trust that once you're all back to normal, you'll be more thorough when guarding her?"

They all nodded without hesitation.

"Good, now go recover."

Vin chuckled as he watched them limp their way out. "You really fucked them up."

"They deserved it," I grunted, sitting down behind my desk.

Vin hummed and I raised my brows at him.

"You don't think so?"

"Arturo, come on. You know your wife. She's a hard-ass and does whatever she wants. In what world do you think those three could have stopped her from doing something she wanted to do? I mean, can you even do that?"

He had a point, but it didn't matter. I needed someone to punish, and those three were still partially responsible. If I could, I would have punished her other bodyguard, Adrian, too. But he was a Bratva man.

I just shook my head and waved my brother away. "Get out of here. I got shit to do."

He smirked, opening my office door. "Didn't think so."

I threw my stapler at him and he slammed the door shut before it could hit him.

Illayana De Luca

We arrived a few hours ahead of schedule, so we ended up taking a cab to Arturo's house. I thought about messaging him and letting him know we had arrived early, but part of me wanted to surprise him. I told my three replacement guards not to call ahead and inform him we were here. They definitely weren't as fun or engaging as Christian, Luca and Lorenzo. They were boring. Barely spoke a word, just stood around with grumpy-ass looks on their faces, like they wanted to be anywhere else except there with me.

I gave the cab driver the address, and away we went. We had to get a maxi cab to fit all of us (and my four huge suitcases) in.

I leant back in my seat and closed my eyes, taking a deep breath. "Alrighty, you can do this. You're just moving to a place where you have more enemies than friends. Ain't no big deal. Easy peasy," I spoke quietly to myself in the back of the cab, trying to reassure myself, but it wasn't working. I was even more nervous at that moment than I was before I left.

"Relax," Lukyan told me, taking a swig from his flask beside me. "You're stressing over nothing."

I glared and flicked him in the ear.

"Ow! Uncalled for."

I rolled my eyes at his dramatics and stared out the window. Truth was, I was so fucking happy that he came with me (not that I'd ever tell the idiot that).

It was like a lifeline, someone to lean on from my old life, to remind me who I was when I got nervous and questioned myself (which I knew I would do).

"Your brother's right, Illayana. You have nothing to worry about. You're strong, smart and cunning. You'll be able to hold your own amongst the Italians with ease," Adrian said, eyes plastered to his phone. "And well, if you run into any trouble, you have us to back you up." He winked.

We drove for at least thirty minutes, the beautiful sights of New York City flying by, until eventually the cab slowed. We pulled up in front of large wrought iron gates and a man stepped out of the security booth, a hand raised in the air to halt us.

The driver lowered the window. "Just here to drop off a Mrs De Luca."

The guard looked into the cab and I gave him a two-finger salute. He pursed his lips in what could only be perceived as dissatisfaction. He nodded to my three temporary guards, and then flicked his eyes over Lukyan and Adrian.

"Who are they?" he asked, voice gruff.

"My brother and one of my guards."

"Names?"

I narrowed my eyes. He was already starting to piss me off. "Lukyan and Adrian."

He touched his earpiece and repeated the names. After a brief moment, he nodded. "Lukyan isn't on the list."

"That fucking bastard," my brother hissed. "He did this on purpose."

"Well, if you weren't such an ass to him all the time, I'm sure he wouldn't have." I looked at the guard. "It's fine. Just let us through."

"Can't do that. I'll need to call the boss for verification."

Anger blasted through me and I growled.

"Oh, no," Adrian sighed.

I undid my seatbelt and opened the door, rounding the car until I was at the guard's side. With zero hesitation, I kneed him in the balls.

A very ladylike shriek fell from his lips and he dropped to his knees, cupping his privates. The second guard in the booth came sprinting out, gun at the ready.

"Down! On your knees!" the guard barked at me.

I glared, unimpressed. "I only get on my knees for one man."

Lukyan and Adrian jumped from the car, pointing their own guns at the guard. "Just give me the word," Lukyan whispered darkly, cocking his gun.

"I said down! On the ground! Now!" the guard shouted.

"You do realise you're pointing a gun at your boss's wife, right?"

The guard paled and lowered his weapon with a shaky hand.

"Better. Now, open the goddamn gates," I demanded.

"Don't do it," the guard on his knees groaned. "We need verification on one of the men first."

"Bitch, do you wanna get shot?" I snapped, pulling my gun and putting the barrel right against his temple. "I'll blow your brains all over the fucking pavement if you don't open that gate right. Fucking. Now." I cocked my gun so he knew I was 100% serious.

The other guard gaped and stumbled to the security booth. The gates swung open.

"Neil! What are you doing?! The boss will kill us when he finds out we opened the gate without checking with him first!"

"He'll kill us for pointing a gun at his wife!" Neil yelled back. He levelled his gaze at me. "I apologise, Mrs De Luca. Please, head on through."

I tucked my gun away and jumped back in the cab. Lukyan and Adrian did the same. I looked at my three temporary guards and glared. "Thanks for the help."

They just shrugged.

I couldn't wait to get Christian, Luca and Lorenzo back.

When we still hadn't moved, I looked at the driver. He was pale, eyes wide open and frozen in fear. I lightly tapped his shoulder and motioned for him to drive up the long driveway to the house.

It was beautiful. A classic, modern-style mansion, somewhere between ten to fifteen-thousand square feet, with thick concrete pillars and tall glass windows. An antique water fountain lay in the centre of the front yard, the driveway curving around it and leading back out the way we came.

When the car stopped, I pulled a $100 bill from my pocket and handed it to the shaky cab driver. "Thanks for the ride."

"Uh, no problem," he gulped, taking the money. "Do you need help with your bags?"

"No, thanks. We got it. Have a good day." I smiled.

I went to the back of the car and opened the boot, dragging my suitcases out. Lukyan and Adrian gave me a hand. My three temporary guards followed along like robots, getting out of the car and waiting at my side like sentries. Once all my luggage was out of the car, the driver sped off like he couldn't get away fast enough.

All Lukyan and Adrian brought was a duffel bag each. Me? I had four suitcases of stuff, and it wasn't even everything I owned.

Lukyan grabbed two of my suitcases, Adrian took the other two and we made our way to the front door. I rang the doorbell and froze, stunned by who answered the door.

"What the fuck are you doing here?"

Gabriella gave a self-satisfied smirk, her eyes alight with mischief. "Didn't Arturo tell you? I live here now."

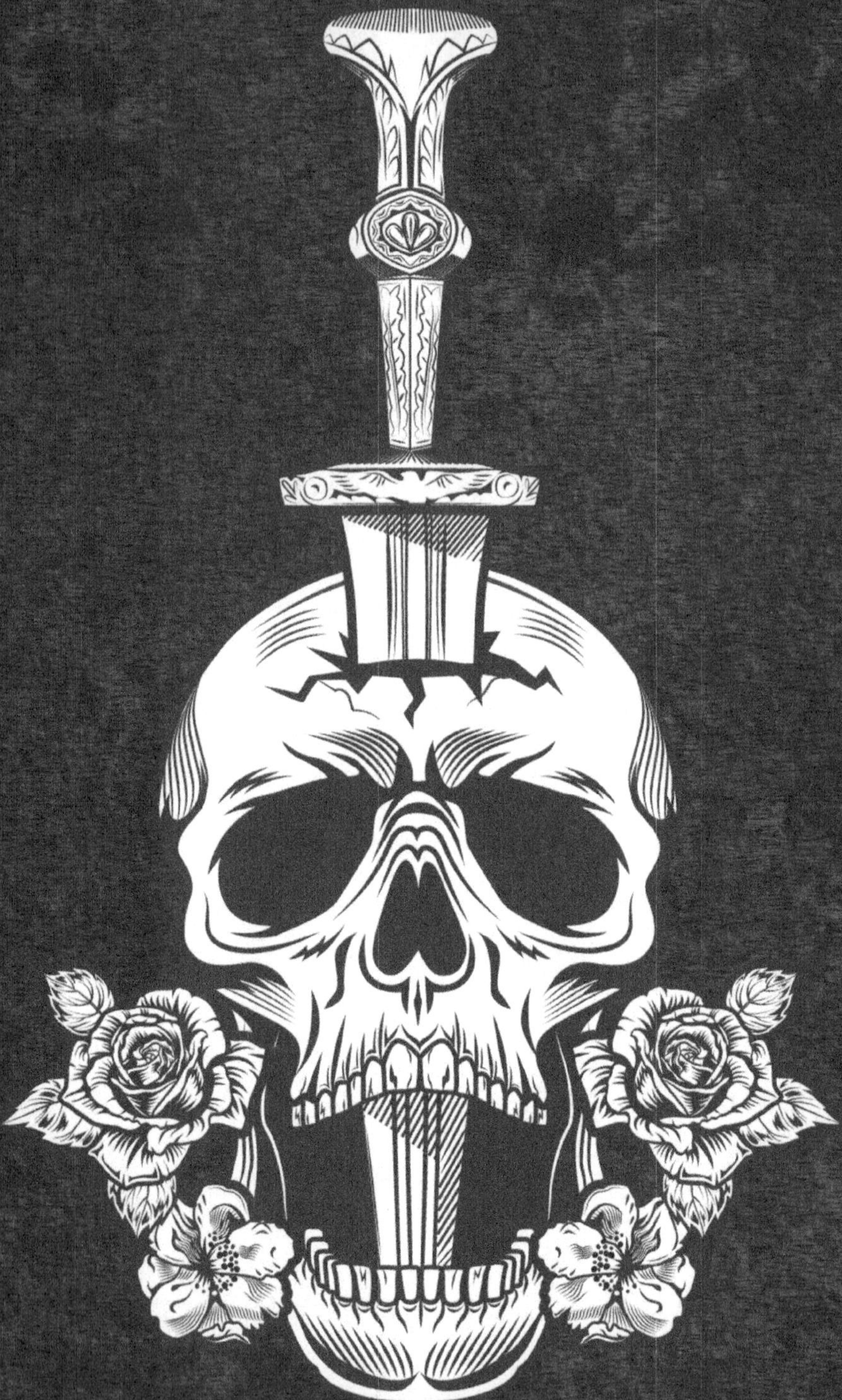

CHAPTER TWENTY-NINE

Illayana De Luca

*O*kay, keep calm. Don't lose it. Smile. That's it. Just. Be. Cool.

Gabriella's stupid face held a certain smugness, like the fact that Arturo didn't tell me about her presence was a good thing for her, and a crappy thing for me.

It probably was.

Lukyan clicked his fingers, giving me that 'something just clicked in my brain' look. "Oh, that's right. Didn't he mention that some bitch was staying at his house for a bit?"

Thank you, brother.

"Oh, yeah," I smirked. "That's right, I completely forgot about that." I looked down my nose at her as I barged my way through the door, making her stumble. Lukyan, Adrian and my guards strolled inside and slammed the front door shut behind them.

A tall, older man dressed in a plain suit walked into the room and gave a small bow. "May I take your bags?"

"Thank you, Mr…"

He blinked, startled, like no one had ever asked him his name before. "Bernardi. Aldo Bernardi."

I repeated my thanks, adding his name with a smile. He gave a shaky smile back.

"Get me a coffee when you're done," Gabriella barked, quite rudely. "And be quick about it."

Aldo jumped and nodded quickly. "Yes, Miss Gallo. Right away." He hobbled to Adrian and took one of the large suitcases, heading for the staircase.

Annoyance flared to life inside me and I glared at Gabriella. I hated people who treated the working class like that, like nothing more than the dirt beneath their shoes. It may have been Aldo's job to serve, but that didn't give her the right to treat him like shit while he was doing it. There was nothing wrong with serving others.

"Help him with the bags, Lukyan."

My brother nodded and rushed to the older man's side, taking the suitcase from him and hefting it onto his shoulder. "Lead the way, Aldo."

A look of gratitude flashed across Aldo's face and he led the way up the circular staircase.

I glanced around the foyer, taking in the opulence drenching the house. The gold-plated antique frames with expensive oil paintings and the sleek Italian marble flooring screamed wealth and luxury.

"I hope you're okay with me staying here. I know you and Arturo are only recently married, but as I'm sure he's told you, this was the only solution."

I put on my best fake smile and turned to face her. I couldn't let her see the jealousy raging inside me. I had to save face. "Of course, anything to help the *famiglia*."

Footsteps thundered and a moment later Arturo burst into the foyer, Vincenzo hot on his heels. My heart thumped hard, looking at him in his black tailored suit, his gorgeous sculpted face making my blood heat and fire scorch through my veins.

His eyes flicked to Gabriella and then to me, unease flashing across his face. He was waiting for me to explode.

Of course, I would, but not in front of an audience.

"Husband," I smiled sweetly, moving towards him. "I'm home."

Without missing a beat, he wrapped his arms around me and kissed my hair. "I can explain," he whispered for only me to hear.

"Oh, you will." I let the venom drip from my voice so he could hear it, and stepped back. He didn't let me go far, keeping me locked in his arms. I looked at Vincenzo over his shoulder and he gave me a warm, comforting smile.

"Welcome to the De Luca mansion. Glad to have you here."

"Thanks, Vincenzo. Appreciate it."

The De Luca mansion was a beacon within the Cosa Nostra, a symbol of wealth and power. It was where every leader of the *famiglia* lived during their reign. First Francesco, Arturo's grandfather and his wife. Then Alessandro and Isabella. And now, Arturo and I. Arturo explained the mansion had been in their family for decades, that it was a tradition to live in it when you ruled the Cosa Nostra. He planned to honour it.

Arturo looked down at me. "You're early. I wasn't expecting you for another few hours. I would have picked you up from the airstrip if I knew."

"I know," I said, placing my hand on his cheek. "I wanted to surprise you."

"Consider me surprised." He leant down and placed a soft kiss on my mouth.

I kissed him back for a second and then bit down hard, dragging his lips between my teeth. He hissed, eyes burning, as he glared down at me. The taste of blood ran over my tongue and I finally released him, smirking at the faint trickle of blood running down his chin. "Missed you," I whispered.

He ran his tongue over his bottom lip and a truly dark, devastating smile graced his face. "Missed you too."

A loud clutter of something falling to the ground made us turn. "Whoops," Gabriella said, looking down at a vase that had shattered all over the floor. "Sorry. Anyway, glad to have you here, Illayana. I can show you around, if you like? I'm sure Arturo has lots of things to do," she smiled innocently, like she was trying to do me a nice deed, but I saw through it.

She was trying to put distance between Arturo and I. I was desperate to let her feel the cool steel of my blade, to carve that pretty little face up until she was begging me to end her life. I smiled at the thought.

"That's not necessary." Arturo looked at Adrian. "Welcome, Adrian. If you'd like to get settled, your room is located on the second floor. I can have someone show it to you, if you like."

Adrian nodded. "Much appreciated."

Arturo signalled for one of the butlers walking past and told him to show Adrian to his room. Adrian glanced at me uneasily and I waved him away.

"I'll be fine, go on. I'll meet with you later."

"Call out to me if you need me." He followed the butler up the stairs, his duffel bag slung over his shoulder.

"Where is—" Arturo began, a loud whooping noise making him pause.

"Illayana!" Lukyan yelled, running down the stairs. "Dude, you've gotta come check this out! The bathroom is like something out of a SciFi movie! There's an iPad in the wall that controls everything—" his words broke off as he noticed Arturo standing at my side. He glared, any trace of excitement vanishing in an instant.

"Hello, Lukyan," Arturo said pleasantly. My brows raised at how civil he was being, considering my brother was looking at him like he just killed his dog. "I'm glad you were able to make it inside without any problems."

Lukyan's glare increased tenfold. "Are you?" he sneered.

"I am. Have you been shown where you'll be staying yet?" Arturo wasn't rising to the bait. Weird.

"No, I just dropped Illayana's bag off in her room."

"Ah, excellent. Here, let me show you." He clasped my hand and led me down the hallway. I glanced behind me and shrugged my shoulders at Lukyan as I followed him. Lukyan trailed after us and we all left Gabriella standing in the foyer by herself.

Later, bitch.

Arturo led us past several rooms, a lounge room, a formal dining area and the kitchen, until we got to the backyard. Frowning, I followed him out onto the back deck and burst into laughter.

Sitting on the grass outside where two dog houses. One had the name 'Brutus' stamped across the front of it with a gorgeous German Shepherd sitting inside, and the other had 'Lukyan' on it. When my brother saw it, he scowled.

"Ha, ha. Very funny," he snapped.

Arturo smirked. "What? You don't like it? I had the best carpenter in New York make this for you."

"You fucking—"

I jumped in front of Lukyan as he came barrelling towards my husband, fists at the ready.

Vincenzo sighed. "I told him not to do it."

"Come on, Lukyan," I said, pushing him away from Arturo. "Even you can see this is funny."

Arturo just kept that smirk on his face, thoroughly impressed with himself. I shook my head. If that was how things were going to be around there, I would end up killing one of them.

After finally managing to wrangle Lukyan away and back into the house, Arturo showed him where he would really be staying. It was a room on the second floor, next to Adrian.

Arturo gave me a quick tour, showing me the beauty of the house and everything it had to offer. It had recently been modernised, little gadgets installed throughout the house that did things for you. It was kinda cool, and made me feel like I was living in the future.

Gabriella hung around like a bad smell, following us around and adding in her input when it wasn't fucking asked for. She kept throwing in little comments that showed she'd been here a million times, like, "I've always loved this room, it's my favourite in the house", or "Isabella and I picked out this painting". She was begging for a beatdown.

We came to a stop in front of a closed door and Arturo flicked his head to the side. "Off you go, Gabriella."

She pursed her lips, her eyes flicking to the door and back. "I thought maybe we could all have lunch? I'm sure Illayana is hungry."

"Illayana is fine," I said, smiling. I wasn't sure what was behind this door, but I could tell she didn't want us going in.

"But—"

"Gabriella," Arturo said sternly. "Go on."

With a huff, she spun on her heels and stomped away.

Now that she was out of my sight, all the anger and rage I had felt seeing her here burst to the surface. The second we stepped into the room and the door shut, I stepped out of his embrace and punched him in the gut.

He grunted, taken by surprise, doubling over in pain. But I wasn't fucking done. I was so mad that he didn't tell me Gabriella was living there. That instead, he had left me to find out by having her answer the fucking door.

I moved to knee him in the face, but he was prepared now, expecting another blow. He blocked, swiping my leg out from under me and taking me to the ground hard, landing on top of me.

My breath whooshed out of me and I growled, pummelling his chest. "You fucking bastard," I hissed, my anger rising.

He gripped my wrists and pinned them above my head, grinding his body into me to keep me immobile. I thrashed and tried to get free, but we both knew it was a wasted effort. I wasn't going anywhere until he let me.

I stopped moving and glared at him towering over me.

"You done?" he asked, his voice deep and rough.

"What the fuck is she doing here, Arturo?" I snarled, baring my teeth.

"If you calm down, I'll tell you."

"Calm down? *Calm down?!* How would you feel if you walked into my home and my ex answered the fucking door?"

"I'd kill him." He said it so casually, so blatantly, like it was the only logical course of action to take in that situation. "But this is different. First, she's not my ex—"

"You fucked her and she was offered to you to be your wife."

"—and second, her mother died at our wedding, and her father burned to death in her family home in an attack by Franco. She has no one now, no one to protect her until she can be married off."

"She can't protect herself?"

He gave me the side eye. "Our women don't fight. You know that."

"Maybe they should start. They're only weak if they choose to be."

"True, but it's not our way."

"Why does she have to stay here? Surely there's somewhere else you can dump her until you find someone to marry her."

He lowered his head into the crook of my neck and ran his tongue over my skin. "As Don, it's my job to offer protection until someone else can. If I'm not seen protecting my people when they need it, it can come back to bite me in the long run."

I shivered and wrapped my legs around his waist. "How long has she been here?"

"A few days," he murmured, finally releasing my wrists to cup my breasts.

A few days?!

I flipped him onto his back with a quick gymnastics move, pulled out a knife and held it under his chin. "And I'm only just finding out about this now?"

Leaning into the knife, he gave me his signature smirk, the blade cutting into his skin. "Don't tease me, *kotenok*, you know I like to play rough."

Oh, I know.

I leant down and ran my tongue over his lips. "I like to play rougher."

He rolled so he was now on top, my knife still at his throat, and thrust hard, grounding his rock-hard cock in between my legs. He groaned. "Fuck, I want you."

He swivelled his hips and pleasure shot through me.

Fuck. I wanted him too. So badly. But I was still so angry, and I wasn't ready to let him off the hook yet. I was going to make him work for it.

I headbutted him, smashing my skull against his (making sure to avoid his nose, so I didn't break it) and shoving him off me with my legs, kicking his chest.

"Ow, fuck!" he yelled, landing on his back.

I scrambled to my feet and went to run, but he was already there. He pounced on me, shoving me down so my cheek pressed against the ground. With a hand to the back of my neck, he held me down as he pressed his body against mine.

I could feel his cock against my ass, and I shivered.

"Is that how you wanna play, *kotenok?*" he purred in my ear. "Fine by me."

He took the knife, still in my hand, and used it to cut my clothes. With precise cuts that showed exactly how good he was with a blade, he slashed down the back of my shirt and ripped it from my body. He moved the cool steel of the knife down my skin until he got to the top of my jeans.

"No," I gasped. "Not the jeans. They're my favourite pair."

"Should have thought about that before you decided to go all 'Warrior Princess'." He sliced down my Dolce & Gabbana jeans until they fell away.

"Argh! You asshole!" I thrashed, and he pinned me down again with his body until I felt like I couldn't breathe.

"I'm gonna take you so hard, it's going to feel like I'm splitting you in two," he whispered darkly, his breath hot on my skin. "And maybe then you'll behave like a good girl." He pulled my underwear down roughly until they stretched across my thighs. The weight of his upper body left mine and I sucked in a breath.

He reared forward and slammed the knife down into the ground so hard it drove into the floor right next t0 my head. The jingle of his belt buckle followed next, and my blood heated in excitement.

My stomach tightened and I squirmed, aching for him. All that strength and dominance he was using made me so fucking hot, I thought I would burn up. Lust coiled down my body, right to my pussy and I clenched involuntarily, desperate to be filled. I felt helpless under his gargantuan form, and I loved it, loved knowing that physically, there wasn't a single thing I could do to stop him.

In the back of my mind, I knew that if I really wanted him to stop, he would. But I didn't. I wanted him to take me like he owned me. To fucking ruin me.

The thick head of his cock touched my entrance and, without hesitation, he surged forward, driving into me with such force that I jolted forward.

A cry left my lips at the pain and then it disappeared, replaced with sweet, sweet ecstasy. Searing pleasure rushed through me and I moaned, long and hard.

"Ah, there's my tight little pussy," Arturo groaned, thrusting into me. He kept one hand at the back of my neck, holding me down while he fucked me like he hated me.

All I could do was lie there and take it. And it was complete and total bliss.

I squealed. I moaned. I chanted his name over and over again like a prayer. All while he grunted behind me, fucking me harder and harder.

Pain flared from my ass cheek and, through my pleasure-induced haze, I realised that he had slapped me. His hand massaged the sting away. He did it again and again, and the sensation was too much. That mixed with his long, thick cock tipped me over the edge. My eyes rolled into the back of my head and I screamed as the most mind-blowing orgasm ripped through me. The rough feel of his clothes against my skin, the thought of him fully clothed while I lay beneath him with barely anything on, made the whole thing so much hotter, so much filthier.

"That's it, *kotenok*, come all over my cock," Arturo hissed between his teeth, pounding into me with such savagery, I was sure I'd have bruises on my skin.

My body tingled and I felt his wet, cold tongue run over my skin. He sucked my earlobe into his mouth.

"You're mine, aren't you, Illayana? All that fire, all that spirit, this sweet fucking pussy. All mine," he breathed against the side of my neck, his thrusts increasing.

"Yesssss," I whined. "And you're mine."

"Always."

His speed and power picked up and his deep voice growled in my ear. "Do you want my cum, *kotenok*? Do you want me to fill you up until you're dripping with me? Until my cum is running down your thighs?"

I whimpered, my body convulsing as another orgasm hit me from out of nowhere.

That fucking voice.

"Yes, please, give it to me, Arturo," I begged, and he gave it to me.

He pressed his chest into my back, his hips smacking into my ass as his cock drove in and out of my tight channel. We slid across the ground with every thrust and he roared, coming deep inside me.

His entire weight collapsed on top of me and I choked, the air rushing out of my body.

Not again.

I reached back and tried to push him with my hand. He rolled off me and slumped onto the ground next to me, his breathing hard.

"You gotta stop doing that," I said breathlessly.

His lips tilted up in a smirk, but before he could say anything, Vincenzo's voice came from behind the door.

"Are you guys done fucking now?"

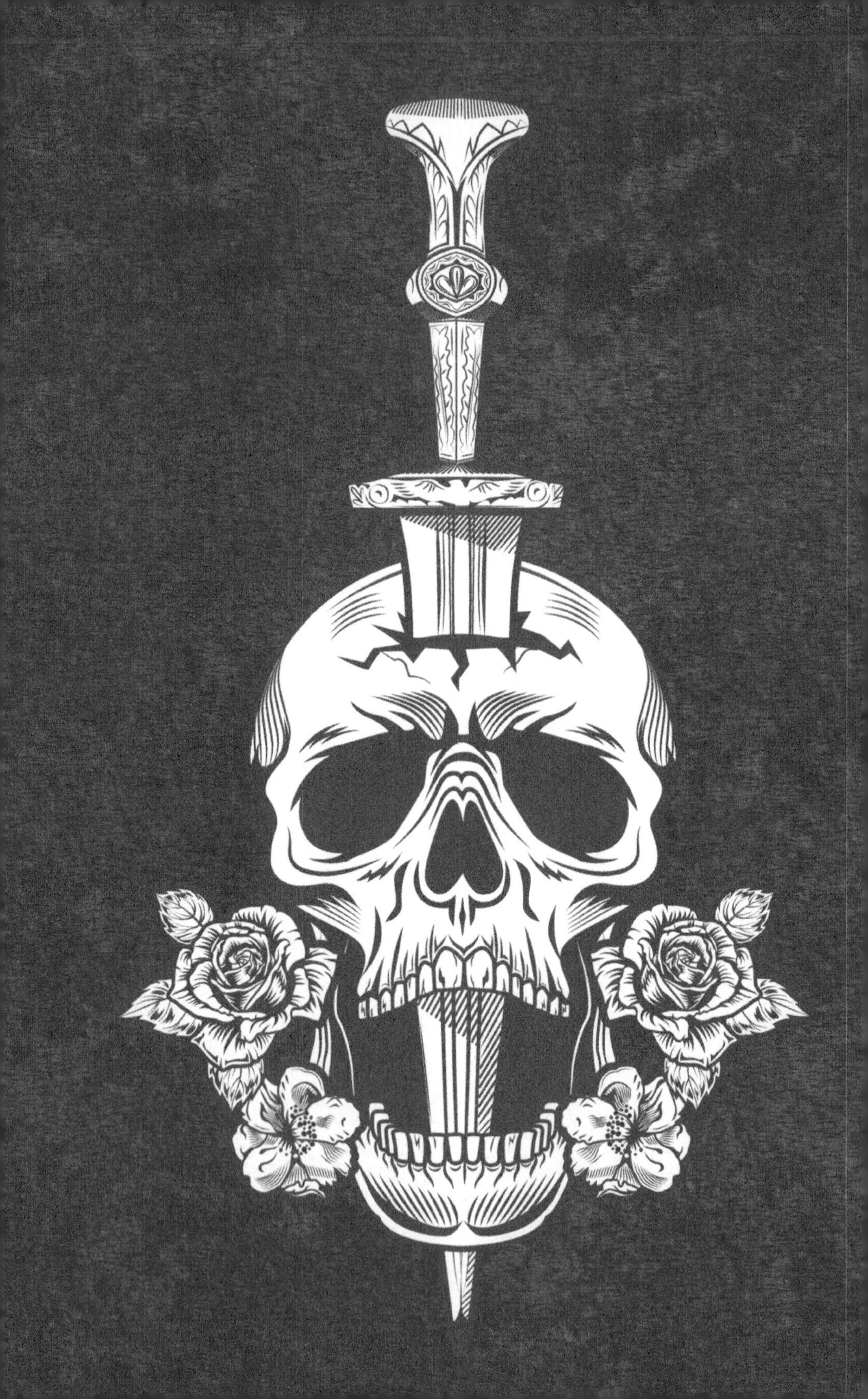

CHAPTER THIRTY

Illayana De Luca

"Yoo-hoooo," Vincenzo sang, knocking repeatedly on the door. "Is it safe to come in, or are you two still humping like bunnies?"

Arturo rolled his eyes and got to his feet, tucking himself back in his pants and doing up his belt. I pulled my underwear back up and stood on shaky legs, my tattered clothing falling away from my body.

Now that we were no longer going at each other, I took the time to look around the room. We were in a large bedroom that was easily three sizes bigger than my room back in Vegas. There was a certain dark vibe emanating from the space, like something you'd feel if you were standing in the middle of the devil's den. It had a king-sized, four poster bed with luxurious black sheets and dark ebony furniture scattered throughout.

The enticing spicy scent lacing the air made it clear that it was Arturo's bedroom (well, my room now too). My suitcases were sitting right next to the bed.

Dressed in nothing but a bra and underwear, I stared down at my ruined clothes and pursed my lips, glancing back to Arturo.

"Don't look at me like that," he chuckled, running a hand through his hair. "You asked for it."

"I'm pretty sure I specifically asked you *not* to do it," I snarked, glaring.

He raised a brow. "Careful with that attitude, *kotenok*, or we'll be right back on that floor and I'll fuck it out of you."

My eyes lit up with excitement. "Promise?"

He took a step towards me, a dark look on his face, and the door burst open.

Vincenzo strolled in and froze when he saw me, a low, long whistle coming out of his mouth. I wasn't the overly shy type, but standing in front of my brother-in-law, basically naked, made me a little uncomfortable.

Arturo shielded me with his body, scowling at his younger brother. "Turn around," he snapped, eyes hard.

Vincenzo rolled his eyes and gave us his back. "No need to get all pissy, we're all family here. Right, Illayana?" He peaked over his shoulder.

"Move another muscle and I'll cut your eyes out, Vin. I swear to God," Arturo warned, and Vincenzo spun back around quickly.

Arturo led me over to a walk-in closet and pulled out a black silk button-up shirt. "Put this on," he barked.

I arched an eyebrow. "Don't get snippy with me. It's your fault I've got no clothes."

"Put. It. On," he growled, impatience dripping off him.

"Alright, alright." I quickly slipped the fabric over my skin. Even though he was taller than me, the shirt barely covered the goods, coming to a stop mid-thigh.

"Is the coast clear now? Can I turn around?" Vincenzo asked.

Arturo responded by going over and lightly pushing him in the back. "What do you want?"

I moved to my suitcases and started sifting through them to find something more appropriate to wear while Vincenzo spoke.

"Thought you'd wanna know I just got a call from Mario. He caught some little shit selling on our territory again. He decided to leave him be and tail him. He followed him to a drop house on the edge of the city, and it was being guarded by Franco's men."

Arturo growled. "Are you sure?"

Vincenzo came over with an iPad and handed it to his brother. Arturo flicked through the images on the screen. "These are the photos Mario managed to get of the men. I cross-referenced them with the information I've been able to gather so far on Franco, and there's a few matches. One of them" —Vincenzo leant over and clicked the iPad— "is one of Franco's capos, Benito."

I pulled out a pair of jeans and a long-sleeved shirt, setting them on the bed. I came over to Arturo's side and glanced down at the screen.

Benito was a beefy guy with huge, thick shoulders. He had short dark hair, light olive skin and a paedophile moustache.

Darkness flashed in Arturo's mismatched eyes. "Call the men. We're moving our plans up. I want them here and ready in thirty minutes."

Vincenzo blinked. "You wanna hit them during the day? You sure that's wise? We don't have anyone in Chicago PD, so we've got no one to cover for us."

"Then we better be long gone before the cops arrive." Arturo handed the iPad back and flicked his head to the side. "Go on."

His brother nodded. "Leave it with me." And he left.

I looked at Arturo. His body was tight, tension rolling off him in waves as he stared into space. His jaw was clenched, hands balled into fists at his side.

"Hey," I whispered, running my fingers through his hair. "You okay?"

He took a deep breath and exhaled, some of the tension seeping away. "I will be, once I put that fucker Franco in his place."

"He's been stepping into your territory a lot?"

"Yes. We've been killing off his dealers every time we find them selling in our territory, but dealers are a dime a dozen. There's always people out there willing to sell drugs for a little extra cash."

I took his hand and sat him on the bed, moving behind him to massage his shoulders. He groaned and leant into the touch. "What's your plan?" I asked, loving the feel of all that hard, toned muscle beneath my fingers.

"We're going to hit him where it hurts. Vin did some research and found out which of his businesses make the most cash. Of course, we're talking legal tender here, not the shit he makes under the table. But by taking out his legitimate businesses, it'll be harder for him to launder his money."

Smart. It would be a real 'fuck you' to the asshole.

"Have you met him? Franco?" I asked, moving a little lower. His muscles flexed under my hand.

"No. And I don't fucking want to, not unless I'm about to slit his throat." He cracked his neck. "He's smart, intuitive. He's managed to do more damage in the week he's been don than Nero did during his whole leadership."

"I've noticed he's a lot more organised than Nero was."

Arturo glanced over his shoulder at me, his brows raised.

I smiled. "We've been keeping a close eye on him, too. The work he did on that MC gang in Chicago?" I blew out a whistle. "Gotta admire the guy's style."

Arturo grunted, turning back around. Tension still rippled from him and I wanted desperately to make it disappear, but I didn't know how.

I sighed. "About Gabriella—"

He groaned, his head falling forward. "Illayana—"

"No, just hear me out. I understand where you're coming from, that if you're not seen protecting your people it could be bad for you. But you need to understand that if she keeps acting the way she's acting, I'm going to put her in her place. I'm just warning you."

He stood and loomed over me. He gripped my face, slipping his fingers into my hair and tilting my head back until I was staring right into his eyes. "I love when you get all bloodthirsty," he murmured against my lips.

I smiled. "Good, because that's 99% of my personality."

He chuckled and nipped my bottom lip before pulling back. "Come on, get dressed. We've got to get moving. It's time Franco realised who he's fucking with."

When we pulled up in front of *Trattoria's*—the restaurant owned by Franco—my heart pounded so hard with excitement and adrenaline, I could barely sit still.

Arturo was planning this offensive attack as retaliation for all the shit that the Outfit had pulled in his territory. One of which was the murder of one of his capos (Gabriella's father) and several of their dealers. He was after blood, and he wasn't going to leave until he got it.

On my left, Lukyan pulled out his gun and checked the chamber. Adrian did the same, an evil look on his face.

"Alright, listen up," Arturo barked, demanding the attention of everyone in the car. His voice rang through the small space as well as in the earpiece in my ear, and all eight of us looked at Arturo, listening intently. "This is a quick in and out, no fucking around. We need to be long gone before the cops show up. When you get inside, light the fucking place up. This is Franco's main restaurant. Everyone inside is one of his, so I don't give a fuck what happens to them. But I want at least one left alive. We enter through the front and leave out the back, where another car will be waiting to take us away."

A laptop sat in Arturo's lap, showing a surveillance feed of inside the restaurant. There were about twenty patrons inside—nearly all men, with a few women as waitstaff. I took a second to familiarise myself with the layout. It was basic, filled with circular tables and a long bar that ran the length of the entire side wall. There was a kitchen in the back and a restroom tucked away on the right.

Arturo put his phone to his ear. "Vin, are you ready?"

Vincenzo was a few blocks away, prepared to hit one of Franco's strip clubs at the same time as we hit the restaurant. His orders were a little different. The place was a front for where Franco made his drugs. Vincenzo was to break in and set the entire place on fire, torching every ounce of it.

It was late afternoon. There were a few people walking down the streets, heading for their destinations without a clue of what was about to happen. It made me twitchy. Pulling something like this in broad daylight with witnesses was risky, but I guess that's why Arturo wanted to do it. Franco would not be expecting it. And Arturo wanted to make a stand, show him that he wasn't going to hide and just take the disrespect Franco was giving him.

Arturo hung up after Vincenzo responded and leveled his gaze on Lukyan and Adrian. "You two are to stay by her side the whole time, got it?"

Lukyan glared. "You're not the boss of me, man."

Arturo punched him in the face, breaking his nose.

"Ow! Fuck!" Lukyan cried, cupping his now-bleeding nose.

"I'm not in the mood for your attitude, Lukyan. Either you listen to my orders, or you can fuck off and I'll get someone else to watch her back. You hear me?"

Lukyan scowled, blood dripping down his chin. "Loud and clear," he spat, eyes burning with anger. "Asshole," he muttered under his breath.

Arturo looked at Adrian. "We going to have the same problem?"

Adrian shook his head. He was a firm believer in the proper chain of command. He would follow Arturo's orders to a tee, unless it was something compromising my safety. Then all bets were off.

"I don't need them to guard me, Arturo. I'm fine," I said, adjusting my grip on my gun.

Arturo just stared at me, darkness vibrating from him.

Alrighty then.

"On my count. Three...two...one...*move.*"

We sprang out of the car and covered the few metres to the restaurant in seconds. The second we stepped through, gunfire rained. Men shouted, reaching for their weapons and ducking under cover. Women cried, running for their lives. It was complete and utter mayhem. I loved it.

Lukyan and Adrian stayed glued to my side as we manoeuvred our way over to a table and flipped it over, using it to shield our bodies. I jumped up, took aim and fired, clipping a guy in the shoulder a few feet away. There was movement to my right and I swerved, catching sight of someone hiding beneath a table, a gun in his hand.

"Adrian, on your right."

Adrian swivelled and fired twice without missing a beat. We moved, staying low in a tight formation with Lukyan in front, me in the middle and Adrian bringing up the rear. Furniture and broken glass lay on the path before us, making it harder to move as we made our way towards the back. Every now and then, we'd pop off shots at people in our line of sight. Some would hit their target, some would miss.

The noise was deafening, the constant *bang, bang, bang* of bullets being fired ringing in my ears. The cries of people screaming in pain were coming at me from all sides, bombarding my senses.

Someone rammed into me from the left, knocking me down. My gun flew across the ground and I cursed. The heavy weight of a body fell on top of me and I swung hard, punching him in the centre of his chest with all my strength before he could do anything else. He grunted, recoiling back slightly, but he stayed straddling my thighs, leaning over me. I locked my fingers around his wrist, sat up over his shoulder, reached under his arm with my other hand and held on tight to my own wrist. I reared back, locked his elbow to my body and twisted, breaking his arm.

He screamed and I let him go, rolling backwards to land on my haunches. A foot came flying towards my face and I just barely managed to get my forearm up to block it. The power of the blow was devastating, pain flaring through me, but I ignored it and grunted, shoving him back. I plucked a knife from my waist and flung it like a throwing star. It hit him in the throat and he tumbled to the ground.

I spun, looking for my brother. Lukyan was on his back a few feet from me, wrestling with someone who was trying to drive a knife into his chest. Blood poured from a cut on his forehead and his face strained as he tried to gain the upper hand. I leapt over broken furniture and dead bodies and delivered a solid roundhouse kick to the guy's face, smashing his nose and breaking a few of his teeth. He fell back, a cry of pain falling from his lips, and Lukyan took advantage, grabbing the knife and ramming it into the guy's heart.

His eyes found mine and he nodded his thanks.

A hand gripped my shoulder and I turned, bringing my knee up at the same time to knee them in the gut, but they blocked me, almost anticipating the blow.

Adrian smirked. "Gotta move faster than that, *malen'kiy (little one)*, if you want to get one over on me." He was breathing hard, splattered with blood, but other than that he seemed okay.

I smiled. "Sorry, it's the adrenaline of the fight." I moved back and scanned my surroundings.

The fight was over. The once-beautiful and elegant restaurant was now completely destroyed, with pieces of broken furniture all over the place and bullet holes through the walls. Blood seeped out of the lifeless bodies littering the floor, pools of it beginning to form around me.

I checked the time on my watch. Six minutes. All the destruction had only taken six minutes.

"Where's Arturo?" I asked, slightly breathless.

Adrian pointed back towards the kitchen and I looked up to find Arturo's eyes already on me. Relief flashed across his face and he beckoned me towards him with a flick of his fingers.

I headed his way, taking long, deep breaths to recentre myself. Adrenaline still pumped through my body, my heart thumping like mad. I worked to slow it down.

In and out. In and out.

When I stepped into the kitchen, Arturo marched over to me and kissed me, his eyes blazing with the rage of battle. He gripped me hard and lifted me off my feet, deepening the kiss, his tongue stroking against mine. His taste exploded on my senses and I moaned, loving the feel of him on me.

Someone coughed and I pulled back, my mind foggy. Arturo ran his tongue over my lips once more before putting me back down.

No words were said. There was no need. He was happy to see me unharmed.

I was surprised he even wanted me to come on this mission. And when I said that to him before we left, he just smirked at me and said, "People need to see my queen in action."

He grabbed my hand and led me over to a man on his knees, surrounded by cooking utensils and food scraps. His clothes were torn and his face dripped with blood as he glared at us.

Arturo walked right over and rammed the butt of his gun into the guy's face. His head flung back and he cried out. Vincenzo was right there, keeping a solid grip on his arm so he didn't fall on his back.

"Two minutes," Vincenzo said, looking at his watch.

Arturo lowered to his haunches until he was eye level with the only man left alive from the Outfit. "I want you to deliver a message to Franco for me," he said darkly, danger and violence dripping from him. "Tell him the

King and Queen of La Cosa Nostra are only just getting started."

A Little Note from Me to You

Thank you so much for taking the time to read Bratva Bride! I hope you enjoyed getting to know Illayana and Arturo!

A little information about the series for you.

As you know, the Bratva series is an interconnected series, where each book is centred around a different couple but the overall storyline and plot actually flows throughout the entire series. Some of the books even overlap with one another, giving you the opportunity to see things that have already happened, but from a different character's perspective.

Any questions that are left unanswered in this book, will be addressed in the book that follows, it is just written in Aleksandr's POV instead.

The next book is centered around Aleksandr and Drea. It will pick up right at the moment where they go to rescue Illayana.

Again, I would just like to say a massive thank you to all of my readers!

If you have time and enjoyed the story, please don't hesitate to leave a review!